Ellen Jurik was born in the outskirts of Perth, Western Australia: the most isolated capital city in the world, where touring musicians often choose not to visit. She has spent her career working in video game development, most notably as Game Director of an adaptation of *Colin Thiele's Storm Boy*. She now lives and writes in Sydney, New South Wales, which is often the top of the list for music tours (or second, after Melbourne).

This is her first novel.

Ellen Jurik

To Axel
who is three years old
and will be upset if Mummy's name is on the book and his isn't.

CONTENTS

Disc 1

One

It was a surprisingly warm Monday morning, the first day back to school, and three weeks before the ARIA Music Awards — something that the calendar on the fridge had reminded Nate about as he put away the milk. He was the one who had written "Term 4 Start," but "ARIAs" had been scrawled on a Thursday — strange, as it was usually held on Wednesdays — by his fourteen year old daughter, Elsie. This year, the ARIAs meant drastically different things to the two of them. As usual, Nate was hoping to find an excuse not to go; for the first time, Elsie was hoping that he would take her along.

Instead of getting ready to leave for school, she was sitting a metre away from the tv, watching some group of artfully ungroomed young men pouting and fawning into the camera. Having made himself a coffee, Nate found himself watching the clip with her.

"You don't know any of these guys, do you, Dad?" Elsie had suddenly become aware of Nate watching her watch the Frothing Mess video clip with too much interest. But, unlike most fourteen year old girls, rather than be embarrassed, Elsie took the opportunity to check her father's connections to see whether she could contrive an introduction.

"No idea. Not unless you know who their parents are." His sarcasm went over Elsie's head. Once in the thick of it, he wasn't the best at keeping up with who was hot in music any more. It made him feel like shit, a reminder of what he once had, and what he'd lost.

Elsie whipped out her phone. "Mmm, I don't think any of them have parents in the industry. But," she blushed into her phone, feigning that she hadn't already done this research. "Tommy cited you as one of his inspirations." She scrolled through one of the pages she'd pulled up, and quoted from it. "Here: 'Growing up, I listened to everything Nate Whitely put out. My goal is to be even half the musician he was.' What do you think?"

"I was kidding, but... That's... which one is Tommy, then?" Nate wasn't sure whether to feel flattered or insulted. He decided it depended on which one Tommy was, whether he'd done the songwriting, and how much of a wanker he appeared to be. On the other hand, when Nate was at his peak he'd probably looked like a wanker to most fathers of teenaged girls who had watched him on tv. Suddenly, he understood how a whole generation of fathers had felt about him twenty years ago; even though he was privy to what it was like to be on the other side of that equation.

"That one."

"Okay." With his narrow elfin features and a darkness reflecting from his green eyes, he was... tolerable to Nate; to Elsie, he was divine.

" '*Okay*'? Okay what, Dad?"

"I don't know. Okay, if you say so, that's Tommy."

Elsie rolled her eyes.

"So, what does Tommy do? Does he write their songs?"

"Yeah, he writes all their songs and plays bass and keyboard and sings and I think he produces them as well. He's soooo talented Dad, and... yeah. They're nominated for like, a *bunch* of awards this year."

"Oh, okay. Great, then I guess I'm flattered he likes what I do."

"Dad? You're going to the ARIA Awards this year, aren't you?"

"I know what you're thinking, Elsie, and no."

"Awwww, not fair. Why?"

"Because you're too young."

"I am not."

Nate chuckled to himself, seeing the indignant look on his daughter's face — the same expression she'd worn when she insisted she wasn't too young to have pierced ears, or walk to school on her own. "You are, for someone like him. Now come on, you'll miss your bus." He smirked, shook his head and walked out of the conversation and back into the kitchen.

Elsie knew how impressed her friends would be if she knew Frothing Mess. She would, of course, love to meet Tommy Freebourne, who was super cute and far more talented and cooler than any of the guys in her class, or at her school in general. In a moment of wanting some of that coolness, she'd told her doubtful classmates that she did know him; a photo of her with any member of the band would be proof enough. The easiest way to contrive that situation was to play on her industry pedigree and go to the ARIA Awards. And then, when they met, would it be so bad if he maybe liked her back? She knew her father's refusal was just a setback: she just had to work on a plan to change his mind. Oblivious to how he was really feeling, she determined that her father must just be an enemy of love. Considering he'd essentially been single since she was a little girl, it was plausible enough: the solution to her problems was to soften his heart. But how? She'd have to think about it for a while. Hoisting her schoolbag over one shoulder, she called out, "Bye Dad!" and walked out the door.

Nate heard the slam of the door, as well as the still-on television. As the adult who paid the power bill, he dutifully walked back into the livingroom to turn it off. He paused and thought about Tommy. He thought about how Elsie thought about Tommy. Even though, all those years ago, there was no social media, and not everyone he met was already a musician or the daughter of one, he remembered knowing that girls stared at his two-dimensional representation and memorised every interview that they could get their hands on. Back then, he'd hated it; but nostalgia has a way of sweetening every sour memory, and he found himself wishing he was Tommy. Or, at least, someone else in their band so he wouldn't be the focus of his own daughter's interest; that would be like a weird reverse *Back to the Future* thing, but even creepier. Or maybe not? He couldn't tell. But, he knew he probably should stop thinking about that anyway.

Something that Elsie had said Tommy said bugged him: 'My goal is to be even half the musician he was.'

Wait — *was?*

The sort of thing that you'd hope to happen when you take in some faulty electronic device or car that's still under warranty is not the sort of thing that you'd ever want to realise is happening to you. Yet, no one is so unique that there isn't someone else who can better fill the exact role that had been identified, until then, as theirs.

Being someone's favourite anything can be fleeting, and is never guaranteed; but realising this is often unexpectedly torturous.

Sometimes it hits hard and suddenly, but sometimes, like Nate, you get the sense that a new-and-improved replacement is confirming your own redundancy.

A click of the remote, and Tommy and his bandmates were gone, leaving Nate in silence.

Two

⏮ ⏸ ⏭

You could almost say Nate had it easy: he still had an opportunity to do something about his impending obsolescence. It didn't happen behind his back like it had for Vera, who had taken the opportunity of losing everything to create a completely new place for herself.

Vera sat down at her usual seat in her usual cafe on a Monday afternoon at the usual time. Recently, her life had become very *usual*. Which, when she thought about it, was rather strange considering that it was only about three months ago that she had worked up the courage to leave her cheating fiance and her well-paying job, packed up her things, and moved from the suburb he'd liked to a tiny place just north of the city centre. She'd needed a fresh start: her old life, she had decided, was too toxic, and staying there even a minute longer would have been too hard. Even speaking to her Mum on the phone was too hard at times, too full of old memories. So she swapped that life for one that was full of entirely different concerns, and a series of new rhythms and routines that brought her comfort, but not pleasure.

Her usual coffee arrived, brought by the usual barista. She opened her laptop as usual, and loaded seek.com.au, like she now did every day. She took a deep breath, and prepared to judge her financial and societal worth by how many of the boxes she ticked and how many applications she'd send and expect to hear nothing back from.

Disrupting her comforting rhythm, an unusual group of teenaged girls in their summer uniforms arrived at the cafe. Vera looked at the date on her phone: was it October already? School must be back. The girls looked just old enough to attempt a mocha in the hopes of giving the appearance of the sophistication of a cappuccino. Just outside, a team of pimply, scrawny boys were egging each other on and pushing one of the pimpliest to head inside, presumably to talk to one of the sophisticated mocha drinkers. He finally walked in, but after taking one glance at the girls, turned and retreated.

"I can't compete with that Tommy guy!" he spat at his friends, who all called him a wuss and slapped him on the back as they turned and disappeared from view.

Vera wondered who 'that Tommy guy' could be, and whose attention he'd gained. She looked back over at the group of girls, trying to spot all the typical cogs that perform certain functions in the group. Which one is the queen bee, who is the concerned organiser, who is the socialite, who is, for lack of a better term, the ugly one? The girls were a couple of years into the age where looks, and the looks they got, became an important part of social standing. If you don't have or get looks, you'd better choose something else.

Vera's brow crumpled, thinking about her friendship group at that age. She didn't have looks. She was smart and unashamed, and the admirers she gained inevitably wanted her to help them gain the favour of some other girl: pretty, silly, flirty, coy, endearing. She had never been endearing, even less, any of those other things. She could never claim that boys were annoying, simply because they didn't annoy her in *that* way: they annoyed her because they always turned out to not be into her.

At least, that was the case until she was in university. Studying Engineering meant that she was in the minority, surrounded by young men who, at worst, were socially awkward, and at best, required a lot of liquid courage to put themselves out there, ultimately finding girls who admired them for their brain or their future pay cheque. The ones who were interested were the ones who, through no deliberate aim of their own, simply made her feel uncomfortable. While other, less understanding girls might call them 'creeps,' she knew they were more along the lines of unfortunate souls; souls who she didn't want the responsibility of having to socialise just to make them decent.

And then, she'd met Steven. He'd started the year after her, a transfer from Arts to Engineering. "*Just to really annoy my parents,*" she could still hear him saying. Both his parents were doctors, his father an oncologist, and his mother a neurosurgeon. They wanted him to be a doctor as well, and while it may have been suspected that a career flipping burgers would have disappointed them more than anything, it turned out that focusing on metal machines rather than flesh ones was more offensive. She and Steven were both outsiders of sorts, and she found herself helping him, not socially, but academically. He flattered her sense of self, the part of her that valued her intellect and her ability to grasp complex spatial and mathematical concepts. Truth be told, she carried him. But she didn't care, because he was handsome, and he adored her for it. It's a powerful thing, adoration.

It even overpowered her ability to recognise that he got on too well with her best friend.

She pinched the bridge of her nose between her eyes, trying to create one pain to distract away from another, the way that someone might dig their fingernails into their palms instead of facing a stronger pain elsewhere. The body's ability to only manage the newest, most immediate pain: it was a tidbit of knowledge dropped into one of those family dinners with Steven's parents.

Even her coping mechanisms reminded her of him!

Instead, she decided to indulge one of her older and oft-revisited coping mechanisms, and stood up to go to the counter in search of something sweet and decadent to overwhelm pain with gustatory pleasure. By this point, most of the girls had left, leaving behind just one. Her reddened face was hanging down, fingers toying with the coins in her palm.

"My Dad will be here soon. He can pay," her eyes flicked up to the group of girls, now outside, chatting with the now-returned boys and waving at her as they started to trail away. "I'm only a few dollars short! Pleaaase," her eyes bulged imploringly, but the surly barista just raised an eyebrow at her.

"You'll have to stay here, where I can see you. I don't want you running off without paying."

"I wasn't... I wouldn't!"

The girl's bottom lip drooped as she watched her friends leave her behind, laughing and waving. Vera couldn't help but feel a surge of sympathy for this girl whose friends didn't care if they upset her.

"I have a few dollars to spare, let me get this for you."

The girl spun around, wide-eyed, to see who had saved her. She mouthed her thanks, as though the shock had made her mute. Vera just smiled and nodded back down to the girl's takeaway coffee, then turned to the barista, whose eyebrow seemed to raise even higher, then fall, defeated. "Fine. And is that all I can get for you?"

"I'll have a slice of the mud cake too."

"Cream or icecream?"

Vera's resolve was either very weak or incredibly strong, depending on what you believed her motivation to me. "Both?"

As the barista rang up the cake and coffee and pulled out a table number, Vera glanced towards the door. The girl was still standing there, looking out. Her shoulders dropped in disappointment, her schoolbag almost sliding off. As Vera watched, she turned back to the counter, disappointment colouring her face. Her eyes met Vera's, and she started over while Vera completed the transaction and took the table number.

"They left already." She sighed. "But, I wanted to thank you. That was super nice. I'll pay you back, I promise. My Dad…"

"Will be here soon? Don't worry about it, it's my treat anyway." Conversing with someone new about an insignificant problem whose significance seemed to escalate so quickly was strangely refreshing. "Why don't you come sit with me until he arrives? I'm Vera, by the way."

The girl nodded, blinked, and held out her hand. "Elsie." She smiled as Vera took her hand and shook it.

"So…" Vera groped for a topic of conversation as their hands dropped. They meandered together towards the table, and were already sitting by the time Vera had given up and gone straight for the one thing she was curious about, that maybe Elsie could answer. "Who's Tommy?"

Elsie's eyes widened.

"Sorry… I overheard something. I was curious."

"Well, he's…" Elsie's face crumpled in semi-embarrassment. "Did you ever like a guy in a famous band?"

"Oh yeah," laughed Vera, as the embarrassment left Elsie's face. Vera leaned towards her to let her in. "Nate Whitely."

"*Nate Whitely*? That's—"

"I know, I know, he's probably super old to you. But—"

"No no, it's not that, it's…" Elsie caught her breath as, beyond Vera's shoulder, she spotted Nate walking in. "Oh, hi Dad."

"Hi. Ready to go?"

Vera turned, and it was like the world was in slow motion. She hadn't felt like this since she was nineteen.

His eyes locked onto hers, and it was as though his face had been composed of sunflowers. His skin glistened gold and the flames in his blue eyes spiralled as they burned into hers.

"Hi," he flashed his cheeky smile and his eyes glistened and glowed. It felt as though time stood still while the zigzag of his dishevelled hair danced above his face.

"Hi," was all that Vera could manage in return. She felt like she was staring, gawping, as she was consumed by the vortex of *Nate Fucking Whitely*. She tore her eyes away from his, feeling as though they were magnets of opposite polarity. She knew she'd stared too long; but if she had, then surely he had too.

Three

There it was: the Look.

Nate drank it in. He drank it in so greedily that it took him a moment to even register anything about Vera. Thank God she wasn't one of Elsie's school friends. That would have been awkward, in a Kevin Spacey in *American Beauty* kind of way. But this was okay; she looked about ten years younger than him. No, he forgot how old he was: he always forgot how old he was until he looked in the mirror. She was younger. Or hopefully, she was ten years younger than him, but just looked even younger. Wasn't there a rule about how much younger someone could be before you were a creep — or, at his age, having a midlife crisis?

"This is my Dad, *Nate... Whitely.*" Elsie had to say something. She thought the adults were being super awkward, just looking at each other and not saying anything.

"Hi, I'm Vera. Hi." Vera didn't know whether to stand or stay sitting. She shifted in her seat and settled on sticking her hand out. Beyond the shock of meeting him in person, there was the additional shock that he'd aged terribly; the years of excess and experimentation causing his smooth cheeks to thicken and begin to turn jowly, the first step before 'turning Harold,' as she and her highschool friends used to joke about. His bedroom eyes now simply looked exhausted. Being a rockstar had clearly taken its toll. Or maybe he was between handsome phases? It didn't matter: he was still fever-inducingly sexy, as evidenced by Vera feeling a hot, wet flush in her ears and up the sides of her face. He still had *those eyes* and that charmingly crooked smile, and seeing them right in front of her felt as though everything was speeding past and yet frozen.

"Nice to meet you, Vera." Taking her hand, Nate briefly considered laying on the charm and raising it to his mouth to kiss, but decided that would probably embarrass Elsie, who he expected was properly embarrassed already; so he should probably play it nonchalant. Instead, he committed her face to memory. She wasn't spectacular, but long ago he'd learned that spectacular usually doesn't mean much. She rather reminded him of a girl he'd dated a lifetime ago. Something about her was softer, though, or puffier; and, he was ashamed to note, she seemed nowhere near as cool. But, her slight dagginess was kind of endearing, in an honest sort of way.

As Elsie watched them locking eyes, she couldn't help but realise what she was seeing, and know what it might mean for her. She'd seen her father be looked at like this countless times, but this was the first time she could recall him seeming to respond in kind. There was potential here! She just had to work out the best way to show Nate that a fan-idol relationship could work. The best way probably included Nate getting only the most superficial and positive impressions of Vera, leaving him wanting more.

"Hey, Dad? I think we need to go."

"Hm? Oh yeah. Nice to meet you, Vera." He let her hand slip out of his.

"Thanks for the hot choc, Vera." Elsie played her card and hoped that Nate would fall into her trap. She knew that he hated them owing anyone anything, especially money. A generous person sometimes has a lot of difficulty accepting that others can be generous towards them.

"My pleasure."

"Wait, she bought you a hot chocolate?"

"Yeah."

"Didn't you have money?"

"Oh, Dad, I thought I would like a coffee, I really did. They smell so good! But it just tasted weird. And then I didn't have enough money for a hot chocolate, but I didn't realise until they'd already made it."

"And you *somehow* got Vera to pay for it."

Before Elsie had a chance to express how kind and generous Vera had been, Vera snapped out of her trance and managed to paint her own portrait.

"No, I saw her and I offered to pay for it; I remember doing the same thing. With trying coffee and regretting it, I mean." Vera blushed at Nate saying her name. Nate *Fucking* Whitely! Saying *her* name!

"That's very generous of you." Nate hesitated, having to change tack from scolding Elsie to thanking Vera. "I don't suppose I can buy you one now before we leave?"

"Oh, no. Absolutely my pleasure. Don't worry about it."

"Maybe if you're here again after school, I can bring more money and buy you one?"

"Make sure you do, Elsie."

"Oh, you don't have to, but I won't stop you if you like. I'm here pretty much every day. Boring, I know. But if you like coffee, this place is great." Vera realised she was ranting. She took in a quick breath to stop herself from starting another sentence or attempting to continue the previous one.

Nate found Vera justifying her repetitive life to be insanely endearing, and smiled at her again, making her blush coyly. Elsie took special note of Vera's admission: a predictable routine made the plan forming in her mind would be so much easier to execute.

"Great! Thanks again, Vera. I'll probs see you again soon, then. Come on, Dad." She stumbled backwards a few steps, grabbing her father's arm on the way. Nate raised his hand and nodded his head, flashing his most charming smile. He felt a twinge of guilt mixed with reassurance as he watched Vera's eyes melt.

After they left, Vera couldn't help but beat herself up. Even though it didn't matter, she couldn't help feeling as though she'd blown some sort of big chance which she'd been dreaming about since she was Elsie's age. She'd met Nate Whitely, the Nate Whitely, and had proven herself completely unremarkable. Or worse — maybe she'd looked like an idiot in front of him, unable to form sentences like an adult, and only occasionally throwing out jittering giggles like a teenaged fangirl. That was it, she was sure; he'd never see her ever again, and even if he did, he wouldn't recognise her. Or he would, and want to steer clear.

But, Nate Whitely had held her hand.

Nate *Fucking* Whitely had looked her in the eyes.

It had felt like their eyes were locked on each other. If she was staring at him, then he was staring at her too.

Surely.

She wanted to tell her best friend, who she'd known since highschool, the one who she'd obsessed over Nate Whitely with through innumerable sleepovers. The one who knew all the words to all his songs as well as her. Pity that it was the same best friend who she'd found having naked sleepovers with her fiance.

The hot, disembodying, feverish horror that she'd felt when she found them in bed together filled her again. She felt like throwing up. The betrayal and disgust over losing the two most important people in her life, combined with her embarrassment over acting like an idiot in front of *Nate Whitely* left her feeling like she needed to get out of there. Her safe haven had been invaded.

The barista brought her mudcake — warm, with icecream and cream — and placed it down in front of her before looking at her with concern.

"Are you okay?"

Vera looked up at her, managing a smile.

Yes, she was, because Nate Whitely had looked at her with *those eyes*, and given her one of his smiles.

Four

⏮ ⏸ ⏭

That night, Vera considered Googling Nate to play catch-up on what he'd been doing for the past decade — aside from raising Elsie. It seemed like an easy, indulgent way to simulate intimacy. However, knowing that either she would have the chance to get to know him as a real person or, more likely, never see him again, she decided against creating an idea of him based on someone else's reports and speculations.

Instead, Vera made herself a bath.

What might have seemed unremarkable was surprisingly significant for her. Steven had always made her feel uncomfortable about taking baths: he only saw the point of them as part of foreplay, so why would she want to take one without him? Even when she'd called him out on that, he found endless justifications that would make her feel like she was being selfish, wasteful, thoughtless. It was expensive. It was uneconomical. It was 'unenvironomical.' Why couldn't she just have a quick shower? Each time, he moved quick-fire through the reasons until one hit — then doubled down on it. He wasn't afraid of swapping out a reason when the old one got cold. Vera was always left with a sense that she was the one being unreasonable, or that it wasn't worth the argument. She stopped even considering taking a bath. When they moved out together, he'd commented that it would be a waste to get a place with a bath. "Unless we got a dog? I'd like a dog," Vera once ventured. He simply laughed as though she'd made a joke. They never got a dog.

When she found this place to rent, she was endeared by it and was compelled to put in an application; but, like a house in a horror movie, she was strangely drawn to and yet frightened of the bath, as though Steven would somehow know from afar that she might take one.

But meeting Nate Whitely tempted her to revert to her old ways, her old desires. She found a plug, ran the water, swashed the dust down the drain, and committed to filling the bath. She felt panic creeping up. She stared at the water pooling up, and forced herself on — but realised that she had nothing to add to the bath. She had soap, of course, but soap seemed too mundane and too *cleansing*: while it might wash away her thoughts of Steven, it also felt as though it would wash away how she felt after meeting Nate. She felt doomed to eternally stand next to the bath, the water either overflowing or slowly turning tepid.

Then she remembered: for her work Secret Santa last year, she'd bought some bath bombs, then felt too uncomfortable to go to the party itself, and had stayed at home instead. She probably still had the bombs: she had no reason to throw them out, and was a terrible hoarder.

By now, the bath was beginning to get worryingly full, so she turned it off while she searched for the bath bomb. She hoped she'd chosen a decent scent. She walked, apathetic about her nudity, into the spare room filled with boxes that spilled out into her living room. The one marked "BATHROOM" in large angry letters was already open, and she rifled through styling utensils she'd never mastered, and soaps and gift packs she'd never opened.

Yes!

Lavender.

Lavender was fine. Relaxing, right?

Vera gazed at the bomb as though it was a crystal ball and began peeling the plastic from it like an inedible orange as she walked back to the bath. She realised she'd never done this before. What's the proper order for a person and a bath bomb? Surely the goal was to have it all sparkly and fizzy around you, so the order would be person first, followed by the bomb? Vera slowly stepped into the bath and lowered herself in, careful not to get the bomb wet, while fragments of purple, scented debris dropped from her hands into the water and fizzed promisingly. As she settled in, she prepared herself (towel behind her head) for the bath, but didn't prepare herself for the outcome of dropping the bomb between her legs.

She felt sexy and glamorous, as though she was Dita von Teese in a giant champagne glass. She should have champagne! Except that felt somehow too decadent, and anyway, she didn't have any. But what if she did? That was a different person. Would that person live a more glamorous life? Would that person have met *Nate Whitely* today?

She wondered: what if that person was exactly the type of person Nate Whitely would want Vera to be? She could be that. She might need to rearrange her budget as it wouldn't be a matter of swapping something like coffee for champagne. Unless Passion Pop was an acceptable substitute? It would be appropriate, she reasoned; but not acceptable. Just because she drank it at school leavers while dreaming he'd tour again and see her from the stage and invite her backstage doesn't mean she isn't more grown up and sophisticated now. She could absolutely wander into that $30-50 sparkling range. She'd just need to stretch the bottle over a few nights. Sparkling doesn't go flat, does it?

Unless sharing a bottle of sparkling was the sort of thing Nate Whitely did casually at home? He'd invite her around and say, 'Hey love, grab the Moet from the fridge and put it in the Esky. Maybe put in a couple. Let's get expensively smashed and make out.'

Vera groaned when she realised how much like her teenaged self that sounded. Time to try again: 'Grab a bottle of real, actual Champagne from the fridge. I'll put it in the car's refrigerative glovebox with the strawberries. Let's go on an adventure. Don't worry, I'll drive. I love spoiling you and watching you enjoy yourself, and then getting you home safely because I'm a responsible adult now.' Sigh! Now *that* sounds so grown up and mature!

The real Nate Whitely, of course, was no fantasy character; but Vera had limited time to think of him this way, so she enjoyed every second of it.

Five

⏮ ⏸ ⏭

There's a game people play when they want to see someone again but don't want to jinx it, especially when seeing that person relies on a certain amount of luck. Suddenly, the banal, everyday life becomes enchanted, because it is impossible to know whether everyday actions will encourage desired results. Simply turning up at the same time at the same place feels desperate, yet varying the pattern may risk missing the other person completely. And, of course, what if the other person's pattern does not match up with what they did on that one day when your lives synced up?

Such was Elsie's search for Vera at the cafe.

She wondered whether her after-school time had been Vera's coffee time for years, and she'd just never noticed her before. Not that Vera was a wallflower or anything, but she was pretty quiet and... Okay, maybe she *was* a wallflower. Elsie feared turning up every day, only to find she'd missed her, or that she'd give up just before Vera walked in. Plus, her Dad wouldn't appreciate her wasting his money on constant hot chocolates. As much as Nate would want her to pay Vera back, Elsie being so keen to fulfill his request would seem out of character. Besides, the whole point was to have Nate and Vera see each other again, not for Elsie to pay Vera back; and yet, it would look suspiciously obvious if she got into the habit of going and asking him to pick her up without ever confirming that they would meet. It *did* help that her friends, who were into boys their age (for some reason), liked to be admired and gossip. That would have to be the angle she'd take. Friends... and maybe helping each other with homework would be an extra incentive? But only after a while, because that would be too obvious.

Conveniently, Nate had an appointment near the school on the following Monday afternoon.

"How about I pick you up... if you don't mind waiting a bit later? We can go out for dinner after."

"Sure Dad; the girls wanted to hang out anyway — I'll meet you at the cafe?"

"And you can pay Vera back while you're there."

Elsie beamed. She didn't need to worry anymore: Vera was clearly on her father's mind. Vera said that she was there most days, so she should be there next Monday. Plus, Nate would be picking her up. Perfect.

Vera *wasn't* there.

Elsie looked all over the cafe. She waited. She bought her hot chocolate. She even got bored enough to start her *homework*.

When Nate arrived, she'd almost finished her English essay.

"Afternoon, Els... Wow, hot chocolates must be conducive to homework. I never knew."

"It's the marshmallows, Dad."

"Of course it is. Are you happy to go now?"

Elsie looked around. Just in case she'd somehow not seen Vera.

"Or is there someone you're here with who you want to say goodbye to? Friends? A *boy*?"

"Nah, I just... thought I heard something weird. I'm ready. Let's go." Elsie packed her schoolbag and slung it over her shoulder. She slurped the last of her now-cold chocolate, disappointed that Nate had seemingly forgotten all about Vera. As they walked to the door, a group of *boys* (Elsie now understood why her father had used this word), aged fourteen, half of them pimply and half of them still looking like children with perfectly smooth and peachy-flushed skin, walked past.

"Elsie!" gasped one of the pimpliest ones, who, despite the effect puberty was having on his skin, had also managed to remain the height and build he was when he was ten.

"Oh... hey David. Sorry, we have to go. Dinner booking."

"If I knew you were here, I would have come sooner."

Elsie closed her eyes hard and feigned a polite smile. "*So embarrassing,*" she muttered to herself. Nate made some mental notes and nodded at David as they walked past.

It appears that burgers and milkshakes are the cure for embarrassment.

"Vera was at the cafe today," Elsie lied through her straw.

"Was she, now."

Elsie analysed Nate's face for any sign of feeling.

Nate watched Elsie, waiting for her to give up. She was a terrible liar. "I hope you bought her a coffee or something as payback for last time."

"Oh. I forgot."

"Ah well, never mind. Next time you see her, eh?"

"Dad?" Elsie had to go for stronger tactics. All those years of avoiding the press had made Nate's emotion-evasion game strong, despite it being weak during the height of his fame. "Do you think she's pretty?"

This non-sequitur knocked Nate off-centre. It took him a moment to prepare his response. "Elsie... there's more to the world than how pretty someone is. I thought I taught you that."

"Yeah, yeah. I know. But... um... is she?"

"What are you getting at?" Nate's sharp response pleased Elsie. It was a sign that she was getting under his skin, and his one unchecked downfall in interviews.

"Nothing, I just... I don't know. She doesn't look like most girls I know her age. All the teachers and stuff. I dunno. I think she is, but I wanted to know what you thought. I'm just curious."

"Elsie. A pretty face can hide the most horrible person. They aren't always, but sometimes they are. Vera *seems* nice. She bought you a drink for no reason. That's nice. That's kind, that's generous. That's... rare," Nate paused, well aware that he was thinking about her eyes and the way she blushed and looked at him. "And... she reminds me of someone I used to..." he paused, thinking about how to phrase it. He gave up.

"Sure, she's pretty. Yeah."

The seed had been planted. Elsie had won this round.

Six

⏮ ⏸ ⏭

Elsie was stopping by the cafe every day now. The only bad part was that some of those boys from school would follow her. They were nice enough, but she wasn't really into *boys*. She was into *men*. Tommy was twenty-one and a *man*. She pushed herself to separate herself from the *boys and girls* by ordering mochas. That's more grown-up, right? She kinda liked them — with a couple of sugars added.

She usually didn't stay long, either. She'd walk in, order a mocha, and then look around nonchalantly. It seemed like Vera would never be there. Her plan was dying. It wasn't worth coming back. Yet every day, she did.

But, after a full five days of going, the mochas were starting to hit her hip pocket. She didn't have a huge allowance, so it meant she had to be clever about it. She had to stop soon.

It had to become an every-second day thing next week. She'd alternate days to get the greatest impact, greatest chance of seeing Vera. Monday would make a full two weeks since they'd met. So, next week: Monday, Wednesday, and Friday, only. As Elsie decided this, she spotted Vera, curled up in a corner and looking super sick.

SHE'D BEEN SICK!

Vera had caught a terrible cold or flu — the type where you don't really want to go out, especially if you might run into the (former) hottest rockstar in the world. Vera simply continued her depressing job searches from home, swapping coffee for Lemsip.

Elsie's mocha arrived, and it was time to play her game. She carried it straight over to Vera.

"Do you like Mochas? I wanted to surprise you, but wasn't sure what you had. Mochas seemed the best of both worlds?"

"Oh! Oh, thank you. You really didn't have to; I meant it. Anyway, today I'm just having lemon ginger tea. This cold… don't get too close!" Vera laughed, then her throat caught and sent her into a coughing fit.

"Damn! I thought I'd got Dad off my back, finally. He's always going on about paying you back."

"That's nice of him to remember. You don't have to, though."

"He's trying to give me 'good morals' or something."

"That's admirable."

"So… you don't want the mocha?"

"Thank you, but no — you have it. Tell your Dad that I had it, so he gives you a break."

"He won't believe me! But I'll try." Time to water this seed. "He was right about you."

"What do you mean?"

"He said he thinks you're very nice."

Nice. It was diminishing — and yet, Nate Fucking Whitely had thought about her, said what he thought about her. Vera felt a hot flush of blood rushing up her neck and filling her face. Elsie watched it.

Vera was both pretty and super cute, Elsie thought. Cuter than her teachers. They were all either super dowdy or trying too hard to be young or hip or sexy. As much as she cared what her Dad thought about Vera for her intentions to get them together, she was also relieved that a guy like her Dad, who had been subject to the interest of so many girls in his life, could find someone attractive who wasn't trying to be *hot*.

"So, how's school?" Vera was keen to change the topic.

"Oh, you know. Boring. It must be nice not to have to go to school every day!"

"I miss highschool," sighed Vera. "It was probably the best time of my life."

"Really?" Elsie was incredulous.

"Oh, yes. I was one of the smart kids, so the homework and assignments were never an issue for me. My friends weren't perfect, but they were pretty fun. Good to have around."

"Did you have a boyfriend?"

"Ha, no... I just dreamt of one. Oh, and the music was good back then, just ask your Dad," Vera laughed, covering her blushing. "Oh! I sound so old. Anyway, I used to play trombone, but I wasn't very good."

"Weird choice of instrument."

"Yeah, well I think I got so used to the discipline and humility that was drilled into me by my parents that I just liked the idea of an instrument with no set keys... and blowing my own horn."

"That's *terrible*, urgh," Elsie groaned, stifling a laugh. "You're as bad as Dad!"

Vera didn't know how to feel about the frequency at which they kept mentioning Nate. If this was a movie, she was sure it'd fail the Bechdel test. It wasn't that she didn't like thinking about him — far from it! — it was more that, every time Elsie did, Vera felt like a silly schoolgirl. There was only one way to defend against this.

"Do *you* have a boyfriend?"

"Ha!" Elsie looked over her shoulder and indicated with a flick of her head. "See those *boys*?" She threw as much emphasis as she could on the word. "Would *you* have gone out with them in highschool?"

Vera regarded the boys: skinny, pimply, under-developed. She remembered how, all through highschool, most of the boys were developmentally delayed, either physically or emotionally.

"Yeah, nah. I don't blame you."

"But there's this one guy... Ah, it's a bit embarrassing," Elsie dropped her head, then flicked the hair out of her eyes. "But you'd understand. I've never met him. He's in a band. A popular one."

They'd talked about this before; Vera was sure. She thought back to their first conversation. "Johnny?"

"Tommy," Elsie beamed, as though saying his name brought him closer to her. "I'm trying to get Dad to go to the ARIA Awards so I can meet him. He's a bit older than me, but..." Elsie had to gather more information before she knew her plan would really work. "Hey, how old was Dad when you were in highschool?"

Back to Vera and Nate. "I'm not sure... late 20s?"

"That's older than Tommy!"

"Musical and physical admiration knows no age!"

"Very wise, my friend Vera. Hey, so... what do you think of Dad now?"

"Oh wow, I don't know."

"He's single, you know."

"Oh... oh, okay."

A horrible thought crossed Elsie's mind. What if Vera was in a relationship? What if she was married? What if she'd sworn off men? What if men were a *phase*? Her Dad had been quite... *pretty* when he was younger. Maybe Vera had liked girlish boys... and now likes boyish girls? She was suddenly hyperaware of her own short hair and Ruby Rose style.

Vera laughed in a clearly self-deprecating way, sneezed, and blew her nose. "Well, it sounds like he probably isn't interested in me, anyway."

"What? Noooo, he thinks you're pretty," Elsie breathed a sigh of relief, while Vera breathed in all her expelled anxiety.

"Really? He said that?"

"Yes!" Elsie, in her excitement, nearly fell on top of Vera. "And more importantly, he said you're really nice, and that being nice is far more important than how you look."

Vera felt like she'd been fantasising in the shower, but must have slipped and hit her head. She looked at Elsie, who was beaming expectantly at her. "Wait, why are you telling me this? You're up to something." She bit her lip. "Are you making fun of me?"

"What? No! Why would I do that?"

As far as Vera could see, Elsie was young, slender, cute, popular, trusting, and confident. While she was full of dreams and hormones, Vera was full of suspicion and heartbreak. She'd been betrayed by the two people who were supposed to be truest to her — how could she trust a teenager who she'd just met?

"I just think it's cute. You're not like the single mums at school. They're all gross and tacky and I know Dad only tolerates them when they tell him they know who he is and cosy up to him. Even some of the married mums do," Elsie shuddered in disgust. "Then he meets you and becomes disgustingly cute and charming instead of cold and mildly irritated."

"Okay, okay, don't build it up. Maybe he was just... I don't know. Laughing at me? I went all fangirly and embarrassed myself." She shook her head at herself. "I've never been very good around guys I have a crush on." She snorted at herself. "CRUSH! Oh, Elsie. I feel like we're school friends; just when I thought I was an adult. I miss those days," she sighed, the nostalgia softening her. "Life was so much simpler. Everything that hurt so much actually felt good to hurt. There was a sweetness in what seemed to be the end of the world." Vera felt Elsie's eyes on her. "Sorry, I'm kind of talking down to you. I'm rambling and being OLD."

"Yep," nodded Elsie. "You and Dad will get along juuuuust fine."

⏮ ⏸ ⏭

Elsie swung her bag down beside the kitchen bench and leaned forward, dropping her face into her hands with her elbows on the cold benchtop. She grinned up at Nate, who was preparing dinner. He didn't really mind that she was coming home a bit later. He knew where she was, and that was enough for him; if it wasn't, he could always message or call her. He thought about what he and his sister had been like at her age: even though they had been less contactable, they were also more unreliable. He felt sorry for his poor Mum and Dad. They didn't deserve their kids' wild ways. Yet, he respected them for being cool about it. If they hadn't, he probably wouldn't have gotten into bands and lived his passion. So, that was good. He should probably call them to say thanks.

"Guess who I saw today?"

"Your latest obsession," Nate paused for dramatic effect. "Dashing David and his Delectable Derriere."

"EW! Dad! You're GROSS! And I bet you've been planning that one all week."

"Saying that only tells me you like him more than I ever expected." He put down the knife, which he'd been brandishing wildly, and leant towards her. "Do I need to be concerned?"

"Urgh, you're literally the WORST." Elsie wrung the disgust from her hands. "No, it was Vera!"

"Oh. Vera," Nate looked down to the chopping board, picked up an invisible food scrap, and flicked it into the sink. "Did you pay her back this time?"

"No."

"Elsie."

"I *tried* to but she already had a drink and didn't want another. She told me to tell you that I had anyway, but I said you wouldn't believe me." Elsie paused, remembering to use the trigger word. "She's just too *nice*."

"Hmmm." Nate picked up the knife and focused back on the celery he had been chopping, as though he was performing complex surgery. "Yeah, she *is* nice. Too nice for you to be able to pay her back." Chop chop. "Well. I guess I'll have to do it."

Elsie didn't want to show her excitement. "Oh, *no*, Dad. Don't make a big fuss. It's okay, I can do it. I'll get there early tomorrow, straight after school."

"It's fine, Elsie. I'll take care of it. And no, I only thought that one up just then. I'm not *that* slow."

Seven

"Hey there. Need a refill?"

It was a voice she'd heard in countless interviews. Deeper now than then, but the same phrasing, the same accent, the same tone. Vera pulled her attention up from her laptop's screen and took him in: scruffy, slightly baggy jeans, and a thin, crumpled t-shirt under a slouchy knitted jumper. Hair: shorter than when he was younger, but just as scruffy and, surprisingly, with only minimal greys.

Yet, once again, it was those luminous deep blue eyes and the lopsided smile that really got to her.

Nate nodded, answering for Vera. "Yeah, I'll get you a refill: your cup is empty. Will you tell me what you have, or am I going to have to engage in some further detective work, Sherlock-style?" He paused, cocking his head slightly before clarifying. "I was thinking Robert Downey Jr style, though if you prefer Benedict Cumberbatch, I could try that, too."

"Oh, um... a flat white."

"I didn't think flat whites existed anymore."

"Well, I ask for it and they give me what I want."

"How about I challenge you to a latte? It's one less word and practically indistinguishable."

"Sure," A coffee conversation was *not* what Vera had in mind when she used to dream of meeting Nate Whitely fifteen years ago. But right now? Anything was good.

Nate muttered "Okay," under his breath, and gave Vera a look that said: *don't go anywhere.* He shot her a wink and spun on his heels. Vera wished desperately that she had someone to sms 'omg' to. She thought about her school friends. She had them on Facebook, right? Or LinkedIn, maybe? Or even their outdated and abandoned email addresses that she could at least shoot an email to, and deal with the discovery of the delivery failure reply that night? Maybe their phone numbers hadn't changed, and she could find someone on WhatsApp or Telegram or whatever other messaging app was new or she hadn't heard of yet?

Vera scrambled on her laptop, opening her various messaging apps and searching for her ~~best friend~~ second best friend, Vanessa. There she was, under her highschool nickname: Ness. Online, too!

VERA: Hey!
NESS: Omg! I was just thinking about you
NESS: I heard about the whole mess with you, bitchface, and the arsehole. I'm sorry.

Well, that wasn't what she wanted to be reminded of.

VERA: Thanks
NESS: Sorry I didn't message you earlier
NESS: Look im at work and i need to go into a meeting but I'm glad you reached out, I'll message you later, k hun?

The universal brush-off.

VERA: Yep, sure

"They'll bring it out in a minute," Nate put down the order number, and sat down next to Vera, uncomfortably close.

Vera snapped shut her laptop. She could feel his heat, and she was sure he could hear her heartbeat and see her sweat.

"So... this makes us even, right?" She said, thinking she was stating the obvious and then completely regretting the words and hating herself for it.

"Well, it just means that Elsie doesn't owe you for a coffee. But, I still owe you my gratitude for putting up with her."

"Oh, ah, no; she's lovely. It's been nice having someone to... I've needed... She's a great girl."

"She is."

WHY. WAS THIS. SO HARD.

"So... Vera," Nate wasn't in the habit of encouraging fans, but something about Vera's hesitancy, her desire to hold back despite her interest, made him curious. "You know what I do. What do you spend your life on? Besides buying hot chocolates for random teenagers in need."

"Well, I'm, um... I'm actually trying to find something different," Vera fumbled, but all the words rushed out again before she could stop. "I quit my job a few months back, and I'm looking for a new one but I just don't seem to be having much luck and I don't know what to do. And, I suddenly realised I don't really have much in my life outside of my last job and my last relationship — which *is* over, thank goodness — so that's..." *Why* had she said that? She had to stop. "Oh, God! I'm rambling and I'm sure you don't really want to hear about a sad person like me."

Nate's face was soft when she looked at him. He'd been watching her pour her heart out, looking like an adorable, frightened mouse. And, he couldn't help noting that she had just confessed to him that she was single. "That's not true. Not at all. I think sad people are great: I write songs about them all the time." He smiled a smile that hoped she would smile too.

The coffees arrived, just in time. "Two lah-days?"

Nate nodded thanks to the barista with the thickest Australian accent he'd ever heard. He picked one of the glasses up and passed it to Vera, their fingers touching during the handover. "Tell me if you taste a difference."

Vera tried to shuffle back, aware of how close Nate was to her. She was worried that she was the one who was leaning into him and being the creep. Nate hadn't touched his coffee. He watched expectantly while she took a sip and swallowed audibly.

"It's good. You're right, it's practically the same, just served in a glass instead of a cup. But really, it's still two syllables so it's not that much easier asking for a latte instead of a flat white."

Nate laughed at her calling him on his bull. "You got me there. But you can't order a flat white at many places, internationally."

"Doesn't 'latte' just mean 'milk,' though? That could end badly."

"Well, that's true. But, in Italy, there's a whole system of what type of coffee you're allowed to drink at different times, so that's a whole other set of complications."

"If I ever go overseas, maybe I'll just order a cappuccino. That seems to be something that would be universally recognised."

Nate paused. "You haven't been overseas? Ever?"

"No… never." She would have gone on her honeymoon, but that trip had been taken by her ex-fiancé and ex-best-friend, she assumed.

Thanks to all his tours, Nate had been just about everywhere — not that he remembered much of it. "Maybe one day soon."

"Maybe. I needed a change or a holiday. I chose the change — maybe I should have gone for the holiday?"

"Did *the change* bring you here?"

She nodded.

"Then, I think *the change* was the right choice."

Vera hid her intense blushing by once again sipping her *caffe latte*. Was she reading him right? She didn't understand why he was being so overtly flirty. Maybe this was just him? He was known to be playfully flirty in some interviews, but it wasn't the way Elsie said he was around the single Mums at school. But maybe that was just the way he set his trap for unsuspecting young women…

Nate loved seeing Vera blush. The women who came onto him were usually so predatory that he could probably tell them he wanted to show them his cock and they'd just ask to suck it in response. Vera, he imagined, would probably either blush, giggle, or get offended. It wasn't that he thought she was prudish or uptight; she just didn't seem to feel entitled to his interest. If he was honest, he'd rather omit the sexual intention in favour of a bit of fun with no guarantees or promises, and jumping to the revelation of body parts would spoil the game for both of them. He liked the game. He hadn't played it for a long time, not without the other party escalating it too fast and ending it for him, which always just led to the whole thing being over too soon, one way or another.

He wondered whether there was a point where it'd be too much for her. It wasn't like she'd indicated in any way for him to stop. She wasn't advancing things at all, but she wasn't really shying away or blocking him, and the blushing *seemed* to show that she was enjoying it. He hoped he'd read her reaction correctly. But, he supposed it didn't matter if he did… except for coming across as an entitled creep, which was the last thing he'd want to do. Once upon a time, he never really thought about whether he came across that way; but, with age comes more self-awareness, more shame. Things that once seemed acceptable no longer seemed fair. Anyway, what if he'd only *imagined* The Look? What if she was just being polite, or starstruck, and he really was being a creep and she was just too nice to tell him where to get off?

She really did seem genuinely nice, if a bit haunted by her past relationship — but she wasn't the only one in that regard. Plus, Elsie had taken a shine to her. Seeing as her mother had left to travel the world and had never really taken an interest in her, he reasoned that it was only fair that she choose her own 'big sister' type, without having to resort to extended family. No, he didn't want to scare Vera away from Elsie, so he probably shouldn't push it by flirting with her if she didn't actually want him to, but was afraid to say so. He looked at her, hunching over coffee, trying to take up the least amount of space possible.

"Sorry; am I making you uncomfortable?" He broke the silence. Someone had to. He wished he knew what she was thinking.

"Hm? No, no." Vera put down her coffee, which she'd been staring into, as though scrying. "Well, maybe a little. No, I don't know." She didn't seem to be able to bring herself to look at him.

Nate shifted away from her. "I'll take that as a yes, then."

"Sorry," Vera half smiled at him. "It's just, you know." She indicated his presence in her humble life. "*Weird.*"

"Okay." Yeah, Nate had no idea what to do here. It'd been a *very* long time since he'd needed or even wanted to flirt like this, and he was sure now that he'd read things wrong and made the whole situation uncomfortable for them both. "Okay."

"Hey, *wow*, your stalker's here, Vera!" They were rescued by Elsie! "I didn't know you were picking me up, Dad."

"Ah, yeah, I had something on that brought me this way. Thought it would be nice. Ready to go?"

"Whoa whoa, wait! What if I want to spend some time with *my* friend Vera? Besides," Elsie looked down at his glass. "You haven't finished your coffee." It must be noted that Nate had not even touched his latte.

"Yeah, okay, you sit down and start catching up, I'll go get you a hot chocolate." *And I'll wait for it at the counter*, he thought.

"Mocha, please!"

"Mocha! Wow, you're like an actual adult now!" Nate grinned at Elsie, but dropped it slightly as his eyes met with Vera's. "Back soon."

Elsie waited until Nate was out of earshot. "Okay... what happened?"

"I— I think I upset your Dad. Sorry. I made things really awkward somehow."

"Okay, well, when Dad feels awkward he usually wants to leave as soon as possible. So… " Elsie pulled a pen out of her bag and scribbled on the napkin sitting under Vera's coffee, then beamed at her. "Talk soon?"

Vera smiled when she saw a mobile number and a love heart with an arrow through it, followed by a big letter E. Elsie was very disarming. She couldn't help but admit that she loved the feeling of being a schoolgirl again. She felt she'd lost a good third of her life to her shitty relationship with Steven, and her one friendship that had remained beyond school? She wondered how long her *friend* had been in it for her.

"You okay?"

Elsie, ever observant, was peering into her face, while she must have spaced out. "Yeah, yeah. I guess I'm just still a little under the weather."

"Okay. I'll tell Dad not to get too close." She laughed at her own joke, a bright peal of sunshine. As cliche as it was, this girl was destined for greatness, if she wanted it.

"Elsie?" She sure was right: when Nate wanted to go, he wanted to go. He was studying the counter, holding a takeaway cup. He raised it and indicated out. "Nice to see you, Vera."

"Urgh, he's such a weirdo sometimes." Elsie rolled her eyes. "Oh, I wanted to ask you something. But, later." She nodded at the napkin, smirked, and started back towards Nate.

Vera smiled and looked down at the napkin. She saw Nate's abandoned latte, still untouched. "Ah, sorry — don't you want your coffee?"

"Consider it… *extra* payback." Absent-mindedly, Nate bit his lip.

Vera blushed. "Sure. Thanks again."

"Yep." Nate considered adding more, anything from, 'anytime,' to 'no problem,' to 'my pleasure,' to 'I still owe you,' to 'see you soon,' to 'let my take you out some time…' but it all seemed too forward, and he didn't want to risk making her any more uncomfortable. "Yep," he said again, nodding and smiling as Elsie took the cup from him and walked past, towards the door.

"Good try, Dad."

The Look

Later that night, Vera looked at her messages. She wondered whether she should message Vanessa again. But, she had another option she might find solace in. She fished the napkin out of her pocket, thought about the coffee Nate bought her, looked at the love heart next to the number. Surely he was just being nice to her; flirting and joking like he would with someone he didn't view as someone of interest. She wouldn't be someone he'd find interesting. Right?

She remembered that Elsie had said she wanted to ask her something. Curiosity got the better of her, so she added Elsie's number to her contacts. Before she had a chance to work out what apps Elsie used, a notification on the other side caused a message alert to come through.

New message from Elsie
ELSIE: VEEEEEERRRRRRRRRRAAAAAGHHHH
VERA: That's me!
ELSIE: I was waiting for you to message me!!
ELSIE: I have an important question.
VERA: Yeah ?
ELSIE: How good are you at maths?

Vera was a Mechanical Engineer, so she was pretty good.

VERA: What type of maths?
VERA: I'm an engineer so I'm pretty good, depending on what type it
         is and if I can remember it
ELSIE: oh sweet
ELSIE: dads shit
VERA: I feel like I should tell you off for swearing
ELSIE: its just cuz I said DAD is shit
ELSIE: oooOOOOoooo
VERA: whatever
VERA: do you want me to help or not??
ELSIE: yeh :(
VERA: Homework or assignment?
VERA: I can talk you through it at the cafe
ELSIE: ooooh thatd be awesome <3
VERA: tomorrow, same time, same place?
VERA: I'll let you get the coffee ;)
ELSIE: Oh man otherwise Dad will harass me

ELSIE: tho I think thats just so he can see you
ELSIE: he's all weird about this afternoon ;)

Vera didn't know how to respond.

VERA: he shouldn't be weird.
ELSIE: yeh. He is tho. But just generally
VERA: :)
ELSIE: <3
VERA: <3 ?
ELSIE: <3 !
VERA: Okay, see you tomorrow?
ELSIE: yep thanx, ur the besssssst

If Vera was totally honest with herself, she wanted to get off her phone and just go to sleep and pretend the whole thing was a dream. But some people didn't want her to have that luxury.

New message from Ness
NESS: Hey Ronnie!! Sorry about b4

It was Vanessa, her ~~second~~ best friend since high school, using her old nickname.

VERA: No its cool. How are you?
NESS: Mega busyyy xxx but good. U?
VERA: Not busy at all
VERA: Going for the "change of life" thing!!
NESS: Ohhh yeah I understand!
VERA: :)
NESS: ne thing new on the horizon?
NESS: Jobs? Men? Best friends? lol
NESS: Srry, 2 soon?
VERA: No :)
NESS: Cool :)
NESS: hey I'm really sorry I haven't been a better friend. I kept
          meaning to message you to catch up
VERA: oh it's on me too
NESS: it got weirdly hard to organise anything with you so I gave up :(
          I feel terrible
VERA: Steven used to make snarky comments if I wanted to catch up
          with friends
VERA: well except for Sarah

NESS: yuck, good riddance to rubbish people
NESS: but I should have made more of an effort for you
VERA: its ok. We're talking now, that's what matters, right?
NESS: yup let's catch up now!!!
NESS: so fill me in. whats happening?

Vera braced herself.

VERA: well... I met Nate Whitely the other day
VERA: You know
NESS: !!!! :O
VERA: THE Nate Whitely
VERA: haha, yep!
NESS: omgggggggggg
VERA: yep!!!
NESS: is he all... old now?
VERA: hahaha kinda yeah
NESS: hot old or just old old
VERA: he's not THAT old!
NESS: just answer me!!
VERA: ...
NESS: ANSWER
NESS: MEEEEE
VERA: hot middle aged ;)
NESS: I knew it!
NESS: silver foxxxxx yeeeaaah
VERA: he's NOT that old!!!
NESS: hahaha ur still as cute as I remember <3
VERA: :P
NESS: soooo what's he like in person? Nice or total jerk?
VERA: super nice
NESS: omggggg tell me everythinggggggggggggggg
VERA: you're gonna wear out your g key!!
NESS: hahaha #WORTHIT
VERA: So I bought this girl a coffee once because she'd ordered but
       not paid and I was being an old creep living vicariously through
       her and her friends, and then she was chatting to me about
       liking a guy in a band while she waited for her Dad and then he
       turns up and its NATE WHITELY
NESS: NATE
NESS: MOTHAFOCKIN
NESS: WHITELYYYYYY OMGGGGGGGGG
VERA: so then now she comes over and hangs out with me at the

cafe when she sees me
VERA: so meanwhile I'm just a nervous wreck around him
VERA: but I SWEAR he was flirting this afternoon but I just freaked out and made it awkward
NESS: wait WHAT
VERA: I just had to tell someone
NESS: GIRL PLEASE
NESS: omggggggg no waaaaayyyyy
VERA: it sounds so made up
NESS: I SO want this for you
NESS: what a rebound!
VERA: omg no, it's nothing
VERA: he's not really interested in me
NESS: what if its not? What if he IS into you?
NESS: okay theres only one way to tell
VERA: ???
NESS: what cafe is this?
VERA: noooo its not like he'll be back
NESS: WHAT CAFE
VERA: its called Blue Jay or something
NESS: the one next to the school?
VERA: yep, thats her school
NESS: MY WORK IS RIGHT NEAR THERE
NESS: TELL ME NEXT TIME HE IS THERE
NESS: SO HELP ME GOD I WILL DROP ALL MY WORK AND BE THERE

Alerts popped up forcing Vera back and forth between the two chats.

New message from Elsie
ELSIE: hey still there?
VERA: Yeah?

New message from Ness
NESS: VERA?
VERA: yep okay okay I will

New message from Elsie
ELSIE: Okay so, Dad's a creep
ELSIE: I happened to mention you're helping me tomorrow and dad said he'll pick me up ;)

New message from Ness
NESS: lol is this a RomCom
NESS: im pretty sure I've seen this one!
NESS: or a few of them that end up being like this
VERA: VANESSA
NESS: WHATTT
VERA: TOMORROW
NESS: !!!
VERA: YES
NESS : I'll be there. Send me a message when he arrives and I will
      stalk

New message from Elsie
ELSIE: he's such a weirdo
VERA: he's just looking after you
ELSIE: he's just lusting after you
VERA: omg no, stop it
ELSIE: lol see you there <3

Eight

⏮ ⏸ ⏭

Vera slept in. She wondered, if she slept long enough, would she wake up from a coma and find out the whole thing wasn't real, that she was back with her fiance, her best friend by her side? Not that she'd want the Nate part of things to not be real — she'd just rather not delay the pain of finding out that it was.

As she lay there, she found herself going over everything Nate said or did, blow-by-blow, like she used to with the cute guys she'd had hopes for when she was at university. She wondered how much of it she was building up, and how much was exactly what had happened.

The agony made her smile — but, unlike some of the agonies she had faced recently, this only promised the potential of something new and better that she could gain, rather than it purely being about how well she coped with something being taken away from her. The desire to be desired is as human as life itself. She thought about all the love songs Nate had written, all the variations of emotion he'd told the world he'd experienced. If romance was a stereotypically *female* thing, that was because the men who said so were too afraid of admitting their own feelings.

She flattered herself, she was sure, thinking that maybe Nate got so 'weird,' as Elsie put it, because he felt things so strongly, and maybe he'd felt rejected? She wasn't sure. She also didn't understand why he'd go from being 'weird' to then wanting to see her, especially when he'd wanted to leave so quickly. When she felt so uncomfortable that she didn't want to be around someone, there was no way she'd go anywhere near them.

Why else did she move so far away from her former life?

Dragging herself out of bed, she walked past the mirror. Glancing across, she didn't know the person in the reflection who looked back at her. It wasn't that cliched thing of not recognising herself: she absolutely recognised that person as the same person who she'd looked at in the mirror every day for the past (she didn't know how many) years. She just had no idea who this person really was, where she came from, or where she was going. She'd become 'An Adult,' but had no recollection of ever choosing to be *this* one. She never realised how far she'd let herself go. Looking in the mirror, she wondered whether she'd been this dowdy when in her relationship. Shouldn't Steven have not minded, and loved her faithfully forever? Isn't that what love is? Or was it her own fault, like the two of them had implied when she found them in bed together?

Vera realised that she hadn't felt like herself in years. Life had happened, and somewhere along the way, 'Ronnie' had transmuted into Vera. She just hadn't really resisted it.

She looked around the room. She'd moved here *three* months ago — unemployed — and still hadn't unpacked. She wondered whether there might be some existential significance to this — that she wasn't ready to move forward with her life — or maybe she wanted to keep all her past memories packed up and throw them out without ever going through them. But that wasn't really like her. At least, she didn't think so. Maybe it was *Vera*, but it wasn't Ronnie. Ronnie was cool, edgy, young; Vera was...

She looked at herself in the mirror and sighed. Vera just was.

⏮ ⏸ ⏭

Nate wasn't exactly sure why he thought it was a good idea to see Vera. He didn't enjoy hearing Elsie talk about her. Actually, he wasn't sure about that, either. But at those stupid times in between, when he had nothing to occupy his thoughts, he found himself thinking of her *AND HE HATED IT EVEN MORE.*

He just knew he had to do something, and it wasn't to ignore and pretend it away. After all, he liked how Elsie acted after seeing Vera. She seemed happy- happier than she'd been in months. She finally had someone to help her with maths! He could help with writing, art, drama, history, and of course, music; but anything outside of the humanities just wasn't him. Neither, it seemed, was it Elsie. He wondered whether this may have been different for him with a different mentor or teacher, someone to sit with him and explain what all these equations and magic tricks were for, and why they were. Music is mathematical, he's heard many times. Maybe he'd just needed someone to show him how.

So, he'd decided that he needed to give his blessings to their friendship, smooth it over, and make sure it didn't stay weird. If he could just go and say hi, thank her again, and prove he's not totally deficient in social graces, that would be best. He was sure of that. So it really came down to just resisting the urge to flirt, to make her blush. He had to remember not to do that, and instead to thank Vera for all she'd done for Elsie, that she doesn't owe him anything (why would she?), and he owes her, but she doesn't even owe him the pleasure of letting him pay her back, as much as he'd like to. He had to remember that this was about Elsie, not him; he didn't want to take this away from her. He could be friends with Vera; that would be fine. He'd just drop in, say hi, thanks, he appreciates it, and that she should let him know if he can return the favour at all. That's it. Calm and cool. Yeah.

Nine

Vera sat down at her now-regular table with a bottle of water and two glasses. "I'm waiting for someone," she mouthed countless times to the waitstaff, who cocked their heads inquisitively each time they passed. She began to regret her decision to put a bit of makeup on. Her mascara had been out of action for so many months that it had become dry and clumpy, so she was aware that her eyes may have looked more spidery than usual. Was it conspicuous? She reasoned that, if pressed, she'd just say she was catching up with an old friend after she finished work. Yes, that's what she'd do. It was true enough, even if she wouldn't specify what their main conversation topic would be.

She wondered what Vanessa looked like now. She'd seen pictures on social media, of course, but they'd looked so different from how she'd looked in school, and Vera guessed that her old self would still shine through. What would she think of Vera? Would she still be expecting Ronnie, and be disappointed when Vera was there instead? Or would she be impressed by how grown up and sensible Vera was, that it was a good idea to leave Ronnie at home in the dirt?

She had become lost in a world of introspection and nostalgia when Elsie arrived, coffees already in hand.

"Here we are; Dad will have nothing to complain about!"

"Oh, you didn't have to bring them over!" Vera picked up the lighter-coloured coffee, devoid of chocolate. "So... what do we have, and how long have we got?"

"Ehhhhh... Algebra, and I'm not sure," Elsie panicked at the thought that her Dad might miss Vera. "Why? Do you have to be somewhere?" *Hopefully not on a date with someone else?*

"I'm just meeting an old school friend; she works nearby." The excuse came out sooner than expected. "No rush, I just want to give her a timeline. She said she might come down for coffee, otherwise, she'll be here after work."

"Oh, right. What time does she finish work? You probably don't want to be seen hanging out with some *kid*," Elsie flashed a smirk before continuing, "But I can keep you company until then. I'll tell Dad."

"That'd be nice, I'd like that a lot." *And it would make it easier to sync up Vanessa to be able to watch Nate.* "Plus, we're in less of a rush. She usually finishes at 5:30pm, I think. That should give us a couple of hours."

"Cooooooooool," Elsie nodded as her fingers sped over the touchscreen of her phone. She looked up at Vera. "Two whole hours of mathematic goodness."

Vera felt her phone buzz.

"Sorry... you set yourself up and I'll quickly check this... if you don't mind?"

New Message from Ness
NESS: I wanted to check that we're still on
NESS: Da doo Ron Ron Ron da doo Ron Ron
VERA: Whoooa, yeah!
VERA: lol I can't keep this up. His daughter's here, she said she'll stay until you arrive and Nate will just have to wait
NESS: this kid sounds like the best
NESS: I can come down earlier if its easier? I'll just make up the hours tomorrow
VERA: 5-5:30 should be fine
VERA: omg I'm nervous
VERA: okay I'm going now
NESS: don't do anything I wouldn't do
NESS: and I would do ANYTHING

"Dad said he'll be here at 4:30ish, but he can, and I quote, *just be creeping nearby while we do maths*," she cringed at Nate's phrasing, then laughed and put down her phone.

"Ha, okay. Well, that was just my friend. She might finish a bit earlier; she'll come down when she's done." Vera looked at Elsie, skinny and with a big smile like a kid, calculator in one hand, pacer in the other, and a big old maths book in front of her. "You know, for someone who isn't good at maths, it surprises me how pumped you seem right now."

It wasn't the maths she was pumped for. Her plan was *working*: she'd been winding Nate up about Vera, and watching him become increasingly agitated by it. "Well, it just feels like there's something I'm missing, like I just had no one that could make maths make sense to me. Plus, robots are pretty cool and I'd like to build them when I get older, and I hear they want you to have maths for that. So, you know. Let's do this!"

Ten

⏮ ⏸ ⏭

"My head hurts."

"Okay, let's take a break. Want another Mocha?"

"I doooo, but I should buy it or Dad will whiiiine."

"Well he doesn't need to know."

"He'll know. Somehow he'll know."

"Well, he should have given you more money."

"He should pay you to be my maths tutor. It's his fault because he's crap at maths and can't help me."

"Well if that's how it works, maybe I could teach him too?"

"Totally. Private lessons."

"Okay, I'm just going to leave that one there. I'll get the coffees. Close your eyes and try to relax."

Elsie closed her eyes, then opened them suddenly.

"ALL I SEE IS NUMBERS!"

"Then think of Robots?"

Elsie closed her eyes again.

"Okay, that works."

"But... keep an eye on our stuff."

"Oh... Oh yeah! One eye open, one eye closed!" Elsie looked at Vera through an extended wink. "Your stuff is safe!"

Vera laughed as she walked to the counter. She enjoyed Elsie's silly humour — the type of humour she remembered seeing in Nate in some of his music clips and interviews. She looked at the offering of cakes and cookies as she waited her turn. Knowing how much she'd comfort eaten these last few months, as her turn came she made the reluctant decision not to order anything.

"Hi, one large mocha and one large flat white, please."

"I'll get that." Vera didn't immediately register what she heard, but the serving barista's glance beyond her, as well as the feeling of a hand on her upper arm, brought Nate's presence to her attention. She turned to look over her shoulder and struggled to move beyond his lips. "And make that two… *flat whites*." As he looked from the cashier to Vera, her eyes crawled their way up to his. "Hi. Don't worry, I've got this. You take the table number and get back to Elsie." He gave her arm a gentle squeeze and let go, turning back to the cashier. He pulled out his credit card and reassured himself that it was just a friendly hand on her arm and definitely *not* too much.

"Sure, thanks." Vera, holding the number, turned and walked back to Elsie. She turned and looked back once as she was about to sit, and found Nate watching her. He turned away quickly when he realised he'd been found out. Vera blushed and sat down across from Elsie again. "I guess we don't need to worry about your Dad hassling you to pay."

"Huh?" Elsie sat up, awoken from her robot dream. She blinked hard and looked around, as Nate got to the table.

"Sorry I'm late. If you need to keep working, I won't disturb you."

"Shit, what time is it?"

"Elsie, don't swear."

Elsie rolled her eyes.

Vera pulled out her phone. "It's 4:5opm," and she had a message from Vanessa, simply asking, "Yet?" *Sure*, she replied. "Oh, I think my friend will be here soon. We should pack up."

"Oh… I can change the drinks to takeaway," Nate took a step backwards, towards the counter. He deliberately didn't interact with the idea of Vera's *friend*.

"No, that's fine. It's not like you need to leave just because my friend will be here."

"Just sit down, Dad."

Nate hesitated, not sure where the best place to sit would be: next to Vera, or diagonally across from her. He reminded himself that he didn't want to crowd her, *plus* she had a friend coming, so it made more sense for him to sit next to Elsie. "So, how did it go?"

"Maths is exhausting. But I think I'm starting to get it. Kind-of." Vera smiled in agreement. She was glad Elsie had answered: she wasn't sure she'd be able to put two words together with those blue eyes kissing hers.

"You did great, Elsie. Much improved," she managed after Nate had pulled his gaze away. "You just need to get into the habit of using more of these tricks, and learning what to use when."

"You'll help me more, right?"

"Of course."

Nate leaned towards Vera, aiming to look as earnest as possible. "I really appreciate this, you know. If there's *anything* I can do to return the favour, let me know." Cool.

Beside her, Vera's phone buzzed. Vanessa's reply, *'yessssssss omw now,'* was permitted to go unread.

"Oh, sure." Vera blushed. She was reading too much into the subtext of his words, she was sure. Elsie, nodding, caught her attention. She mouthed, '...*anything*!' Vera looked quickly away from her and back to Nate. "I'll... let you know."

Nate sat back in his seat, the intensity of his eyes relaxing. "Great."

They sat together in silence, suddenly uncomfortable. Nate avoided Vera's eyes, Vera avoided Elsie's. Elsie, amused by this adult awkwardness, kept trying to catch Vera's eye so that she could wink or raise her eyebrows suggestively. Their silence was broken by the arrival of their coffees.

"Two flat whites, one mocha?"

"Yesss, mocha!" chirped Elsie.

"I decided to try your poison," Nate pushed one of the flat whites to Vera. "I reasoned that if I can't break your habit, maybe I can break mine."

"Hi, what habit are we breaking?" A tall, slim, beautiful woman bearing blonde hair with a life of its own had appeared at the table.

"Oh, hey Ness!"

"My girl Ronnie!"

"Ronnie?" Nate's question was delivered to Vanessa. Vera saw him looking at her. She was beautiful; even more beautiful than she was at school, or in her social media photos. It wasn't fair. Vera became aware of how plain and daggy she'd become in comparison, and again thought of the allure of comfort eating that she'd succumbed to. She looked down into her flat white: running her fingers around the rim of the little plate it had been delivered on, fiddling with the spoon.

Elsie watched Vera seeing Nate look at Vanessa. *No Dad, No!* She hated Vanessa instantly.

"Ronnie, as in, Ver-*Ronnie*-ca," Vanessa purred.

Nate grinned. "And Vera," he looked at her with affection. "As in, *Vera*-onica?"

"Either works," Vera mumbled into her coffee with what small amount of feigned good humour she could muster.

"Well, no need to stand there," Nate motioned to the seat next to Vera, directly opposite him. "Please, sit down, join us."

"Oh, I hope I'm not interrupting anything?" She slid into the chair, leading towards Nate as she settled.

He couldn't help the flick of his eyes. "Not at all."

Vera felt sick: the blood draining from her face and heart and pooling deep in her guts. Her wounds were still fresh; and, worse, a friend who she thought she could trust was tearing the scar tissue right open again. She inhaled sharply and shakily reached for her glass of water, just as she felt Nate's eyes turn toward her.

"You alright, Vera?" Without thinking, Nate reached out for her hand. She snatched it away instinctively, knocking over the glass and spilling the (thankfully) small amount of water on the table. Nausea from horror, betrayal, and now embarrassment at being noticed by Nate swept over her. Everyone rushed to grab napkins and blot the spill.

"Yeah, just... no, I'm okay. I just suddenly felt..." Vera's eyes flicked between everyone at the table, only finding safety with Elsie's. "I'm not sure what happened."

"Too much maths?" Elsie offered.

"Maths?" Vanessa asked.

"Yeah. *Vera* was helping me with my maths."

"Hmmm," Vanessa closed her eyes and tapped her lips with her fingers thoughtfully. "I'd usually agree that it *was* the maths, but this is *Ronnie* we're talking about. It's more likely post-maths downer." She opened her eyes with sudden urgency. "Quick! Say maths things!" They all looked at her, puzzled. "Derivatives!"

Vera couldn't help laughing, but buried her face in her hands. Vanessa had never had the patience for mathematics, and at school she had teased Vera that maths was the only thing that made her happy. 'Say Maths Things' was an old joke of hers, something Vanessa had used to cheer Vera up when things weren't going so well for her at home. It didn't always work to make her laugh, but the schoolyard memory did.

"Quadratic Formula!" Elsie quipped — proudly showing off that she'd absorbed what Vera had just explained to her — before turning and nudging Nate.

"Hm? Oh… Uh… times tables?" offered Nate.

Vanessa looked at Nate in horror. "Seriously? That's pathetic! Don't you want to help Ronnie? Try harder." Nate wasn't used to being called pathetic by anyone except Elsie, and certainly not by a stranger. He blushed.

Oh man, he thought. *I'm terrible at maths, Vera knows this. It's a good thing I'm swearing off her.* "Ge…ometry?"

"Don't bother: you'll kill her!" Vanessa's mock seriousness triggered another wave of giggles from behind Vera's hands.

"Division! *Long* division! No?" He started to understand the actual goal of the game. "Wait… I… I can think of more!"

"Stop it," Vera laughed, pulling her bright-red face out from her hands and gasping for air. "I'm alright!"

"Wait, I've got it!" Nate smirked. Making Vera laugh was almost as good as making her blush. He put his hands up in the air, palm-out, to command the table, before putting them down, leaning forward, and looking pointedly at Vera, as though she was the camera lens and he was shooting one of his music clips. "*Arith-metic.*" He formed the syllables so sensuously that, as soon as he saw Vera's expression change, he felt uncomfortable and full of regret — but he couldn't look away.

Elsie watched Vanessa. Vanessa watched Nate. Nate and Vera's eyes were locked so intensely that the rest of the world was blocked out. A slow smile spread across Vanessa's face as she turned to look at Vera, and then to Elsie.

Elsie's scowl dropped as soon as she saw it— Vanessa was *not* a threat, but an ally to her plan! She beamed back at Vanessa and was granted a wink in return.

"Daaaad?"

"Mmm?" The spell was broken.

"All that maths made me hungry. Can we go get something?"

"Oh. Sure," Nate felt horrified and he wasn't sure why. "Are you… ready?"

"Sure. Mocha's gone."

Nate looked down at his flat white, then smiled sheepishly at Vera. "I guess I didn't touch this one, either. He bit his lip, and revealed that girlish-boyish charm of his youth. "Maybe a takeaway cup for me, next time." He stood up, patted down his pockets to check for everything, then leaned forward, holding out his hand. "I'm sorry, I've been terribly rude. I didn't introduce myself. I'm Nate, this is my daughter,

Elsie."

"Vanessa." One last attempt, her name purred, one hand placed in his and the other draped on her collarbone. "Call me 'Ness.'"

"Vanessa, right. Nice to meet you." Nate gave her hand a single pulse, let go, and pointedly looked away. "You two have fun. Vera... See you next time?" He didn't see Vera's coy smile.

"Nice to meet you, Ness! Talk to you later, Vera." Elsie walked around behind the table and gave Vera a hug. This solidified in Nate's head that he should back off: he didn't want to ruin this blossoming friendship, especially if it meant that Elsie might do better at school. And, besides, she'd pulled away her hand when he reached for it. She probably thought he was a sleaze. He felt bad disappointing her: don't meet your idol, right? He couldn't bring himself to look at either Vanessa or Vera. Shoving his hands into his pockets, he threw a half-smile at Elsie when she came past, schoolbag in hand.

Vanessa grabbed Vera's hand and waited until they were alone in the cafe.

"Hun, sorry about earlier. I probably shouldn't have done it, *but* I kinda wanted to protect you."

"What?" Vera didn't realise that Vanessa had done anything.

"I just didn't want some sleaze grabbing you. I don't care who he is... Or used to be!"

"Okay?"

"I shouldn't really have done it. But!" She squeezed Vera's hand. "I think you're absolutely right about him!"

"Huh?" Vera had been totally confused by the whole explanation.

"Nate. He's... *really* interested in you." Another hand squeeze. "I don't think he can help it. It's all over his body language. And not even a bubbly blonde in a skintight dress distracted him!"

Vera finally caught on. "Oh, so... all of that? You were testing him?"

"Yup. Work friends call it the 'Ness Test.' Apparently, I'm generically pretty enough to catch men. Not that I really want to... though, that's probably part of the appeal!"

"Wait, so you were...?"

"Yeah. Just a few bits of meat to see if he'd bite. But I didn't really think it through... Seeing me flirt with him was probably the *last* thing you wanted, after..." She trailed off, then suddenly shook her head and frowned, looking like a beautiful demoness. "That fucking *bitch*."

One corner of Vera's mouth peaked. It was too much information to process.

"Sorry hun, you okay? Promise I'll never do it again. Urgh. No offence, but he's *definitely* not my type!" She laughed, her blonde curls shimmering as she threw her head back.

Vera finally caught up with the outcome of Vanessa's detective work, having finally understood her process. "So, you think he *likes* me?"

Vanessa nodded and reached over to help herself to Nate's untouched coffee. "Oh, absolutely."

"Elsie—his daughter—she's always teasing me about him liking me. I don't know, I thought it was just a joke because she knew I liked him when I was in high school." She paused. "I thought he might just be treating me like anyone else, and that my own fantasies were making me imagine that he might like me, especially with Elsie encouraging me."

"I don't think so."

"But then he gets so weird sometimes, like he doesn't want to be near me."

"Well, how have *you* been acting?"

"Umm…" Vera blushed. "I don't know. I just feel awkward about the whole thing. I don't want to just be his next conquest."

"Which is exactly why I wanted to test him for you. He doesn't seem like he's just looking for a conquest!"

"So, what do I do?" Being totally honest with herself, Vera didn't know how to take Vanessa. She hadn't heard from her for years, which, she recognised, was as much Vera's own fault as Vanessa's. She couldn't hold anything against her just for that. But, then she wants to catch up the moment Vera mentions Nate, and when she gets there she's all over him, then *claims* she's doing it to test him and protect her? That's just awfully convenient.

Right?

Fine, whatever. She can have him.

But Vanessa was telling her that she could see Nate was interested. She didn't know Vanessa anymore, so she wasn't sure if she was the type to be playing some sort of game; meanwhile, Vera was too bad at game playing to be able to recognise one even if she wanted to. Her conclusion was that Vanessa *may* be teasing or manipulating her, but it could only be for the purpose of trying to get Nate for herself. But she said he wasn't her type… but Vanessa was one of the girls in their group who had always dated older guys; had she changed *that* much in the ten-plus years since they'd last seen each other?

Maybe this was just her paranoia talking. Vera attempted to reassure herself that Vanessa wasn't going to do anything; that she was true to her word.

Vera had never thought her *best* friend would betray her. She'd thought that she and Steven would be together forever. But, she supposed it was better to find out now, when she was still young enough to have kids if she wanted, but didn't already have any that would remind her of that… arsehole.

"Hello, Ronnie? Have I lost you?"

"Yes, sorry. Just, um," she forced her face into an attempt at a smile. "I don't know."

"Okay. Well, I was just trying to say that you should have fun with this. Stop holding back. Enjoy that *Nate Fucking Whitely* wants you! Let him have you. And let yourself have *him*!" Vanessa put her arm around Vera and looked at her with an affection that reached back twenty years, to when they went to year eight camp together and whispered secrets together in the dark instead of falling asleep. "You deserve it."

⏮ ⏸ ⏭

Nate ran his hand through his hair, as though trying to brush out his self disgust. "Christ, I'm sorry, Elsie."

"What?" Elsie stopped in her tracks.

"Next time I won't come into the cafe. She's your friend, and I make her uncomfortable." He paused, then put his arm around his daughter. "I don't want to make either of you uncomfortable."

"Dad, you don't—"

"I don't know what gets into me when I'm around her. I just feel so…" he groped for a word. "…familiar, I guess. And then, I overstep, and it clearly makes her feel uncomfortable."

"Dad: she's uncomfortable because she *likes* you."

Nate took a moment to process this. "She likes me?"

"Dad she's had a crush on you for like… Forever. And I mean that literally. She liked you when she was in *high school*."

"Elsie, that doesn't mean anything. Tastes change." His brow crumpled. "People change. I was a lot younger, and a lot… cooler, then."

"Okay, but, she likes you *now*."

Nate was silent as they continued walking. He hadn't really prepared for this. He'd concluded that all of Vera's blushing must have been because of her being polite and uncomfortable and possibly starstruck. He thought he was imagining the chemistry: that he was merely projecting his growing interest onto her, like some love-sick teen.

"So, she likes me?"

"Yup! It's gross. But cute."

"She's actually said she likes me?"

"Well, that would be an awkward thing to say to me!" Elsie laughed. "She just told me she gets shy and awkward around guys she likes, and when you appear…"

"Shy and awkward?"

"Yup!"

"Hmm."

Elsie watched the cogs turning. "So…?"

"So then, that decides it. I'm definitely not going to run into her again, then."

"Whaaaat?"

"I don't want things to get weird for you. It probably wouldn't work out, anyway. She's a nice person and I want you to feel free to be friends with her."

"Oh, Dad. I'm friends with her now, but friends are *shit*." Her voice faltered on this last word. "Who knows how long we'll be friends. Friendships are no more stable than relationships."

"That's profound. But what are you saying?"

"I'm saying, just go with it. You both like each other. Ask her out." Her voice dropped. "Just try not to be such a creep, like *pleaaaase* don't check out her friends in front of her."

"What? I didn't!"

"Oh, come *on*, Dad…"

"You mean Vanessa?" Nate laughed, knowing he'd been caught. "Don't be stupid. Since when have I liked blondes?"

"Anyway Dad, I saw you."

"I was being polite!"

"It's okay, Dad," Elsie brushed it off with laconic sarcasm. "I know she's gorgeous. She looks like a Victoria's Secret model."

"I don't even know what you're talking about." Nate peered up into

the sky, shoving his hands into his pockets.
     Elsie sighed. "Fine, Dad; whatever you say."

Eleven

Vera couldn't stop herself from thinking about Nate. It felt insane, the most implausible of serendipitous coincidences — a scenario that she would have dreamed up half a lifetime ago. But, when she thought seriously about it, her teenaged self would have imagined him as he was then and not as he is now: middle-aged and with a daughter her own age. But, the overall fantasy was there — gossiping with a school friend about whether *Nate Fucking Whitely* had fallen for her!

Her phone buzzed, snapping her out of the circular thinking she had resorted to as a form of procrastination and distraction from looking at job ads; from trying to put her life back together.

It was Elsie:

ELSIE: Hey!
ELSIE: coffee this arvo?
ELSIE: tell me u dont have more friends 2 hang out wit
VERA: Sure we can hang. No friends. Just jobseeking and hating on myself
ELSIE: aww no dont
ELSIE: ur the best <3
VERA: hahaha <3
VERA: everything okay your end?
ELSIE: yep just wanted to hang
VERA: after school, usual time?
VERA: I'll be the one on their old laptop with a furrowed brow, working

>   on my frown lines and old lady wrinkles
> ELSIE: hehehe :*
> ELSIE: yep after school, seeyaaaaaa

⏮ ⏸ ⏭

Vera frowned. She wasn't sure she could look at another job description without crying. She'd forgotten how demoralising the whole process was; not only that, the last time she'd had to look for engineering jobs was when she and Steven were graduates and looked together, prepared their resumes together, wrote their cover letters together. And now, they definitely were *not* together.

"Hey, you weren't joking about the frown line," Elsie's bag slumped down before she did.

Vera forced a smile. "Hey. Good timing! I need a break." She closed her laptop. "So what's going on today? Need more maths help?"

Elsie looked down as her phone buzzed in her lap. "Nope, just..." she looked up, hiding her discomfort by looking Vera straight in the eye and forcing an insincere smile. "Just want to hang."

"Oh, okay. Sure."

"So!" Elsie's phone buzzed again. She glanced at it, batted her lashes, and looked at Vera. "Tell me about you. Why the furrowed brow?"

"I think I need a change of career."

"Oh?"

"Yeah. These job ads just remind me of..." She trailed off. "You know. Worse times." The pain was clear on her face. "I'm just not sure I should be looking at engineering jobs anymore."

"You're giving up engineering?" Elsie's phone buzzed again. This time, she didn't even glance at it. Vera did.

"Yeah. Well, no; not exactly." She eyeballed the phone. "But maybe just mechanical. Maybe I'll look for jobs in a different type of engineering?"

"Maybe *robotics!*"

"Maybe, yeah. I haven't looked for robotics jobs yet. I did pretty well in my mechatronics units."

Elsie's phone buzzed again. Again she ignored it.

Vera couldn't ignore it any longer. "Okay, what's going on? Are you fighting with your Dad or something?"

"Huh? Oh yeah, Dad!" She picked up her phone, scrolled through the messages, and put it down. "No, not Dad." There was a brief pause as she avoided Vera's questioning eyes. "You could be a maths teacher! You're better than my crappy ones. Today mine said he's impressed by my 'improvement'!" she beamed. "Not that he had anything to do with it. Anyway, he said if I keep going well, I will get to go into higher maths next year!"

"Hey — congratulations! That's great news! You'll be building robots in no time!"

"Yeah!" Elsie was glowing — but that quickly faded when her phone buzzed again. She caught sight of two girls from her year giggling at her from behind Vera.

Vera had noticed that Elsie was prone to intense fluctuations of emotion, but this was odd — it was like the sine curve of her moods had been translated down. Rather than being endearing, it was worrying.

"Elsie, what's going on?"

She frowned and shook her head. "No; nothing."

Vera cocked her head, then turned around to look behind her. The two girls yelped and turned away, giggling and snickering. She turned back to Elsie. "Is that about me?"

"No! No, it's… it's about me." Elsie felt adrift, wanting to escape to her phone, but she knew there would be no solace there. She didn't want to look at Vera, because if she was anything like Nate, she'd be scowling. Eventually, she gave in and looked up. The expression on Vera's face was unexpectedly sympathetic and attentive. Elsie still squirmed in her seat. "I don't want to talk about it."

"Okay. That's okay. Just let me know if I can do anything to help."

"Just don't tell Dad, please?"

Vera had kept secrets from her own parents. She had kept them from her friends' parents. She could see the familiar pleading look in Elsie's eyes, recognised the tension in her shoulders as she huddled towards her, her pout seeking Vera's confidence. But now, Vera was older and could see it from both sides; she thought Nate could offer support and guidance in a way that school friends never could. She wrestled with it briefly, and concluded that if she played the role of confidant, there might be a way for her to strike the balance between school friend and concerned, experienced adult. So, as much as the idea of withholding anything from Nate rubbed her up the wrong way, she hoped that if he ever found out about it, he would trust that she was doing it from a place of good intentions. "Got it."

The confession and lack of prying buoyed Elsie up. Her entire posture changed, the light returning to her eyes. She even managed to glare back at the girls sitting behind Vera, rather than being defeated by them. "So, back to you. Why do you want to give up engineering?"

"I don't want to talk about it." Vera attempted a smile, but her eyes gave her away.

"Well, you've been cool about me not wanting to talk, so I won't tell my Dad about that either. But, um, that reminds me…" She reached into her pocket and brought out a note. "Dad and I have been talking about how nice you've been to me, and I thought you might want to come over for dinner one night? Dad's actually really good at cooking." She put the note down on the table. "I'm not sure when you're able to, but it can be like, anytime. Here's our address, and Dad's number." She winked.

Vera laughed at Elsie's blatantness. She remembered what Vanessa had said, took a deep breath in to brace herself, reminded herself she was an adult, and asked, "So… should I call him *now*?"

⏮ ⏸ ⏭

Nate was picking up groceries when his phone rang. He was so used to people noticing him that he almost always ordered groceries online, but this time he'd forgotten and found himself with some extra time on his way home. He reached into his pocket to pull out his phone and saw a number he wasn't familiar with. From past experience, these calls were risky — would it be someone he knew, or someone who had tracked down his personal number? As he held the phone in his hand, he considered hanging up on it. He looked around, and decided to take a chance on answering it based on his luck at there being so few people in the Supermarket around him.

"Hello?"

It was Vera.

"Oh hi Vera, I didn't know you had my number. What's up? Everything okay?"

She thought he'd given it to her? That didn't matter. Elsie had told her that they'd wanted to invite her over for dinner as thanks for everything, and that she should organise it with him.

"I think this is all Elsie's doing." He regretted it the minute he said it. "But, it's a great idea. How about this weekend?"

Saturday night would be great for her, if it was okay for him.

"Yes, that'd be great. Saturday night, then? I'm... actually at the supermarket now, so that's good timing. Is there anything I should keep in mind, food you do or don't like? Or can't eat?"

Anything is fine. She eats anything.

"Great. See you Saturday, say at about six o'clock?"

That would be great. She's looking forward to it. She says bye.

"Me too. Bye."

It was only when he put his phone back in his pocket and looked over at a cool, crisp iceberg lettuce that he realised how fast his heart was beating.

Twelve

⏮ ⏸ ⏭

Vera arrived at Nate and Elsie's house a little earlier than she was meant to, braced herself, and knocked on the door. She felt like she was being foolish, hoping that something would happen tonight. Elsie would be there all night, trying to help get them together and yet inadvertently be chaperoning. But a kiss would be nice…

She shook the thought out of her head as the door swung open. Nate's lopsided smile appeared from the other side. "Come in," he stepped back and let her in before closing the door behind her. "There's been a slight change of plans tonight. Elsie has been invited to a sleepover, so it's just going to be you and me for dinner." Nate picked up his gaze, which had fallen down Vera's figure, just as she turned back to look at him.

"A Sleepover?"

"I hope that's alright."

"She's not…" Vera thought he was asking her permission for Elsie to go on a sleepover, then realised that it was the change of plans and the two of them being alone together that he was checking on. "Oh, never mind. Yes, that's fine." That hope that something might happen popped back into her mind, and she did her best to suppress it. "She must be excited."

"She is, actually. And, uh," he stepped closer to her, lowering his voice in case Elsie might somehow overhear, despite not being in the room. "I've been worried about her: she hasn't seemed herself lately. But then, maybe fifteen minutes ago, she came in and said she'd been invited to a friend's place. She looked so happy that I couldn't say no. I would have told you sooner, saved you the trip if you wanted to reschedule." He was about to place his hand on her shoulder reassuringly, but remembered the last time he'd done that and thought better of it— give the poor girl a chance to escape. He took one step back and offered her some space, shoving his hands in his pockets and shrugging. "If not, you'll just have me to deal with."

Vera was feeling brazen. She stepped closer to Nate, looking him up and down. "I *think* I can deal with that."

Nate found himself taken aback by this move — the coy girl who he loved to make blush seemed to be gone. He felt a little disappointed in one way, but in another, it gave him a clear signal. He weighed his options, biting his lip. "Elsie? Vera's here," he called, without breaking eye contact.

Vera regretted her decision and scolded the Ness inside her head when she saw the sudden change in Nate's demeanour, but was quickly distracted by a teenage squeal incarnation of her name, followed by its physical form hurtling towards her with arms outstretched. Vera was unused to seeing Elsie out of uniform, and just how pretty and *cool* she was unsettled her a bit. But, what time is there to be unsettled, when those arms were flung around her with such warmth?

"I'm *soooo* sorry, Vera! But I just gotta go... Will you forgive me?"

Vera made a show of betrayal. "Well... maybe if you take me clothes shopping another day."

"Huh? OH!" Elsie let go of Vera, holding her at arm's length. She looked down at what she was wearing. "Is it okay?" Nate sighed disapprovingly, but then shrugged and turned away. Who was he to judge?

"Elsie, you look amazing! You've got more style than I ever had."

Elsie laughed and hugged Vera again. "I wish you could come to the sleepover."

"Thanks, but I'd feel out of place: too many people I don't know. Plus, I'm old."

Nate laughed at Vera calling herself old.

"No way, you're not!"

"Don't worry Elsie, I'll accept a rain-check. We can have a sleepover another night."

Elsie's eyes lit up. "At your place?"

"Sure, but," she looked around. "Your place is nicer."

"I don't care!"

"Elsie?" Nate glanced at the clock on the wall. "You ready?"

"Ooh! Yes! One minute!" Elsie scurried back upstairs.

Nate turned to Vera, his hand reaching up to rub the nape of his neck. "So, we were *going* to make home-made pizza and watch a movie together, but if you wanted to do something else, we—"

"That sounds great, actually."

"Yeah?"

"Home-made? You mean, from scratch?"

"Yeah, making pizza dough was our lockdown hobby of choice."

"Ahh. Sauce making, for me."

"As in: tomato sauce?"

"Yeah, for pasta… or pizza," they smiled together as they realised the complementary nature of their hobbies, before Vera turned shy. "Oh, and other sauces. Hot sauces. And pickles. I don't know why."

"Just something to do? You wanted to… spice things up a little?"

Before she had the time for her mind to think about Steven's own way of spicing things up during lockdown, Vera's attention was caught by Elsie calling out to them. "Okay! Ready!" Elsie tumbled down the stairs and back to the two of them holding her bag, filled with all manner of teenage sleepover equipment.

"Okay, great." Nate patted himself down, and finally pulled out his keys. "Oh — Vera. Will you come with us? It's not a long drive. If not, you're more than welcome to wait here. You can look through what's on Netflix, start making pizza, or… make a sauce?" Nate smiled cheekily at Vera. She smiled back.

"I'll come."

Thirteen

The drive was short, as Nate had promised. Elsie sat in the back seat, beaming quietly to herself while Vera and Nate chatted about pizza toppings: Nate fretting about whether he'd have what Vera had wanted, Vera reassuring him that she didn't mind, and that she was excited to taste their base. After the drop-off ("Don't come in, Dad, here's fine. You two go."), they turned their conversation to movies they'd seen advertised, ones they'd seen recently (or not), and their absolute favourites.

"Anything *Monty Python* is guaranteed to make me laugh. Elsie doesn't get it," Nate smiled, turned to Vera. "Whose side are you on with this? Elsie's or mine?"

"I'd join the Ministry of Silly Walks any day," Vera said after a pause. Nate laughed and turned his attention back to the road. Steven had been firmly on Elsie's side. Any suggestion she'd made that they could watch it was met with a sneer, as though the mere idea of liking such silliness was far below him. He'd say, "Oh, but if *you* want to watch, we can." The first time he'd said this, she'd taken him at face value, only to have him huff, sneer, and try to distract her throughout. She learned never to suggest it again.

"What are your other favourites?" Nate hadn't caught the drop in Vera's mood.

"*Zoolander*?" Vera offered.

Nate's mouth twisted a little, but he smiled. "Less my style, but if it makes you laugh, I'm sure I can enjoy it."

"No, that's okay." Vera had learned her lesson from Steven, and never wanted to repeat it.

"You can show me why you like it."

"I think I'd prefer to watch something we both like. Or haven't seen."

"It's okay, Vera," Nate reassured her, pulling into the driveway. "I can watch anything on there anytime I like, on my own. This is the first time I'll watch something with you, and I'd like you to enjoy it." He parked the car, turned off the headlights, and turned to her. She looked so hesitant, suddenly. Small, her head downturned. He wanted to take her in his arms, comfort her about whatever had made her feel that way. He wanted to kiss her.

"Are… you sure?" She looked up at him, doubt on her face.

Nate scoffed, like it was the most obvious thing in the world that he would want her to enjoy herself. The car was not the ideal place for a kiss. Movies make it look like it's not awkward and uncomfortable. If Nate was going to kiss her, he was *not* going to make it awkward and uncomfortable. He hoped. He thought about stroking her face, taking her hand. He bit his lip, took a deep breath, pulled himself back together. "Come on, let's make pizza. We can see what takes your fancy inside." Nate sure as hell hoped that he was what would take her fancy.

Vera was surprised by how much fun they had doing something as mundane as making pizza together. Nate lost count of the number of times he wanted to kiss Vera, while Vera marvelled at how incredibly natural and normal it felt to be in each other's space. Nate was clearly more used to causal touch than she was — or so she thought, assuming he wasn't being set ablaze in the way she was every time they touched. But she was wrong: he was.

When the two pizzas were finally in the oven, Nate directed them to the lounge, turned on the tv, and gave the remote to Vera. "I'm in your hands," he said, smiling. A thought struck him. "Sorry, I've been a terrible host. Can I get you anything to drink?" He wondered what she'd ask for. She didn't seem nervous anymore, but there was still that hesitance, especially when he handed her the remote. Would she ask if he had alcohol? He did, but he had stopped drinking. In the past, it had been an easy escape for him, a way to feel safe from his emotions. But years ago, he'd decided he couldn't do it anymore and swapped it for therapy. It wasn't that he swore off it — he'd never been an *alcoholic* — but he just interrupted his impulse, took deep breaths, and told himself it was alright and that the feelings would pass. It seemed to work for him. Most of the time. He still slipped, but slipping usually just made him feel ashamed later, and the feelings and fears were still there, waiting to be dealt with. He'd resolved to only drink on happy occasions. He wasn't sure exactly what occasion tonight would be — yet.

"Oh, just water. Or whatever you're having."

Nate nodded, and turned back to the kitchen. "Water it is." He'd started noticing Vera's easy compliance. Was it just politeness on her part? Was the same true of what he'd seen as her 'niceness'? As the taps filled up the glasses, he thought about Vanessa and her talk of 'Ronnie.' That person sounded so self-assured, so confident in her tastes. *Say Maths Things.* He chuckled to himself, and wondered what else was within Vera, ready to be explored.

He took the two glasses of water back to the lounge. Vera froze as he entered, as though he was a parent who had caught their child watching a sex scene. Instead, she was looking at music documentaries.

"Oh, sorry, I must have gone on a tangent. I was just curious," Vera quickly backtracked to the main screen.

"You're fine," Nate sat down next to her, putting the water down. "Find anything interesting?"

"No. I don't know," Vera looked away, held the remote out to him. He looked at it, but didn't take it. She extended her arm to push the remote towards him again. "You can choose for us."

"Well, what were you looking at?"

"It doesn't matter. I don't know what I want to watch." That strange coyness again. No, not coyness, he realised: fear. Nate sat next to her, not saying anything, not taking the remote. Vera grew tired of holding it and put it down on the coffee table, and picked up her water. "Thanks." She hid herself in the glass, as Nate watched.

He looked back to the tv, unsure of how to reassure her. They sat together for a while, in silence, monitoring each other. The smell of melting cheese gave him an out. "The pizza will be ready soon. I'm going to check on it. Honestly," he picked up the remote again, and handed it to her. "Pick anything. The movie's not what I wanted to see tonight."

There was such earnestness on his face, such concern. Vera took the remote and cursed herself, cursed Steven for how much stress she was putting herself through: all over choosing something to watch together. She decided to pick what she knew would be the safest option, selected it, and paused it.

"*Fuck!*"

Vera rushed into the kitchen; seeing Nate hunched over in front of the oven, she feared he'd burnt his hand as he tried to take the pizza out. One pizza had slid and splattered onto the floor — Vera's. Nate stood up — completely unharmed — and looked up at her, his anger at himself visible in his entire body.

Vera looked down at the pizza, back at Nate, and shrugged. "I guess I'll just have some of yours? We were going to share anyway, right? I'm sure there'll be enough."

For a second, Nate looked at her like she'd spoken in a foreign language. Then, he ran his un-mitted hand through his hair and laughed. "You're right. You're right. I'll just..." He pulled the other pizza out and carefully placed it on the benchtop to cool. "Here, you cut it while I clean this up." He handed her the pizza cutter, their fingertips touching.

Vera busied herself, trying to work out how many cuts would make how many slices. She didn't want to do too many or too few, but decided that too many was probably easier, and cut the slightly misshapen circle into the most even eight slices she could. "I thought you'd burnt yourself."

"Well, that probably wouldn't have been surprising," Nate wiped the last of the pizza sauce and grease from the floor. "Maybe Elsie is right, a dog would have cleaned this up quicker than me." He threw the paper towel into the bin and came over to see how Vera was going.

"You're thinking of getting a dog?"

"Maybe. We'll see."

"I like dogs."

"Do you have one?"

"No."

Nate was given another icy answer, a conversation blocker. He looked at the pizza. "Wow, nice and even. Very professional. I'm glad I asked you to cut. You'd be ashamed of how I would have cut it. But," he was trying his best to make her laugh, "It means that I can tell myself I'm only having a couple of slices, while still managing to eat half the pizza." He got a half smile from her. She didn't look him in the eye. "Come on, let's see what you chose for us to watch."

⏮ ⏸ ⏭

They sat together but on opposite sides of the lounge, hyper-aware of each other's presence. They ate the pizza bar two slices, but they'd never really returned to the playful banter at the start of the night. *Monty Python and the Holy Grail* was meant to be fun, a nod to the fact that Nate had mentioned it, and a chance for Vera to enjoy it for the first time in years, knowing they both liked it. Instead, she felt shame — as though she was watching something she shouldn't — and she felt guilty for killing the mood. She hadn't heard Nate laugh for a while. She turned to look at him, and he was watching her with concern.

He was trying to understand what he'd done to upset her. "Everything okay?" A nervous smile flicked across his mouth. "I'm starting to think that you don't actually like *Monty Python*, and you just said you did for my sake."

The irony of the accusation made Vera crack, a laugh erupting from her mouth before she could stop herself. "Sorry, I do. I really do, actually. It's just... never mind. I can't focus on it."

"Let's just stop watching, then. Because I can't focus on it either." He reached out for the remote. Vera didn't stop him stopping it. He put the remote back down and turned to her, looking at her earnestly. "I'm worried I've done something to upset you. You'd tell me, right? You won't just... bottle it up?"

Vera watched him, the pain and fear in his eyes contrasting with the easy smile and posture he'd taken on. "No, Nate. It's not you. I'm sorry. I've been caught up in my own head."

"You're alright," he shifted closer to her. Put his arm around her in a way he hoped would leave it open to being platonic if that's what she wanted. He expected her to shy away, but she didn't. This, he decided, was also not the time to kiss her. She looked at him, smiled, gazed into his eyes. Possibly, slightly more the time to kiss her—

"I..." Vera broke eye contact. "I have a random question."

The way she said it worried Nate. "Yes?"

"Do you think you'd ever tour again? With any of the band, I mean?" Vera didn't expect the dark energy she found herself surrounded by. Nate kept his arm around her, but it felt like he was holding her tighter.

"No."

"Is it... because of Elsie's mother?" Their love story had been compared to the drama of Fleetwood Mac, and so many unresolved rumours had swirled about the band's breakup, her pregnancy, and tensions with other band members.

Nate's energy lightened. He actually laughed, and shook his head. "Not at all. But…"

Vera cocked her head at him. She didn't expect him to tell her the real reason. The band basically went silent aside from the announcements of the hiatus and split; even Elsie's birth and Nate's single fatherhood had been pieced together from paparazzi shots and gossip magazines. She tried to give him an out, justify her question. "I was only curious, because I just saw some of those music documentaries and some of them are about reunion tours. And it got me thinking… I never did get to see one of your concerts. But I loved you so much then."

Nate wasn't listening. He was being thrown back decades. "No. No way, never. I wish… you wouldn't understand." He pulled his arm away from her, retreated into himself, picked at his thumbnail. "You think you know someone through and through. For years. You think you know every part of who they are. You'd never, ever think they could… You'd never think…" He ruffled his hair to pull himself out of it. He didn't want to talk about it. He'd talked about it enough in therapy. It didn't need to exist here, with the two of them, tonight. He was trembling, trying to control himself. He swallowed it all. He heard Vera take a deep breath and felt her hand on his back. He glanced at her, not really seeing her. "I'm sorry. I just… there's something I really wish I'd done differently. I don't like thinking about my part in all of it."

Vera said nothing, but reached her arms around him. Holding him.

Suddenly, he pulled his head up, wiped the tears threatening to emerge from the corner of his eyes, and feigned a laugh. "What a fun time we're having tonight." He turned and looked at her. She was watching him with quiet concern.

She placed her hand on his cheek, a little smile teasing the corner of her mouth as her thumb toyed with the idea of touching the corner of his. "I'm sure you did the best you could at the time."

The intimacy frightened him. That she was still there. She'd seen a crack into his darkness, and she was still there. That she got closer. The reassurance she gave him that happened to be right on the money. He could so easily let her in, let everything tumble out… but she could so easily walk away when she heard it all. He needed a break. He pulled himself out of her arms, stood up, turned away.

Vera looked at the coffee table and the pizza they'd had so much fun making together. She cleared her throat. "The pizza was really good. It *was* fun making it. Next time, you'll have to let me help you make the base." Nate remained silent. Vera tried again. "I'll make us some sauce to use."

"Want... a coffee?" Nate managed. He needed to recompose himself. He needed to recover the evening. He could escape to the kitchen, focus on the coffee task, get his emotions back on track. He knew she liked coffee. But it was also late — just past nine o'clock. He turned back to her. "If it's not too late."

She smiled, standing up from the lounge. "It's not too late," her tone was soft, accidentally sensual. Vera could tell Nate was struggling. His gaze dropped down her body, and he batted his eyelids to collect himself. She was sure he'd held himself back a few times already this evening, seen him look at her mouth. She'd managed to bring the whole evening down though her own fears and by triggering something in him. Somehow, it felt like they were working through every part of it together, giving each other space. She could feel that it was her turn to close the gap.

As Nate calmed himself, his guilt and shame and feelings of betrayal gave way to nerves about Vera and what she thought about him. He turned and retreated to the adjoining kitchen. "Okay, coffee. I have... your choice of pods. Green, purple, silver. Oh, there's a light blue one, too." He pulled two mugs out of the cupboard and placed them on the bench. He turned back to find Vera right behind him.

"I don't know... what's your favourite?" This time, her hand on his arm as she looked over his shoulder.

"Purple." He glanced back at her — at her biting her lip as she smiled.

"Then I'll have what you're having." She gave his arm a little squeeze. It helped him find his way back to a bit more playfulness.

"A latte?"

"Ha." Vera had never seen one of the coffee pod machines in action. She'd been thinking about getting one, but if she wanted a coffee in the evenings, she'd either find a cafe (even if it had to be McCafe), or just ended up with instant if there was no point going out. She stroked his arm, absentmindedly. "Show me how to use it?"

"Sure. It's really simple. I put the milk in earlier; it looks like there's still enough. The pod goes in here," he dropped one in. "The mug goes here. Press the button," he demonstrated. "And it does it all for you." He stepped back and crossed his arms. They watched together as the machine spluttered into action, expressing dark coffee and creamy milk.

"Can I try?" Vera edged in front of him, deliberately brushing herself against him.

"Sure." Nate had to reach around her to take the filled mug out, and, feeling game, placed his hand gently on her upper back as he handed an empty one to Vera, standing half behind her, waiting to see whether she'd shrug him off. She didn't.

"The pod goes in here," she repeated, dropping one in. "The mug goes here." She put her finger on the button, but stopped and looked over her shoulder at him, feeling utterly awkward in her attempt to appear something resembling sexy. "This button?"

He nodded. She pressed, without looking back to the machine.

"And let it do it all for you," he whispered, letting his hand slide down into the small of her back, as his gaze slipped down her face and onto her lips. He wasn't sure that he could stop himself this time.

It was like a Moccona coffee ad on tv. Vera had no idea how she'd managed to be so *smooth*. All she did was get into his space, and not let herself freak out. She couldn't turn back now — so she raised her chin and let her lips meet his. They melted into each other; he pulled her closer to him as she turned so that her whole body faced his. Even if he'd never been famous, if she'd never dreamt of him and built him up in her mind to be the idea of someone worth wanting, their chemistry would still be this strong. No fantasy needed to be added to this kiss.

From the coffee table in front of the tv, Nate's mobile phone buzzed insistently. He wanted to ignore it, but the nagging feeling that it might be his daughter distracted him. He sighed in disappointment, dropped his head and looked up at her through his eyelashes. "It could be Elsie. Sorry."

"It's okay. Get it." Vera slid her hands to his chest and gently pushed him away. Reluctantly, Nate peeled himself from Vera and rushed to pick up the phone. Vera leant back against the kitchen counter, feeling groggy and validated, before looking back and reaching for her freshly made coffee.

Nate looked at his phone. "It's her," he said, answering. "Hey."

Elsie watched as Nate's expression changed from mild disappointment to concern.

"What's the matter? ...yes, she is, do you want... Yes, we can. No, that's fine. Where are you now? Okay, got it. Okay, bye." Nate hesitated.

"No, I'm not. Well, yeah, I am, actually. But no, no, don't worry. No, I haven't. I haven't. Do you want me to put Vera on?" Nate's tone was moving from concerned to defensive. "Here. She'll tell you. Oh, you don't? Maybe I should leave you there!"

Vera watched on, uncomfortable about the changes of emotion she witnessed, seeing the echoes of behaviour that reaffirmed Nate as Elsie's father. "Nate, give me the phone." He handed it over without a word. "Elsie? Elsie, slow down."

—Vera? Oh, I told Dad not to put you on!—

"Elsie, what's going on?"

—I just… I need to be picked up. I don't… I can't be here anymore.—

"That's okay. Are *you* okay?"

—Umm, not really. No, I mean, I'm fine. I just, I want to go home.—

"I understand. We'll come get you."

—Okay. Is Dad okay?—

"Yeah, I think you upset him, though. What did you say to him?"

—I just told him to let you pick me up if he had anything to drink.—

"Ah. Well, we haven't."

—I also asked him not to be angry about this.—

"I'm sure he's not. He's just…" she looked at Nate's stormy face. "…disappointed you didn't have a good time."

—Oh.—

"Okay, we'll come pick you up?"

—Okay.—

"Okay, see you soon."

—Okay. Vera?—

"Yes?"

—Sorry if I ruined the night you guys were having.—

Vera looked across at Nate, who had cooled down and was watching her with gratitude and admiration. "Don't worry, you didn't."

Fourteen

Vera sat in the back as Nate drove. As much as they wanted to stay close to each other, they'd agreed that it was best for her to sit behind him so that Elsie would have the choice of who to sit next to, and wouldn't be left alone in the back seat. Vera leant across to the middle to see Nate through the rear-view mirror. His eyes told of his concern, his powerlessness. She couldn't tell whether he was trying to avoid her gaze or not, but he never looked at her or spoke to her throughout the fifteen-minute trip. He pulled over at the bus stop outside a Maccas, turned the radio down, opened both windows, and looked out.

Elsie peered in, then opened the back door to sit beside Vera. She'd barely stopped crying, but she was doing her best to look like she'd never started. "Hi. Thanks."

"You okay?" Nate asked from the front seat. The tension in his voice revealed his desire to control his emotional response, rather than the emotional response itself. His attempts to control himself had gone neither unnoticed nor unappreciated by Vera and Elsie.

Elsie looked at Vera. "Yeah." She reached over to hold Vera's hand. When she glanced up, she saw her father's eyes in the mirror, flicking away without catching her gaze. He sighed, releasing the tension like air slipping from a slashed tyre, and turned the radio back up. "Okay."

Nate dropped his keys in the bowl on the bench. He was desperate to speak with his daughter but knew better than to push to find out what had happened. "Did you eat? There's still some pizza."

"I'm fine, Dad. I'm going to my room." Elsie sped up the stairs.

Nate moved to follow her. Vera stepped in his way, her hand resting on his chest. The unexpected intimacy made them both pause, the tension distracting them briefly.

"No, let me. But first, I just want to give her a few minutes. A bit of space," she paused, "but not enough for her to think we don't care."

Nate shook his head — this wasn't what he would do, but it made more sense. He caught her hand as she tried to pull away, holding it against his pounding heart. "Why weren't you here for the last fourteen years?" Their eyes met, and a flippant remark about understanding his daughter took on more weight than he'd intended.

"I'll... check how Elsie is." Vera pulled her hand away and turned, not wanting to focus on the thought of meeting Nate instead of Steven. She hurried up the stairs, and Nate backed off into the kitchen to tidy the undrunk coffee. He couldn't help entertaining the thought experiment of what it would have been like if he'd met Vera back then — what would have she been like? Would she have been crazy for him the way that Elsie seemed to be for Tommy? And considering what he had been like back then, riding the height of his fame, would he have taken what he would have assumed was a stupid teenaged girl for granted; would he have ignored her — or worse, taken advantage of her, damaged her, and made her a completely different woman? Just like...

As Vera reached the top of the stairs, she heard Nate let out an uncomfortable sigh. She realised she had no idea of the lay of the top floor, and began opening doors at random until she heard Elsie's voice — quiet and emotional — coming from behind her.

"Wrong way."

Vera turned, and Elsie opened her door wider, looked past Vera to check that Nate wasn't behind her, smiled weakly, and retreated into her room. Vera followed, and closed the door behind her.

The walls of Elsie's room were covered with printed pictures and posters purchased or pulled from magazines, just like Vera had done with her Smash Hits, TV Hits, and occasional Rolling Stone Magazines. One band took pride of place, and one of its members got extra wallspace: this must be Tommy.

"Cute," she said, nodding at him. Elsie gave a weak smile. "So, are you going to tell me what's been happening?"

Elsie sighed and launched herself onto her bed. "I guess." She rolled onto her back and stared at the ceiling. A lava lamp shed patterns of liquid emotion onto the walls. "Have you ever... My friends don't... they don't seem to be my friends anymore." Vera sat down on the bed next to her, watching her as her eyes filled with tears. "I don't know what I've done. They're making things up about me. Oh," Elsie sat up suddenly, staring at Vera with wide eyes. "Don't tell Dad about any of this, okay?"

"Of course. I promised before. What are they saying about you? Do you want to tell me?"

Elsie's face went dark. "They're saying that *David* — this guy at school — they're saying," she says these words quieter and darker than Vera had ever heard her speak, and she spat out David's name like rancid milk. "They're saying that we had sex, and that he's been spreading all of this nasty stuff about me," she pulled her knees up to her chest, tears spilling down her cheeks. "I don't know what to do."

Vera paused. She remembered when Vanessa lost her virginity — she was about thirteen — and wondered whether she actually had, or whether it was someone else's story and she'd run with it. In the end, Vanessa was, and still is, the one who seemed the most together. She was the one who lost touch with the group first, off on her own adventure. A rumour, or the truth, didn't seem to hurt her in the end.

Vera felt Elsie's arm sneak under hers and suddenly realised she didn't know what to say to help. She didn't have experience with this; Vanessa did. Maybe she could ask her for help?

Elsie sniffed. Vera looked over at her, and her watery eyes looked back. "Vera, you're my best friend. Thank you for listening." Elsie let go and threw herself back onto her pillow. Vera, still at a loss for words, shuffled to lay down next to Elsie and wrapped her arms around her. Elsie let go of her emotion, and the harder she cried, the tighter Vera held her, until she quietened enough to fall asleep.

⏮ ⏸ ⏭

Vera wiggled out from next to Elsie. She quietly opened the door and found Nate, arms and legs crossed, slumped against the wall on the other side. He'd been pacing around downstairs until he couldn't stand it anymore, at which point he crept upstairs — but couldn't hear anything from Elsie's room.

He looked up as Vera stepped out, his eyes dark with concern. She smiled and stepped forward to him.

"It's okay," she said, quietly pulling the door closed behind her. "She's asleep now."

"Mmmm," Nate bit his lip. So many emotions threatened to flare up, each one of them only spending an instant playing across his eyes. "Anything I should know about?"

"Ah, no. Just, you know: teenage girl stuff. It'll blow over soon enough."

Christ, I feel so old, they both thought to themselves.

"Thank you for doing this."

"You need to stop thanking me."

"I can't help it. You're the nicest girl I've met in a long time, and I don't want you to think I take that for granted."

Vera was used to being called 'nice.' That's what she always was: nice, cool, a good friend; never hot, sexy, incredible. Her heart sank. Any points she'd gained that night, she was sure she'd lost. She looked down, ready to say goodnight as friends.

"Actually," Nate had noticed that his compliment hadn't had the desired effect, and decided to double down. "I think I'm glad I didn't meet you fourteen years ago: I doubt I would have appreciated you." Hesitantly, he moved towards her, navigating one hand to her waist and letting it slide to her hip. She looked up in surprise at his touch. When she didn't pull away, he slipped his other hand behind her neck, his thumb brushing against her cheek, his fingers sliding into her hair. He felt her soften at his touch. His eyes blazed as he looked deeply into hers, several emotions combining to send one clear message; but he held himself back, wanting to give her whatever space she might need.

She studied his face, the way he was looking at her, the way his touch made her feel, and Vanessa's voice came back into her mind. She placed one hand on his arm, leant towards him, and gave him a gentle, hesitant kiss.

As he added to her kiss, she felt herself begin to press against him. He pulled her away from the door and back towards him.

Fifteen

He was amazing.

In the half-light, Nate looked like he did in her dreams, and acted nothing like Steven. When she thought about that, she found herself almost feeling sorry for her supposed 'best friend,' who now had to deal with *that*.

Yet, Vera was haunted by an uncomfortable, niggling feeling that she couldn't quite place.

"You okay?" Nate breathed, noticing the tension in her arms as she lay in his. "Is there something else I can—"

"No, no, I'm perfect." She cut him off.

"Okay... okay. Great." He nuzzled into her, kissing her reverently on the neck. She felt him relax — but she couldn't. Realisation dawned: he was amazing, but how did he get that way? Vera wasn't stupid, she knew he had Elsie with his ex — she knew where babies came from! But he was a rockstar, and the truth was, when she was in her teens and adored him from afar, he could have had — no, *would* have had — countless partners already. She suddenly felt like no matter what she did, she was another notch on his belt, another score on the scratched-up bedhead. If asked, he'd probably have no idea how many people he'd slept with, while Vera knew exactly, and could count on one hand. She felt anxious — how did she so easily go along with it? She was nothing special. She was, compared to him, inexperienced and naive, probably really boring in bed. He was probably really disappointed.

She didn't know how to think of him now. Growing up, of course, everyone had that joke: "What do you call a male slut? A champion." It was a gross and sexist remark. When she was older, *Sex and the City* taught her that a female slut can be a champion, too (as long as it was what she wanted), but those early teen years were incredibly formative in everyone's moral life — unless they were given special scrutiny.

Nate sighed behind her, and shifted.

"I think I'll check on Elsie," she whispered.

He sighed, "Mm-hmm. Thanks," and let go of her. She sat up, aware of her less-than-supermodel physique, and scrambled for her clothes. She grabbed them and dressed in the half-light. She found her way to the ensuite, freshened up, and smoothed her hair.

She watched Nate, now asleep, as she crossed the room and opened the bedroom door to the hallway. There was light under Elsie's door. She knocked gently, then opened the door when she heard no reply.

Elsie was sitting on her bed with her headphones on, reading a novel. She looked up when she saw movement at the door, then smiled and took her headphones off. She'd long stopped crying, but her eyes were still puffy and red.

"Vera!" she hissed, and beckoned for her to sit down. "Oh my God… did you and Dad…?" Vera didn't have to say anything for Elsie to understand her answer. She closed her eyes and waved her hands in front of her face, as though she'd just eaten something disgusting. "Oh gross! But… I knew it was just a matter of time!" She shook her head, trying to clear the cognitive dissonance between disgust at what had happened, and the excitement that the first step of her plan had worked. She was closer to meeting Frothing Mess, she knew it. She could win back her status in the schoolyard now; rise above the rumours. She'd ask her father about the ARIAs again in the morning. Maybe Vera would help convince him! And maybe this could bring a happily ever after for all of them: even Nate would finally no longer be sad and lonely, despite his claim that he wasn't. "Oh, now I feel even worse. You two were probably having *quite the evening* until I ruined it."

Vera laughed. "You didn't ruin anything." She thought about what to do now. She didn't feel comfortable going back into the room with Nate; in fact, she wasn't sure she could bear to see him again tonight. Or ever. She couldn't quite gather her feelings together. She needed to go and unpack it all. She needed to talk to Vanessa: find out if she was being crazy; find out how she could help Elsie. She had to get out of there.

"I think I need to go," she ventured. "I didn't really expect to be out *this* late tonight."

"Oh, okay." No Vera to help her in the morning. Hopefully, it wouldn't matter; Nate would be happy and in love enough to let her have the chance to meet Tommy. "Cool, cool. Is Dad asleep? I can let you out."

"Yeah, he is, thanks." Vera and Elsie got up from her bed, opened the door, and walked downstairs. Elsie opened the front door with a sniff and a smile. "You know I'm serious about us going shopping together, if you think you can help an old lady like me look a bit cooler." She gave Elsie a hug, holding her tight.

"It would be my honour! Then *everyone* can know how amazing you are the minute they see you."

She stepped out of the front door, smiled back at Elsie, and walked to her car. She got in and drove around the corner — far enough to be out of sight lines — and pulled out her phone. Not thinking of the time, she sent a message to Vanessa.

VERA: Ness? I need to talk
VERA: I know its late. If youre up Id appreciate it
VERA: or if we can meet tomorrow for a coffee?
VERA: Monday if needs be
VERA: a lot happened tonight and it would help

She put the phone down for a second, then realised how panicked she sounded.

VERA: Im okay though so no stress

Sighing, she dropped the phone back down into her lap and looked down the street, full of beautiful homes with leafy embellishments, moonlight making them look mysterious and foreign to her. Her phone buzzed in her lap.

NESS: hey hey
NESS: im up!
NESS: what's going down
VERA: oh yay!
VERA: can I come over maybe?
NESS: yeah of course
VERA: amazing! What's your address?

Vera copied the address into Maps, and set a course for half an hour away.

The radio played one of Nate's songs.

DISC 2

Sixteen

⏮ ⏸ ⏭

"Hello, hello!" Vanessa was more chipper and alert than Vera expected for after midnight. "Welcome to my mansion." Vanessa's tiny two-bedroom flat felt jammed to the walls with her soul.

"Sorry to come by so late."

"You're fine! Seriously. For once I was having a… *quiet* night," she laughed. "And by that I mean I didn't go out tonight. I was just watching crap movies on tv. Can I get you a tea or coffee? Vodka? Beer? Wine? I have it all!"

"Just a cup of tea would be fine."

"Too easy!" Vanessa navigated to the kitchen and poured water into the kettle, before placing it back on its base and flipping the switch. Vera watched her, so at ease in herself and her body. She envied her. "So what brings you here this time of night? I didn't know you were the stay-out-late type."

"I'm not. I was with Elsie," she paused. "And Nate."

"And Nate," Vanessa echoed, turning to lean against the counter, nodding to encourage the rest of the story. "You were out with them?"

Vera ran her fingers over her lips and shook her head. "At their house."

Vanessa raised her eyebrows and sucked air in while looking Vera up and down. "What. Did. You. Do?!"

"I don't know how it happened," Vera's excitement overtook her shame. "We *did it*."

"DID IT!" Vanessa threw her head back and laughed. "It's like you're still a teenager! You mean you *fucked*?" She smirked as Vera turned red, horrified by Vanessa's deliberately crass choice of words. "Sorry. You *made love*?"

"Well, yeah. I guess."

"*And?*" Vanessa stepped toward Vera, intent on seeking out every detail of her friend's hopefully transformational rebound sex. She reached out and put her hands on Vera's shoulders, tilting her head to look her square in the eyes. "How was he? Is the rock god also a love god?"

Vera's face fell.

"Oh. That bad?" Her hands slid down Vera's arms, ready to take her into a comforting hug. Instead, Vera took hold of Vanessa's arms, holding her back.

"No," Vera looked up at Vanessa, a strange embarrassment and excitement flicking through her. "No, he *is*. That's why," she paused, palpating Vanessa's elbows, trying to think through how to explain it, how to justify her repulsion. The car ride wasn't long enough for her to finish sorting out what to say. "Steven—"

"I'm sorry, you mean: *the Arsehole*."

"Yeah. He was *terrible*. I didn't realise how bad." Vera shifted away, dropped Vanessa's arms, turned and leaned against the kitchen counter. "You know I... I haven't been with many guys. And it just felt so *obvious* that I'm just the last of who knows how many for Nate, and it just felt... like he... was *gross*." She sighed. "Is that crazy?"

Vanessa moved to Vera's side and draped her arm over her shoulders. "Yes, yes it is." She smiled. "Seriously though, I don't think so. I'm sure he *has* slept with a lot of people. But the question you need to ask is *why* it gets to you so much, *why* it makes him gross."

The kettle beeped its tea-readiness.

Vanessa moved to the cupboard to retrieve two mugs and teabags. Her brow furrowed as she dropped the bags in and covered them with boiling water. "Is this really about *him*? Are you maybe worried that *you're* not good enough? That you didn't satisfy him?"

"I don't know. I guess? I mean, what if I'm bad?" she blanched as her mind skipped ahead. "What if that's why Steven did what he did? What if I'm just... not enough?"

"Oh, hun. A person isn't just who they are in bed."

"Then why? Why did Steven cheat on me? It's not like he outright left me. It must have been that. Right?"

"Seriously? I have no fucking idea why he did that to someone like you. But…" She shook her head, her golden curls scattering. "Forget it. Those two aren't worth your time. I don't even wanna waste my time thinking about them anymore." Vanessa brought the two teas around to the coffee table in front of the tv. "Take a seat. I wanna hear every detail about Nate and his amazing skills."

What was intended as an attempt to create connection and distract from someone not-worthy back to how-someone-showed-you-you're-worthy fell flat. Vera turned green and snapped at Vanessa. "Wait, why do you care so much what he's like in bed?"

"What? I'm excited for you. I want you to revel in your encounter with a rock-slash-love god, while living the excitement vicariously through you. But if it upsets you, just… forget it."

Vera picked at her nails, realising the erroneous conclusion she'd jumped to. "I'm sorry. Just, what with Steven and…"

"It's okay. You know, now that I think about it, it'd probably unsettle me a bit, too." Vanessa turned the tv on, flicking through to ABC, where RAGE was playing, and Prince was crooning *Little Red Corvette.* "And check it out– even *Prince* was unsettled by it."

Vera smiled, but remained quiet.

Vanessa, feeling her attempts falling flat, turned back to the tv.

"Ness? I wanted to ask you about something that happened back in school. It's okay if you don't want to talk about it."

"Highschool? Well, go for it. I can only say no."

"Okay," Vera breathed in, bracing herself. "Remember when we were like thirteen, and you lost your virginity to Andrew Jones?"

"Oh! Andy Jones!" She laughed. "Okay, what about it?"

"Well, did you *actually…*?"

"Did I what?"

"Did you actually lose your virginity to him?"

"Oh." It was Vanessa's turn to go quiet, turn sullen. "No, I didn't."

"What do you mean? What happened?"

"I don't remember details anymore. But I think it was that he wanted to, and he knew I wouldn't, so he started saying it. He said I'd deny it as well, so what was I supposed to do? Denying it would confirm it, and confirming it would confirm it; just one big catch twenty-two." She looked at Vera earnestly. "I thought: I'll own it, make out like it was *my* choice, and turn it around that he was bad in bed. That was the only way I could think of where I could come out on top. No pun intended." After a brief smile, she sighed. "I worried that I would be branded as a slut forever, and that all the guys would try to have sex with me, but really it just made them afraid I'd spread how bad they all were. Which didn't really bother me."

"So, would you say that was the right choice?"

"Oh God no," she laughed. "I hated lying. I hated making him look bad. I wish I'd been able to clear my name, or that there was someone who could call him on his bullshit. Really, I wish someone would teach these boys to be men when it comes to someone not letting them stick their dick where they want."

Vera nodded, and went quiet.

"Why do you ask? Do you wish you'd slept with Andy Jones and had a bad lay, because that's more your style?"

"Well, Nate's daughter, Elsie? Her friends are all spreading this rumour that she slept with some kid in her class. Which she didn't."

"Shit." Vanessa went silent. She sorted through all the options in her head. "She should talk to Nate. But, I'm sure she won't."

Vera nodded.

"I don't even know what he could do, but he has to do something. Someone has to. Something like this changes how people see you."

"Well, it's slander."

"It is. But, you know, Nate seems like a genuine guy. Beyond protecting his daughter, he seems like someone who would legitimately not treat people like shit. As evidenced by the love god side of things."

"I hope you're right. But, I told Elsie I won't tell him. So I'll have to convince her to." Vera sipped her tea. "And actually, I think I'm fine with the rock-slash-sex god, now that I think about it. I'll have to pass on Andy Jones."

Seventeen

⏮ ⏸ ⏭

Nate woke, unexpectedly alone in his bed, the crumpled sheets and his nudity a sign that last night wasn't just a dream. Vera must be already up; but not in the en suite, as the door was open and the light was spilling through. He pulled some clothes on and decided to investigate. Gingerly, he stepped out from his room and into the hallway, walking down towards Elsie's room. The door was slightly ajar, so he only needed to gently push to see inside. Elsie was asleep in her bed, face-down and snoring. He opened the door further, trying to see the remainder of the room. There was no one else there but the representation of Tommy. He grunted and closed Elsie's door quietly behind him.

She must be downstairs. She loves coffee, she's probably making coffee. He couldn't smell coffee; maybe she was trying to remember how to make coffee.

She's not downstairs, she's not making coffee.

Nate opened the front door, stepping outside to pick up the morning paper. Her car was gone.

She'd left during the night.

He felt anger and humiliation flare inside him. Did she regret it? He had noticed she seemed non-plussed after they'd finished. But she'd seemed to want it. And when he offered to keep going, she said that no, she was *perfect*. Had he read her wrong? Had he done or said something to upset her? Did he fall asleep too quickly? The last thing he remembered was that she wanted to check on Elsie. But she'd gone.

No note, nothing.

She'd snuck out in the middle of the night. She did the walk of shame and left him there, alone, without even saying goodbye.

She must have regretted it. She must have regretted *him*.

He walked back inside, and stood at the coffee machine. All he could think of was last night, when he showed Vera how to make coffee. That kiss. He shook his head to snap himself out of it. Which pod today? Not purple. Anything but purple. He still couldn't shift the memory out of his mind: it kept coming back, haunting him. But, truth be told, he didn't want it to leave him. He sat down with his coffee and the paper and tried to read, but all he read was that kiss, those embraces, her eyes, her lips, the curves of her body, his fingers trailing down and her shivering at his touch, grabbing at him, pulling him closer. And now: her absence.

Was he just some sort of trophy to her?

No, that didn't seem like her.
It seemed like him.

He'd certainly fucked to prove to himself that he was desirable when deep down he was sure he wasn't, to form some sort of physical proxy for the emotional intimacy he craved. A decade ago, the simple solution was to pick someone who idolised him, who made him feel like he was the rockstar that the record sales claimed him to be, who adored him. It's a powerful thing, adoration.

But then, that all fell apart. It was too easy. He didn't care about them, and he didn't really want them to know him. So he changed his tactic; then, he'd fucked because of the challenge, the satisfaction of charming someone, winning their adoration to prove to himself that it wasn't flimsy and hollow.

Maybe that was the case here: despite The Look when they met, Vera hadn't been an easy target, throwing herself at him because of who he used to be. It was almost the opposite. And yet, he was able to seduce her with who he was now, even after initially holding himself back. It was proof that, even if he was older, he was still desirable. He knew it wouldn't be long before he simply lost interest in her because the chase was over.

He didn't want to admit it, but this was a lie. He'd never *really* been the type to lose interest once he got someone in bed. It was just an easy lie that he — and previously, media outlets — would use to cover up the truth: it was only a matter of time before *they* lost interest in *him*. He'd only started going for those who were harder to win over because he'd hoped he would have more time to develop a deeper intimacy with them before their image of him was shattered apart.

Even with Vera, he knew that one of two things would happen: he'd get scared of her disappointment and close down, emotionally distancing himself until she got bored of him and left; or he'd open up to her and she'd see him for the horrible, unlovable thing he knew himself to be. In the last ten years, he'd never let the second thing happen, and now he had put himself once again on the path to the first.

In her mind, he hoped he was still the version of himself that she thought she saw in interviews and music clips, someone who magically knew her intimately because he spoke to her through music. It wasn't worth the risk of breaking this apart, so as always, he had tried his hardest to stick to the superficial, so that she would never know the truth of who he really was back then, what he was really like, of the disappointment he could be. He wasn't much different now, except he was missing the exciting glamour of being on the cover of Rolling Stone.

And what did he know about her? She was a fan of his when she was a teenager; she likes him now. She is single. She is younger than him. She is nice. She knows how to make pasta sauce from scratch. She makes him feel both incredibly nervous and incredibly calm. But, aside from that, he hadn't really attempted to learn much more about her at all. This was a strategy he used subconsciously to keep her at arm's length, to never allow himself to feel safe enough to open up.

And yet, the night before, he almost couldn't help himself, and it frightened him to feel how easily she could disarm him. He'd let his guard down for a minute, shown his wound — and she'd only wanted to get closer. A thought tickled his mind: maybe she didn't realise what she'd seen until they were together in his bed, and backed out while he was asleep.

Nate found it easier to buy into the lie that he would use her and throw her away, rather than admit that he was afraid that she would throw him away. He started wondering whether she had bought into this lie too: maybe she'd seen the headlines that put words in his mouth that no one could be a good enough mother for his daughter, no one could compare to his ex, no one could keep his attention for long. Words he'd never said, but started to believe, so he'd stopped hoping for love — until Vera. It wasn't worth stringing along a nice girl like her, who really deserved more, who was becoming friends with his own daughter.

Maybe she let herself be his trophy? She seemed so attentive, so perceptive, so agreeable; maybe she knew what he was after even before he did, and left because she thought that's what he'd want. Maybe it was pity. Or maybe it was just something the both needed? Simple, mutual, fun.

But couldn't she have left a note? Did she feel that uncomfortable, or afraid of him? Maybe she did feel coerced, after all. Cornered, in his house; powerless. Nate felt his breathing quicken. He felt sick — horrified in himself, that he'd shown even more darkness than he feared, that he wasn't so different from those he despised.

He got up to look for his phone — maybe she'd sent a message that he hadn't seen?

That would make sense. It might all be okay.

It was on the coffee table, low on battery, and free of messages.

He hoped that nothing bad had happened to her. He looked through his call log, and saw nothing except more missed calls than he'd expected from Elsie. He felt a new pang of anxiety, layering on top of his self-disgust: if he'd coerced her and she'd regretted everything, if she wanted nothing to do with him, how would this affect Vera's friendship with Elsie? Everything would be ruined now, wouldn't it? He shouldn't have let it go this far. He'd known it was doomed from the start. And, if it wasn't too late, if she wasn't upset with him, it would only get worse if they kept seeing each other. It was headed to an inevitable, messy end. He needed to call her. He needed to make sure he hadn't really upset her, but more than that — he had to end it.

Vera was lying in bed, awake, the morning sun harassing her. In her mind, she was running through the events of the night before, every little thing that led to the moment when she felt that disgust. Her attempts to be brazen; his attempts to make her feel safe. The times she'd realised too late that he was looking at her like he wanted to kiss her. The times Steven's ghost got in her way, the times Nate's fears were visible past his facade of confidence. The way they both just tried to understand and be patient with each other. The way they both startled as they got closer, then yielded. The *way* they yielded to each other.

Maybe she shouldn't have left the way she did. But she couldn't cope with how disgusted she felt, thinking about all of his previous conquests. She knew he'd settled down before, with Elsie's mother — and they'd been together for years before her birth. Vera didn't really know what his dating life had been like after that: she'd started focusing more on her own and given up on worrying about the life of a Rockstar she'd never meet. But, maybe settling down was what he liked, despite him being single. Maybe he was actually just very picky?

Had she been too easy? Should she have resisted, acted cooler, harder to get? And all those moments where she felt confident to push forward, to get the attention and affection and validation she had craved, was she coming on too strong? And after, was he disappointed in her? Was he expecting her to be *more* for him? To *do* more for him? He'd seemed to want to *keep going*. Would she, too, one day find him in bed with someone else... with *Ness*?

Her phone rang. It was Nate.

"Good morning," he purred, trying to hide the strain in his voice. "I noticed you aren't here. Is everything alright?"

"Oh, yes," she lied, and recounted the reason she'd given Elsie. "I just have a lot to do today, and I hadn't expected to be out so late."

"Mmm," he left the words to her.

"I..." She cursed herself. She shouldn't have left. "You were asleep; I didn't want to wake you."

"Okay, that's okay," he lied back.

They both paused, at an impasse of trying to guess how each other was feeling, of wanting to make the right move. Vera knew she needed to say something, reassure him that she hadn't freaked out, even though she had. "Thanks again for everything, it was..." she thought back to the pizza making, about Nate's joke when she'd accidentally upset him about his past. "It was fun."

A quick breath in. Hesitancy. Had Vera used the wrong word? "Yeah, it was. I, uh," there was an audible sigh from the other side of the phone. "I wondered if you'd like to catch up again on Wednesday, over coffee, at the cafe?"

"And see where we go from there?"

"Something like that."

"Sure."

"Great."

"I'll see you then?"

"Yeah, about… five-ish?"

"Okay, see you on Wednesday at about five-ish, at the cafe."

"Great."

"Okay. Bye, Nate."

She hung up the phone and examined her feelings. He wanted to see her again, yet he hesitated when she said the night was 'fun'; maybe he did want something more than just one night. Maybe she wasn't a disappointment. Maybe she was everything he wanted.

Vera thought about everyone he would have slept with before her, all the different styles and positions and bodies and flesh and smells. Ultimately, he'd rejected almost all of them. But he wanted more of her. It was like getting tasters of all the icecreams before settling on one tub of your favourite to take home. Well, maybe he wasn't taking home the tub, but he was certainly ready to commit to a double-scoop waffle cone.

She seemed fine to Nate. And she didn't seem fazed by not seeing him for a few days. She didn't want to run away, she wasn't upset or anything. She said she'd had fun. Maybe, if she thought he just wanted to use her, she was okay with that.

He wasn't sure if *he* was okay with that.

Vera was just too *nice*, and he didn't want to hurt her by leading her on in any way. He didn't want to use her to feel good about himself. He didn't want to have *fun* until he hurt her — he wanted to protect her from that side of himself. So it was important that this week, he decided on the best way to tell her that it would never happen again.

Eighteen

⏮ ⏸ ⏭

"Elsie, can you come in here?" Nate was bracing himself for how Elsie would feel when he told Vera it was over. He felt rotten — he knew that she would be angry at him for leading Vera on, or taking advantage of her. He knew that she would tell him that it'll be weird now, and that her romantic little heart was going to burst out of disappointment. But this was just how relationships were, he'd found. One person always leaves for reasons that the other will never truly understand, and not from lack of trying, but more often than not, for noble reasons: the desire for a better life for both of them. Nate knew it wasn't worth the future pain that they'd both endure, and it was better to stop everything and give Vera back to Elsie.

When Elsie's mother had finally left, it had ripped him apart. It was great for him musically, leading a way to the blues, to revenge songs, anger songs. It had been one of his most productive and successful periods, redefining him as a solo artist: it turned out that most people want to hear their pain reflected in others so they know they're not alone; otherwise they want to hear the pain that they've missed out on so that they can appreciate their own lives more. Every failing relationship after this felt like poking a sore spot, like reopening a wound that would never heal.

Elsie had dragged herself from the couch and was standing in the kitchen in front of Nate. "Dad? You *did* ask me to come in, right? You didn't just, like, space out on me, did you?"

Nate blinked. Could he possibly warn her that he was going to drop Vera, and *not* expect Elsie to immediately message Vera to tell her? He was a short-sighted idiot. But he needed something to tell her. He clicked his tongue. "Yeah, yeah I did, Elsie."

"Okay, weirdo. And *why* did you want me to come here?"

Nate glanced around for inspiration. He noticed that Elsie had written 'ARIAS' on the coming Thursday. "Er, I thought about what you said. If you're interested in coming to the Awards, I, ah, *was* given two tickets." It wasn't a lie, but he hadn't quite sent through an RSVP for it yet. He knew that he only had to say it and he would be squeezed in somewhere, cameras plotted and trained on him. It was one of the things he hated about going to the awards, a reminder of both being of importance and yet, with no nominations, of being past-it.

Elsie's eyes widened. She could hardly believe it — her plan had *worked!* "Do you mean it, Dad? I thought you'd forgotten!"

"Yeah, I do. It's only a few days away, so you'd better start thinking about what you'll wear."

Elsie let out a squeal of triumph and ran back to the couch where her phone lay, barely remembering to double back and throw a hug to Nate, yelping, "Thanks Dad you're the *best!*"

Nate watched her typing a message, almost dropping her phone in excitement. Was this the right decision? He didn't like the idea of a fourteen-year-old at the ARIAs. Execs frequently drank too much and let their inhibitions down, and that included their visible admiration of pretty young girls. He knew that not only would they be there, but so would other musicians. They were a mixed bag, some the kindest and most honourable people you'd meet, but others? He thought back to his bandmate and the night that ultimately launched Nate's solo career. He'd just have to keep a close eye on Elsie; especially around that Tommy guy who she seemed to like so much. He didn't know him, it was true: but he knew exactly the type of person that he *could* be.

"I just messaged Vera she's going to be so excited when she hears!" The words rushed from Elsie without any punctuation. "You really are the best Dad this is awesome I don't need any birthday or Christmas presents this year if EVER," her breaths fuelled her words like oxygen fuels fire. "I wish Vera could come too but I guess you said it's only two tickets but... oh my GOD!" She ran back into the lounge room and threw herself on the couch, convulsing in nervous excitement.

The smile slowly faded from Nate's face. Vera.

ELSIE: omg dads the bestttt
ELSIE: what? Why
ELSIE: IM GONNA MEET TOMMY
VERA: ??

Vera stared at her phone, trying to will comprehension.

ELSIE: oops soz
ELSIE: ARIAS
ELSIE: IM GOING

The squeal of delight that pulsed in Nate's ears never made it through text, fortunately for Vera.

ELSIE: TOMMYS PLAYING
ELSIE: ILL GET TO MEET HIM
VERA: OH
VERA: EXCITING!!
ELSIE: YEEEEEAH
ELSIE: you must make him happy hahahaha
ELSIE: dad I mean
ELSIE: im so excited
ELSIE: im sad you cant come with us but dad said he's seeing you soon so hes probly planned something to make it up to you
VERA: ha, I don't mind not going
VERA: I'm excited for YOU!
ELSIE: yaaaaaaaaaaaaaas
ELSIE: what r you n dad doing next time neway?
VERA: just goin to the cafe I guess
VERA: nothing exciting
ELSIE: thats near ur house rite
ELSIE: ;)
VERA: ha
VERA: it is
ELSIE: lol youre cute
ELSIE: ok gtg
ELSIE: BYEEEEEEEEEEEEE
VERA: bye Elsie!

Vera didn't want to jinx it. Her imagination started running away with itself, thinking about what Nate could have had in mind for their 'date.' How was she going to pass the time before then? She should busy herself with job applications, especially as she'd let those slide recently. She could actually unpack the boxes that still haunted her after her move. But what would she find in there? Clothes that didn't fit, and reminded her of spending time with Steven?

It had been *years* since she could justify shopping for something nice. *'Who are you trying to impress?'* Steven would say. It had become easier for her to just fade into the same unimpressive clothes than try to explain that it was enjoyable just to be able to see herself in the mirror and feel good about who she saw looking back at her. He somehow couldn't understand this: to him, it was all about the male gaze, about her as an object of desire for others. So, he'd just reassure her that he didn't need her to dress up for him, so why should she? He was so *persuasive* about it that she felt like an idiot questioning it, because of course he *loved* her, and that's really all she needed. So she tried to only buy things that weren't showy, but then he'd question why she needed new clothes at all. He'd concede, though, and the non-showy things were okay. Her no-makeup look was best.

She realised now that he was trying to make her fade into the background, make her a shadow of *Ronnie,* and she was so willing to be what she thought he wanted. This must have been how she'd become so plausible as Vera, even to herself. Somehow, she'd just bought into the whole thing. It had seemed so gradual that she hadn't even noticed. She'd lost so much of herself that she couldn't even seem to find her way back. But, she couldn't let him keep defining her. She needed to start doing that for herself.

Nineteen

⏮ ⏸ ⏭

Nate arrived first. He had spent the days leading up to this busying himself in the studio, mentally rehearsing what he was going to say, and trying to ignore what he wished he could say instead. He ordered them two lattes and sat down at a table to wait. He sat, nervously looking out the window and checking his phone periodically. The coffees arrived in takeaway cups. He hoped that he hadn't ordered them too early. He didn't want them to get cold before Vera even arrived—that would be a waste of good coffee. For her, at least. It wouldn't be unusual for his coffee, he knew: he tended to not drink his coffee almost every time he was with her. Fortunately, she arrived only a few minutes later, beaming at him.

"Coffees already? You *are* on top of things."

"I started worrying that you'd be late."

"Late? Not for you."

Nate winced, and wound himself up, ready for The Talk.

"Vera, we need to talk," he began. As soon as he said it, he knew he'd phrased it in a bad way — the universal code for *I'm dumping you*. "Look, this *has* been…*fun*," he made sure to use her word, "but I think we both know it's not going anywhere." He paused to give her space to respond. She just looked at him, and gave a slight nod that meant no more than 'continue.' He took a deep, shaky breath in, to steel his nerves. Usually, he was the one being left and playing it cool, not the other way around. He closed his eyes, afraid of the pain he knew he was going to cause. "I just… I want to apologise for the other night. It never should have happened. I don't want you thinking it meant any more than it did. I was just feeling a bit down about myself and I was flattered by your interest. I overstepped, and I'm sorry."

Nate had been rehearsing this since Sunday. He knew it was going to be tough, and it would hurt her, but he thought it could be like a bandaid where he just ripped it off in one go and she could get upset and do whatever she needed to do and then she'd hate him and get over him and it would all be okay. When he finally looked up at her, she had tears behind her eyes, but she smiled, looked down into her lap, and simply said:

"Okay."

He was deflated. He'd expected a full-scale attack, but instead he'd won the war without a single shot fired back at him. He didn't expect her to swallow it and accept it. But, she did. And that was the hardest part. He hoped she'd yell at him, scream, call him every name under the sun. He deserved it. She deserved to tear him to pieces. Instead, she just looked down into her lap, looked at the pattern on the dress she was wearing, fiddled with the fabric. She'd been dressing better since their first meeting, he could tell. It was nice — not because she looked hotter or sexier, or even because he thought she might be doing it to impress him, but because she looked like she was blooming, finding a part of herself that had been lost somewhere along the way, something that had been found through their time together. Or maybe it was her time with Elsie.

He cleared his throat. He didn't know what to say now. His script had been derailed.

Vera couldn't bring herself to meet his gaze — it was impossible to look into those beautiful eyes of his, soft yet intense, almost sad, and such a deep blue. The eyes she'd looked at on a hundred magazine spreads, watched in music clips, interviews, behind-the-scenes videos. She felt like an idiot. Of *course* he was just playing with her. He was just being kind to even suggest that she thought he might not be. Or was it an insult? It didn't matter.

All she knew was that she needed to leave, to deal with this. So it was better to just assume it was the end, and deal with it later. At least he'd had the decency to tell her that she wasn't enough, and that he would be looking for something, *someone* more the following night. She appreciated that. She collected her things, reached out and, smiling, squeezed his hand, and slipped away.

This time, it was the fate of Vera's coffee to go cold.

Years in the spotlight had made Nate uncomfortable being in a public place while he felt vulnerable. He downed his coffee and left. He'd planned to get dinner on the way home so he could prepare to tell Elsie that he'd broken it off and he was sorry for being a creep and he hoped that she and Vera would still be friends, that they could bitch about him to each other, that they were good for each other and he was finally out of the way. But now, he was so unsettled by her reaction that he didn't know what to do with himself. He'd lost his appetite. She was just so *nice* about it. And he'd been such an *arsehole* about it. Subconsciously, he was relying on an assumption that she would get upset, turn nasty, and make him feel less about her because she was suddenly no longer the *nice* girl he was falling for.

But instead, he found himself thinking about her more. *She was okay with it.* She even looked slightly relieved. *Relieved?* What was she relieved about? Was she glad that he'd lost interest, that she didn't need to deal with his advances anymore?

He thought back to how he felt waking up, expecting her to be beside him. The sting of her absence, the hope and disappointment as he searched the house, the worry and frustration when he realised that she'd left him in the middle of the night — as he'd done to so many others.

But it wasn't like they'd come to a conclusion; they hadn't talked it through. He had no idea what she was feeling, whether she was avoiding it, whether she'd be avoiding him and, by extension, would she be avoiding Elsie?

He cursed himself, thinking what an idiot he was: that this must have been his worst idea ever. The whole thing was terrible. He walked the streets around the cafe, near Elsie's school, and his mood only mulled and increased as he walked. Eventually, he walked back to his car, got in, and drove home.

Twenty

⏮ ⏸ ⏭

Nate tried to close the door quietly behind him, but Elsie had already heard his car pull up, its door open and shut, and the key in the front door.

"Hi, Dad! You're back early. Is Vera with you? I'm in here, watching tv!" she called from the living room, the sounds of Frothing Mess music obscuring her voice and her standing up and walking out to him.

He couldn't deal with Elsie right now. He regretted the decision earlier that week to agree to take her to the ARIA Awards. Set against the roar of music that he was ashamed he couldn't identify but could guess correctly, he couldn't look at her without thinking about how that lowlife 'rockstar' Tommy would chew her up and spit her out, just because she would make it so so easy for him, and that he has access because of who her father is. Jerk. He was sure that if he told Elsie this, she'd come up with a list of excuses. And she was probably right; Tommy was probably not that much of a jerk; he was probably a very nice and reasonable and hard-working young man. Because, as much as Nate wanted to make this about Tommy and Elsie, he knew it wasn't. It was about him and Vera. He was ashamed of himself and ashamed to let down Elsie (his only daughter, the one who loves him and looks to him for guidance on how a man should be) and show her how much of a jerk 'rockstars' can be. He'd used Vera for her attentions, and he knew it. *He* was the jerk. And he had to protect Elsie from that, and the only way to do that was to tell her that he'd changed his mind and she couldn't go tomorrow night, even if it meant that *he* would break her heart.

But, he wanted to break Elsie's heart even less than Vera's. It was easier to hurt Vera because he could take her out of his life and it would go back to the way things were. He told her it was over. He told her the 'truth' — for ultimate jerk cred and maximum certainty that it was over and she would never want him back. He failed to admit that it was digging the knife in his gut as much as it was in hers, that he was ashamed of himself for being such a jerk; so much of a coward. That he just couldn't take the pain of her adoring him so much, of being so *nice* to him when he couldn't even be that nice to himself, and knew it was only a matter of time until he let her down, too.

And Elsie, ever-perceptive, was now standing in front of him and had picked up that something was upsetting him; she was hassling him, asking what was wrong, why he isn't talking to her. Where's Vera, what's the matter?

"Elsie, just forget it."

"Forget what, Dad?" Elsie pestered him like an insistent blowfly. But he couldn't let her know.

"It. Everything."

"Everything? What's 'everything', Dad? That something is wrong? That you're not talking to me?"

"Just... I need to be alone for a bit, Elsie."

"Why? What happened? Was it Vera? What happened with Vera? You come home super late and—"

"Elsie? Leave it alone."

"Why?"

"Elsie—"

"I'm calling Vera to ask what happened."

"Just... drop it, Elsie."

"Too late."

He could feel a mashup of emotions — guilt, rage, shame, fear, frustration, grief, horror — all blending together, his control over his voice and actions waning. He tore his jacket off and growled, "Elsie, I told you to *drop it*."

"Hm. She's not answering."

A flush of panic rose over Nate's face, silencing him. He hoped nothing had happened to Vera on her way home: it would all be his fault.

"She always answers. Why isn't she answering?"

"I don't know! Maybe she's in the bathroom. I don't care!" All he knew was that he had to get out of there.

As he stormed off and slammed the door to his room, he heard Elsie slam the front door.

⏮ ⏸ ⏭

She was being an idiot — she knew this.

Only an idiot would be surprised or upset that their teen idol wasn't exactly as they'd imagined them to be, some perfect blend of talent and looks and absolute match-made-in-heaven compatibility. She knew that she was lucky if she got the first two. The first two should be guaranteed... of course, not taking ageing into account. She thought she'd been quite lenient on the looks department.

"Oh my God!" she said to herself. "Listen to how petty I am!" Suddenly she was overcome with the most intense feelings of shame and guilt. She couldn't be angry at him for not living up to her fantasy, even if he *had* just been a total arsehole about it. She wasn't enough for Steven, and she knew for certain now that she wasn't enough for Nate. Why would she be? She was lucky enough that she'd attracted his attention at all, even though he wasn't at his peak.

Anyway, she'd loved the thrill of it. She loved that she could say she was *right* about her adoration of him, her fourteen-year-old dreams of being able to draw his interest, her hopes for their perfect life together. She wanted to be angry that this was being taken away from her. Surely she could be angry at him for that?

Who was *she*, anyway? Someone who flattered his ego. There was nothing at all special about her in the scheme of things. He was just vulnerable, feeling down about himself (as he said), and she was there, right-place-right-time, ready to adore him and get swept up in her own fantasy. He took advantage of her, surely. Or... did she take advantage of *his* weakness for *her* fantasy? She knew he'd never be interested in someone like her any other day of the week. And who better for her to use to find a way back to valuing herself than someone who she had adored back when she did?

Vera dragged herself to the mirror.

"Look at yourself!" she muttered. "Who do you think you are: some great seductress?" Her eyes were red and blotchy. Her face was puffy.

But she hadn't yet changed her clothes, and despite their crumpliness, she could still see a snippet of something resembling sexiness. Maybe the advantage-taking *was* all hers, after all…

The thought was interrupted by her phone buzzing. It was Elsie - the last person she wanted to talk to. Well, maybe the *second* last. Vera ignored it. She dropped her phone on the bed, pulled her dress off and threw it in the corner, and took a shower.

While the hot water ran down her, washing away so many things, her phone on her bed continued to buzz — alternating between attempted calls and a string of messages.

ELSIE: What happened??? Dads acting super weird
ELSIE: Srsly hes being weird
ELSIE: I asked what happnd tongith n he said 2 forget it?
ELSIE: Whyyyyy? I dont get what im ment to forget
ELSIE: Ok now u rnt answering either
ELSIE: Damnit im coming over

⏮ ⏸ ⏭

Vera took her time: washed her hair, scrubbed her face, did everything she could think of to make herself feel cleansed of everything. She didn't even pick up her phone from her bed when she returned to the bedroom, focused as she was on wanting to forget everything and just exist in her own sense of nothingness, being in the moment. She looked in the mirror; the life had returned to her face. Her eyes were still red, but now that the smeared mascara and eyeliner were gone, she looked fresher, more alive, purer.

She tried to position what had happened logically: it was flattering, really. For a short while, *she* had been what Nate wanted. She couldn't deny that. It wasn't that she thought he would *love* her. Oh no— she wasn't that naive. Hopeful, maybe; but not naive. They'd just both wanted the same thing: to feel wanted, to feel desired. It was mutual. When thought about that way, it really was a pure and sweet thing.

It *was* life-changing; to deny that would play down its significance. Vera had been one person before they'd met, and another after it was all over. She'd attracted the attention, if somewhat briefly, of the man who she'd considered *the* most desirable in the world, ever since she was in her teens. Not bad for a rebound.

She smiled at herself, proud of how she'd worked through her thoughts.

A few hours passed, and Nate had begun to worry. He checked his phone; nothing from Elsie. This wasn't like her! Usually, she'd have sent a message to say where she was or at least to abuse him for being a jerk to Vera. That's what he'd expected. But there was none of that: instead, it was just silence.

He sent her a message to ask her to check-in. He trusted her, of course; but it was late, and she'd stormed out, and she hadn't contacted him. Did she get lost? Did she get grabbed by some lowlife? Was she hurt? He didn't know where she was, and he couldn't protect her.

She must have gone to Vera's house, but he had no idea where that was.

He looked at his phone again. Still no reply. He looked at the time — 10:38pm. Far too late for a fourteen-year-old girl to be wandering around on her own. Thinking about all the options, he settled on the fastest… which unfortunately would also be the most painful.

He groaned and scrolled through his phone to one name: Vera.

Vera was lying on her bed, eyes closed, drifting into dreams when her phone buzzed insistently in the way that could only mean a call. Waking again, she reasoned that she was ready to speak to Elsie — or whoever else was trying to call — but seeing *his* name on the screen, her heart dropped; all the rational positive thinking of the previous few hours gone, vanished like water in a too-hot frypan. She thought about ignoring his call just as she'd ignored Elsie's, but decided that this would be an opportunity to prove to herself that all her reasoning had stuck, that she really was *okay*.

"Hello?"

"Yes, hi Vera. It's… Nate," as though she wouldn't instantly recognise his voice. As though it wasn't burned into her memory. "Sorry to call you so late. I just…" he paused momentarily to collect his thoughts. "Is Elsie with you?"

"What? No, she isn't. Is she meant to be?"

"She left home a couple of hours ago, saying something about going to see you. You don't know anything about this?" They both spoke as though the last week, even the last day, had never happened.

"No, no idea. I mean, I know she called me earlier, but I missed it. I didn't call her back. But, honestly, this is the first I've looked at my phone since then."

A pause; faint sounds of Nate wrestling with his thoughts. Vera — usually so happy to respond to Elsie — had inadvertently shown him the pain he'd caused. "Well, she's been gone for a while, and isn't answering her phone. Seeing as she was trying to make her way to you, can I..." he trailed off. He didn't want to have to ask her. Maybe he could back out now?

Vera knew where his question was heading, and it was the last thing she needed. He'd already imprinted himself into her cafe, she didn't need his presence invading her home, too. She considered cutting him off, saying that she'd just keep an eye out for Elsie, that she'd call if or when she turned up.

Nate's thoughts were leaning the same way. Asking Vera to just let him know if Elsie turned up would make things easier for him— but he couldn't bring himself to sit around and wait even longer. He might catch up to her on the way, he told himself. But he needed a destination, and knowing that Vera's place was Elsie's goal, he couldn't find himself an alternative. He cleared his throat and said with as much firmness as he could manage, "It's probably best if I wait for her at your place."

"Oh. Um, sure. That's fine," b*ut not really*, she thought, *but there really isn't much choice is there?*

"Okay, thanks. I need your address. I don't have it."

"Sure. I'll text it to you. It's just around the corner from Elsie's school and the cafe."

"Okay. Thanks." Nate didn't know how to end the conversation. Saying 'See you soon' felt utterly tactless, even if it was correct.

"She'll turn up, Nate."

"Yep."

The phone went dead. Vera wondered whether Nate felt as uncomfortable about this as she did, or whether this was something he could gloss over. She looked down at herself, clad only in her underpants and a singlet. If she was someone else, she might have considered taking advantage of the situation. But Vera was *nice* and this meant respecting that, while Nate had seen her in fewer clothes than she was wearing now, he probably didn't want to think of her that way again, and was better off finding some clothes to shield herself with.

Twenty-One

⏮ ⏸ ⏭

It only took Nate about twenty minutes to drive to Vera's — certainly not a long drive, and if Elsie had been clever and saved properly, she could have used her allowance on a taxi. Nate wondered why she would be so stupid, walking out, without a plan of where she was going, at six thirty at night. He'd moved from concerned to angry, something that frequently happened to him. He knew he could be a slave to his emotions. Elsie had inherited his flashing changeability, but whereas she flicked from joyful to sassy to teary, he flicked from cheeky to fearful to angry. It was never long-lived, but it was one of the things about him that tested so many relationships, one of the things about himself that he hated. The more vulnerable he felt, the more volatile he was; so if he didn't freeze a partner out, his fury often burnt them out. Another reason he resisted letting his guard down: there were so few people who could rise above those moods without taking damage.

As he sat in the car outside Vera's house, he started thinking about her, and how she'd reacted when he told her that he wanted to stop... whatever it was they were doing. She just took it so *well*. Had he really meant that little to her? He had secretly hoped that he hadn't, but presumed that he had; as a result, her apparent apathy felt less of a relief and more of a disappointment. He didn't like to be disappointed, and his hatred of his own behaviour combined with how little he affected her, layered over with concern and anger at Elsie, had pushed Nate close to the rage that had created some of his best songs, and yet destroyed so many of his personal relationships. He reached over to open the glovebox, and looked at the half-empty bottle of gin he found himself reaching for when he felt his emotions well and truly getting the better of him. He thought better of it and slammed it shut. His hands gripped the steering wheel and squeezed, a squeaking sound releasing under his knuckles. He turned and looked up towards the house as an outside light flicked on, and the door opened.

There Vera stood, looking towards his car.

He hoped to see Elsie's face peer out from behind her, but instead, he just saw Vera shift uneasily from one foot to the other, close the flyscreen door behind her, wrap her cardigan around her waist as though to protect herself, and head towards his car.

He supposed it would be rude to stay in the car.

Sighing, he released the steering wheel from his grasp, feeling the blood rush back into the fleshy parts of his fingers. He unbuckled the seatbelt and, without looking, opened the door— slamming it into Vera's leg.

"Shit." He grumbled to himself, looking down, avoiding her eyes. "Sorry." He knew his voice was infused with anger. He could still feel all the shame and disappointment and frustration and *powerlessness* of the whole night.

"That's... okay." Vera's voice wobbled. She stepped back, put her hand on the top of the car door. "I checked my phone after you called. I, uh... I have a few messages from Elsie. She must have sent them while I was in the shower. She said she was heading over here, but..." she shrugged. Even without Nate watching, he could see it. "I tried to call her back, but I got the same as you. No answer."

She wasn't crying, she wasn't angry, she wasn't screaming. She sounded worried, hesitant, small. Nate looked up at her, finding her puffy eyes looking down towards the street, noticing how she stood, hunched into herself. Diminished again. *He'd* done that to her. He felt as though he'd stabbed himself in the chest, as though he'd drunk burning poison.

"Do you..." she hesitated when their eyes locked. "Want to come in for coffee or something while you wait?" Her hand squeezed the frame of the car door. "It's better than waiting out here, alone."

Her eyes flicked between expressions of pleading and pushing. It was like a lighthouse light flashing: I am here, but keep away.

Nate thought about what he'd said. He should take it all back.

"Vera, about earlier—" His phone rang: Home. Elsie. He scrambled to answer it without a thought. "Hello? Elsie, is that you?"

Vera watched Nate on the phone with Elsie. He stayed quiet for a long time, listening to her. Vera couldn't make out any words, but she could hear Elsie's timbre, her tone carried through the tweeter of his phone. She watched his expression, flicking between relief, anger, shame. Back to anger. He looked up at Vera, took a breath to calm himself, and closed his eyes.

"Okay." He said finally. "I'll come home now. No, you can go to bed. That's okay. We'll talk tomorrow. Yes, we're still going. No, I'm not angry."

The muscles on either side of his jaw flared: telling his lie, showing his control. Vera couldn't help but think he looked beautiful and vulnerable and everything that his most painful songs hinted at. She felt herself faltering.

"See you soon." He hung up and fiddled with his phone. "Well, she's home."

He looked up at her and she prayed that he couldn't see the pain and adoration in her eyes. "That's good. So I guess you'll go home, too."

His expression shifted when their eyes met. He looked unsure, boyish: he was toying with conflicting thoughts. "Mmm."

Vera pushed herself away from the car door, "It's pretty late. I should get to bed," a brief flash of electricity passed between them. *Her bed.* "And you... should go home. Drive safe." She turned and started walking towards her door. *Don't look back,* she told herself. *Just get inside.*

She held her reserve until she turned around to close her front door. Nate had stepped out from the car to watch her walk back to the house, instinctively following her. His posture relaxed when their eyes met, and he sent her a hesitant, sweet smile. She felt herself blushing despite herself, felt her head drop in coyness, before looking up at him again. His smile was firmer, more assured; but then something changed in him, his face blanked, he looked at anything but her, he turned back to the driver's side of the car, and, after one final pained glance back at her, he got in.

Suddenly all those logical, rational, stable thoughts of hers weren't so solid, and her stance on the situation wasn't so clear — because neither was his.

She closed the door behind her, and the yearning, the frustration, the desire for him came flooding back. She staggered to the couch and, flopping down on it, curled into a ball and cried herself to sleep.

Twenty-Two

⏮ ⏸ ⏭

Vera woke, overheated, the curtains wide open and the eastern sun heating the living room more than she expected. She dragged herself to the bathroom to splash her face. She stood staring at the basin with the water running, searching the water trailing down the drain for help. It was hard to know what to do. She couldn't bring herself to go to the cafe — it held too many bad memories about Nate. She needed a fresh start from her fresh start, but she didn't know where to go. It felt as though what had happened had poisoned too much of her life. All that music she used to listen to, through high school and university? Gone. It all had an extra layer of pain and heartbreak, and as such was of no consolation to her now. She needed to go somewhere else, do something else, talk to someone else.

Her phone lay beside her, two new messages. Elsie.

ELSIE: Dad told me. He's a jerk!!! He's just an enemy of love n doesn't know how to be happy.

ELSIE: Don't worry im gonna change his mind ok?

Okay, she knew she didn't want to talk to Elsie. Maybe she could talk to Vanessa?

She scrolled through her phone, checked the time, and being a reasonable pre-work hour on a Thursday morning, decided to call rather than text.

"Ronnie!" came the chipper greeting. "How'd things go with Elsie? Is she gonna talk to Nate?"

"Oh, uh," Elsie's troubles at school had been forgotten in the mess of the last day. "I haven't really had a chance to talk to her much about that, actually."

"You sound... not... great. You okay, hun?"

"It's over, Ness. With Nate. It's over."

"Wait, what? When did this happen?"

"Yesterday. He uh, he said we both know that it's not going anywhere, he'd just needed an ego boost or something. I..." she broke off, stopping to recompose herself and failing.

"Bullshit."

"It's okay. I was okay with it... until he came over later on."

"*Excuse me?* Was he there for like, a breakup fuck or something?"

"Oh, no no no. Elsie went missing and he thought she'd tried to get to my place, which she had but she hadn't got here, so he came around. He was only here to look for Elsie. But," Vera let out a big sigh, and gulped air back in. "I was fine, I'd told myself that there was nothing more to it, it was just a fun rebound hookup or whatever; I was feeling flattered that I'd got his attention and we'd made each other feel good for a little while, and I was sure that I could be mature and be okay when I saw him. But then, seeing the look on his face when we were talking?" Vera shook her head even though Vanessa could never see it. "I don't know anymore Ness, I don't know."

"Honey." Vanessa let Vera cry, letting her get it out. "Urgh, I honestly didn't think he'd be an arsehole like this. I tested him and everything! Do you want me to come over for a bit? I'm having breakfast with my girlfriend, but I can drop by after? I can take the morning off work. I just have a 2pm meeting I can't skip."

Vera sniffed up her tears. "No, that's okay. I just needed someone to talk to."

"I'm glad you thought of me." Vanessa paused, her tone shifting. "Shit. I didn't want him to do this to you. I honestly thought maybe he'd be an adult and not a cock and be sensible."

"It's okay. I'm not really angry with him."

"Well, I am. What a dick."

"No, Ness, I'm upset at myself for thinking I had a chance with him."

"Ronnie, he *gave* you a chance with him. But then he took it away. For what?"

Vera could feel herself getting more upset. "It's okay Ness, I think

I'm okay now."

"Okay. But: hey— you call me anytime. Today, tonight, anytime. Well, not between two and three this afternoon. If I don't answer, leave a message. I will call you back. I am here for you."

"I really appreciate that, Ness."

"You deserve it. You're one of the most amazing people I know. He may be a rockstar, but you're so smart and kind, funny, and nice. Shit. I really hoped that Steven would make you happy, but he was an arsehole, and then I hoped that Nate would see you for what you are, but he's an arsehole too."

"Thanks, Ness. Clearly, I just choose the arseholes."

"You do. One day, someone nice will choose you, and you'll choose them, too."

Nice. It was what Nate said he was able to appreciate in her now, despite the number of times that others had used it as a way to turn her down. If she was so nice, didn't she deserve nice, too? Vanessa was right. She was going to be nice to herself, and not waste her time on anyone who didn't do the same.

"Thanks. I hope so."

"I love you, you know? Just... be kind to yourself."

Vera smiled and hung up, unable to respond to her without crying. She was still so exhausted from last night's ups and downs that it wasn't long after sitting down on her couch that she fell asleep again.

A few hours passed before Vera roused again. Tired of the sound of her own thoughts, she turned on the television before getting up and moping her way into the kitchen to boil the kettle and rummage in the fridge, only to give in to the loss of appetite from fresh heartbreak. Soon she was back, surrounded by pillows and spent tissues, holding in one hand a mug of tea, and in the other, a remote. She flicked from channel to channel, hoping to find something that would make her feel better, not worse. Since Steven had left her, she hadn't felt so acutely aware of how much entertainment was cued to evoke romantic yearning in those whose own romances had dulled or had never happened, while those who were feeling the sharp sting of abandonment were left bitter at the lack of happy ending in their own lives.

She opened YouTube on her tv and was offered the livestream of the ARIA Awards Red Carpet, and sat up slightly, a pang of fear and hope that she'd see Nate. She scrolled away quickly, then flicked onto Free-to-Air channels, and onto another RomCom and its sickly sweet promise of a reality that doesn't exist outside of a writer's mind. Groaning, she flicked onwards, but eventually, her curiosity got the better of her, and she found herself once again streaming the ARIA Awards Red Carpet on YouTube. Per her luck, they were interviewing Nate; he looked tired and worn, impatient and almost bored by the whole thing. This wasn't outside his usual interview disposition, but Vera was sure she saw more pain in him. She wondered how many times he'd been hurting during all those media appearances he'd endured, what sorts of things that gruff and evasive exterior hid.

Elsie was standing next to him, half excited nerves and half coy. At least Vera could focus on her, and how excited she must be to be there this year. She looked young but intensely pretty, having been more lucky than some celebrity offspring, for whom their parents' perfect features mixed in a less desirable way.

"And are *you* going to get into music?" the interviewer asked her.

She blushed and batted her eyelashes, before smiling up at him and saying, "I don't think so. I'm more interested in robotics right now!"

"Not much of a chip off the old block then, eh?"

"I don't know where she gets it from. But I'm very proud of her." The set of Nate's face softened as he slapped his hand on Elsie's shoulder and looked at her with pure affection. It was the sort of thing that could charm a million hearts: seeing the aloof rockstar turn gooey and sweet.

Vera couldn't hate him, as much as she wanted to. She could see he was such a loving father, and a good man. He wasn't perfect — no one was. She thought about the evening in the cafe, when he'd told her that they never should have slept together. He didn't even know that they were *both* just looking for some verification that they were attractive, acceptable, okay.

They had chemistry, that was undeniable. But he was right — it wasn't going anywhere. It wasn't serious for either of them. Not really. It was just a fantasy for her. It was like living in a daydream — until reality hit. And, to be honest, she was kind-of glad that he was the one to say it, not her. How on earth do you say *that* to your icon? So when he said all of that, deep down, she was glad it was over. She didn't have to worry about avoiding him, trying to explain her awkwardness, her being ill-at-ease. He'd freed her.

But, what ruined all that reason and logic was that she wasn't even sure if he'd really meant it.

She thought back to all those high school and university years before Steven, all those guys she'd liked who didn't like her, for whom any sort of 'relationship' lasted no longer than a weekend at most, a hookup at a club, only to see him the next week with someone else. All those nights she'd go home and listen to sad songs. She'd pulled those sad songs out again when she left Steven. She found herself mouthing those words from those songs again as she watched Nate and Elsie smiling, looking amongst the crowd that they had started blending into.

Standing up suddenly from the couch, shedding all the pillows and blankets and crumpled tissues like a dandelion sheds its seeds in the wind, she launched herself towards the cardboard moving boxes sitting opened but never accessed. Plunging her hands in, she started to sing, her strained throat croaking.

Her fingers clawed at the contents of the box, not really processing what was inside, just wanting to have something to distract from now — even if it meant processing something from the past. She pulled out a frame, tore the tissue paper off it, and looked down at a picture of her and Steven on the first night they were officially a couple. She didn't know why she still had it. Had she packed it and forgotten? Had he packed it as some sick parting gift? She looked up from the photo of them, both younger, slimmer, and happier, and caught her reflection in her window.

Before she even had the time to process a thought, her phone rang.

She considered ignoring it, but thought it better to at least find out who she would be ignoring should she choose to ignore them. Grabbing it from the coffee table, she turned away from the television and missed seeing Tommy introducing himself to Nate and Elsie in the background as the host focused on some other musician of significance to the world but insignificant to Elsie or Vera. Instead, her focus snapped to her phone, and as though the universe had decided to punish her in one big hit, she saw a number that she didn't need a name to recognise: Steven's.

Twenty-Three

⏮ ⏸ ⏭

"Nate Whitely, we meet at last." A youthful, husky voice crooned his name. Nate turned around and found himself looking up into a pair of intense green eyes. The same green eyes that seemed to stare him out from Elsie's bedroom walls.

"Ah, you're..." his eyes flicked to Elsie; the shocked look on her face confirmed that he had identified him correctly. "Thomas, right?"

The intensity of his eyes faded and the edges crumpled. "Aw man, you know who I am? Oh, man... You're my hero, man!" The over-frequent use of the word 'man' unsettled Nate. Not because he had any problem with the word itself, but because it had become such a foreign part of his vocabulary, reminding him that he was no longer either hip or cool. Tommy thrust his hand out to Nate, who removed his own from his pocket and offered it to him. Before Nate knew it, Tommy grabbed at his hand with both of his, bracelets jangling as they shook. "Please... call me Tommy."

"Tommy," Nate repeated. "Well, it's a pleasure to meet you. And congratulations on everything." What was intended to be a rather offhand remark took on additional weight as Tommy leaned forward to him, eyes widening and hands still wrapped around Nate's.

"Thank you. Oh man, that means so much coming from you!" Nate looked down at his hand and back up at Tommy's face. He wasn't letting go. "I mean, when I was growing up, seeing you, you'd made it. You were amazing, man: a real inspiration."

"Thanks." The use of past-tense was mildly unsettling, an

innocent backhanded compliment.

"…Dad?" In the discomfort of the extended handshake, Nate had forgotten about Elsie. He soon realised that she could be his way out, making Tommy feel as awkward as he felt.

"Oh, Elsie. Tommy, this is my daughter, Elsie." Tommy was forced to drop Nate's hand as he was pointedly introduced to a third party. "Elsie, this is Thomas, call him Tommy."

There it was.
The Look.

Nate had known it was likely to happen, which is why he didn't want his *fourteen-year-old* daughter to come to the Music Awards. It was too risky. But she was there, and as much of a rockstar as he may have been in his previous life, now he was a Dad, and his rockstar heritage simply made him flare with a more aggressive sense of protection.

Tommy, meanwhile, quickly nodded at Elsie, said, "Hey," and looked back at Nate. "So uh, I don't know if you've heard my latest album, it's up for an award; but really, I'm looking for a collaborator-producer for some of my new stuff, and… uh…"

Nate looked at Elsie. She was beside herself, beaming longingly at Tommy. Nate looked at Tommy. He, too, was beside himself — because he was talking to Nate. Although he was more guarded and self-aware than Elsie or even Vera, Tommy was singularly and intensely focused on Nate, not the young girl who Nate had feared he was dangling in front of a wolf.

Tommy suddenly bit his lip, a flash of fear crossing his eyes. "I'd be *thrilled*, like, really *honoured*, if you would even *consider…*" Nate's silence shook the last of Tommy's resolve. "Oh shit; that was probably really presumptuous of me, man. Forget it. I'm just — it's an honour to just meet you." Tommy looked around for an escape path. "Catch you later, maybe." His eyes landed on Elsie, who raised her hand in an attempt at a goodbye. He gave her a nod, swallowing his embarrassment, before turning and weaving into the crowd.

Nate could feel Elsie's heart drop. She turned to him, hands on her hips, a look of fury and disappointment on her face.

"What?"

"*Wow*, Dad. You just… stared at him."

"I didn't know what to say."

"Why? It's not like he's the first fan of yours you've met recently. It's not like you had trouble talking then."

"Well, what did you want me to do? *Flirt* with him?"

Elsie paled at this suggestion. "Why can't you help me out with anything?"

"Elsie," Nate laughed.

"Don't laugh at me!"

She turned and ran, slamming face-first into someone, spilling his drink.

"Elsie... are you okay?" The man asked in a quiet tenor, remarkably high pitched for his age and build, and shook the droplets of pale ale from his hand.

"No!" She yelped at him, before glaring back at Nate and weaving forward into the crowd.

Nate blanched. "I'm so sorry, Jason."

"Kids," he quipped, rolling his eyes and grinning, thinking of his three between the ages of five and twelve at home. "You're a braver man than me, bringing her along. I guess though, you don't have the missus around to help, and Elsie's probably too old for a babysitter."

The unexpected mention of his failed marriage stung, adding fuel to the fire of emotion that Nate was beginning to build about Elsie.

"No friends would have her either, then?" Jason slurped through his words.

"She's... not doing well with her friends right now."

"Ah. Sorry to hear that, for her sake." A masculine slap-on-the-shoulder of solidarity underlined the sentiment. "Next time, you call me up. The boys would be glad to have her around."

"Thanks, Jase." Nate had met Jason early in his career. He was harmless, warm, and kind, and the type of music Producer that anyone would be lucky to work with. Nate had the fortune of working with him and his label in various professional capacities over the years, but Jason always left the door open for Nate if he ever wanted to move the relationship from professional to personal. He'd been sympathetic when the band split up, reached out when the news of Elsie's mother leaving hit the papers, and turned up on Nate's doorstep with meals in hand, ready to entertain Elsie and be a shoulder for Nate. And when Nate came to him with a series of demos, scared that he was weak as a solo artist and would never sell another record, Jason was the one who pulled it all together, got him the right support, and advocated for a promotion strategy that didn't rely on touring. He was perpetually supportive and understanding, and he did it again and again, despite Nate continually holding him at arm's length. Nate suddenly felt horrible for taking him for granted; he'd had a hard time trusting anyone after the band's dissolution, but Jason was someone whose taste and professionalism he could always rely on — so why was it so hard for him to trust him personally, after knowing he'd been beside him for so many years?

Jason clapped his hand onto Nate's shoulder again, roughing him up with a fond smile. He was no stranger to Nate going silent and moody on him. "Oh— by the way, have you seen any members of that new group, Frothing Mess? They're really tearing up the charts. They remind me of you lot when we were all young. I guess it's no surprise: I heard that one of them's a big fan of yours. I'd love to work with him, really push them to do something interesting."

Nate bit his lip. Usually, he wouldn't care less, he would say something flippant and retreat into his own shell of self-preservation, feeling justified that all these people just wanted to take advantage of him and of each other. But, Tommy was looking for a Producer; Jason was looking for Tommy. Jason had always been generous to him, and Tommy — Tommy had been starstruck, but held himself back from overstepping or presuming, despite how successful he already was. Maybe it was time to trust that it would be okay to be supportive of someone else again. "Actually, you know — I just met him. I'll let him know you're looking for him. Oh, and Jase? Maybe," Nate felt sick to his stomach from fear, but the steadfast look on Jason's face reassured him, "maybe we could all get together on this one?"

Twenty-Four

⏮ ⏸ ⏭

There was no logic in why Vera answered Steven's call. She just found herself accepting it, saying hello to the phone at her ear.

"Hey, Ronnie?" It felt painful when *he* said it, even though Vanessa's use of it pulled her back to an earlier, purer time when her identity felt unadulterated. "It's me. Steven."

"Yes, I know your number."

"I know you probably don't want to talk to me."

"Well, no; I guess I'd kinda hoped that you'd lost your phone and someone was calling me because they'd tried calling everyone else in your phonebook," she paused. "Or that you'd sold your number to telemarketers."

A forced laugh echoed from the other side of the phone. "You always had the most droll sense of humour, Ronnie. It's what I always liked about you."

Vera could feel something curling inside her. Something negative but indescribable. "Why *are* you calling me at eight o'clock on a Saturday night?"

"Oh, no reason."

No reason? There had to be a reason. She could tell that he was pretending that there wasn't. A spark of hope flared in Vera's heart. She didn't know exactly what that hope was about, but there was some sort of hope. "It can't be *no* reason."

"No, I uh, I just wanted to hear y—" he quickly, yet perceptibly, changed gears, "hear how you're doing." It was a bad cover up to make him proud. "How *are* you doing, Ronnie?"

"Fine, actually." Hopefully, he wouldn't hear the crackle in her voice. "Actually... I think I'm coming down with a bit of a cold."

"That's no good," Steven was skirting around something. "Well, as I said, I just wanted to see how you're doing. I, uh," he paused, and Vera wondered if he was searching for whether it was the right time to end the call. She decided that it was.

"Yeah. Thanks for calling. Take care." And she cut him off again.

Glancing at the television, she caught sight of Elsie, seemingly on her own. That was odd: what happened to Nate?

"Tommy? Tommy!" Elsie chased after him, reaching out thoughtlessly to grab hold of the crook of his arm. At the unexpected touch, Tommy shot a hostile glance: his eyes fierce, ready to shrug off danger. When his eyes met Elsie's, she was taken aback slightly, but she glanced away in coy embarrassment before she had the chance to process it. "I'm sorry about Dad. He's—"

"Right, you're Nate Whitely's daughter," Tommy hadn't really taken in what Elsie looked like when he'd met her: he'd been so focused on Nate that everything in the periphery was a bit of a blur.

"Elsie, yeah."

"Yeah, Elsie, that's it. Cute name. El-sie."

Elsie blushed at the sing-song way he said it.

"Sorry, you were saying?"

Elsie, still reeling from Tommy saying her name and *complimenting* it, fumbled. "Oh, um, ah... I... really like your music."

Tommy laughed; tension broken. "I'm really glad to hear that, Elsie." Her cheeks got redder every time he said her name. He kept repeating it so that he could remember, so he wouldn't offend her later by getting it wrong, and by proxy, offend Nate. "How old are you, Elsie?" He was trying to remember if he knew — or could work out — how old Elsie was. Her birth was big enough news, and there were absolutely adorable quotes about it from Nate in every interview he gave; it was also not long before he had retired from touring, and aside from an incredible first solo album, the music he put out became less and less frequent. Understandably, really, as the rumour was that he'd taken over primary caregiver responsibilities early. But Tommy's quick calculation didn't quite line up with how old she looked; the careful styling of her hair and makeup could have made her a punkish, babyfaced nineteen-year-old, or—

"Fourteen."

"Fourteen," the same age as his kid cousin.

"Almost fifteen."

"Right." He was glad she wasn't lying to him. She could have, but it was an easy enough fact-check to do later on. Tommy looked around, thinking of some of the types he'd encountered throughout his time in the industry. The things they might do to her. The things they'd wanted to do to *him*. "Where *is* your Dad?"

"Oh!" Elsie snapped out of her trance. "That's what I wanted to talk to you about. He didn't mean to be rude. He's just... going through something at the moment."

Tommy could tell that Elsie was doing her best to try to protect Nate's personal life, but he couldn't help but both feel slightly concerned for his hero, before the thought struck that this might all be a lie and that he had, in fact, left a bad impression. "I dunno, Elsie. It was pretty presumptuous of me. I just... admire him so much, y'know?" He let out a huff of amusement. "If he knew how many pictures of him I had on my walls, growing up..."

He looked up to see Elsie watching him intensely. He couldn't quite read her. Out of the corner of his eye, he noticed that people were starting to move out of the foyer. He checked his watch.

"C'mon, let's get you to him."

⏮ ⏸ ⏭

Vera's phone rang again. She answered without even looking at the number. "Hello?"

"Yeah, hi, it's me again."

"Steven?"

"Yeah, I—" he was faltering again. "I wanted to say. I'm really sorry," his voice was wobbling.

Vera continued watching the television, keeping an eye out for Nate. She willed the television Producer to swap cameras, the cameraman to pan out to another section of the crowd, and the presenter to investigate the crowd on her behalf.

"I'm really sorry Ron, I truly am. It was a rotten, fucked up thing to do. I didn't realise it at the time. I didn't realise it until," he swallowed. "Just today, actually."

"Mmm-hmm?" Come on cameraman. Just pan across the crowd.

"Ron?"

"Oh, uh, sorry. Missed that. I have a lot on my mind." A pause. "You still there, Steven?"

"Oh yeah yeah, I am. Sorry, of course, how silly of me. Of course you have a lot on your mind. You've moved and probably have a new job and a new *boyfriend* and everything," the word *boyfriend* came out all strangled. It hurt them both more than a single word should hurt two people. "Sorry. I'll leave you to it, then?"

"Yeah," Vera continued watching the television, but now neither Elsie nor Nate were anywhere to be seen, and they were moving inside the venue for the awards, and the presenters were wrapping up the Red Carpet coverage. "Yeah. No! Sorry. I can talk now."

"No no, that's fine. I'll—" he paused yet again. He was pausing a lot. He was pausing more than he used to. "Can I call you some other time? Just to check in on you, hear how you're going."

"Oh, um," Vera, confused, scratched the back of her head. "Sure."

"Okay."

"Okay?"

"Okay, uh… goodbye?"

"Goodbye, Steven."

That was the strangest phonecall she'd ever had with him.

Vera turned her attention back to the television. She didn't want to process what Steven had said. It looked like the live stream of the Red Carpet was over. If she wanted to see any more, she'd have to wait for the special presentation on Free-to-Air later that night.

Twenty-Five

⏮ ⏸ ⏭

Aside from meeting Tommy, who had surprised him by delivering Elsie back to him with the utmost respect and disappearing into the crowd before Nate had the chance to mention Jason, Nate found the awards about as unremarkable as expected for something where he had no nominations. Spending time with all his industry acquaintances and seeing performances by musicians new and old was always nice, and enough to take the edge off being haunted by his thoughts of Vera. However, as the night went on, he became more and more unsettled by seeing those so much younger and more relevant than him getting awards. Having Elsie with him was meant to be a comfort, but instead, their discord earlier in the night had made her bristle, adding to his discontent.

He thought of Vera, of what she might be doing now, of the puffiness and the flighty look in her eyes and the defeat in the way she stood, the way she'd just accepted his rejection, her dedication to civility and acting as though he hadn't hurt her even though it was written all over her. The way he wanted to take it all back and take her in his arms.

"Can I tempt you, Nate?" Jon, a portly publicist with a twinkle in his eye that not even the thick glasses he wore hid, offered one of two bottles of craft beer to Nate as he settled into the seat next to him. In one regrettable instant, Nate nodded and held his hand out. Jon beamed and let Nate choose which of the bottles he would use to block out thoughts of Vera.

Elsie watched as Nate took a swig of beer. She knew that his starting drinking would likely mean that the night would go from bad to worse, but that he wouldn't take kindly to her 'embarrassing' him in front of his peers.

"Oh, how rude of me. Are *you* old enough to drink?" Jon was nothing if not inclusive. Elsie glanced at her father, who avoided her eye contact.

"Well, not really, but I'm sure Dad won't mind."

Nate's eyes shot up, locking onto hers with a warning. She smiled sweetly and held out her glass for Jon.

"Alright, just a little bit then!" he chuckled, delicately dribbling some of the golden liquid from his bottle into her glass. "You just let me know if you want some more." He turned to Nate. "Little girls have got to grow up one day."

Nate felt the anger burning again, but hid it in a forced laugh and a gulp of the beer, keeping his furious thoughts at bay. Elsie blushed into her glass as she heard Tommy's band being named as the winners for the first of their nominated awards of the night.

Earlier, as they had been just about to go inside to their allocated seating, Tommy had walked with her back to Nate. After presenting Elsie to him, Tommy turned back to her and winked before squeezing her shoulder as he walked past, filling with her a hot excitement and nervousness. It was incredible to her that she was here, having met him, having been recognised by him, and waiting to congratulate him when he won an award or share her disappointment and tell him that he'd been robbed if he lost. She focused so hard on the moment that she didn't notice Nate downing the entire bottle of beer.

"That's the spirit," Jon chuckled and nudged Nate with his elbow and looked back to the stage. "This is already my third; I know you can keep up — I'll get you another in the next break."

Elsie's eyes were glued to the stage as Tommy and his bandmates were called onto the stage. Nate's eyes flicked to his daughter, still so young and vulnerable, watching her much older crush walk onstage.

"Wow… This is a dream, man. We're so grateful to everyone who has helped us on our journey, to our families and friends, and to you, our peers, our constant inspiration. And," he paused, looking left and right at his bandmates, "I want to say a special thank you to my idol, whose music meant so much to me growing up, who I finally met tonight. Nate Whitely—" Tommy scanned the crowd, only to have the hands of various people around Nate — including Jon — help him catch his eye as he raised the award in the air, "this is thanks to you, man."

Nate wanted to hide his face, but knew enough about the way these nights worked to know that there would be a camera trained on him at that very moment, ready to film his reaction. He feigned coy embarrassment and smiled and nodded to the stage in an attempt at humble recognition. He supposed that the only way to keep Tommy from Elsie was to stay between them.

For the first time, Elsie looked over at him. Her face dropped at seeing the bottle of beer empty so soon; he wasn't the type to drink to celebrate. She couldn't predict how he was going to act now. Following her father's model, she drowned her nervous tension in the bitter drink in her own glass.

Twenty-Six

Vera sat, numb, her mind flickering between Steven's phonecall and the previous night with Nate; the way they'd spoken, the way he'd looked at her.

When she was young, and speculation about his relationships and news of his wedding were dispersed in magazines, she'd felt a kind of naive heartbreak over the loss of a future she knew she'd never have but always hoped for. When Elsie was born, Vera had heard the news and mentally completely broken up with him. It seemed that he would have a happily-ever-after, and that she should grow up and focus on hers. But then she'd lost her chance at that when she'd lost Steven. She didn't even know how.

So here he was, *Nate Fucking Whitely*, leaving her in the most honourable and honest ways. He admitted what he did, he admitted he was an arsehole; and really, she supposed, they'd both done the same thing to each other, both got the same thing from each other. So that was fine.

But he did it despite still longing for her in some way, she was sure of it. The look on his face had said he hurt himself more than he hurt her, and he hurt himself more *so that* he wouldn't hurt her.

Vera realised that she wasn't really heartbroken by him, but rather was disappointed and angry that he'd been able to be courageous in a way that Steven had not. If anything, this showed her that she did mean something to him. And because she was worthy of his honesty, but he wanted to see other people, it stung. It just didn't sting for the reason she'd expected.

But every time she'd really seen *him*, when he'd actually allowed her in and relaxed around her, she found herself falling for him. She didn't even really see him as a combination of his interviews and his music videos and performances anymore, but she saw him in his kindness, his vulnerability, his emotions: everything he'd poured into his music that had made her *feel* every time she listened. The greatest art affects you because you get to see yourself, your emotions, laid bare by someone else who has the courage to say: *you and me, and everyone around you? We're all the same.*

Nate Whitely's music had told her that, and when she stood in his presence and he fretted over whether he had the right pizza toppings for her, or how to comfort Elsie, or whether she was safe, and his eyes told a story about his vulnerability that his words and actions tried to hide, she felt that same feeling.

With Steven, it always felt like there was a facade, a challenge to get through to those moments of vulnerability. That facade made it feel all the more rewarding when you could get inside: a feeling of being in the inner sanctum of his mind. Vera was sure that he had opened up to her, and that they were sharing everything with each other: secrets that no one else knew. But, the problem with people who are very guarded is that you never know what they might be hiding from you; what secrets they might only share with someone else.

That's why Steven was able to have one relationship with Vera, and yet develop another with Sarah. It wasn't that he was necessarily *bored* with Vera, he didn't intend to hurt her, he didn't hate her or feel trapped; he just had different parts of himself that he felt comfortable sharing with different people. It was just the way he worked. With Sarah, he could reveal another part of himself, talk about different things, act in different ways. Vera was lovely, she was sweet and funny and romantic and intelligent and stable; Sarah was volatile and passionate and challenging and dramatic. They were two totally different people, and Steven loved them both. Vera was the one he wanted to settle down with, Sarah was the one that it was exciting to be around. That's how he'd explained it to them both, at separate times. Sarah didn't care that he was still with Vera, she kept wanting him despite him never choosing her over Vera. Vera, as he found out, couldn't stand that idea. She was *nice*, but her sense of self-preservation meant that she didn't take kindly to being second fiddle. Or even having there be a second fiddle. Vera didn't want to be in an Orchestra

— she wanted to be a soloist.

Vera looked at the tv. It was showing highlights of the nominees, cycling through their music clips. In one of them, there was a group of young men that, now that she thought about it, she recognised from Elsie's wall. The clip cut to a close up of green eyes: Tommy. She wondered whether Elsie would get the chance she wanted to meet him, to bring him off her wall and into her life, just as Vera had been able to do with Nate.

She sighed, shaking herself out of her old habit of thinking of Nate as a beautiful distant thing she adored and admired; remembering that he was a human and real thing, a real thing that she's spoken to and touched, who had shared his life with her, had touched her, had... loved her? She laughed at herself as her thoughts trailed that way. If he'd felt anything close to that for her, it was over. He'd made it clear, hadn't he? It was over. Whether he'd truly wanted it to be over, though — she wasn't sure. But it didn't even matter. Here he was, free of her, able to do and be with whomever he wanted.

It wasn't worth watching any more. She flicked from channel to channel, finding RomCom and drama and documentary. She turned off the television, which had turned into the final light on in the room. She sat in the dark, thinking about Nate, thinking about Steven; thinking about who she'd been and who she was, then turned her energy to who she might become.

Twenty-Seven

⏮ ⏸ ⏭

Vera had slept on the couch again. The morning sun peeked through the crack in the living room curtains, which she had remembered to draw, but she'd also turned to face away from during the night. Her phone was more insistent, the ringtone harassing her enough to wake her up. She didn't even look at who it was before answering.

"Hello?"

"Hi, it's me again," *Steven*. "Did I wake you up?"

In the past, Vera would have insisted that he hadn't. She didn't want him to accuse her of being lazy or cause him to feel like she was angry at him — something that would just make him patronise and diminish her. But *he'd* cheated on *her*, he'd cheated on her with her *best friend*. She didn't care. He was on the other side of the phone, he didn't even know where she lived. She could just hang up and block his number if she wanted.

"You did, actually."

"Oh," he was uncharacteristically polite. "I'm sorry. Should I call back later?"

"No, I'm awake now." She propped herself up, rubbing her eyes and looking around. "Is there something that you want?"

"I just... I wanted to make sure that you, uh, *understood* my apology last night."

Vera had to focus hard to think about what he'd said to her. She remembered him calling, but she was more focused on what might have been going on with Elsie and Nate at the awards to really think about the phonecall. "You apologised for *cheating* on me," she sighed. "Now, maybe I've misunderstood how apologies work, but I thought you were meant to be free to go on your way again, relieved of the burden that you've been carrying; meanwhile the wound has been reopened for me and I have to get over it all over again."

Steven paused. "Well, I mean... I wanted to say, to *admit*, that when I apologised before, I guess I was really just sorry for getting caught. But I realise now how much I hurt you, how much I took you for granted, and I'm sorry for that. I um, *understand* your pain now."

Understand. The word rang through Vera's ears. What did he mean by that? She wasn't sure she cared, and she needed a bit of time to process and unpack everything he'd said. She'd previously suspected that he didn't really care that he hurt her, and now he'd confirmed that. But he'd just said that he now *understands* her pain? Something must have happened.

"Why are you saying this to me now? What happened?"

Steven cleared his throat. "Well, I guess that's what I was trying to tell you last night." Vera could hear his characteristic patronising tone creep into his voice. "I, uh—it's quite funny, actually— I had a cancellation yesterday afternoon, so I thought I'd go home early and surprise Sarah. And..." he trailed off. "I guess I was the one who got surprised."

If she was someone else, and this was someone else she was watching on tv, Vera would have just snorted in laughter and said *it serves you right!*

But Vera was Vera, and she was *nice*. She didn't try to be, she just was. It was part of her core identity. "I'm... sorry to hear that."

"Yeah, so. I just wanted to say, I understand now. And I'm sorry."

"Oh."

"If there is any way — *any way* — I can make it up to you, I will. I didn't realise how lucky I was to have you, and I wanted to let you know that. I was a rotten person to you, but..." Steven paused. Vera suspected she knew what would come next, but she wanted to see whether he would say it. "I wish it hadn't happened. I wish I could have you back."

Vera wished that instead of thinking about whether he was going to say it, she'd thought about what she would say in response to when he *did* say it.

"I know you've... you've probably moved on, you probably have someone else. He's—" he let out a small laugh. "He's probably right next to you now, wondering who has called you, is talking to you this early."

"I don't, actually," it slipped out before Vera could stop herself, more a reactive impulse to her frustration at Nate than anything else. She knew what he was doing: it was a trap, a ploy to see whether she was available.

"Oh," Steven stopped, changed gears. "Well if you don't, how would you feel about catching up?"

She regretted saying it. "I don't know if that's a good idea."

"Oh, it's no pressure! I mean, just as a catch up. To say hi," his voice got warmer, softer, more intimate. "You know we didn't end on *good* terms. My fault entirely. But I want to make it up to you."

Vera paused. She looked over towards the photo of them together and thought about when they'd first started dating, about all the fun they'd had. All their shared moments, all the secrets they had together and hid from the world. He knew her more deeply than anyone else in the world.

"Surely we can be… *friends?*"

Vera sighed. It would be a good break from fretting over Nate. Nate had made his feelings clear when he'd spoken to her: he'd rather stay away than hurt her more. She had to trust what he had said and not fuss about it anymore. And this was just a catch up. Maybe it could be a good opportunity for some closure.

If she could set it on safe ground, on *her* territory, maybe it would be okay. But not her house — no way. Maybe the cafe? It was ruined enough by her 'breakup' with Nate that she might as well ruin it more by catching up with Steven.

"Fine," she sighed. "I mean, okay. I'd like that. Coffee? There's a nice cafe near me."

"Thanks, Ronnie. Anywhere you want to go. My shout, no obligations. I owe *you*. Are you free this afternoon, say… one o'clock? I only work half days on Fridays."

Fortunately or unfortunately, Vera was.

What do you wear when you go to meet up with the man who you loved with all your heart, who had thrown it all away because he had feelings for your best friend?

The man who had been hurt by your best friend, just as you had?

Clothes are costume, they tell a story of who you are and how you are. They have the power to defend you, to keep you hidden; or to make you vulnerable, to reveal your truth. They can wound, they can comfort. Vera didn't know how she wanted to affect Steven; she just knew that she needed to. She needed to make a statement about who she was now that she wasn't with him. She knew she needed a statement of success: the problem was, she felt as far from success as she could imagine.

In so many movies, a transformation in a person's spirit is shown through a makeover. They decide that they don't want to hold onto whatever they were clinging to, whatever was hurting them, before, and letting something underneath emerge from underneath. Vera walked to the mirror and looked at herself. She could hardly recognise herself, so it wasn't even that she needed to change: she already had, whether she'd wanted to or not. Her hair was longer than she had noticed, and her 'around-the-house' clothes sat like paper bags, obscuring the physicality underneath. Looking at her face, she knew that the last week had affected her more than she'd expected — at once it showed more joy and loss than she had shown in the years before. She felt as though she was standing next to herself, looking at something that wasn't who she'd grown up as. In the past, she'd felt as though she was a collection of attributes. In her mind, she was ranked high on her intelligence and skills, and low on her attractiveness. Recently, her inability to secure a new job belied any of the intelligence or academic skill that had been attributed to her. Her ability to draw the attention of a man who could have any woman he wanted belied her mediocre looks.

So this person staring back in the mirror felt completely disconnected from who she saw as herself. How do you dress when you don't know who you are anymore?

All that Vera knew was that she had to dress as someone other than the girl who had found her fiance in bed with her best friend. She just needed to be someone who had moved on with her life, who wouldn't just go back to that time and that place when she saw him. She needed to see him as a completely new person, divorced from all the pain he'd made her feel, and instead as someone who she hardly knew, yet knew her more intimately than anyone in her life.

She turned her tv back on, loaded up YouTube again, and found someone's 'get ready' playlist. She let the music move her, as she stripped off and walked to have a shower, letting all the hopes and pains of her relationship with Steven and her fling with Nate come to an end, flowing down the drain. She stepped out with her mind clear, and didn't care what she wore. Steven didn't matter enough for her to care what she wore or how she looked anymore.

Twenty-Eight

⏮ ⏸ ⏭

Not long after lunch, Vera walked to the cafe, light and full of life. She walked into her regular cafe, intending to sit in her regular seat after ordering. At the counter, the regular waitress asked what she'd like: a latte or a flat white? Vera looked at the table where she and Nate had sat together in the past, the first time he held her hand, and the time he'd told her that he wanted to be free of her. She wanted to be free too, and all it took was to make a new decision.

"I'll have a cappuccino."

She chose a seat at another table, and sat with her eyes closed as she waited. She felt warm and glowing in a way she'd never felt before, previously weighed down by a fear of rejection that had a way of continually coming true.

"You look relaxed." She opened her eyes to see Steven. "I almost didn't recognise you." She expected to feel something when she saw him. She expected to shrink into herself, the way she'd had a habit of doing when she was around him. She expected a twinge of regret or desire or anything; instead, it was like seeing a stranger. He was clearly dressed to impress: wearing the shirt she loved on him, the cologne she remembered lingering on her own clothes after the first night spent with him. He sat down in front of her, tentatively. His dark eyes — like molten chocolate — searched her, their warmth trying to thaw her heart the way they had done so many times before.

"Your cappuccino. Can I get you anything, sir?"

"Er," The cappuccino seemed to catch Steven off guard. "A flat

134

white, thanks."

The waitress nodded, and gave Vera an amused look.

Steven was still staring at the anomalous cappuccino. "You've changed a bit since I last saw you."

Vera felt suddenly defensive, the old flare of needing to hide in plain sight kicking in again. She picked up her coffee, and smiling at him, took a sip. Steven's fingers began drumming on the table nervously. She put the coffee down, and looked at him, critically. He looked legitimately shaken, not the confident rebel who had chosen her to be the object of his adoration. His eyes were searching hers for how to feel. He leaned back in his chair, puffing out his chest and trying to look as unaffected and cool as possible. Vera breathed in through her nose deeply, glancing outside to the sunlight falling on the ground, shattered by the leaves.

"Yes, I've changed. For the better." She looked back at him, looking him up and down. "You've changed too."

Her unflappable confidence flapped him. He was used to being able to drape his interest on Vera and have her swoon back at him, or get under her skin and have her yield her interest to him, that he didn't know what to do when she was suddenly so icy. He tried an appeal. "I missed you, you know," he ran his fingers along his lips as he spoke. "You know I never stopped loving you."

A small, icy dagger pierced Vera's heart. She couldn't let him know. His flat white appeared, and the perceptive waitress merely slipped it in front of him without more than a brief smile before retreating back to the counter to watch.

"Did you love Sarah too?"

Steven's mouth twisted like barbed wire. "I thought we already talked about this?" He took his time, sipped his coffee, waiting for Vera to speak. She didn't. He took a deep breath in. "I did, actually. I loved both of you. Can you blame me?" He smiled gently and leaned towards her, this line intended to flatter her falling flat.

A small laugh escaped Vera's mouth. "How long?"

"Did I love you both?"

She looked him right in the eye, unwaveringly, and outright asked the question she'd previously been afraid to know the answer to. "How long were you *fucking* her behind my back?"

Steven shifted in his seat. "Ronnie, I was hoping we could talk about something else. You look really good, you know. Did I say that already?"

She wanted to press on, ask how long their relationship had held his secret, but there was a small part of her that still wanted Steven's admiration. He'd laid it on so thickly before, she'd become dependent on it. She was beautiful when he said so, she was smart when he said so. He'd told her that she was everything she wanted to be. She felt herself soften, blush, feel good to be told that she was still worthy of his attention, despite Sarah.

Steven saw his *in*. "But then, you always were beautiful, and absolutely unique. And we both know I never would have made it through university without you." He knew how to play her better than Nate could play piano. His words hit all the keys with more certainty now, and the harmonies moved her in the way he always used to. "Do you remember all those nights you'd come over to my parents' house for dinner, and they'd try to get you to agree that I was wasted in engineering, that I should have switched to medicine?" He shifted forward in his seat, the touch of his fingertips on the skin of her wrist so familiar that she didn't even notice, his molten eyes searching hers.

But *his* eyes weren't the ones to captivate her; she was drawn to someone staring at her from over his shoulder. Noticing Vera looking past him, Steven turned around, one brow arching.

It felt as though a million hands were pulling down every part of Nate when he saw the proof that he meant so little to her, that she was already moving on. She'd probably been dating a few people at the same time — what made him think he might be special, the only one she was interested in, or the only one interested in her? He felt a crushing feeling on his throat and chest, as though his shoulders were pushed down and his knees would buckle under the weight, as though he was crowd surfing but they wanted to tear him down, not lift him up.

Their eyes locked for a second, and it was as though a mirror had been shattered between them. Then, his eyes met Steven's, and he took a few steps backwards away from the counter, forced a blokey nod, waved 'never mind' at the barista, and left before he knew what to do with the rising swell of emotions.

Steven shook his head and looked back at Vera. "What a weirdo. Anyway, Vera," he leaned towards her, a smile flirting with the corners of his mouth. "I guess what I'm saying is, I realise what I did to you, what I lost. I want you back, Ronnie. I want," his eyes were downturned; he was playing earnest, pleading with her. "I want another chance." He locked his eyes onto hers. "Can you find a way to trust me again?"

She saw on his face the same expression that she had seen on Nate's two nights ago, as he looked up at her after finding out that Elsie was safely at home. Steven was putting in words what she now realised Nate had said without words. "I... I'm sorry, I have to leave." Vera stood up, pulling her hand away from his and grabbing her things from next to her.

"You need time to think about it, I understand."

She looked down at him. "Sure, something like that."

Vera rushed out to the street, but Nate was gone.

Disc 3

Twenty-Nine

Nate knew he'd been stupid to go there. Despite everything that happened at the ARIAs the night before, everyone he saw, and no matter how much he drank, he couldn't get Vera out of his mind, *still*. But when he tried to think about why she haunted him, all he could think was how *nice* she was, how she looked at him, how she made him feel. It was a stupid, selfish reason to like someone, wasn't it?

But he knew that the way she made him feel was the way he wanted to make her feel. If he could do that — if she'd let him — maybe it wouldn't be so selfish? Maybe he could open up to her, let her have the part of him that he'd withheld from so many others? Maybe he could trust that she could love even the parts of himself that he hated?

So, with Tommy's prompting, he'd decided that he should take back everything he said; he would stop by the cafe, and bring her a coffee to try to sweeten her and beg her to forgive him for what he said, to give him another chance. He hadn't expected to see her there. There had always been the possibility, of course, considering that she lived around the corner from the cafe. But he hadn't expected her to be there that day, and especially not on a *date*.

Now, driving, he didn't know what to do or where to go. Burnt into his head was the image of Vera with someone who she was clearly emotionally very intimate with, someone her age, and handsome, and well dressed. Someone more suitable for her than some emotionally unavailable has-been who she'd had a superficial crush on when she was a teenager. How could he have thought that he was more than just a plaything for her? He didn't even know why he was surprised. He should feel relieved, really. He had been right about their relationship being doomed. That was why *she'd* looked relieved when he told her; she knew he was right, and they could easily both just move on with their life, having had a bit of fun together.

So now he knew for sure that he wasn't the be-all and end-all of her life, he supposed he didn't need to understand why she seemed so captivating to him. He'd seen how much she was *glowing* in the presence of this other man. He was glad that she was being saved from someone like him by someone else who made her glow and shine.

He supposed that part of how he felt must be embarrassment — firstly, he was embarrassed at having assumed that, because she had been enamoured with the idea of him all those years ago, she would therefore automatically feel a deep, intimate bond with him when they met in person, like so many of his fans had. He'd assumed that she would instantly value him more than was reasonable to expect. After all, he was a lot older now and was no longer in the prime of his life, physically or musically. He hadn't put out an album for a while; even when he had, it never reached the sales he once made. He just wasn't the man who he used to be, he wasn't who or what she'd been so obsessed with all those years ago. That he thought he could be was, admittedly, also embarrassing.

He also felt ashamed that he had only liked her in the first place because of the way she acted towards him, the way she looked at him. He was used to people staring at him with fascination, admiration, or intent, but not looking at him the way she did, the way they used to when he was much younger.

Did he ever really care about her? Or was the whole thing a sort of self appeasing ego stroke, using her apparent interest in him as a way to feel that he was still desirable, still valued? It wasn't as though he hadn't come across someone who had outright hit on him, it wasn't that. It was enjoying how he had affected her, how he had watched her blush under his gaze. Her response had always felt somehow purer, less calculated, more instinctual. He supposed it made him feel that she liked him, yes, for who and what he was, but not *because* of who or what he had been.

Nate tutted as he struggled to understand his own feelings, his own reactions.

Did he feel this way because he'd lost her? Or was it because he'd opened himself up to her entirely, without even realising it, and it seemed like she'd still pulled away at the end of it? All he'd wanted to do was make her blush, make her coy, reach out and touch her, hold her. And the nervous excitement he'd felt over the idea of that affected him, made *him* blush, made *him* coy. He'd felt embarrassed to be so nervous, and yet he'd loved every minute of it. He hadn't felt something so innocent for such a long time, if ever. It was pure chemistry.

He couldn't lie to himself any more. He didn't like her because she wanted him, he'd liked her because it seemed like she'd liked him, but not wanted anything from him. She was quiet, and nice, and he felt himself relax around her. And really, he didn't want anything from her. He was simply drawn to her; he wanted to see her smile, wanted to make her blush, wanted to make her feel nervous like she made him feel nervous. Not because he wanted to feel wanted, but because affecting her made him feel alive, full of fear and hope and regret and peace all at once. He couldn't explain it. He just felt it.

He just *felt* it.

He felt the impact of the other car into his.

Thirty

Vera hadn't been able to find Nate, but she couldn't go back to Steven and his confession. As she walked back home, she realised that while Steven was so keen to have her attention that he lavished his on her in order to secure it, it was the uncertainty of Nate that had made her so nervous. She never saw herself as anywhere near worthy of him, so the idea of him finding her the least bit interesting was flattering enough. She'd been thrown by the idea of him being interested, and originally considered any interest he showed to be fabricated in her head, and she never would have believed it if it wasn't for Elsie's insistence. Had the whole thing been orchestrated by Elsie? That seemed like an odd thing for someone to have done.

But soon it became clear that he *was* interested, for some reason she couldn't understand. And, egged on by Vanessa, she thought: screw it! This was her chance. She'd dreamed of this since she was Elsie's age, and she was damned if she let her chance go. But she was thrown, hugely, when it hit home about just how many ghosts she'd be sharing his bed with. She knew it was stupid to think about it that way, but she couldn't help it. Knowing that she hadn't been enough for Steven, and knowing that Nate would have slept with so many people, it was just unfathomable that she would be enough for him. And after she'd been with him, the horror at the reality of how different their lives had been was amplified by subconsciously connecting it to a betrayal by someone else whose life had been so similar to hers. She didn't want to believe that she was just one of a long line of lovers for him, but she knew deep down that she was — whatever that would mean for the two of them.

She just couldn't get herself to crawl back into his bed, not then. No matter how much he looked like her dreams, the reality of him was just too much for her to deal with then and there. It wasn't worth the pain of going back in, knowing she was putting herself on the line, putting her boring self out there, ready for judgement and ridicule and rejection — like she'd found herself subjected to by Steven only a few months before. And then, only a few days later, Nate had told her that she wasn't good enough for him. It was no surprise for her: she knew it was only a matter of time before he realised and freed them both from the charade of their flirtation. She didn't hold him responsible, not at all.

But, damn him, it was only a few hours after that he turned up on her doorstep looking for Elsie, and the way he looked at her—? It stung with longing. She knew that look: it was how she'd looked so many times before, longing for men who weren't interested in the funny, smart, nice girl; how she'd looked every time she'd been told that it was 'just a bit of fun' — even when it hadn't been for her. She had seen it before on the faces of those few of her university cohort whose interest she didn't return. But this was different: here was her *dream* man, looking at her as though it tore him up to claim that he didn't want her, that they weren't right for each other.

She had never considered that he might go to the cafe. It was *her* local cafe — why would he go out of his way to be there at that time, long before Elsie would finish school for the week? Was there a girl at the cafe — maybe one of the baristas? — younger and prettier than her, who had recognised him and shown that she was a more suitable trophy girlfriend than some miserable, chubby, socially awkward woman who was an average lay?

No, she was kidding herself. She saw how he'd reacted when he saw her with Steven. *She* was the one who had the attention of someone younger than him: someone who, at first glance, was more beautiful, in his prime. But Steven was also someone who was more superficial, who had connected with Vera less despite knowing her more. He'd managed to hide more of how he felt over that whole time than Nate had managed to hide in the last few weeks. Nate's emotions were on show, and when she'd seen his face drop, it hurt her as much as he was hurting. She'd considered herself quite unremarkable, quite rejectable, but she'd never stopped to think about him. She may feel that she was past the 'prime' of her twenties, but his prime was more like twenty years ago.

She stopped mid-step when she realised that her inability to face him, overwhelmed by the ghosts of his lovers past, was *her* closing off, was *her* rejecting *him*. She'd been so caught up in how she felt, how affected she was, how undesirable she'd been taught she was, that she was unable to put herself in his shoes. She'd just assumed that he — famous, talented, adored — was likely to be so above and beyond her, as he'd then said he was. She had no reason to question it. It wasn't fair to him to assume that, but she already had. For a man who had revealed his love and heartache so many times in his music, she'd failed to see him as someone even more afraid of rejection than she was.

Now she understood this. She could see his vulnerability, and how fundamentally and unabashedly honest he was, and she regretted not being able to see it before; because, underneath it all, he was someone who just wanted someone to love them, to be *nice* to them.

"I can't help it. You're the nicest girl I've met in a long time... I think I'm glad I didn't meet you fourteen years ago: I doubt I would have appreciated you."

It was only now that the pieces all fell into place in her head. And it was entirely possible that she'd thrown it all away because she was worried that *she* wasn't enough.

She had to find him. She pulled her phone out of her pocket, but as she was about to find his number, her phone started ringing.

Elsie.

Thirty-One

⏮ ⏸ ⏭

A strangled sob came from the other side of the phone in response to her greeting.

"Are you okay? What's happened?"

"It's Dad…" Elsie gulped air, trying to continue.

"What about him? Did he do something?"

"He's… I just got a phonecall. He's in hospital. There was an accident."

Vera's world turned high-contrast. This was the last thing she had hoped to hear. Right when she'd decided to chase after him, to open up to him, he could be gone. And he was in front of her not even half an hour ago. He couldn't be far away: she could get there. "Where is he? Which hospital?"

"It's near you. I'll send you the address. Vera, I'm scared."

"Can you get there? Do you need me to drive you? Are you at school?"

"I'm at home. I can get there. You go. Let…" she gulped. "Let me know how he is."

The phone line went dead.

Vera ran home, pulling the keys out of her bag, running past where she remembered Nate parking when he came looking for Elsie only two nights before. She sat in the driver's seat and held the steering wheel. She had to breathe, to calm down. It wasn't worth two accidents. She pulled out her phone, and messaged Vanessa.

VERA: Nates been in a car accident im going there now

She found Elsie had sent her the hospital address and forwarded it to Vanessa. Throwing her phone to the passenger side, she started the engine and drove to the hospital.

⏮ ⏸ ⏭

Celebrity can bring unexpected difficulty in times like this. Who was Vera, how was she related to Nate? Sorry, they can't simply let her in. She's an unknown: she could be press, she could be a rabid fan. Need to wait until family arrives. No update, no information. No, we can't ask him to confirm.

So Vera was relegated to the waiting room. Elsie would be along soon, she hoped, and able to clear it all up. But as soon as she sat down, Vera saw a flurry of golden blonde curls. Vanessa.

"Ronnie! There you are, you haven't been answering your phone!"

"My phone? I... " Vera rummaged in her bag. She must have left her phone in the car. "Shit."

"Relax, relax. Forget about your phone." Vera couldn't follow Vanessa's advice: she kept rummaging, as though finding her phone would be finding Nate. "How is he?"

"I have no idea. They won't let me in, they can't prove that I'm close friends or family... I have to wait for Elsie." Rummage, rummage, rummage.

"She's on her way?"

"Yeah, but I didn't ask how she was going to get here. I can't find it!" Vera finally put her bag down in defeat. "Oh, shit. I should have gone and got her. She said she could get here, but..."

"Hmm." Vanessa's brow furrowed. A short woman with dark hair and round, cute features cleared her throat behind Vanessa. "Oh, right. Ronnie, this is Emma. Emma, Ronnie."

"Ronnie? Nice to meet you. Sorry I didn't meet you earlier, or in a better situation." She extended her hand with an apologetic smile. "I'm Vanessa's partner."

"Oh, nice to meet you. I uh, I actually go by Vera these days," In other circumstances, Vera would have taken a moment to process this properly, making the connection with when Vanessa had said that Nate wasn't her type. Instead, in her singular focus on the accident, everything unexpected lost its significance.

Emma placed her hand on Vanessa's lower back. "Hon, why don't we talk to Reception, and Ronnie... ah, *Vera* can go find her phone?" Her bright eyes flicked to Vera. "Sorry for eavesdropping. Maybe it's still in your car? I assume you drove?"

Vera swallowed, her stress thick in her throat. She forced an appreciative smile and nodded at Emma, then turned to Vanessa. "Okay... Keep an eye out for Elsie, in case she gets here while I'm out there."

"Of course."

As she turned to head back out the giant sliding doors, Emma grabbed her hand and squeezed it. "He'll be okay, Vera."

"I hope so."

Emma let her hand slip away.

Vera turned, the doors parting, giving way to an unexpectedly cool breeze and warm sun, tickling her skin and making her shiver.

⏮ ⏸ ⏭

Vera walked back to her car, numb. She opened the door, rummaging around inside, looking for her phone. Stubbing her fingers as she searched, prying into cracks and crevices, she finally found her phone between the passenger chair and the door, where it must have slid while she was driving. She looked at the screen: eight missed calls; five new messages.

She scrolled through but her eyes could not see, could not read. Giving up, she shoved the phone into her pocket and sat in the driver's seat. *He'll be okay.*

Wiping the tears from her eyes, she opened the car door and began the walk back to the hospital. She didn't hear Elsie's cries for her before she felt the arms around her, felt her clothes wet with tears.

"Elsie? How did you get here?" Vera wrapped her arms around her and held her tight.

"Tommy..." Vera turned to see a scruffy young man, eyes red from emotion.

"He's... he's my hero, man. Shit." He held out his hand as though to offer it as greeting, but instead patted Vera on the shoulder before running the same hand through his hair.

"Have you seen Dad yet? He's okay, isn't he?"

"They didn't let me in," she took a deep breath in. "There's no proof that I'm a close friend."

The three of them bundled together as they walked towards the entrance, out of the light and into the dim sterility of the hospital. Vanessa and Emma were working on the Receptionist, trying to explain how Vera was involved with Nate, that she was practically family. The poor Receptionist was just following protocol, trying to prevent any snoops from taking advantage of the situation.

"Ness, Emma, it's okay, thanks," Vera interrupted them. "This is Elsie Whitely, Nate Whitely's daughter."

Elsie gulped, then turned to Vera. "I... I don't think I have any ID."

"Just Google them," Emma offered from the back.

The receptionist, herself about twenty-three, locked eyes with Tommy. A flash of recognition crossed her face. If Nate had been there, he would have recognised The Look. Clearly feeling the effect of giving The Look and assuming she'd stared too long, she quickly looked down, red with embarrassment.

"Hey," he pushed himself to the front. "I'm Tommy Freebourne of Frothing Mess. Elsie and I were with Nate at the ARIAs last night."

"R-r-r—right." The receptionist stammered, unsure what to do. "I'll... yes, I guess you and Miss Whitely can go in."

"No," piped up Elsie. "Vera needs to come. She's Dad's girlfriend." She reached out and grasped Vera's hand. Vera was confused. Surely he'd told her that he'd dumped her? Was this just Elsie's way of working the system?

The receptionist pinched the bridge of her nose, then looked between them as they all nodded emphatically — except Vera. "Right. Well, okay. Here's the sign-in book. Only you two." They looked between each other and nodded. The receptionist couldn't help looking at Tommy again, admiring the way he stood with his hands in his pockets, looking moody and aloof and like she was staring at a cover of a magazine made flesh.

Vera went to the sign-in book first. She filled in her name, date, time, and Nate's name. It was surreal to consider that it was *his* name that she was signing. She found herself wishing that it was Steven's. Elsie stepped forward, copying Vera's entry. She cleared her throat as she put the pen down. The receptionist finally pulled her focus away from Tommy and checked the entries.

"Okay. One minute, I'll call the nurse for you." The receptionist stood up, surprisingly tall and lanky when she wasn't behind her desk.

She picked up a phone on the next desk over, pressed a few numbers, and waited, briefly pushing her face into a smile designed to be delivered to Elsie and Vera. In response, they clung onto each other's hand, before the receptionist mumbled a few words, ending in, "Thanks." She looked up at them again. "One minute." She closed her attention off from them again, moving to sit down at her seat. Tommy hung over the desk, forcing her to look at him.

"Thank you," his words pressed into her. She blushed as he pushed himself away from the bench, and looked from Elsie, to Vera, to Vanessa and Emma. He stuck his hands in his pockets again and shrugged dramatically. "I guess we wait." He pulled one hand out and placed it on Elsie's shoulder. "Good luck, kid." He turned away, pacing towards some chairs in the corner, and dramatically slumped down. His charisma forced all their eyes to follow him until he was seated with his feet on the chair opposite, his head hanging back against the wall, and his eyes closed.

Emma turned to Vanessa, and reached out for her hand. She looked to Vera and Elsie. "He'll be okay."

Vanessa pressed her lips tightly together, and nodded. "You just let me know if you need anything. And keep us posted, when you can."

"Ms Whitely?" An unexpectedly perky voice spoke up from behind them. Vera looked at Elsie.

"Yes?"

"You can come with me." The nurse backed briskly towards the door to the Emergency wards, scanning her pass as she pushed the door open for them to follow.

Thirty-Two

⏮ ⏸ ⏭

Endless corridors, endless elevators. Door after door after door. Every time they turned, Vera hoped it would be the last turn. She wasn't sure whether she was imagining how long it took; was she just trying to delay the inevitable in her mind? Was she somehow playing with time, slowing it down, in the same way as it felt it had when she'd first met Nate's eyes?

Finally, the Nurse started slowing down. She stopped at the board in front of a door. A chart was hung on the door outside: *Nathan Whitely.*

"Here we are," she smiled, before looking at his chart. "Oh."

"What do you mean, 'Oh'?" Elsie yelped. "What does that mean?"

"Oh, um," the nurse was almost as bad at emotional vocal control as Elsie. "He's... he's in a coma. I thought he would have woken up by now. I'll... the doctor will be around soon. You're welcome to go inside." She turned on her heel and pumped away.

Vera looked at wide-eyed Elsie. She repeated Emma's mantra. "He'll be okay."

He'll be okay.

Vera reached out, her hand shaking. She grasped the door handle and turned it. Her heart was pounding. She felt Elsie's hand slip away as she stepped forward and pushed the door open.

"...Dad?"

He was bandaged, monitor hooked up, tubes to keep him hydrated,

152

an arterial line to monitor his blood pressure. Fortunately, he was able to breathe by himself, though his face was half visible from all the scrapes. His closed eyes looked relaxed, as though he was having the most beautiful dream and someone had made him up with special effects makeup for a Halloween party. Vera hung back; the scene was incomprehensible. Elsie flew to her father's side, searching for a hand to clutch, squeezing it to try to pump life into it.

"Dad, Dad!" She shook from the effort of holding in her cries.

Vera stepped closer and closer, slowly.

He'll be okay.

That'd be easy to think if you hadn't seen the state that Nate was in. Vera couldn't even hear Elsie's wails and sobs over her own pounding heart. She thought about him, half asleep, just after they'd slept together. The restful look on his face then, echoed here now. She scolded herself for not climbing back in bed with him then, for enjoying the moment and the man without being hounded by her own neuroses. Without noticing how, she found she'd arrived at the other side of the bed, opposite Elsie, as though they were going to hold hands and pray over him. Her eyes searched his face for a sign of movement. He looked so like he would wake up, but yet there was Elsie, clutching his one good hand and squeezing and shaking it as though she were a little girl again, begging him for attention. Vera reached out and hesitantly stroked his face; his lack of response contrasted sharply with the warmth of his skin, his breath against her hand.

She edged away, shutting her eyes. She couldn't stand looking at him. She didn't want to believe that they were here, that this had happened. She wanted to rewind time to when he'd seen her in the cafe. She searched for a moment when she could have stopped him, held him, kissed him and told him that she felt like an idiot girl: that she was falling for him and wanted him to love her, too.

He'll be okay.

"Ms Whitely, and ah, Ms Cunningham?" An old, weathered doctor was standing in the doorway with a sad, worn look on his face. "I'm Dr Hastings, I've been attending to Nathan."

Elsie turned to look up at him, her pretty round face flushed red with emotion, cheeks saturated, her eyes swollen and unfocused. She nodded once and turned back to her father.

Vera hesitated, then stretched out her hand to the doctor. "Nice to meet you." His eyes softening, his mouth shifting into a sympathetic smile, he took Vera's hand gently.

"So, I want to get right to it. As you can probably tell, Mr Whitely is in critical condition. The other car ran through a red light and slammed directly into his car." His lips pressed together, and he paused, waiting for the weight of his words to settle in. Vera only nodded slightly. "He hasn't woken since he came in, and we're monitoring him. There's, uh," he cleared his throat. "There's a chance that his brain may start to swell, and we don't know the current extent of the head trauma."

"He's in a coma now?" Vera wanted to know what was happening *now*, not what *could* happen.

Dr Hastings nodded. "Well, it's quite common in a closed head injury. Even then, uh," he gesticulated with his right hand, as though spinning through airborne wheels to find the right thing to say. "Even then, he may deteriorate." He was stomping all over the line between downplaying and exaggerating the potential severity of Nate's condition.

Vera nodded. "And right now, you're thinking..."

"Right now we're monitoring him."

"I see." Vera looked over to Nate, with Elsie, now quiet, staring at her father.

"I'll leave you to it. If you have any questions, you know who to ask." Dr Hastings looked towards Elsie, not really expecting her to look up; then looked back to Vera with a nod.

Vera watched him go, the bearer of bad news. She couldn't blame him. She picked up a chair and moved it back to the other side of Nate. She sat down and looked across at Elsie.

"Did you hear—"

"Yep."

Vera bit her lip. "Anything you wanted to ask?"

Elsie sighed. "Just... why?"

"I wish I knew, Elsie." Vera reached out to touch Nate, trying to find a part of him that hadn't been unsettled by the impact of the crash. She looked at the hand nearest her for the first time: it was wrapped, raised. Not to be touched. She gave up and tucked her hands together between her thighs. "He'll be okay."

Elsie looked up at Vera, doubt in her red, watery eyes. "I hope you're right." She let out a garbled gasp, and added, "I don't want him to leave me, too." They sat together for a while, quietly, on either side of him; the only sound was the heart monitor's constant beeping.

Finally, Elsie stirred. "Well, at least he got to talk to you."

"Talk… to me?" Vera blinked. "He didn't talk to me."

Elsie looked up, her brows furrowed. "But, he sent me a message. He said he saw you, and that he was going to go to the studio for the rest of that day. Work on something." She sniffed, leaning forwards. "He didn't talk to you?"

"He saw me, but…" Vera shook her head.

Confusion clouded Elsie's face. She bit her lip. "He was… he'd told me he was going to go to see you. He'd made a mistake. He…" Elsie choked. "He was going to tell you he wanted to take everything back. He was wrong. He wanted you to give him another chance." Her brows furrowed. "He didn't tell you?"

"He didn't say anything," Vera looked at Nate, his face bandaged, the drip taped to him. Her heart bled as she realised what had happened. "I… I was with my ex. Steven was trying to get me to give *him* another chance," she huffed a bitter laugh. "As if. But… Nate just looked at me, and left. He must've thought…"

"Oh my God," Elsie sobbed. "I thought, I mean, I was relieved that he'd told you. I thought you were both going to be happy." She shook her head and squeezed her father's hand. "So he never said it, and he has no idea how you feel?"

"No. He probably thinks I'm back with my ex?" She shook her head. "I tried to chase after him, but he was gone. I… had a feeling that he might have changed his mind. Maybe. But I thought for a while, and decided that I wanted to talk to him about it properly, either way. I was about to call him when…" her voice wobbled. "When you called me," she dropped her head into her hands. "It's all my fault. I'm sorry Nate," she looked up to him and brushed her hand over his hair, and heard a whimper of disagreement from Elsie. "I'm sorry."

She wished to see his eyes again, see the way he looked at her. He wanted to see the fiery sunflower magic that surrounded his face the first time they'd met, she wanted to go back to that moment and hold it forever and never let it go. It wasn't fair, it wasn't the slightest bit fair that they'd only had one night together before their neuroses split them apart. She thought of the way he'd looked at her, kissed her, held her. It was like she was the most important thing to him, more important than himself. She'd *never* had a lover like that, and it frightened her. Why would she deserve someone like that? No wonder she didn't put up a fight when he'd told her that she didn't deserve him: she'd never believed it in the first place. It was always a hope, the type of hope where she never believed that it could come true, and even when it did she had to sour it with her own feelings of disbelief. How had he taken that?

It didn't matter how many meaningful or meaningless flings and relationships he'd had in the past. He was always honest with her, and he had been about to tell her that he chose *her* when he saw her with Steven.

"Fucking Steven, why couldn't *he* have been in the accident?" Vera's sharpness and anger, her raw emotions, startled Elsie. Vera always seemed to be in control of her emotions, but the method of her control was to bottle them up and hide them, deny them. She over-thought everything, over-analysed, never *felt* her way through anything. Elsie, who was a slave to her emotions in the way both of her parents also were, had admired that about her. She reached out her hand to Vera, over Nate. Vera's lip wobbled, and she let out a long sigh filled with her frustration and disappointment, reached out and grasped Elsie's hand.

"Do you think he can hear us?" asked Elsie. Vera looked up at her, surprised at how their emotional states had swapped: Elsie now was post-hysteria, while Vera's slow-burn had led to her current state of devastation. "You know, on like, movies and medical shows and things. They say that people in comas can still hear things, so people are always talking to them. Do you think Dad can hear us now?"

"I... I really don't know, Elsie." She let go of Elsie's hand, and wiped the tears from her eyes. "I need to go for a walk. Are you okay here, or do you want to come with me?"

Elsie looked down at her father. "I'm going to stay here. I need to talk to Dad for a bit."

Vera nodded. She didn't know for sure whether Nate would be able to hear anything, but if it made Elsie feel better, it was better for her to do whatever she wanted.

Vera stood up, picked up her phone, and quietly left the room.

Thirty-Three

Vera wandered the corridors. She'd messaged the short form to Vanessa:

VERA: We're here. Critical condition. In coma. Its "wait and see" territory

To which she'd received a message full of expletives and sympathy. She sighed. Meeting Nate had been her most surreal experience for a long time, but now this? She felt as though she couldn't stay in any one place for long, or she'd get lost somewhere in the mess of her emotions, of her existence. Her own parents had been so weighted down, so driven by their emotions. Unlike Elsie, she'd been the one sane one amongst the mess of her parents, and it had managed to wire her to become more and more *logical*, as she called it. Really, it was more than she avoided everything, suppressed everything, denied everything. She feared that if she didn't, it would take her over, and then she would, like her parents, affect anything and everything around her. She didn't like that idea. She wanted to be the stable, safe, sane one.

Which is why, rather than deal with her reaction properly, she fled his bed — both in the middle of the night, and again now. The first time, she went to Vanessa to seek help analysing it all: she wanted to nail down why she felt the way she did, so she could understand it and move forward with the right action. And when Nate dumped her, she rationalised it away, so that she didn't get overwhelmed by emotion. She knew that, like her parents, once she got overwhelmed, that would be *it*. Which is why, after Nate had visited the following night and looked at her with such regret and longing, she became such a mess. She didn't want to become a mess again, not now, not in public, not when Elsie needed her support more.

"Ronnie?" A kindly doctor was looking at her. Vera blinked away her tears and strained to focus. "How are you?" Recognition hit Vera.

"Ah sorry, Sandra. I'm, uh," she wiped the tears away from her eyes. "I haven't seen you at work, in your uniform and everything."

"I'm glad I ran into you. I have something I wanted to say. I know you and Steven aren't together. And I know that I'm his mother and I'm supposed to love and support him no matter what, but you were so good to him, you helped him achieve, and he treated you like you meant nothing."

I don't need this now. Vera sighed, avoiding Sandra's eyes.

"What I'm trying to say is, we — Steven's father and I — still care a great deal for you, and if there's ever anything we can do for you, please let us know."

Steven's parents weren't exactly known for their sense of social appropriateness. "Thanks, Sandra."

Sandra looked around, and then looked at Vera's red eyes, and seemed to suddenly put two and two together. "Is everything alright? Are you here for someone?"

Vera couldn't control her emotions, and she actually didn't even care who got in her way or who she hurt. She shuddered, her fear and grief and regret flowing out of her. "Car accident... Coma," she felt Sandra's hand on her arm, an attempt to hold her, to soothe her. "He's critical?"

"Shh, it's alright, I understand." Sandra pulled Vera to her. If anyone's parents were logical and rational, it was Steven's. Colder than dry ice, they had the advantage of being unflappable, uninjurable in the face of emotion. It just washed over them and never caught hold. Maybe that was one reason Steven seemed to delight in disappointing them: at least then he would get some evidence that they cared about what he did.

Vera let herself go, no longer afraid of any repercussions of her emotions, no longer afraid that the emotion would catch and be amplified. Sandra just held her tighter, breathed steadily, until she began to relax in her arms.

"Ronnie, I'm glad to see you like this," again, that lack of appropriateness. "I always worried that you were holding in your emotions too much. It's not good for you. But you're so free now. It's beautiful." Vera pulled back, her face twisted in confusion and offence. She saw admiration and kindness on Sandra's face. "Sorry, I didn't mean— oh. Ronnie, I'm bad at that sort of thing. I intended it as a compliment. It was bad timing, wasn't it?" Vera, having purged her emotions, simply sniffed and nodded. "Now where's your friend? In ICU? Maybe I can take a look at their chart."

Vera nodded. She felt strangely light and clear after the catharsis. It was like her senses had focused, shifted. She somehow felt centred, inside her body. She never realised how disconnected she'd felt before. She felt more honest, more herself than ever before. All she'd needed was the safety to let down her guard.

Thirty-Four

⏮ ⏸ ⏭

Vera didn't realise how far she'd strayed while in her daydream. It was almost impossible for her to find her way back, save for Sandra's knowledge of the labyrinthine maze of the hospital wards. Finally, they found Nate's room. Elsie sat up as Sandra walked in and picked up Nate's charts. Elsie watched wide-eyed, her eyes practically bulging out of her head as she looked for some indication of anything from Sandra. Vera followed behind, not wanting to look at Nate for fear that her acknowledging his condition might suddenly worsen it.

Sandra bit her lip, making a slight ticking, tutting sound as she flicked the page over, her eyes absorbing everything, her mind analysing everything.

Elsie's eyes drifted towards Vera, questioning.

"Oh uh, Elsie, this is *Sandra*, she's my... she's my ex's mother."

Sandra looked up at Elsie, nodded, and looked back at Nate's charts. Elsie blinked, overwhelmed with questions of why Vera would bring her ex's mother into the room. Questions she didn't have the energy to focus on.

"She's a neurosurgeon. We ran into each other and she's..."

"Yup, I can guess what she's doing." Elsie squeezed Nate's hand and let it go. "I... I'm gonna find a bathroom." She stood, edging around the outside of the room and towards the door. She looked back at Sandra and Vera, at Nate, then sighed and walked out.

Sandra looked up at the sound of the door closing. "His daughter?"

Vera nodded.

Sandra's eyes pierced through Vera's exterior. "He's your new boyfriend?"

Stunned, Vera met her eyes. She wished it was that simple. Her lip quivered. She shrugged, nodded, shook her head, shrugged again.

"You love him; I can see that." She moved closer. "I hope he loves you. We do care for you a lot. We would have loved you as a daughter, and we still love you like a daughter." She sighed, putting the chart down. "I'm sorry to say, I don't have much more information than you already have. He seems stable, but there's always a chance for a clot, and always a chance that clot will travel to his brain. Always a chance that his brain will swell. CT scans look fine, but there's always a chance of complications. There could be an internal bleed that wasn't picked up. That's why we have to keep an eye on him. Look," she moved beside Vera and put her arm around her. "I can volunteer to be the surgeon on-call for him in case of emergency."

Vera nodded, "I'd appreciate that." Sandra noted something down on Nate's chart.

"It's the least I can do. I'll... I'll be around." She backed out of the room, as though watching to see whether Vera or Nate would lunge at her.

After Sandra left, Vera suddenly found herself alone with Nate for the first time since they sent each other those mixed messages out the front of her place in the middle of the night.

Her brow knotted, she sat down where Elsie had been sitting, the less-damaged side of Nate, and took his hand. It had a drip, an arterial line, and a heart monitor attached to it, but it was still more exposed than the other hand. She held it, expecting to feel some resistance, some twitch of movement, something. Anything. Tears stinging her eyes, and sobs burning at her chest, she held it to her lips, feeling his skin against hers, hoping for familiarity and safety. He smelled of disinfectant.

She looked up at his restful eyes, looked for some movement under the heavy lids, looked at the stubble prickling through on his cheek and chin. She'd never felt more aware of his life than this, when he seemed closest to death. She leaned over, kissed his brow in some attempt to be as close to him as possible, to bring them both some comfort. Swallowing sobs, she sat back in her seat, looking him over, wishing again that it was a week ago and she'd never left his room and instead stayed with him all night. Would he still have broken it off with her, if she had?

She knew she could only have ever guessed how he had felt, and what his intentions had been. It seemed as though he had wanted her, and had felt for her, but the truth was that his words had spoken louder than actions, and she'd had to trust that. She couldn't blame herself for misunderstanding. She had to push through to where she was before, knowing that he had freed her.

But here he was, essentially alone.

She didn't care if it hurt. She would love him.

She wanted to say it out loud, but she felt stupid. He couldn't hear anyway, right? And even if he could, would he want to hear her saying she wished she could backtrack on what she'd done, that she was sorry, that she wanted to keep him, and let him keep her? He'd started out as some fantasy, perfect, flawless. But she'd found his flaws one by one, and that had made him more beautiful, more loveable, over time. Had he felt the same way about her?

He'll be okay.

But what if he won't be? What if this afternoon was the last time she'd ever see him look at her, the last time he was more than a memory and a focus for tears?

Vera felt the heat of her bursting heart spilling through and onto her cheeks. She couldn't remember what it felt like to not be crying. She knew in her heart that he'd wanted her back. She knew that what Elsie said he'd told her was right, that he'd come back to try to win her over. So why did he leave when he saw her? Why didn't he come over? Why wasn't he like the hero of a Romantic Comedy, happy to charm her back from the man who had cheated on her anyway? Why didn't his temper and his jealousy flare, compel him to steal her back from anyone who might have been a threat incomparable to him? He was *Nate Fucking Whitely*, he was famous and talented and beautiful and he was the most amazing person she'd ever known; he was the most amazing person she'd imagined knowing; he was the most amazing person that she'd only started getting to know.

Would she never get the chance to really know him?

Would he never get the chance to know that she wanted to know him?

She was furious with him, furious that he hadn't walked over and pushed Steven off his chair or punched him in the face, pulled her up from her seat, wrapped his arms around her, kissed her, and let the credits roll. Why hadn't that been what he'd done? If he'd done that, they could have walked back to her place together. Or they could have got in his car together. They could have been in the accident together. They could have been *together*. Instead, he was alone.

He was alone in his mind, somewhere in there. He didn't know that she wanted to know him, that she wanted to love him, that she wanted to tell him that she loved him. She wasn't sure she could bring herself to say it, but felt compelled to say *something*.

"Nate?" her voice wobbled. This was stupid. "I know you won't answer, so I'll just… I hope you can hear. Because I'm saying some things because I want you to know." She felt so embarrassed, like she was talking to him in her imagination, but out loud. "Nate, I… I'm sorry. I was scared. I liked you *too much*. I was scared. I was scared I wasn't enough for you. And that's exactly what you told me. And… I was okay with that. I was okay with that because you told me exactly what I expected to hear, and I was already okay with that. It was a relief." She felt so stupid saying it out aloud. "It was a relief. I didn't have to keep worrying that you *would* reject me because I wasn't enough for you, because you did. You did it, and I was free. You did it a few days after we slept together, not years after, when we were engaged. Well, not *us*, but," she reached out to touch his chest, gently, softly. "Well, I never told you about my last relationship. It didn't end well. And I wasn't really ready to meet you, I guess. And I'm sorry I wasn't ready. But I'd only needed one night." She curled her fingers gently, making spiral shapes in the material of the hospital gown. "Did you know I ran after you?" She found herself gasping for air. "But you were gone. You were already gone. You were… *gone*." She grasped the material in her hand. "I don't want you to be gone, Nate. I still have to get to know you. You've been so open with me, and I haven't been open with you, and I haven't been open *to* you. I want to be, I am ready," she shook her head. "I don't want it to be too late."

She stared at him, expecting *something*. Wasn't he meant to wake up now? Or at least, go into some sort of spasm or cardiac arrest? Everything she'd seen in movies and on tv suggested that people in comas only stay in there as long as dramatically necessary, and then come out the other end in one way or another.

Nothing. She let go of the material bunched up on his chest, smoothed it down, and collapsed down into the chair, burying her face in her hands.

Thirty-Five

⏮ ⏸ ⏭

The door opened, and Elsie slipped into the room. "I have juice," she handed Vera a foil-sealed cup. They peeled off the lids with sunny red apples printed on them, and drank together in silence.

"Do you want to stay at my place tonight?" Vera's eyes stayed on Nate. "It's... it's a bit of a mess, but we can find a way. You can sleep in the bed or on the couch. I'm happy with either."

Elsie looked at Vera. "Do you think he'll wake up?"

Vera's lips wobbled. "I hope so."

"I'll need some things."

"We can do a round trip."

"You don't want to stay at ours?"

"Not really."

"Mmm. You *are* closer. To here, to... school."

"I don't think you'll be going to school on Monday."

"Probably not."

It felt easier to talk about anything but Nate.

"Is school... any better?"

"No."

"You should really talk to—"

"I don't *want* to talk to him about it."

"No, I mean..."

Elsie's brow furrowed, and her lower lip stuck out.

"Elsie, you should talk to Ness about it. She had a similar thing happen when we were in highschool." Vera looked down at her phone, where unread messages from Vanessa sat expectantly. "I'm not the best person to help you through it. I didn't get much attention of any sort until—"

"I didn't ask you to help me."

"But I can't do nothing!"

"I just wanted someone to talk to! I don't need you and Dad to solve everything for me! Oh my God! I can figure it out! I'm not a kid anymore."

Vera closed her eyes.

Nate coughed.

Vera and Elsie both shot to his side as his eyes flashed open, glossy, confused, his eyes flicking from face to face and around him. His mouth opened as if to speak, but his tongue swam in his mouth, and his eyes rolled in response, his brow furrowed in frustration.

"I'll find someone," Vera yelped as Elsie rushed to take her place next to Nate. Elsie found the alert button and pressed it as Vera fled the room. Nate watched her go, his eyes reaching out for her.

Vera slid down the hallways, to the first medical attendant she could find: an orderly.

"Can you help us? We need someone in 1501."

"Yes, of course, at once."

She backtracked as the orderly pushed the empty gurney against the wall and paced in the opposite direction.

When Vera got back to his room, Nate had relaxed a little, but looked exhausted. His eyes were on Elsie, who was crying again — happy tears this time — and stroking his face. She looked across at Vera, the happiness tinged with some sort of apprehension. She stood up straight, wiping the tears from her eyes. Nate's eyes turned to Vera, expressing a mixture of mild concern and fear. He flicked them back to Elsie questioningly.

"He... he can't seem to... talk," Elsie stepped back from him as she spoke.

Nate moved his jaw as though trying to speak, then let out a small grunt, somewhere between sighing and clearing his throat. Vera's lips trembled as she thought about the implication: his beautiful voice! Surely Sandra could help, tell them if it was something they had to worry about.

"Nate," she whimpered, moving to his side. His eyes followed her, his expression lost, unsettled. "Nate, are you okay? Are you in pain? Do you understand what I'm saying?" He screwed up his face, looking away, as though someone had asked him to think back to something unremarkable that had happened on a drunken night, years ago.

Mentally, he was wading through cotton wool. It was as though a veil had been cast between him and his memory. He reached in, struggling for an answer. He could grab fragments of the last question: he understood them, yes. He tried to say it. No good. It was too hard. He just couldn't seem to coordinate everything. He sighed in frustration and exhaustion.

Elsie looked at Vera, wide-eyed. "This is what he's been like since you left. I just… gave up asking him. He seemed really stressed so I just told him it's okay." She looked down at him, his eyes now on her, softening again. She smiled gently at him. He gave her a sullen nod.

It was hard to follow more than one thing he heard. It was like he was floating … like everything was floating … like the words were written on floating scraps of paper that he needed to catch and try to make sense of in some abstract order, except they kept slipping away. Tone of voice, stress, emotion. That was easier to follow. Here was his daughter, who he wanted to hold and to comfort, because he could tell that it was him that worried her. He wanted to tell her that it was okay, whether he believed that was true or not. He didn't want to be causing her pain, causing her worry. But every time he tried, he couldn't make the parts work. The words he wanted weren't there for him to grab from the air. Feelings couldn't be turned into words. So instead, he just tried to focus on the feeling and look at her. It seemed to calm her down.

"He nodded! It seems like he can understand us," Vera grasped his hand, leaning towards him. "Nate, did you nod because you understood? You can hear us, but can you understand? You don't need to try to speak, just nod."

Vera… the last Nate remembered, they'd been flirting in the cafe. He strained to recall — but they didn't know each other enough for her to be holding his hand, did they? Had he forgotten things? What had happened anyway; how long had he been here? Nate's mind swarmed with intangible questions. Why was she holding his hand so comfortably now? This seemed surprisingly intimate to him. Was she some crazed fan, who thought she knew him better than she did? He'd encountered this before. Why wasn't Elsie doing anything about it? He tried pulling it away, but it was as though his body didn't want to move the way he wanted it to. He could only manage a twitch.

His eyes read as concerned, alarmed, overwhelmed. He just stared at her, his blue eyes rimmed with red, the exasperation clouding his features. Vera dropped his hand and stepped back. "Elsie? Do you think... What do you think he's thinking?"

Elsie slipped beside Vera. "Dad?" his eyes flicked between them, increasingly agitated.

There was a bustling sound as a pair of Nurses entered the room. One picked up Nate's chart and rushed to his side, pushing Elsie and Vera out of the way. "Hello, Nathan Whitely. You've been in an accident, and have been in a coma for a few hours. Do you understand?"

Vera edged forward, and tried to speak to her. "Hi, sorry, but Dr Sandra Aitken... she said she'd look after him."

The nurse ignored her, looking at Nate's heart rate monitor and vital stats, adding notes to the chart. "No, it should be Dr Hastings." She squinted at a note elsewhere. "Oh, I see. One minute." She nodded to another nurse, who nodded back and left the room. "Okay, Mr Whitely. How are you feeling?"

How was he feeling? Lost. Like he had a phone he wanted to scream into, but someone had cut the line — and his vocal cords. The nurse never seemed to look at him, just paused long enough to make him feel like he had a chance to answer her questions.

"Any pain?" She checked the bag of clear fluid at the helm of his IV drip. "Nausea?" She looked down her nose at him, leaned down so that she was peering up into his eyes. "Confusion?" She brought out a little light and shone it in his eyes, making his pupils shrink and his lids snap involuntarily shut. "Okay," she said finally, adding final notes to the chart and putting it back down on the bed. She turned to Vera. "Dr Aitken should be along shortly."

"He's not saying anything," Elsie chirped as the nurse turned to go.

"Confusion and difficulty speaking can be common after any sort of head injury, including whiplash. Don't worry, Dr Aitken will be able to give a better assessment." She paused on her way out. "But I haven't seen anything I'd immediately worry about." She pushed the door open and stepped out.

Elsie and Vera looked at each other, checking for their stress levels. Nate cleared his throat again, closing his eyes. His brows slowly knotted together as they watched. He drummed the fingers of his good hand on the hard, thin hospital mattress.

He didn't remember the accident. Only a few hours, that's good. No, he wasn't in pain. No, not nauseous. Yes, very confused.

The answers came when he gave them time. The lag was frustrating. He thought about what he wanted to say, what he wanted to ask. A slow, burning pain began to creep up one of his arms, his hand feeling like it was burning from the inside. His eyes shot open, and down to his hands. One was bandaged, splinted. His hand. He had no idea what was under those bandages; was there anything left?

Nate let out a groan and a sob. He looked towards Elsie, then forced his damaged hand a few inches up into the air.

"Dad! Dad, stop it, put it down, it's okay, it'll be okay!"

He suddenly felt incredibly ashamed in front of Vera. The embarrassment and shame flushed hard on his cheeks and filled his mouth. He bit his lip and shut his eyes hard, trying not to let the tears escape in front of her. But he just felt so weak, so powerless. Hot needles prickled his bandaged hand.

"Sorry I took so long," Sandra shut the door behind her. "Ronnie, Elsie; hello Nathan." She picked up the clipboard, and reading the notes from the nurse, came over to look at Nate. "Did the nurse tell you that you were in a car accident?"

Nate forced his eyes open, attempted a nod.

"You're in pain."

Nate shot out a gasp and twisted his face into a thankful smile.

Vera was impressed — Sandra had always seemed so clinical, so prone to saying the wrong thing. Her bluntness was legendary. It had rubbed Steven up the wrong way more times than she could quantify. Yet, her skills of observation were amazing. It seemed only fitting that someone who was so quick to offend should see her effect so quickly. She was just lucky that she didn't hate herself for the weakness of her strength.

Sandra checked the notes again, then fiddled with one of the bags. "You should feel better soon."

"He's not talking," Elsie had started feeling like a broken record.

"No, but he seems alert. Nathan, are you with us?"

Nate's eyes roamed the room, ending on Sandra. She watched him with still patience. He looked like he was going to say something, but instead chewed once and swallowed, then nodded clearly.

"I'm Dr Aitken. You can call me Sandra. We haven't met before." She waited until he gave her another, smaller nod. "And your daughter is here." He looked at Elsie and let out a sigh of relief. Elsie gave a half smile and raised her hand in a wave. "And Ronnie is here." The panic flashed on his face. He nervously looked over to her, the panic giving way to puzzlement.

Assuming it was the mismatched nickname that had confused him, Vera leant towards Sandra and whispered, "He knows me as Vera."

"Vera's here." Sandra took the correction without missing a beat.

Nate's response didn't improve. For Vera, it felt like a blow to the heart, not knowing what thought caused the reaction painted on Nate's face.

The way that this Sandra had said it, Nate was sure he was meant to feel something for Vera. But, he didn't know what. There was nothing there for him to pin anything on — no memories of her beyond flirting once or twice. Though... he felt somehow emotionally bound to her. And when he looked at her? Well, she looked different to how he remembered. She looked more sure of herself, more beautiful. There was something familiar about the way she was looking at him now, so different to the coyness and awkwardness of the Vera of his memory. But it was like that was hidden once again behind that veil.

"You don't quite remember Vera?" Sandra watched and waited as Nate kept his eyes on Vera, pressing his lips together, the expression of his face shifting to an apologetic set. He half-nodded, half shook his head, opened his mouth.

"A... little...?"

Those two little words were so hard to navigate.
His voice was crackly and his tongue seemed fat in his mouth.
But those two little words moved Elsie and Vera to tears.

He stretched the fingers of his good hand towards Vera. "Sorry."

Vera shook her head. She hadn't thought that maybe he didn't remember her — some sort of short-term memory loss, she supposed. She didn't know what he did or didn't remember. *A little.* What did that mean? He recognised her, but he couldn't piece everything together. What did he remember doing with her, talking about with her, seeing in her? Did he still want to try again with her?

Sandra sighed, and smiled. "Okay, Nate, you're improving. That's good. I'm going to ask you some questions, and then every half hour a nurse will be by to ask you the same questions. We do this so that we know if you're improving. Do you understand?"

Questions, half hour, I'm improving, understand. "Yes."

Sandra asked him questions: his full name, where he was, why he's here, what year it is, what month it is. His answers were slow, took effort, but were correct — except it was November, not October, as he'd thought. Sandra fussed and took note of them, but didn't seem to show any concern as she jotted down the adjustments she'd made to the morphine. Elsie beamed at her father. He was going to be okay.

Vera stopped paying attention. He was here, but something was missing. It was as though he'd never said the things he'd said, never looked at her that way. Sure, in his mind she'd probably never left his bed, but they'd probably also never become close enough to sleep together in the first place.

Sandra interrupted her thoughts. "He's looking good. As I said, a nurse will be by in half an hour. In the meantime, if he has any pain, seems more confused, or gets nauseous, press the call button. If he gets tired and needs to sleep, that's okay. Okay?" She looked from Elsie, who had moved to sit next to her father, beaming at him, and Vera, who nodded. Sandra took her by the arm and walked with her towards the door. "I don't know what you're expecting him to remember about you, but it's in there. It will take time." She paused. "I hope you get it back." Sandra pushed the door open, leaving Vera alone in front of it.

"Should I leave?" Vera looked at the floor, aware of the division between her and Nate that she couldn't breach. Elsie looked at Nate, who looked back at her.

"No?" Nate offered.

"Maybe," Elsie overrode, "you should let the others know he's okay."

"Others..?" Elsie smiled at Nate's confusion, shushing him gently.

"Okay, yeah," Vera nodded. Nate looked at her apologetically, and Vera could swear she saw a hint of the way he'd looked at her the night he'd visited her house, looking for Elsie. "Good idea. I'll be back... soon."

After Vera left the room, she stood outside the door and cried. Tears of relief mingled with tears of loss. Would he ever remember? And if he did, would he feel shame? Regret? Would he want her, or would he feel it was better left alone? Would he ever tell her if he remembered but decided on a different course, one without her?

She inhaled deeply, sucking down all the questions and the pain. They didn't matter for now. She looked at her phone, ignoring the messages from Vanessa, and sending a new one.

VERA: He's awake. seems okay.

A few seconds later, a reply.

NESS: only OK?

Vera weighed up her options, then found a member of the hospital staff to take her to Emergency Reception where the others were waiting.

Thirty-Six

Elsie put her hand on the side of her father's face.

"I was so scared you'd leave me."

"Never." The thoughts formed words more easily now. "I'll never leave you."

Elsie blinked back tears, pulling a chair close and sitting beside him. The lie was sweet, even if its tell was the nature of life giving way to death. They looked at each other for a long time.

"Are you in pain?" Elsie needed to break the silence.

"A little. Not really." More lies — or maybe they were lies that the brain told Nate about his body. The truth, as always, was in his eyes.

"You don't remember Vera?"

"I remember Vera." He had to prove himself. "She's going to tutor you in maths, right?"

Elsie, ever the romantic, gave out a huff of air that constituted something between a laugh and a cry. "Sure, Dad."

"That's not right?" He racked his brain for more. That's all he could remember. "… she's *not* going to tutor you?"

"She *has* been tutoring me. A few weeks now," she gave him more evidence of his memory loss. "But," she leaned forward and examined him through the corner of her eye. "You don't remember *anything* else?"

Nate tried to read what he was meant to remember from her face.

"Come on, Dad."

He stared at the door, hoping that he could will the answer to walk through. It was like looking through a wall of ice. There was nothing, and the effort exhausted him. "I'm…" he felt embarrassed by his failure, and unsettled by the idea that he couldn't remember. "I'm really tired, Elsie. I think I need a nap."

She sighed, leaning back in her chair. "Okay. Okay."

"I'm sorry, Elsie."

"Mmhm."

"So the tutoring… has been going well?"

"Dad, it's okay."

He frowned, pursing his lips. He looked back up at the ceiling, then giving up, closed his eyes. He heard Elsie shift, sigh, get up and walk to the other side of the room.

It felt like the next moment, he was woken by a knock at the door. A slim Nurse with bright eyes and a nervous quality appeared at the doorway. "Mr Whitely? Sorry to wake you. I've come to check in on you," he busied himself, checking Nate's charts against the monitors, noting down changes, stabilities, anything. Elsie watched from next to the window, the light falling through against her face, her arms wrapped around each other. The nurse asked the questions, got the right answers. Nate remembered that he had been told that it was November. "Are you in any pain?"

"Just…" Nate held up his damaged hand. He was scared to ask what was underneath those bandages, but he knew it was burning. He didn't want to think about what the repercussions may be.

"Just a little bit? You were able to sleep, so maybe I'll just give you a liiiiittle more," he stretched out the word as he fiddled with the bag. "Okay, that should help." He looked between Nate and Elsie. "Anything I can get you? Drinks, something to eat, anything?"

Elsie shook her head. She'd lost her appetite.

Nate cleared his throat. "Maybe something, some juice? Lemon in the water? My throat hurts a bit."

"Of course." The nurse nodded, then disappeared out of the room.

"You okay, Dad?" Elsie seemed somehow older, more worn.

"Yeah, why wouldn't I be?" His small laugh belied the rasp in his voice. Elsie nodded and looked through the window.

"I think I'm going to find Vera."

"Okay, love."

She picked up her phone, walked over, squeezed his hand, and turned for the door, which opened in front of her thanks to the return of the Nurse and two containers of apple juice, one of which he promptly opened and handed to Nate with a smile and left to follow through on the remainder of his rounds.

Elsie had already slipped out. And he was alone.

Vera found her way back to Emergency. She'd lost track of time; the glow from outside was a deep blue. Emma saw her and elbowed Vanessa, who was half asleep from waiting. She opened her eyes and stood bolt upright. She strode over to Vera, gathering information from the set of her face, and then hugged her, holding her and making it safe for her to let go.

"Tell me *everything*."

Vera sniffed, pulling herself back from Vanessa. "He's lost some of his memory. I don't know how much. But it was like he hardly knew me."

"Did he know who you were?"

"I think so? Or maybe he just thought he ought to know me."

"Oh, honey," Vanessa held her close again.

"What if he'll never love me again?"

"Don't be stupid. Of course he will. Come, sit with us."

Vanessa led her back to their little corner, kicking Tommy's legs to make sure he took them off the seat opposite him so that Vera could sit down.

"So?" he repeated what Vera had sent in the message, seeking reassurance. "Nate's awake? He's okay?"

"He's..." Vera watched Tommy nervously biting his thumbnail; she thought about him playing music, thought about Nate playing music. "Well... His hand seems pretty messed up, I think. It's all in bandages. But he's awake. He was pretty confused, but seems to be getting better?" She treated the statement as a question. "At least, he was when I left. They're still keeping an eye on him."

"His hand? Oh, man. What happened to his hand?"

"I think maybe you should just sit with us, you don't need to say anything, okay?" Emma cut over the top of Tommy's questioning.

"Thanks, Emma. That would be nice."

"Shit, his hand. Shit." Tommy mumbled to himself. "Shit, man."

Vera stared at the foyer television screen, watching but losing focus, just as an excuse to not look at anything, to fill her mind with anything. She didn't want to think about the idea that this week was resetting her back to a place where she was before: just under a week ago, she'd lain in bed all day, fretting over how she felt about sleeping with Nate. Now, he didn't even remember it, as though her relationship with him had never existed except in her mind as a fantasy. Then, for reasons she couldn't exactly justify to herself, when Steven had called, she'd gone to meet up with him, instead of telling him how she really felt: that she wanted nothing to do with him, and she wanted to move on.

It's incredibly hard to be angry at a situation, to recognise that some things happen through freak twists of timing, for good or bad. Human brains developed to be able to find patterns, to trace every event back to possible causes, to lay blame in order to prevent a bad thing from happening again. It's an evolutionarily sound tendency, but also meant that Vera wanted to blame someone, so she played the 'if only' game in her head until she came back to the one thing that she felt had truly ruined things. Sure, she'd walked out on Nate. He'd dumped her. But he was going to visit her, and everything would have worked out — if only she hadn't said yes to seeing Steven. If only he hadn't called! He was the one she could blame, she decided. And while she consciously blamed him for Nate's accident, she subconsciously blamed him for so much more. This blame felt justified.

Fuck Steven!

"Ronnie!" Fuck that smarmy voice. "Ronnie, Mum called me. She said that you were here, that someone you know was in a car accident!" He ignored everyone and kneeled in front of Vera, his hands on her two armrests, fencing her in. She shrunk back from him. It was like she'd thought his name and he'd been summoned.

"Oh. Hi Steven."

"Are you okay? I was worried that maybe you were in the accident as well."

"Oh. No, I wasn't. I got the call right when I got home after meeting you at the cafe today."

"I wish you'd never left. Hearing this made me realise: I need you with me."

Vanessa's ears pricked up. "Steven?" She sat forward, glancing back at Emma, who raised one eyebrow and gave her a smile. "I remember you."

This time, Vera was prepared for it, *and* appreciated it: *The Ness*

Test.

"Oh, uh, hi," Steven gave her a double-take. Vanessa's long legs and boisterous golden curls were nothing if not captivating.

"I'm Vanessa," she reached her hand out to him, and smiled her big, charming, wide smile as he took it. "You and I met at a party a *long* time ago. Maybe you don't remember me, but I remember *you*. I went to school with Ronnie... *and* Sarah."

"Oh," he glanced at Vera, who nodded. He raised his eyebrow and looked back to Vanessa, smiling. "I see!"

Tommy watched on, confused and disgusted. He looked over at Emma, whose straight face gave a little bit when she saw his expression.

"So, Steven, Ronnie is feeling a *little* overwhelmed. Someone she cares about almost died. Let's you and me go and get her a coffee from the cafe?"

"Oh, absolutely." He beamed at Vanessa. The Ness Test was taking its course.

"Urgh," grunted Tommy when they were out of earshot. "Sorry, but what the fuck just happened? Emma... isn't Vanessa your girlfriend?"

"Well, yes. She doesn't really like men at all, but men like her an awful lot," she beamed. "She uses her powers for good, not evil."

Tommy blinked and turned to Vera. "And who is Steven anyway?"

"My cheating ex. I ran into his mother — she works here."

"Sorry, Vera: did I imagine it, or did you say you saw him today?" This time it was Emma.

Vera looked between them. There was no reason to hide the truth. "He begged me to catch up with him. I should have said no, but... He claimed it was just as friends. I wanted to believe him; I thought I could get some closure. And then he tried to coerce me to get back together with him. That's..." she faltered. "Nate walked into the cafe and saw us sitting together. I didn't have a chance to explain to him; he just turned around and walked out."

Tommy's eyes turned almost triangular with devastation. "Aw man, *no*." Like Nate, his emotions shone through at the surface. "Wait — did he talk to you? Or he just... *saw* you."

Vera rolled her lips together. "Elsie told me everything."

"Oh man... Wait, he's awake now, right? Did you two talk it out? Are you, like, on the same page now?"

"Nate, doesn't, um," she scratched her neck distractedly. "I don't know how well he remembers me."

Tommy slumped back in his chair. "Shit," he shook his head. "Hang on — do *you* love him? I mean, is it a good thing or a bad thing that he doesn't remember?"

Vera looked at him and bit her lip. She didn't need to answer.

"Shit. Well, I hope he remembers you," a dopey smile crept onto Tommy's face, his eyebrows tilted up in the middle. "Hah. The way he talked about you last night!"

"He... talked about me? To you?"

"Yeah," Tommy laughed. "He's my hero, you know? The reason I got into music. I don't think he really liked me at the start, because I was such a fucking fanboy when I met him."

"Well, you know Elsie adores you. That would put any father at unease."

"She does? That's... cute. She's — like — a kid, though."

"I'm sure she wouldn't want to hear that."

Guilt flashed over Tommy's features, his eyes seeming to shine greener.

"But wait, you drove her here?"

Tommy blinked the discomfort away. "Yeah, old man Nate got himself drunk at the awards, the silly goose. I didn't drink because I wanted to be, you know, really *present* for the awards! And it was a good thing too, because even with a singular celebratory drink, I was still under. I drove them home. We got to talking, and he kept going on about you."

Vera blushed at this admission.

"Elsie said he's a mess when he drinks, but all he seemed to do was cry and talk about how nice you were, how he fucked up; how he must have done something that he didn't understand to upset you, and all this other junk." He shook his head. "We put him to bed, Elsie and I fell asleep watching tv. When we all woke up," he grinned, proud of himself. "I told him to tell you how he feels about you. He looked *so* scared. Super cute. I told him: pick up your car, drive to her place, tell her you love her, that you want another chance. Sweep her right off her feet and into your arms!"

Tommy was too busy enjoying retelling the events of the previous night and the morning that he failed to watch Vera's facial expressions and responses. When he finished, she took a deep breath in. "Well, he never got to do that. He saw me and Steven, and probably got the wrong idea, and... And now he doesn't remember any of it. So it's a good thing for him."

Tommy's face dropped. "Nah, man, it's terrible! It'd only be good he forgot if you were going to say no to him. Elsie was sure you did, which is why I gave him a push. And she was right, right?"

"Supposedly the memory loss won't be permanent, so..."

They sat together, Emma quietly watching, Tommy thinking about how he could possibly trigger a memory and bring Nate and Vera back together, and Vera mulling over what would have happened had she refused to meet with Steven: would they be having their happy ending?

Steven and Vanessa returned, Steven mesmerised while she carried the coffee and gave it to Vera. As she leant in, she caught Vera's eyes and rolled her own dramatically.

"Thank you," Vera wasn't just thanking her for the coffee.

"Elsie," Tommy stood up. He saw Elsie wandering towards them. When she saw him, her eyes lit up and she rushed over, launching herself into his arms. Tommy exchanged a worried look with Vera, suddenly seeing Elsie's affections in a new light. "Hey, *kid*; how are you? How's your Dad going? Vera said he's awake and seems okay," he did the best impression of a big brother that he could manage.

Elsie swung around to look at Vera. "Can I still stay at your place tonight?"

"Of course."

Steven let out a small, nonsensical whimper. In his head, any hopes he had of getting with Vera tonight had been dashed by a fourteen-year-old girl.

"I think... I think Dad's okay. I'm ready to go whenever."

"Can *I* see him?" Tommy asked.

"I don't know if he'll remember meeting you."

"Hm, and he didn't like me the last time I met him for the first time."

"Yeah, maybe now isn't the right time."

"Have you told him you're leaving?" Vera asked.

"No, I just said I would go and find you."

"Ah. We should go say goodbye, then, and find out when they think he'll be able to go home."

Elsie nodded. She let go of Tommy, and looked around, looked at Steven but didn't make any effort to introduce herself. And of course, neither did he. "Let's go."

Thirty-Seven

⏮ ⏸ ⏭

Nate was alone with his thoughts for a while. He tried to go back to sleep, but this time he couldn't. He started to think about what he'd been told: he'd been in a car crash, he'd been in a coma for a few hours, the last thing he remembered about Vera was from a few weeks ago. If he had only been in a coma for a few hours, why couldn't he remember weeks worth of life? He couldn't even remember what date it was. If he had his dates straight, the ARIA Awards would have been last night. Did he miss them, as he'd planned? Or, worse: had he gone but drank and caused the accident himself?

The door opened again, and it was Elsie and Vera. Elsie looked strained, Vera looked… unsettled.

"Hi," he ventured.

"Hi Dad," Elsie came to stand next to him. "We're gonna go. The doctors said you need to stay here under observation for a few nights. Something about surgery, too. Vera said I can stay at hers — she lives pretty close to here, so we won't be far from you."

"Okay. That makes sense. Thanks, Vera," Nate looked at her appreciatively, but that seemed to do nothing to affect her. Nate switched back to locating himself in time. "Elsie? Were the ARIAs last night?"

Elsie flushed. She hadn't thought that maybe he didn't actually remember *anything* from the past few weeks. "Yup, we went to the Awards last night," she smiled, thinking of her evening spent with Tommy. "It's Friday."

"Ah, okay," he frowned. Elsie would be more angry, more sullen, and given him an earful if the accident had been his fault, so he ruled that out. "I, uh, I thought that was weeks away. We went? God, I can't remember anything." His eyes flicked to Vera. "I'm guessing we've gotten to know each other better since I last remember, Vera."

"That's an understatement, Dad," Elsie was very effective at making both Nate and Vera feel embarrassed. When their eyes met, though, there was a spark of shared delight — the first hint of proper connection they'd had since he'd woken up. Something stirred in Nate's mind, a memory that he couldn't quite reach. It didn't matter right now, he was sure. He grinned at her, and she blushed in response. He loved doing that. He wanted to do it again.

"Okay Dad," Elsie leant forward and kissed him on the cheek. "The hospital has both our numbers. I *think* they might have your phone and things somewhere."

"Bye, Nate," Vera walked to him, and hovered awkwardly by his bed.

"See you soon, Vera. Right?" He held out his hand to her, motioning her over. Her eyes twinkled, a flush of colour playing against her coyness. She reached out, hesitantly, her fingers brushing his; he tickled her hand into his, jostling to get a better hold of her. He felt her hand soften into his. "And, uh," he inclined his head towards Elsie. "Again. Thanks."

Vera nodded, and Elsie put her arms around her. He smiled at them, they smiled back, and turned to leave the room.

By sheer luck of timing, another Nurse came in to check on him. He was glad he could relax, knowing that Elsie would be safe with Vera. She was a nice girl. Really nice.

Thirty-Eight

⏮ ⏸ ⏭

Vera and Elsie sat together in silence in Vera's car as she drove them to Nate's house.

"Do you want to get your school things? You know, for... Monday?"

"I don't want to go to school again, ever."

"We'll see how things are on Monday. If you're not up to going, I'll call them. Tell them what happened, that you won't be in."

"Mmm," Elsie switched the radio on. It was just something to hide the silence that she wanted to hide in for the rest of the drive.

They pulled up in front of Nate's house, dark and looming. Vera remembered the first time she saw it, both unsurprised and jealous at its size and location. Elsie had never been to Vera's house, but of course she knew the types of houses in that area.

Elsie opened the car door, and turned for Vera. "Do you want to come in? I might take a little while to get everything."

Vera nodded. They walked to the door in silence, Elsie jangling her keys in the lock. She stepped into the darkness, running her hand along the wall to find the light switch.

The flood of light exposed Vera's memories. She walked past the kitchen, looking in at the coffee machine.

"Make yourself a coffee if you want," Elsie said, flatly. "I'm sure Dad wouldn't mind. Just wash the cup when you're done."

It was the second time Vera had used a pod machine to make a coffee, and she couldn't help remembering the lessons from her teacher the first time. She found herself making small choices that represented much larger ones: should she have the purple pod again, or try another? She was well aware of the effect that scent had on triggering memories and emotions. Was it worth remembering more about that night, or was it better to try to forget it, as he had done?

The difference was, she'd had a choice. It didn't seem like he had.

Purple.

Elsie stomped upstairs. In her room, she looked at the posters of Tommy, in awe of the fact that she'd actually met him. She was glad he hadn't gone into her room. Would he think she was weird? Maybe he'd be flattered. Either way, it was probably good that he hadn't seen it. Plus, Nate wouldn't have been at all happy about Tommy being in her bedroom, with or without her. Even though he teased her about David, she knew he only did that because she *didn't* like him. Urgh, David. Another reason she didn't want to go to school. She'd rather quit and just follow Tommy around. Plus, Vera could homeschool her, right?

She found a bag to fit everything in. She opened her drawers and began throwing things in. She didn't know how long she'd stay — she didn't know how long her Dad would need to be in hospital.

Her hand hesitated at her school uniform. Vera was right, she supposed. She grabbed a couple of dresses, her jumper, her shoes and some socks. She shoved them in her schoolbag. She picked up her homework from her desk and put it in, as well as her laptop, and wandered to her bathroom. She grabbed some toiletries and put them back in the bag she'd packed only last week for her sleepover. Just her toothbrush, moisturiser, cleanser, deodorant. Everything else, she could figure out at Vera's. She stopped in the laundry to collect some fresh underwear and some clean comfy clothes from the dryer, both for herself and Nate.

After she dumped them all in her bag in her room, she took another look at the posters on her wall. She climbed up on her bed and started pulling them down. She couldn't bring herself to rip them, so she carefully unpicked them from the wall, then folded them all up and hid them in her wardrobe.

Standing back, she looked at the bare walls of her bedroom. She picked up her two bags, turned off the light, and walked downstairs.

Vera was hunched over her coffee mug. She wasn't exactly crying, but maybe that was just because they'd both made themselves dry from all the tears they'd shed over the course of the day. She looked up at Elsie as she walked in, dropping her bags in front of them.

"I'm ready whenever."

Vera nodded slowly, and looked down at her coffee. She sighed, straightened up, and dumped half a mug of coffee down the sink.

"I didn't mean to rush you," Elsie apologised. "I just meant—"

"No, I was done." Vera smiled briefly at her. She began rinsing the mug out, squirting a little detergent to help it along. She placed it beside the sink, clean and slick with water. "It just didn't taste as it did last time. Let me help you." She blotted her hands on her pants, leaving damp handprints on her thighs. She picked up one of Elsie's bags, and looked at the other. "Your schoolbag?"

"Yeeeah. I don't *want* to go back to school, but I guess I'll have to. I don't want to be bugging you-all-day-every-day, either."

Vera smiled, and turned towards the door. Elsie picked up her schoolbag, turned out the other lights, and followed her, closing the door behind her.

Thirty-Nine

"I don't really have a spare bed," Vera stated, shifting things from her couch. "And I've been sleeping on the couch this weekend, I don't know why. So you can have my bed."

"No, the couch is cool," Elsie looked at the tv. "I'm not really sure I'm gonna sleep, anyway."

Vera nodded. "I was thinking the same thing."

"Your place is cute," Elsie wandered around the room, then stopped in front of the boxes, with the photo of Vera and Steven still on it. She picked it up and looked at Vera—captured when she was around the same age as Tommy. "Oh, so you knew that guy at the hospital? *He's* your ex?"

"Yeah," Vera walked to the kitchen. "Want a tea? A hot chocolate?"

"Umm a hot chocolate would be good. I can see why you'd meet up with him," She looked up pointedly, then in her best attempt to sound nonchalant, asked, "d'you still love him?"

Vera let out a laugh. "No, I really don't. I used to think I might, but really I think I just liked the attention he gave me," she reached down, collecting two mugs from the cupboard. "He was my first serious boyfriend. No one really liked me much before him." She ignored the incredulous look Elsie was giving her, got the milk out of the fridge, and filled both mugs up. "He seemed to adore me, told me I was everything: smart, beautiful, talented, his saviour." The milk went back into the fridge. "He told me everything I ever hoped to hear, praised everything I valued in myself." She dug some powdered hot chocolate out of a drawer, and grabbed a spoon. "He was the first guy who didn't tell me that I was *cool,* or *nice.*" Elsie swallowed. *Dad called her nice.* Spoonfuls of chocolate went into the milk. They were stirred. "Usually, when a guy said one of those things, a minute later, he'd turn and try to flirt with one of my friends. One who was hot, one who was sexy, one who was cute. Not the *cool* girl, not the *nice* girl." The mugs went into the microwave, and a few buttons were pressed. The microwave hummed into existence, agitating the milk. "Well, except for your Dad, of course."

"He used to talk about how nice you are, *all* the time," Elsie reassured her. "He really likes it about you."

"I know," Vera smiled. "He told me." Her face started to fall as she thought about how he'd said it that night. Would he appreciate it again, the way he did a week ago?

"So, what happened with this dork. I mean, he's pretty hot, but he also seemed a bit weird."

"It's weird that you think my ex is hot."

"Well, I mean," she turned the photo to Vera. "Let's be honest." She grinned.

"Okay, well, yes he is." She laughed to herself. "But looks aren't everything."

Elsie nodded earnestly. "Dad says the same thing."

"Does he?"

"Yep. I asked him if he thought you were pretty. He said it didn't matter."

"Ah, so when you told me that he said I'm pretty, you meant he said it didn't matter."

"Nah, I pushed him and he said you are. But that it's not the most important thing, that's all."

The microwave beeped. "Hopefully they're hot enough," Vera fished the two mugs out of the microwave.

"Hot enough like your hot ex-boyfriend," Elsie continued, keen for the full story.

Vera scrunched her nose, and took the bait. "My hot ex-fiance, actually."

"Oh, whaaaat?"

"Yeah. He proposed to me and everything. But then apparently he was also in love with my best friend."

"Who, Vanessa? Was that why he was like, half hanging off her?"

"No, Vanessa was one of our good friends. My best friend was Sarah. I came home earlier than he expected. Caught them in the act."

"Huh, impressive. And clichéd."

"Well, this was especially impressive considering how quick the act usually was with him." She handed Elsie one of the hot chocolates with a smile.

Elsie blushed. She wasn't used to talking so candidly with *adults* about sex. Everything came from Reddit, movies, and their fantasies.

"So that's what happened. And it snapped me out of it. I wasn't enough for him, despite what he said. I knew I could never take him seriously again."

"And that was it?"

"That was it. I threw away ten years of my life, quit my job, and moved in here."

"Wow."

"Yeah."

"So why was he at the hospital?"

"Do you remember the Doctor, Sandra?"

"Oh yeah, you said she was your ex's Mum."

"He said she called him to say that I was there. Besides," Vera cleared her throat. "He *was* in the area."

"Yeah. So, I don't get it. Why'd you meet up with him, if you don't even want him back?"

"That's what I keep asking myself. But, he kept calling me, and I guess I thought that if I met up with him, maybe I'd have some sort of... closure? And I'd sort-of been fretting over your Dad so much, I just needed to get out."

Elsie nodded, sitting down with her hot chocolate. She couldn't really blame Vera. Nate had been an arsehole to her. He'd actually deliberately been an arsehole to prevent himself maybe being an arsehole some time in the future, as she'd learned from his drunken confessions to Tommy.

"You know, I was kinda okay with what your Dad had said to me, until he came to my place looking for you."

"Why? Did he say something to upset you?"

"Not really."

Elsie frowned. "So why weren't you okay anymore?"

"It was the way he looked at me. When I was sure that he wanted nothing to do with me, that was okay. It was clear: it was just another rejection." She smirked. "I'm quite used to those. But, the way he looked at me that night? I wasn't so sure that he wanted nothing to do with me. It meant he felt something, but he *chose* to not be with me. It meant that it wasn't *just* another rejection. And I couldn't figure it out."

Elsie nodded again. "Sorry."

"For what? Elsie, this isn't your fault," Vera sat down, putting her arm around her.

"It is, though. I was trying so hard to get you two together."

Vera smiled gently at her. "Well, you didn't do everything. It wasn't like we didn't like each other from the start."

Elsie sighed. "Can we put on the tv, maybe?"

"Of course."

Vera flicked through the channels until they agreed on a movie to watch. Elsie tucked her legs up onto the lounge, making herself tiny. Vera pulled the doona up and onto both of them.

Forty

Elsie's phone buzzed.

NATE: Got my phone back. I'm bored. I hope you're okay
ELSIE: I'm ok, vera's asleep. Have they said u could leave yet?
NATE: No. Same as before. A few dayd
NATE: days
ELSIE: Ok. Want us to visit tomorrow?
NATE: Itd be nice.
ELSIE: Okay, I'll tell vera

Elsie screwed up her face as she considered just telling Nate everything about his last few weeks with Vera. After a long pause, her phone buzzed again.

NATE: Elsie I don't know why I dont remember anything, I cant
      remember anything from a few weeks ago

Elsie's brow twitched with concern.

ELSIE: Its ok dad
NATE: Is it? I'm sure things happened that I don't remember. And I
      know there are things, but its like forgetting where you put
      your keys
ELSIE: lol dad no don't say it like that
NATE: Thats what it feels like though!i know I had my keys but where
      did I put them. Right?

Elsie looked down at Vera, asleep, emotionally exhausted and worn out. How could he forget?

ELSIE: Do you want me to tell you?
NATE: No
NATE: I just want you to know that its bugging me, I know its upsetting you, I know it upset vera
NATE: It must b something important and I'm sorr
ELSIE: Its ok dad. We'll visit you in the morning. Maybe ull dream about it or somehting?
NATE: I hope so.
NATE: Love you very much. Goodnight. Goodnight to vera
ELSIE: Dad I told you shes already asleep

There was a long pause before her phone buzzed again.

NATE: Did you? Scrolling up is hard with one hand
ELSIE: Love you too dad. Go easy on the nurses. Goodnight

Elsie put her phone on silent, and snuggled down next to Vera.

Nate put his phone on his lap. The reality of his hand injury hit home. He didn't like to think about it, he didn't want to think what it would mean for his work. He had got into the habit of spending most of the week in the studio, tinkering on the keyboard or strumming his guitar, listening for interesting sounds. What if he could never use his hand anymore? He's always prided himself on his ability to pick up and play almost any instrument as long as he gave it some attention. His fingers were precise, quick to learn.

Well, at least you really only needed one hand to play Trumpet. So there was always that.

Even in his head, he tried to distract himself by making himself laugh. He also knew that there was no point worrying until the doctors were ready to have another look at it. That's what the nurses said: making sure he was alive and wasn't brain damaged or bleeding internally was top priority. All his questions about it had been dismissed: basically, they told him that yes, it was broken, but it wasn't more pressing than making sure he didn't have any other trauma-related complications that could put him at risk during the surgery. And he supposed they were right. But, he was a musician, and he relied on his hands. They were his tools, his life.

He cleared his throat. He'd worried about the hoarseness as well, but the nurses said it was probably just from the tube they'd put down his throat when he was brought in, to make sure his lungs didn't collapse. They suggested getting Strepsils or something similar when he got out.

When would he get out? A few more days, they said. They wanted to make sure he was stable and safe before they let him go home. Another night at least, another week at most. Hospitals were always overcrowded, so the minute they felt that it wasn't malpractice to discharge someone, they'd ask them to leave.

He'd been watching the news. He'd caught short mentions of himself being in an accident, no formal statement from family or agents. Just one from Tommy Freebourne, saying that he'd only met him the night before, but they'd hung out all night and he was shocked and worried for him. Nate couldn't tell whether he was lying, but had no reason to doubt his honesty — especially as the interview was filmed in front of the hospital. He was relieved that he wasn't big news anymore, and that Tommy would probably be the one who would attract people's awareness and make him more important. Everything else being featured on the news felt like a continuation of the same. No new big political issues, no new great social events. Just the usual, the same noise as before.

He switched off the tv. He looked down at his phone. Elsie was probably already asleep. He looked at his call log. Elsie, Vera, Jason. He went to his messages, and looked through them. Messages from Elsie, Tommy, Vera. He opened the message history with Vera. Recent, but nothing of significance. Clearly, they'd called each other, rather than messaged. He wanted to say something to her. Elsie said she was asleep, so a message would be best. It could be something nice for her to wake up to.

NATE: I'm sorry

He stopped writing. He didn't know what he was sorry for. He deleted it, laying back and looking up at the ceiling.

NATE: Thanks again for looking after Elsie

That seemed to diminish who she was to someone who just looked after Elsie. They'd both hinted that there was something more. That got deleted too.

NATE: I know it didn't seem like it, but I'm happy you were here.

He chewed his lip. He felt filled with nerves. Was that appropriate? It didn't really matter, he supposed. It was honest. He pressed send. He stared at the phone for a few minutes, hoping for a reply that he knew she couldn't send while she was asleep. He looked at the message again.

NATE: See you soon.

Something about that felt right. She was really nice, Vera. So nice. And it seemed to upset Elsie so much that he couldn't remember the last few weeks and what they meant for them. He was glad that Elsie had someone like that to look up to, someone grounded, someone smart, someone kind, someone nice.

He fussed with his phone. Looked at the photos. There were a few from the ARIAs, one with Tommy in it. He could see a half-drunk beer bottle in his own hand. He worried. He scrolled further back. No photos of Vera. None at all. He sighed.

Sometimes, while out, he'd record audio of him singing an idea for a song, so he could work on it later in the studio. He often copied them across to his studio computer and then deleted them from his phone, so he didn't have a large backlog. But maybe, given it was Friday night, he might have a couple from the last few days. He navigated through to his mic, and went to playback.

And in a rush, everything came back.

Forty-One

⏮ ⏸ ⏭

When they arrived in the morning — fresh from a night spent cramped on the couch, showered and fed with takeaway coffee and hot chocolate — Nate was sitting up in his bed, a nurse gently unwrapping his hand as he looked on in a mix of fear and curiosity.

"Hi Dad," offered Elsie. Nate grunted, his eyes flicking up once, then twice as he saw Vera there as well. His eyes lingered for a second as she smiled politely, before the pain of his hand drew his attention back down. He couldn't quite bring himself to look at his hand, instead watching the Nurse's response. She gave him nothing.

Elsie and Vera moved closer silently, standing off to the side.

Every time he had a chance, Nate glanced up at them. He felt a mix of emotions: embarrassment, anger, frustration, need, yearning, comfort.

Finally, he looked down at his hand. It wasn't as bad as he feared, more disfigured than destroyed. The nurse gently squeezed each of his fingers, stretched apart his palm. Nate tried to hide the pain, but his body tensed and relaxed, his unshaven jaw bulging as he clenched his teeth involuntarily.

"Can you move your fingers?"

Nate focused on his hand. He looked at his fingers, tried curling them. He managed a minor twitch, flames of pain shooting up his arm.

"That's fine, Mr Whitely." The Nurse barely looked at him as she turned to jot something down on his chart, and he kept looking down to hide his feeling of shame and his inability to achieve something that should be so easy for him. She reached over to begin rebandage his band. "The surgeon will be by later to discuss options with you."

"Mmhm," Nate couldn't even manage a proper response. "Thanks."

"Be careful of this," the Nurse gave him a terse smile, let go of his hand, collected what she needed to, checked his drip, the grazes on his face, and quickly escaped.

The three of them waited as the weight of the silence built in the room, none sure what to say, all wanting to speak first, yet no one knowing the right thing to say.

"Thanks for coming by," Nate finally said, his eyes still avoiding them.

"Are you okay, Dad?"

"Sure, I will be." He had always been a bad liar. "The doctor said I should recover fine."

"But, your hand," Elsie reached out to him. He snatched it away, wincing from pain.

"It will be fine."

Vera wished she wasn't there. She just didn't know what to do or say to connect with him. There was something different about the way he had looked at her when she came in; it didn't match the message he'd sent her the night before. Maybe they'd just arrived at a bad time?

"Vera, I'm..." His face twitched. "Sorry I interrupted you yesterday. On your *date*."

Elsie and Vera looked at each other, both letting out a brief laugh of shock.

Vera bit her lip and looked back to him. "You remember?"

"Yeah, unless there's even more I don't know about."

"Dad, it's okay. That was Vera's ex and he's a jerk and she doesn't like him."

Nate regarded Vera. She held his gaze firmly, intent on reassuring him. He looked so vulnerable and hopeful and young; it was a look he used to flash for the camera, but this time it was the original, true version of that look that he'd taught himself to play on cue, repeated and hollowed out. "Really?"

She nodded, feeling herself turn into cotton candy in front of him.

"Vera, I..." He closed his eyes as he drummed up the confidence, yet again, to open himself up to her rejection. "I went there to surprise you with coffee, and I wanted to say... to tell you..." When he opened his eyes, he sought out Elsie, who gave him an encouraging nod. "I'm... sorry about what I said that day. I didn't mean it." He looked down at his hand. "I just thought," he sighed. He didn't *not* want to tell her the truth, but he didn't really understand the truth himself. "I don't know." He looked up at her.

She stepped towards him, let out a shaky breath, and, smiling, reached out to take his good hand. As soon as she touched him, he grabbed hold of her hand and quickly brought it to his lips, kissing her fingers, holding them to his face and looking at her as though he feared she would disappear if he let her go again.

Elsie rolled her eyes and giggled. "Should I be the one to leave the room this time?"

There was a knock on the door, and a kindly man about Nate's age entered the room. "Mr Whitely, ah! Sorry to interrupt," Nate smiled and let go of Vera, who moved away and stood next to Elsie, who beamed at her and elbowed her playfully. "I'm Doctor Preskov, your surgeon." He had a faint European accent that Nate found hard to place. "Nurse said your hand is crushed, but you have little movement." He gently shuffled over, placing a folder of papers on the bed next to Nate's legs. "I look?"

"Sure, take a look." Nate lifted his hand. Dr Preskov looked at Nate again.

"I open?"

Nate had a feeling that he'd be asked every step of the way. He didn't really mind it. "Sure."

"Okay, I open." He made faint trumpeting sounds with his mouth as he looked at Nate's hands, his swollen fingers, his fat palm. "No bone sticking out, good." His bluntness was simultaneously shocking and amusing. He turned Nate's hand over and stroked the back of it as though he were petting a cat. "Mm, I hear you are musician? So you use hands a lot."

"Uh, yes," Nate looked towards Elsie, who looked back with anxiety.

"So we need the surgery to make sure the hand is all good. Maybe one, maybe two."

"Okay."

"Is expensive, but you have health insurance?"

"Money is not a problem."

"Okay, okay; good." He gently re-wrapped Nate's hand. "This morning's X-ray, I had look and it was, pff," he made a small plosive and emphasised with his hand. "It need a little help."

The colour drained from Nate's face.

"But you musician so we need to be very careful, too. It's your playing hand?"

"It's my playing hand." Nate nodded.

Dr Preskov tilted his head down to his chest and looked up at Nate through his eyebrows, before tilting his head back and looking down his nose. "Is okay, I take good care of you. We can have surgery today, okay?"

Nate looked at Elsie and Vera. They nodded to him, despite it not being their decision at all. "Okay."

"Okay. I have some forms, maybe ladies can help you fill out?" He pulled some papers out of his folder with a brisk tug, then took a pen from his pocket; he moved towards Nate and then spun on his heels and handed the paper and pen to Elsie. She unfolded her arms and took them from him uncertainly. "Okay, I leave you now; I add you to my afternoon, I look after you and then: hand? Good as new. Okay!"

"Okay," Nate, Elsie, and Vera echoed him. He nodded, spun again, and barrelled towards the door and his next patient.

Nate bit his lip.

"That sounded… good?" Vera tried.

Nate groaned. He knew she was trying to be optimistic, but it felt like she downplayed the repercussions of the injury.

"I mean, he seemed confident, and he'll fit you in right away."

"It doesn't fix my hand does it?"

"I think that's what he's trying to do, though. I mean, I think that's the point of the surgery."

Nate shot Vera a glare that frightened her a bit. Until now, when he'd looked at her, his eyes had always been soft, seductive, wounded, scared. This time there was fury, and it was directed at her. She took a step back without realising it.

"Dad, Vera's just trying to—"

"Elsie, my hand is *fucked* and we all know it."

Vera stared at her feet. Elsie crossed her arms and looked out the window. Nate looked between them both, then took a deep breath.

"I'm sorry, I just… my hand is fucked. It's fucked. Even Dr Strangelove knows that — what did he call it? My *playing* hand? Well yes, my *playing* hand is fucked. It's not just a little battered and bruised. It's broken and I need surgery, and who the fuck knows what after that.

Will it even heal right?" He blinked away the tears of fear, shame, and frustration that clouded his vision.

Vera looked up at him, her face soft with pain. "You've made lots of beautiful music, you don't need to—"

"What?" Fury played with his features again. "I don't have to *what*? Make more music? Jesus Christ, Vera: I'm a musician. I don't do anything *but* make music. It's like me telling you that you've breathed a lot of good breaths before, so you can just stop breathing."

His words, his face, stung Vera. She didn't respond well to being snapped at like that, especially when she'd been trying so hard to make him feel better.

"I should stop talking."

"Yes, you *fucking* should."

"Dad!" Elsie stood over him, arms akimbo. He looked away from her, burying his chin in his chest, pouting. Vera wrapped her arms over her, stroking one arm with the opposite hand, soothing. Elsie looked from one to the other. She dumped Dr Preskov's paper and pen between Nate's legs. "Vera, Dad's being rotten. Let's just go."

Vera looked at Nate, but he continued staring down, avoiding eye contact like a sullen dog. She nodded slowly.

"I *am* sorry. About what I said, about your hand; about..." She trailed off, trying to decide how to phrase the rest of her thought, "Other things."

The muscles around Nate's left eye twitched, so he closed his eyes as his brows knitted together and did his best to stop himself from collapsing into tears.

"Come on Vera," Elsie took her arm, and led her out of the room.

"So the ladies did not help you with form," Dr Preskov laughed, seeing Nate struggling to fill in the last of the paperwork. "Mean ladies."

"No," sighed Nate. "Mean me."

"Mean *you*?"

"Yeah, I yelled at them."

"Ah, you were angry, but not from them; but you got angry at them. Not about them."

Nate smiled with relief. The Doctor at least understood.

"Is normal. You musician. A good one, I remembered: I know your song," he went back to trumpeting with his lips, but this time it was a song Nate wrote twenty years ago.

"That's the one." Nate smiled.

"I take care of you, I fix you up. After, it will be hard, take a while to get better. But you will be better. You will need help. So... be nice to ladies."

Nate nodded silently.

"Okay?"

"Okay."

"Okay, I go clean up. You will be brought in."

Forty-Two

⏮ ⏸ ⏭

Vera hung back as Elsie bowled into the room, clambering like a little girl onto her father's hospital bed with no regard for the way he might be feeling. He winced as she settled at the end of the bed between his legs, a sparkling smile plastered across her features in anticipation.

Nate had pushed himself awake from the anaesthetic and was doing his best to ignore the plastered, splinted, and slung symbol of what he thought was the hard end of his slowly degrading career. The struggle was showing on his face, which he tried to rearrange into a hopeful smile in line with Elsie's, hoping it would egg her on.

"Guess what, Dad?"

Nate batted his eyelashes in an attempt to push back everything he was thinking and focus on Elsie. "What, love?"

Elsie bit her lip and glanced back over her shoulder at Vera, who had hardly moved inside the room. "The doctors said we can bring you home!"

Nate had followed her gaze back and been caught in Vera's eyes. She gave him a shrug and an insincere flash of a smile, before looking away. Nate's visible reaction to realising he'd pushed Vera away — just when he had got her back — clashed with the reaction Elsie expected.

"Didn't you hear me?"

"Oh — sorry. That's great, Elsie!" The insincerity rang in his voice.

Elsie slumped back, defeated. "I thought you'd be happy to leave. It… it means they think you'll be okay."

Nate flinched his eyes shut. He knew he should be happy. But he also knew that if he went home, the reality of his broken hand would be sorely felt. He wouldn't be able to go back to his daily routine, and he'd know it. He couldn't drive, he couldn't play music — what could he do? Just mope around the house? He inhaled deeply, then looked at Elsie, forcing a smile in an emulation of relief, while his eyes continued to tell another story. "Sorry, I'm just a bit," he swooshed words around in his head. "Overwhelmed?"

Vera cleared her throat, but still didn't look at him. "Well, it'll be one more day of observation, and the nurses said you'll feel off for a while. You'll need someone to be around you at all times." Elsie shot her hand up. "You *really* don't want to go to school, do you?"

Nate was too fixated on Vera avoiding his eye contact to be worrying about Elsie avoiding school. "Nice of you to want to look after me, Elsie, but maybe someone who can drive?" Vera finally looked at him — a pointed glare that seemed to accuse him of bad parenting. "And, you know, doesn't have to go to school?"

A smile crept across Elsie's face as she watched her father keep looking back over her shoulder. "You mean... Vera?" Elsie raised her eyebrows suggestively. "Smooth, Dad. Smooth."

Nate flushed red. "Actually, I was going to ask..."

"Who?" A flicker of hope revealed itself in Elsie's voice. "Tommy?"

Nate was caught by the suggestion unexpectedly. "No, not Tommy." The brief memory of his drunken confessions was blinked away as Nate recomposed himself. "I thought maybe Jason could help." For all the offers of help Jason had ever given him, all the times he came by or called him or helped out unasked, this would be the first time that Nate had actually considered actively reaching out to him for help.

"Dad, Jason is pretty freaking busy."

"Well, I'm sure Vera has a lot to do as well."

"I don't, actually." She mentally scolded herself for letting the words slip out.

"*See* Dad? And didn't Jason tell us they were going on a family holiday next week?"

Nate's brow furrowed. He couldn't remember that discussion at the ARIAs, but then, there were a lot of details about that night that he still couldn't remember — blame that on drinking, rather than the accident, though. He decided to give Elsie the benefit of the doubt. "Well, then... Vera, could Elsie stay with you for a while? And I'll just... stay home."

"But then who will look after you?"

"I'll be fine. I can look after myself. I've always managed before."

Elsie looked dubiously at the sling on Nate's arm, while he clenched his jaw in defiance.

After a long pause, Vera dropped her crossed arms, and broke the silence. "Why don't you both just... stay with me?"

Elsie and Nate both turned to look at her, the three of them thinking through the logistics.

"But you only have one bed and a couch," Elsie wiggled her eyebrows again. "Even smoother, Vera!"

Vera rolled her eyes and addressed Nate. "We... can find a way? Or I could stay with you,"
she faltered as she saw a shift in his expression, a cheeky smile threatening to spread across his face. "It's up to you."

Nate mock-frowned, seeing what he hoped was an opening. "Well, that *is* a difficult decision."

Disc 4

Forty-Three

Nate's journey from his bed to Vera's car the following afternoon left him feeling as powerless as he had when constrained to the bed.

From the moment he'd swung his legs onto the floor, it felt like they were going to slip out from under him. He'd been under the influence of a number of substances in his life that had affected his coordination and locomotion, so righting himself in this situation, he thought, would be a breeze. But, the removal of the catheter and the nurse helping him to the bathroom for the first time made him realise that he would be more dependent than he'd feared. He hoped that it was just a matter of getting used to being on his feet again — his hand was the only part of him that had sustained notable injury — and that by the time Vera and Elsie were able to escort him out, he would be back to normal. He had assumed that, aside from his hand, he would be basically back to normal. Instead, while the effects of the anaesthetic had worn off, the symptoms of whiplash persisted. His entire body ached when he moved, and he felt like falling asleep at every moment. Maybe it was his body's way of telling him that he should let himself heal? Most likely, it was his body suffering through an amount of trauma that he hadn't really been given the chance to recover from.

He refused the wheelchair offered by the hospital. "It'll only take us to the front of the hospital, anyway," he joked, but only to justify his stubbornness. Stepping away from the bed, he stumbled, causing Vera to reach out and grab him, scolding him when he tried to snatch his arm away. He thought of Dr Preskov and his advice: once again restating when he'd done his discharge checkup, of being nice to his ladies and accepting their help. He gingerly allowed her to put his arm over her shoulders while she slipped hers around his waist to steady him and catch him should he fall. The feeling of her hand holding his body against hers did nothing to actually steady him; instead, it brought to mind more and more details of their one night together.

Finally, they arrived at the car, painkillers acquired from the overpriced hospital pharmacy. Nate felt aware that he likely smelled like shit, and regretted that his sense of self-sufficiency and pride caused him to refuse a wheelchair. He was aware enough that smelling like shit isn't the same as having a *masculine musk* and that it couldn't be endearing him to Vera. He hoped that he was wrong, that his quick shower at the hospital and the new clothes Elsie had brought him had been his allies.

He regarded Vera, still avoiding eye contact, but being as pleasant and helpful and *nice* as ever. Despite having physically supported him all the way, he could tell she was angry at him. If he was pressed to put in a complaint, there'd be nothing he could find. It was more the absence of openness that he felt, rather than anything cruel or mean. He felt an ache in his chest — he hadn't intended to hurt her, but he could tell that he had. He was used to people either getting over his outbursts quickly, or deciding that he wasn't worth being around. It felt like Vera couldn't decide. He didn't want her to make that decision.

"Hey," he squeezed her shoulder, then let it drop down, grazing her back. As she stepped away and pulled her arm out from around him, she looked up at him. This time, he was ready, the full intensity of his gaze on her. "I'm sorry about snapping at you, before. I was—"

"It's okay; I understand." She rubbed the back of her neck absent-mindedly; she knew he'd snapped at her because he was upset, that he wasn't angry at her, that it was misdirected. It wasn't fair, but neither was the accident or the injury. But the way he looked at her now, the way he was apologising? It brought up memories of Steven trying to gloss things over with seduction. As much as Nate's luminous eyes could catch her, she tore herself away. "Let's get you in the car. Here," she reached out and opened the door, holding it between them. "Want me to help you to get in?"

Nate half-smiled, the rebuffal triggering a fear that this was all just sympathy on her part; that he'd misread her and she didn't really want to give him another chance. But, he didn't want to let it drop just because of his own fears. If she really wasn't interested anymore, then fine. But he had to try, even if it meant he could get rejected properly.

"It's really not okay. But thank you for understanding."

Vera nodded, and rolled her lips together. Nate reached up and placed his hand on hers, on top of the car door. She looked down at his hand, his *good* hand, a thousand conflicting thoughts drowning out any decisive action or reaction.

"Hurry up!" Elsie called from the back seat, a welcome call to action to hide Nate's retreat. He slipped his fingers from hers, then eased himself down and into the passenger seat, an awkward shuffle of dizziness, weak legs, and only one hand to steady himself while he tried not to bump the other on anything.

Vera looked in at him, her face painted with concern. When he was settled and buckled in, he smiled up at her and batted his eyes sheepishly, the stubble on his grazed face turning his boyish charm into masculine vulnerability. She felt herself blush against her will as she closed the door for him.

Elsie leant forward to touch Nate on the shoulder. He placed his good hand on hers and squeezed it tight, as Vera climbed into the driver's side, clicked her seatbelt on, turned the ignition, flicked the lights on. She sighed, "Okay," and glancing back to Nate and Elsie, gently eased the car forward.

A memory of the accident tugged at Nate's memory, and he closed his eyes to try to shut it out. Fifteen or twenty minutes was all he needed to survive. The car slowed down and sped up a few times, rocking and soothing him, but the post-accident nausea kept him alert.

"Nate?"

He opened his eyes to see Vera looking at him, glancing back at the road periodically.

"You look pale. Should I pull over?"

He winced. "Just feeling a bit off. I'll be okay."

"Okay. We're almost there; see, Elsie's school, and now the cafe…"

"Mmhm," Nate nodded, closing his eyes again.

Before long, the car started slowing. "Okay," Vera unclicked her seatbelt. Nate followed suit, and made to reach for the door. "Don't get out without us helping you!"

Frustration flared once again in Nate. He was sure that he could do something as simple as getting himself out of the car. But, by the time he'd opened the door and swung his legs out, Elsie was there in front of him.

"I'll get you up," she cooed, an echo of what he used to say to her when she was a little girl. He couldn't help but concede, offering his arm to her and allowing her to pull him out, then draping his arm over her shoulder. "God, Dad! You stink." Confirmation.

Together they meandered up the path to the doorway where Vera had stood and looked back at him only four days earlier. This time, when Nate smiled at her shyly and she glanced down and back up in coyness, he let his smile grow more and more until they were close enough for her to back backwards to let him into her house.

"You get the couch," Elsie steadied Nate as he sat down. "Want a hot choc? Vera makes an awesome one."

Vera had backed herself nervously into the kitchen doorway, more aware of the boxes and afraid of Nate's judgement than she had been of Elsie's.

"Um, you can also have a tea or if you want coffee, I could make you instant, or quickly run to the cafe?" She checked her phone. "It might still be open." She glanced around at the disarray of her life, avoiding looking at Nate collapsed on the couch where she'd been sleeping the last few nights. So, he was well and truly in her life, now: not just on posters, but here, in the flesh.

"That's okay, I think I just need to lay down for a little bit." His attention was caught by the picture of Vera and Steven, lying forgotten on the coffee table. He recognised Steven and his dark good looks from the cafe, and was hit with the awareness that his own looks had faded, while Steven's had not; if anything, they'd improved since the photo was taken. Well — Steven was still young and in *his* prime, so that wasn't unexpected. He wondered: how long had they been together? How deep was their connection? Was Vera really as 'over' him as she had claimed? Elsie snatched the picture up, gave Nate a brief smile, and nudged Vera into the kitchen, dropping the picture in an open box on the way. Still unsettled, he shuffled himself back, kicked the slippers off his feet, and `manoeuvred` himself on the couch. He lay back, eyes closed.

"Should I take the hint that you'd like a hot chocolate, Elsie?" Vera put Nate's prescription painkillers on the kitchen counter, then propped her hands on her hips.

"What the hell, Vera?" Elsie hissed, her humour gone.

"What?" Vera turned to pull a pair of mugs from the cupboard.

"I mean," Elsie sighed, draping herself against the countertop, as though she could absorb the correct phrasing from its strength. "I dunno. You with Dad. You're being so... *cold*."

Vera looked back at her over her shoulder. She considered

defending or explaining herself, but instead let out a sigh of defeat.

Elsie watched her, focused on waiting for her response rather than trying to assume an answer from the lack of one. While she really wanted to wait long enough for Vera to get herself together and come to a cohesive conclusion, patience had never been her strong suit. "I just don't get why you're just... shooting him down."

"I'm not shooting him down," lied Vera.

Elsie scoffed. A faint snore from the lounge reassured Elsie that there was no chance that Nate was eavesdropping.

Vera's shoulders dropped, her bluff called. "I feel stupid. I know he didn't mean it. But—"

"Yep, he snapped at you. And he'll do it again," Elsie shrugged and shook her head. "That's him."

"It just... scares me a bit."

"*Scares* you?" Elsie blinked at the admission. "He's not going to do anything. He's just loud."

Vera conceded to herself that Nate's singing had often featured impassioned screams. He wasn't what she imagined he'd be like when she was Elsie's age, or even a few weeks ago when they'd first met. When she was young, he was older and a rockstar, brazen and reckless, yet with an unfailing mature warmth that she imagined he'd surround her with, and passionate anger that she imagined he'd use to protect her. Instead, she'd learned, he was just the same as her: damaged, flawed, prone to reacting out of fear more than logic, and wanting to be loved and accepted. She knew that he was trying, and Elsie was right: even though Elsie didn't really understand what Vera was so afraid of — that Nate would treat her as Steven, or even her own parents had — Elsie was right that he was just loud and was lashing out at a time when he felt not only scared, but that his fear wasn't being heard. She knew that his apology after had been sincere and deliberate, not manipulative. It wasn't fair to assume he was like Steven. It wasn't fair to Nate, and, Vera realised, it wasn't fair to herself, either.

"You're right," she sighed. "Now, did you want a hot choc?"

"Not really," Elsie smirked, then turned and walked back to the other room.

Vera sighed and put one mug away, then filled a mug with tap water. She found Elsie sitting on the floor in front of Nate. Vera put the mug down on the coffee table within arm's reach of Nate, and sat on the armchair. Elsie sighed and rested her head against Nate's hand, waking him accidentally.

He looked around the room, then focused on Elsie. "What are you doing on the floor? I should get out of your way."

"You're not in our way, Dad," Elsie giggled. "But I think we need to discuss sleeping arrangements." Even though it wasn't late in the day, this would be the first time any of them had been able to relax in a few days, and the prospect of an early night appealed to all of them.

Vera cleared her throat and did her best to seem warmer. "Are you comfortable where you are, or would you prefer the bed?"

Nate looked from one to the other. "I'm pretty sure I can sleep anywhere, but you two look like you've had it worse than me. I'll stay here, you two take the bed." His eyelids were heavy from codeine: discomfort wasn't part of his current experience.

"Are you going to be okay though, if you wake up in the middle of the night and don't know where anything is? I can sleep out here and you and Elsie sleep in my bed."

"No no, just put the telly on and I can find my way."

Vera looked at Elsie. "Okay, if you say so." She turned on the tv, turned down the sound, and put the remote on the coffee table next to the mug of water.

Elsie stood up and helped Nate get comfortable, rearranging the cushions under his head and the doona over him. He smiled like he was drunk, but in a soft, sweet way, then involuntarily yawned.

"You're tucking *me* in now?"

Elsie smiled, leant over and gave him a kiss on the forehead, another act that he'd done to her countless times. She walked to the bathroom, turning the light on and calling out, "Toilet's in here, Dad!" before walking inside to brush her teeth, closing the door behind her.

Nate couldn't help but laugh at his daughter, ruining a sentimental mood by switching her focus to function. He turned to Vera, who had eased herself from the armchair to kneel where Elsie had been, by his side. She gazed up at him, the first time since the previous morning that she'd held his eye contact. He wanted to take her in his arms, but realised he wasn't very capable of pulling her up to him. "Come here."

"But, I *am* here?" The sober look on her face eased when she saw the effect she had on him when, unexpectedly, she reached out and slipped her hand onto his chest.

"You know what I mean," he breathed out. He looked at her, no energy to do anything but adore her with his eyes. He put his hand on hers, pulling slightly to encourage her towards him.

She rose up and, as though taking a leap of faith, reached her other hand forward, wrapping it around his neck, pulling herself towards him, landing her lips on his, kissing him softly and sweetly. She pulled back to look at him, and he at her; absolute vulnerability and care. They both breathed a coy laugh, a flush on both their faces.

"Well, if there's anything you need during the night, call out. I'm a pretty light sleeper," her fingers tickled the hair at the nape of his neck as she hoped he'd pick up on the gentle allusion.

He did. "Maybe I'll just need you."

"Well then, you should have said you'd sleep in the bed." She slid the hand that was on his chest out from under his hand and brought it to his face, brushing her thumb along his jawline. He grabbed hold of her wrist to keep her from pulling her hand away.

"Is it too late to change my mind?" He pulled her thumb against his lower lip.

"Probably," she pulled her hand away gently and stood up, took a deep breath and ran her hands against her hips to recompose herself. She looked around, mentally checking that the tv was on, the remote where it should be, the mug of water filled, the curtains closed, and there was nothing in Nate's way.

"Night," he cooed, drawing her focus back to him.

"Good night," she adjusted the blanket around him, felt him graze his fingers along her arm. "Sweet dreams," she whispered before turning and making her way into the bedroom, glancing back to him occasionally.

Briefly disappointed but quickly overcome with fatigue, Nate settled back into the couch as he heard Elsie open the bathroom door, then fell asleep so quickly that he didn't hear any more.

Forty-Four

Nate woke to the room filled with light. The same sliver of light that had tried to wake Vera up previously was now snaking across the doona. His hand was searing with pain and he needed to pee. He opened his eyes and looked around, seeing Vera sitting on the armchair near him, watching the tv quietly. She noticed him moving and smiled.

"Good morning."

"What time is it?"

"Nine."

"Elsie needs to go to school."

"She already did."

The night before, while they were curled up facing each other as if they were *both* teenagers on a sleepover, Vera had warned Elsie that if she didn't go to school, she'd have to explain why to Nate.

"But I just want to stay with him while he recovers."

"But he won't want that. He'd want you to go to school."

Elsie pouted, sullen. "Mmm, but wouldn't he want me to look after him?"

"He'd want you to look after your education."

"Hmm," she searched for more excuses. "But what if *I'm* not ready? What if I need more time to process it all?"

"Elsie," Vera sighed. "You can't avoid this forever. If you don't go to school, you have to tell him why. The real reason. I still think you should talk to Vanessa about it, too."

Elsie sighed, snuggling down further under the blankets. "I guess I'll go to school."

Even though she'd dragged her heels that morning, she was true to her word.

"That doesn't seem like my Elsie."

"No; but I can be persuasive."

Nate smirked at the thought of Vera, seemingly so gentle and soft, being able to get her way through unknown skills of rhetoric. "I really appreciate you looking after her, I hope you know it's not something I *expect* you to do."

Vera could see the pain on Nate's face as he sat up. "Are you okay?"

"Painkillers wore off, I guess?" he attempted a smile, and held one hand with the other. He braced himself to get up, but realised that Vera had brought them in, and he didn't know where they were. Even if he did, getting them out of the blister pack would be impossible for him. "Can you get some for me?"

Vera got up quickly, found them where she'd left them on the kitchen counter. She read the instructions as she popped a couple of pills out, picked up the mug of water from the coffee table, and handed them both to Nate, one after the other. She counted in her head. "Next are at three in the afternoon."

He nodded, drowning the pills with water. The coffee table was barely out of reach for him, prompting him to shuffle and swing his legs off the couch to get up. Vera moved to help him, but he batted her away. "I'm fine, really."

"Come on, let me help you."

"I'm fine," he reaffirmed, as he let her take the mug off him.

She placed the mug on the coffee table and sat down next to him. "I know." She eased her hand under his arm, snaking it around to cautiously hold his. "I'm glad." She placed her other hand on his cheek, turning him towards her. Her thumb trailed down to his lips.

Nate looked from his hand to Vera's face. She was staring at his lips, biting her own slightly in anticipation. Amused, he watched while she mustered up the courage to lean forward and kiss him. He pulled back from the kiss, rolling his lips together to prolong the feeling of her lips on his. "Sorry to break the mood, but I feel gross, and I bet I don't taste much better. Do you have a towel I can use? And a spare toothbrush?"

"Sure," Vera, feeling slightly slighted, stood up and retreated into the bathroom where she rummaged around for a towel and a new toothbrush, while Nate proved that he didn't actually need her help to stand up. "Hm, you'll need a plastic bag or something, won't you?"

"What?"

"For your hand," she walked back to him and indicated his bandaged hand. "You're not meant to get it wet, are you?"

He looked down at the stump of bandages showing a hint of dried blood. "I guess not."

Vera continued her rummaging: this time, in the kitchen. "Cling wrap?" She pulled the plastic out from the box and advanced towards him.

He stuck his arm out and absorbed the plastic film onto his wrist and around his hand. "Gently?"

Vera hesitated, and carefully wrapped until his arm resembled a glossy cocoon that no water could penetrate. She nodded and looked pleased with her work, but it just made Nate more aware of how hard it would be to do *anything* in the shower. He smiled quickly in thanks, and headed to the bathroom. He closed the door behind him, but left it unlocked.

He turned the taps, and waited for the warm water, fiddling with one tap after the other until he got the water just right: warm and soothing, reassuring. He took twice, three times as long as usual to do anything. Shampoo got in his eyes, he dropped the soap more than a few times, and brushing his teeth with the wrong hand was a minor nightmare.

While towelling off, he saw himself in the mirror, unexpected bruises and shallow grazes dotting his form. He realised he didn't have any clothes aside from the now-dirty ones that Elsie had given him at the hospital. *Shit.* He tried wrapping his towel around his waist, but it was seemingly impossible to get the towel around him with one hand. He gave up.

"Vera?" he called. Predictably to anyone but him, she opened the door to answer him. He quickly hid himself with the towel, half-dropping it in the process. "Er, um, no need to come in," he informed her, too late to matter. She turned away from him, hiding a coy smile. "I just wondered if you had any spare clothes I could borrow?"

Vera hadn't thought of that. She knew Elsie had grabbed a couple of things quickly, but that was probably what he wore home. She couldn't really blame her for only getting one set of clothes — Nate staying at Vera's hadn't been the plan that night. "Just let me see, I might have something." She closed the door behind her.

Shit. What could Vera give Nate to wear? She wracked her brain for something that might fit him. She probably had some spare tracksuit pants, and an oversized promotional t-shirt she would have won somewhere along the line that made the assumption that Men's Shirts are Unisex Shirts. She rummaged through her drawers and triumphantly found both a shirt she used to wear to sleep and tracksuit pants that should work. As for underpants, she'd have to look through Elsie's bag to see if she'd grabbed more than one pair for him. She decided not to worry for now and rushed back to Nate; at least he would have *something* to wear. She knocked on the bathroom door, and slowly pushed it aside. Knowing she would see Nate naked apart from the towel filled her with a nervous tension.

"I found a t-shirt and some tracky dacks, you can borrow socks but it's probably best if we take a trip to your place to pick up things you need — what do you think?" She placed the clothes down over the towel rack, doing her best to avoid looking at anything.

Nate looked at her, flushed and nervous. He was feeling bad about pulling back when she'd attempted to take the lead this morning. He'd been thinking about how best to reassure her that he wasn't rejecting her; he decided to employ all the tactics in his arsenal. "Well, *Vera*... maybe everything I need is right in front of me?"

She looked up at him, startled. She was caught by the expression in his eyes, intense and magnetic. Her gaze dropped to his mouth, trailed down his neck, to his collarbone, down his chest... before she caught herself and met his eyes. He was smiling, enjoying watching her look at him. He stepped forward to her, his mouth finding hers, locking down, drawing her into him. He dropped the towel and wrapped his arms around her. She gasped, feeling him against her, reflexively running her hands along his neck and back, her fingers touching bare skin all the way down; one of his own hands moving down beyond the curve of her hip and pulling her closer. Her eyes stayed closed, the intoxicating fresh scent of him seducing her and making her feel groggy with desire. He kissed her cheek, her neck, her shoulder. She nuzzled into his neck, her lips catching against his skin, finding herself wanting to devour him.

She opened her eyes, but in a flood all her fears came chasing her. Would she ever live up to what he'd experienced before? Was she good enough? How long before he looked for her replacement? She recoiled, her desire extinguished. She pulled away from him, knocking his bandaged hand with her shoulder. He swore, wincing in pain, and looked at her: rejected and confused.

She threw her hand over her face, pinching the bridge of her nose. "Sorry," she mumbled. "I can't right now." She turned and fled, slamming the door behind her.

Nate stood, staring at the door in shock. It had happened so quickly that he didn't know whether it was something he'd done, and picking up the t-shirt that she'd left him, he began running everything through his head. Did he come on too strong? Maybe she needed more time. Maybe he should let her take the lead. He really didn't know. He should apologise, just in case. Cautiously, he slipped his bad hand through one sleeve, his head and his other hand through, putting the t-shirt on with more ease than he expected. The tracksuit pants were more of a struggle, but nothing he couldn't achieve with focus. He looked around and found a pink tube of aerosol deodorant, and decided that smelling like flowers was likely better than the alternative. He looked down at his hand, still wrapped in plastic and perfectly dry. He picked away at it, pulling at it with increasing frustration that merely built to make it harder and harder to unwrap. He finally gave up, opened the door, and stepped out.

Vera was sitting on the couch, and turned to look back as he came through the door.

"Sorry," they both said at the same time. Vera furrowed her brow. "What are *you* sorry for?"

"I don't know," he admitted. "I'm sorry I don't know."

"You don't have anything to be sorry for. I just, um," she blinked a few times, and breathed in to steady herself. "I think I'm still a bit… hesitant."

When Vera could follow her thought process, she was always able to unpack things perfectly, and move towards resolving them. But this was a flood of illogical emotional reactions to something that *should* have been pleasurable, desirable, correct, and good. She liked him, she wanted him, and he liked and wanted her. And yet, her subconscious mind evoked images of him enjoying himself with faceless figures whose forms were all more perfect than hers. Her mind blurred this with the image of Steven and Sarah, the victorious look on the latter's face, the hopeful look on his. '*Sorry,*' he'd said to her. But even he'd admitted it was '*Sorry you caught me,*' or, '*Sorry you found out this way,*' not, '*Sorry I hurt you.*' And then there was Nate, '*Sorry I don't know.*' There was a selflessness to him that didn't seem plausible to her. Not after being with Steven for so long.

Defeated, she dropped forward, her face falling into her hands, her elbows on her knees.

Nate edged around the couch and stood in front of her. "Can I sit with you?"

Softened by his softness, she looked up. "Of course."

He sat down, inspecting her face, chewing his lips in thought. "You know," he cooed eventually, picking absentmindedly at his plastic and plaster wrapped hand, "I don't expect anything of you. I just wanted to," he batted his eyelashes and swallowed. "I don't know. Make you feel good."

She let out a puff of a laugh, and leant against his shoulder. She took his bandaged hand and started working on unwrapping the plastic. "I know; that's what gets to me."

It was a concept both totally foreign to Nate, yet absolutely known. He'd had so many girls and women want to make him feel good, to force him to verify their desirability and worth, that it had become disgusting and repulsive to him. Vera's hesitancy was one of the things that drew him to her in the first place. But it wasn't as though Vera had been through this, had she? He supposed that he still didn't really know her enough to know this. He didn't know what her past relationships had been like, what her parents had been like, who had done what to her to make her feel uncomfortable when someone wanted to adore her.

She turned to him apologetically. "Stupid, isn't it? I don't even understand it."

"Well, whenever you're ready..." he trailed off, letting her fill in the rest. He'd made up his mind to trust her, that her pulling back wasn't about him; he wasn't going to let her fears get in the way of that. He snuck his face next to hers, giving her a gentle, tender kiss on the cheek. "Until then? Maybe let's get me some more clothes. These tracksuit pants are really *not* cut for men." He went to stand up, but she gently pulled him back down.

"Thank you," she said, her eyes welling up.

He grinned. "Come on."

Forty-Five

Vera and Nate sat in silence, the radio filling in the blanks in their conversation. Vera kept watch on the road; Nate's jaw clenched, some primaeval part of him going into self-preservation mode in an attempt to protect against past trauma. As they pulled to a stop at some lights, Vera looked across at him. He sighed and looked out the window, not wanting to see her regarding him with disappointment or, worse, pity. She reached out, placing her hand on his knee. It just made him slump further into the seat.

Turning back to the road, Vera stared at the street in front of her, waiting for red to turn to green. Nate looked down to his bandaged hand. He stared at it as though he was willing it to just burn off. Vera could feel his anger radiating from him.

She wanted to say something, but she didn't know what. She wanted to tell him that it would be okay, that it would heal, that he just had to take it slow. But she knew that wasn't the type of reassurance that he needed. She'd learned that now.

Green.

She eased on the accelerator. Trees and houses flew past. Still, he sat staring at his hand. Finally, he sighed and looked up.

He'd been trying to wiggle his fingers. He knew that it was hard to move them even before the surgery, but he'd somehow hoped that was just from the pain and that he'd be able to move them now that his bones had been reinforced. Instead, it felt like there was even *less* movement than before. How was this supposed to help? He wished that his hand had just been torn right off. At least that way there'd be no hope left, and he could just grieve it and get on with his life. But now? He didn't know whether he'd recover or not. Dr Preskov had reassured him that he likely wouldn't need a second surgery, and that there would be no long-term damage as long as he allowed it to heal and took his physical therapy seriously — but was there even any point?

One of his songs came on the radio. It started with a brilliant piano intro. Instantly, without a word, Nate reached across and switched the station. It flicked to the classical station — another piano concerto. He flicked again- jazz. Jazz *piano*. The radio was taunting him. He switched it off.

"You know this means you have to talk to me," Vera teased, an undercurrent of nervous hesitation in her voice.

"Mm, yes, sorry," Nate responded quickly, if not enthusiastically. "Sorry, it's not that I don't want to talk to you—"

"It's that you don't want to talk. I get it."

"Yeah," he turned to her. He watched the way the late morning sun attacked her eyes as she drove east. The sun sparkled from her face, evoking sounds and harmonies in his mind. If he could get to his keyboard...

She turned at the sound of his frustration.

"You look beautiful, you know?"

"You sound angry about it."

"It's really not that. I'm sorry," he reached out as they slowed to a halt at another set of lights. He stroked her arm gently with his good hand, reaching around awkwardly.

"You don't need to be sorry. I just want to understand."

Nate turned back to look forward. He didn't like talking about his thoughts. Feelings he could put in poetic nonspecific phrases, translate into music. Thoughts felt verbose, periphrastic. It was probably his own lack of practice, but it always felt laborious and other people misunderstood everything he said, just making it even more frustrating. He looked down at his hand again, the source of his power, lost. What if he never got movement back?

Vera pulled up and parked along the leafy street in front of Nate's house. She gave him a look that said, *stay there*, and opened her door to get out. Nate opened his door and waited patiently for her to appear in front of him, to help him out. He looked sullen, so she made a big show of putting out her hand to him as though they were meeting for the first time. "Oh my God — are you *Nate Whitely?*"

Her unexpected playfulness broke him out of his spiral. "Why yes, I am. And," he was looking at her with a softness that suddenly turned cheeky, with a grin he was unable to suppress. He placed his hand in hers and together they pulled him up, then, leaning forward, he pulled her towards him and whispered into her ear, "I'm not wearing any underpants."

She'd almost forgotten how quickly he, like Elsie, could change from one mood to the next. She laughed, pulling back and looking up at him. She was relieved to see a real smile on his face for the first time since she'd visited in the hospital — if not before. It really was beautiful, the energy that was in his face; it was the sort of thing that buoyed you up and made you feel really special. The charisma that had earned him a billion fans and admirers, once upon a time, was all directed at Vera.

"Come on, let's go inside," she laughed.

"Not into a bit of exhibitionism?"

"Stop it, come on."

His face dropped in feigned disappointment. "Worried someone might see? The tabloids would love it. Could re-launch my career…" With a wink, he let go of her, resigning himself to the duty of unlocking the door using Elsie's keys. He went to unlock the door with one hand and turn the doorknob with the other —

"Fuck this."

"What?"

He turned to her, sullen again, held out the keys. "I need both hands."

"You can have my hands."

"That's a dangerous offer."

She tutted at him, to which he responded with a cheeky wink. She unlocked the door and opened it for him, stepping back to allow him to step inside before her. He walked up the stairs, into his room to collect what he'd need for the next few days.

Vera wandered around downstairs, looking out the windows. This was the first time she'd been there during the day, and the light shattered in through the leaves of the trees outside. It was the kind of space that felt inspiring.

There was a bang from upstairs and a shout. Vera ran up the stairs, taking two at a time. She stood at the threshold to Nate's room, expecting to see him on the ground in pain. Instead, there was a mess of clothes on the floor, including an open bag.

"I thought I could carry it," he looked up at her, ashamed. Hesitantly, he forced out the next part of his thought, "I don't want to ask for your help."

She walked forward without saying anything, knelt down, and picked up the bag. "What do you want to take?"

Together, they collected enough clothes to ensure Nate wouldn't look too much like a hobo.

Nate started yawning as they zipped the bag up.

"Are you okay?"

"Yeah, just tired." He sat down on the bed. Vera sat next to him. "Do you mind if I just nap for a bit?"

She brushed his cheekbone gently with one hand, where he was nursing a graze. "Of course not." She stood up, watching him struggle to get on the bed. She helped him take his shoes off and manoeuvre himself until he was lying down on his back. She climbed onto the bed next to him, coyly sitting at his side until he looked over at her and reached out. She found her space beside him, his arm curled around to bring her closer, his heartbeat playing music to her ear. Every part of him was a musician.

Her fingers ran along his breastbone, and she felt him breathe deeper and deeper, slower and slower, until he was peacefully asleep. Vera found herself to be sleepier than she expected, too. Maybe it was because of the strain of the last few days, or maybe it was because of the safety she found next to him. She opened her eyes and looked up at him: *Nate Fucking Whitely*. The reckless rockstar she'd adored in videos, whose voice she could recognise on the radio, whose reflections on life had echoed and given meaning to her own. She was there, in his arms. So many times, she'd fantasised about what it would be like to meet him, to know him, to be with him, but she'd never imagined it would be quite like this. He was both the person she'd imagined, yet wildly different.

He brought his bandaged hand up to rest over his stomach, suddenly in her line of sight. *His hand.* She knew he relied on it: it was one of his tools for expressing himself. She wished that she could heal it, make it better. But, he was so much more than just his hand, or his music. His music was just a channel for his emotional honesty and courage to be expressed. He was capable of doing that without the music, but the music he was capable of creating had captivated her and half the world with its sincerity and its resonance. What she'd adored him for when she didn't know him was the same thing that caused her to fall for him when she met him. It was the same thing that was so lacking in Steven: Nate was emotionally honest. She might not always understand him or the thoughts going through his head, but she could always trust in knowing how he felt. And when he looked at her the way he did that morning, she knew he felt a lot for her.

Forty-Six

⏮ ⏸ ⏭

Nate woke up, the pain in his hand steadily increasing. Vera was asleep next to him, her hair fallen haphazardly over her face. He looked towards the window, relieved that they hadn't slept for too long. He struggled his way into a seated position, then looked down at Vera again. Her eyes were now open. She sniffed, and checked her watch.

"Oh wow, it's almost three," she stretched out. "Oh! Three — you need more painkillers. Are you feeling okay?"

"Ah, actually it's what woke me up."

"Okay, well, we'd better get you back home. I mean," she shook her head. "Back to my place. Hm, Elsie will be back soon as well." She reached over to him, rubbing his back gently. "You okay?"

"Yeah," he swung his legs over, pushing himself up with his good hand. "I, uh," he looked coyly back at her. "I want to get something before we leave." He slid his feet into his shoes and sighed. "And I'll need help with my shoes. Why did I never buy loafers?"

Vera smiled to herself as she moved to crouch at his feet, tying his laces like an adult ties a child's. She stood up and picked up the bag they'd packed hours ago. "Okay, what do you need to get?"

Nate was already out of the room and down the stairs. Vera followed him, weaving through doorways to what looked like a basic home studio setup. He walked over to a mini keyboard synth and picked it up. "I don't have to lose use of *both* my hands," he smirked. Vera helped him pack it up and bring it with him.

Together, they packed everything into the car, the synth and the bag in the back, and the two of them in the front. Vera started the ignition. "Can I turn the radio on?" She turned to Nate.

"I will," he said, reaching over. He flipped between a few channels until he found one playing a song he'd once covered as a b-side. He chuckled and started singing along. His voice was hoarse and his throat sorer than expected, but that just made it sound like he was mimicking the original artist. Vera got lost in the freedom and spirit of his impromptu performance, reminding her even more of the Nate Whitely who she'd seen on the television, whose voice captured her heart all those years ago. His voice had the same humour, the same expression, even more control and a hint of cynical sorrow that made it all the more bittersweet to listen to. Vera wished he'd sing forever, and that she never had to stop listening. She felt too self-conscious to sing along with Nate, as much as she used to imagine it. She just smiled, enjoying this side of him in person for the first time. She realised that this was the first time she'd actually heard him sing *live*. The thought of this, of the yearning she'd had for him to tour, made her feel young and giddy, and it was the closest thing she'd felt to the way she'd imagined him all those years ago when her admiration for him was a schoolgirl crush. She could only imagine how Elsie would have felt meeting Tommy. But how had Tommy treated her? It sounded innocent enough, but were the two of them on the same page? She made a mental note to ask her about it, to get the gossip that had been denied in the last two nights.

They pulled up at Vera's house not long after three-thirty, and Elsie was sitting on the doorstep. Her face was covered in tears and she was staring down into her phone.

Nate's face fell, and he and Vera exchanged glances. An unspoken agreement passed between them, and Vera parked and hopped out of the car, as Elsie stood up and rushed over to her, hugging her.

"Did we worry you?" Vera walked her towards the passenger door, which Nate had pushed open. "We were just at your house, picking up some things."

Elsie wiped her face and looked up at them. "No; no, this isn't about you two."

"Did something happen at school?" Nate tried his best to control his tone, but the question still came across as accusatory.

"I told them I met Tommy and they said they saw on tv and they bet that I, um…" Elsie's chin quivered. She hid her eyes from Nate and turned to Vera to confide in her, "…they bet that I slept with him."

Nate felt anger rising, bubbling up between them. Vera glanced back at him, placating him with a stern 'let me handle it' look.

"I was going to ask you about Tommy, I realise we haven't had a chance to talk about him," Vera cooed.

"You didn't, did you? I'll break his neck if you did," the words slipped out of Nate's lips before he had a chance to catch them.

"No! Oh my God, Dad," she strained against Vera's arms. "Why would I even do that?" She shook her head, then turned to Vera. "We just, like, talked, is all."

"Why are they saying this about you then?" Nate's tone remained accusatory.

Elsie hung her head and cried, feeling the strain of having nowhere to turn without being accused.

"Some horrible kid named David has been spreading rumours," Vera spat at Nate pointedly.

"David? You mean that pimply kid that has a crush on you?" Nate leant back in the car seat. "What a little dickhead. Why aren't your friends shutting him up? Are they listening to him? Is this why you came home from that sleepover?"

"Dad," Elsie wanted nothing more than to make the whole thing go away, and especially didn't want to dodge Nate's spitfire attack. "Just forget it, okay? It'll blow over."

"It really won't, Elsie."

"Yes, it will! And anyway, what are you going to do? Punch him with your broken hand?"

Nate was dumbfounded by the attack, more embarrassed than angered. The pain, fueling but forgotten during his anger, throbbed as a reminder of his weakness.

"Come on Elsie, that was unfair." Vera tried to soothe her, prepared for Elsie to turn and spit her venom on her. She could take it.

Instead, Elsie just nodded. "I know. You just want to protect me. Sorry, Dad."

Vera was impressed by Elsie's self control, and hoped that there wasn't sarcasm that she couldn't detect. She looked from Elsie to Nate. She looked defeated, but he looked destroyed. "Elsie, will you take my suggestion and talk to Ness about it?"

Elsie looked up at her, glanced at Nate, and nodded.

Vera pulled out her phone, and scrolled through, looking for Vanessa's number. Elsie and Nate both stared at nothing while Vera waited for her call to be answered.

"Hey, Ness? Can you come to my place after work? Or to the cafe? As soon as possible... yes, everything's okay. Just need your advice." She watched Elsie, her lip trembling, avoiding eye contact with her father. "Yes, it's about what I talked to you about before."

Nate couldn't stop himself from spiralling out of frustration, his protective drive going into overdrive. He turned in his seat, pulled himself to stand, and started spitting attacks on both Elsie and Vera. "Wait, you've talked to Vanessa about this? How long have you both been hiding this from me? How long has this been going on?"

"I don't know Dad."

"What do you mean, you don't know? You must know. How long?"

"I don't know! A couple of weeks?"

"A couple of weeks!" he turned to Vera, stepping forward threateningly. "And you knew about this?"

Vera turned pale. "Kind-of."

"What do you mean, *kind-of?*" he rubbed his brow and staggered back, sitting down in the car again. The pain of his hand merged into the pain in his heart. "Why did no one tell me anything? You're already avoiding telling me things. *Fuck's sake!*"

"Dad, it's not Vera's fault! I told her not to tell you."

"Why didn't you tell me, Vera?"

"I..." her jaw shook with fear. She felt herself paralysed, learned helplessness silencing her.

"Dad, stop it! This is my problem." She threw her hands up, standing up suddenly. "God! This is why I can't tell you *anything!* You just explode if you can't fix it instantly." She walked to the car, spitting her words in his face. "You can't fix *everything*, Dad!" She turned and stormed off. Nate awkwardly went to stand again, reaching to try to grab her wrist. His reflexes were too late — she was soon out of their sight.

Nate looked across at Vera. Why hadn't she told him? Didn't she trust him? This was his own daughter, too — he should know what she's going through. Vera didn't have a right to know more about Elsie's life than he did. He suddenly felt as though he couldn't control anything: not his daughter, not his life, not anything. He sank back into the car seat, and turned to the person still with him.

Vera could feel his eyes burning into her. She felt it building, melting away all of the feelings of calm and joy that she'd felt for him that afternoon. She couldn't find a way to say all the words she wanted to say — about him yelling at her, about him not helping things, about him not understanding, about him needing to calm down, about him scaring her, about him breaking her heart when he was like this — instead, she swallowed them, picked up her bag, fished inside for her keys, and let herself into her house, closing the door quietly behind her.

Nate was left alone, sitting in the passenger seat of Vera's car, full of rage and feelings of betrayal, feeling out of control and lost. He just had the two people he cared about the most walk away from him. He just wanted to love and protect them, but instead, it seemed that all he did was let those desires get the better of him and hurt them until they couldn't take him anymore. Was this who he was: someone who pushed people away so easily? He'd always assumed that people were always so quick to walk away from him, but he wondered whether it was always all his fault, that he was the one who pushed *them* away. He sunk back into the seat, full of disappointment in himself.

Vera still hadn't come back outside, and Elsie hadn't come back. He needed to go after them, not the other way around. He knew that. Elsie would be easier to placate — she was used to him, unfortunately. Vera? Well, he didn't want to let his anger push her away, too. He sighed, and spun his legs out of the car. Standing up, he steadied himself with his good hand, and opened the seat behind him. He looked at the bag and the keyboard. He looked to Vera's front door. He made the decision that he probably couldn't carry either of them and be able to open the door. So, he shut both doors on the passenger side, and walked to the door.

It was locked.

He wasn't sure whether Vera had intended to lock it, but it was locked.

He walked back to the car, re-opened the back door, picked up the keyboard, and sat in the back seat. He gave himself a mental pat on the back for getting one with battery power. He turned it on, and started picking out notes with his one still good hand. He had to forgo picking out a melody, but he still was able to console himself, picking out melancholy harmonies to match his mood. He hummed along and tried using his bad hand to pick out one note at a time, but the pain began to be unbearable. He thought of Dr Preskov's warning not to over-strain his hand now while it was healing. He blinked back his tears, and leant back in his seat. He started planning what he wanted to say when he saw Vera. '*You locked me outside,*' would be his complaint. '*In pain.*'

Breathing in a shaky breath, he saw movement out of the corner of his eye. Vera stood in the doorway — like the night he'd first come here to look for Elsie — watching him, her eyes red and her face blotchy. She held his painkillers in one hand, and water in the other. Her mouth twisted when he looked at her; she took a breath to steady herself, and walked over to him. The locked door must have been an accident, he reasoned.

"I'm sorry," he said, when she got within earshot.

"You can't just keep... saying *sorry* all the time," she handed him the pills, then the mug.

He swallowed them and hung his head, nodding it like a little kid. "What do you want me to say? I feel bad enough as it is, and I mean it."

"It's not about what you say, it's about what you do." Confusion flashed across his face, forcing her to clarify. "I don't like when you talk to me like that. When have I ever done anything to make you think I'm hiding anything from you?"

"But you were — you didn't tell me about this."

"That was in Elsie's confidence. As her *friend*. And, seeing how you reacted, I see why she didn't tell you."

Nate's face fell. He grasped for an explanation, a reason.

"Nate, Elsie is going through something really hard. She doesn't need you attacking her as well, doubting her, asking what she did to bring this on herself. That's really not fair."

"I don't need you telling me how to treat my daughter!"

"Do you really think she deserves any of this happening to her?" Vera scoffed. "I've only known her a few weeks and even I know that she's utterly undeserving. It's these horrible kids at her school, not her, who are to blame. No one taught them how to lose well."

Nate looked down, his hands on the keyboard. He looked at his bandaged hand, the part of him that he was losing, that he was still struggling with. He closed his eyes tight and took a deep breath.

"Does her father know how to lose well?"

"Maybe not." She'd expected him to say yes, to say something about teaching these kids what it meant to be an adult, and that it meant that you lose sometimes. "I mean... I thought I'd lost when you left in the middle of the night. But I wasn't sure, and I didn't want to lose. So I made you lose." He paused, avoiding her eyes. "I don't like losing."

Vera was taken aback by his admission. After a while, he looked up at her and smiled apologetically, hopeful she'd understand. She blinked back tears. "I... don't think anyone does." She reached out and stroked his hair. He softened, reassured by her touch. "All I could think of was how I couldn't compare to you. If I wasn't enough for my ex, how could I be enough for you? *Nate Fucking Whitely?*"

"But that's such bullshit," he laughed. "Why would you—"

"No, seriously," she was taken aback by his laugh. "All I could think about was all the... I dunno, *thousands* of people you've slept with before, and how I was probably the worst of the lot. So why would you want *me?*"

He looked at her incredulously, lost for words.

They swam in their silence, her standing, him sitting. Snatches of thoughts passed through both of their minds: did she think that's all that mattered to him, did she know so little about him? Is he silent because it's true, he doesn't want to lie but he doesn't want to admit the truth? And neither could know what the other was thinking, the questions they had, the fears they held.

Nate drummed his fingers on the keys, letting out a little trill. He looked up to her. "Not that something like *that* even matters, but... you shouldn't think that you're not enough for me."

Vera nodded, hearing what he was saying but not sure she was agreeing.

"Vera, you are so much more than me. You're smarter than me. More talented. Kinder."

"I am not more talented, how on earth can you think that?"

"I worked hard. Music is skill and inspiration. You have so many talents. You're just good at so many things — things that you can't just grind away at, things that have to be natural at before anything else. And whoever made you feel you weren't, well they should fuck right off."

Suddenly she could see him as a little boy, a young man, spending hours doing exactly what he was doing now: drilling his fingers on instruments, working up the skill and coordination through practice, determined to make it feel natural, feel effortless.

"Well, whoever made you think you're not smart should fuck off, too."

Nate smiled, almost blushing from the flattery. Vera *was* very nice.

Vera looked around. "So how long does it usually take for Elsie to come back after storming off?"

Nate's face fell. "Oh, uh, it's more about how long she thinks it will take *me* to cool down, I think." He avoided her eyes.

Vera felt her phone buzz. She looked down at it, and saw a message from Vanessa saying she'd be at the cafe in ten minutes. "Hm, hopefully she's gone to the cafe."

"Would she, though? That's where she used to go with her supposed *friends* and that little underdeveloped shit David."

Vera realised that between her schoolmates at the cafe and Nate at Vera's place, Elsie had essentially been stripped of any known safe refuges: tracking her down might be hard. She reached out her hand to help him up. He put the keyboard down on the seat next to him, and took her hand. "Why don't you start taking your things inside?" She picked up his bag and handed it to him, then started replying to Vanessa, asking her to re-route to her place. "Oh, and get changed. It's obvious that you're not wearing underwear."

Nate nodded, taking the bag from her and slinging it over his shoulder, then attempting to pick up the keyboard as well. Aware that it was going to be too much, his face took on an ashamed set that Vera wouldn't even see. He couldn't carry everything — so he placed it back on the seat, and took his bag inside, trusting that Vera would bring it for him. Vera dialled Elsie. It rang, and rang, and rang. It went to her messages. Vera hung up. She sent her a quick message:

VERA: Ness is on her way here. Your Dad has calmed down, I'll lock him in the car if I have to

Then she leaned into the car to pick up the keyboard to take it into her home for Nate.

Forty-Seven

⏮ ⏸ ⏭

Elsie crouched on the side of the road, her phone against her ear, pouring out her heart into the microphone. On the other side, Tommy was having his heart broken about his musical icon, and getting a healthy reminder of the behaviour of young boys who want power over someone who has power over them.

"I don't know what to do about him," she sighed. Which *'him'* she was referring to was starting to get unclear to Tommy. He made a noncommittal, sympathetic sound of agreement. "I don't know how much more I can take it."

"It sounds pretty rough," he tried, hoping that if he stayed with her train of thought, he'd find out whether she meant David or Nate. "It's really not fair to you."

"It's *not*," she agreed. "I don't even understand why. Does he think it'll make me like him more?"

Ah, David. "Well of course not. But it's... I don't think it's about that."

"Why, then?"

"It's more about... it's about, like, desecrating you, I think?"

"I don't get it."

"Well... Have you heard the fable of the dog in the manger?"

"I... don't think so."

"It's about a hungry dog that goes into a barn. All the horses and cows are like, 'sure, our food is in the manger, help yourself.' The dog looks in, sees it's all hay and corn, and says, 'I can't eat this!' and climbs in to sleep. When it's dinnertime for the horses and cows, he like, won't move, and tells them, 'If I can't enjoy it, no one can.' So, I mean, if he can't have you, then he wants to make you *unwantable*, for him or for anyone else."

"That... that's kinda messed up."

"Yeah kid, it is."

"Is that seriously what he's doing?"

"Well, I'm not him. I can't really speak for him!"

"So why did you say it?"

"I hate to say it, but... I've *seen* it. Some guys I've known, they'll talk down a girl, pick on her, shit on her, anything they can do to, like, *punish* her... all because she said no to him. And we didn't know; we just assumed he was being honest with us because, you know, why would he lie to us?"

Elsie listened silently. There was a long pause that Tommy took to mean that he should continue.

"And it's *so* much easier to ruin people than to redeem them. People are... crazy, kid; and they want to feel like other people are shit, so they don't feel so wrong for being so shit themselves."

Tommy heard faint sobbing on the other side.

"Hey... Elsie? Where are you, anyway? I... I can come to you."

Elsie composed herself through her sniffles. "We're staying at Vera's. But I'm not there, I didn't know where to go. Dad just gets *so* mad and I can't deal with him, too."

"Where did you go?"

"I don't know. Not far. Just... somewhere on the side of the road."

"Can you find your way back to Vera's?"

"I don't know if I want to yet. Dad's probably still shitty."

"Nah, he'll be cool. As you said, he's just pissy that he can't help you."

"Why can't he just... stop being that way?"

"I dunno, kid. Maybe he just... can't. Maybe if he stopped, he wouldn't be able to make music? I always wanted to have anywhere near the level of... *rawness* that he has in my music. It's one of the things that I admire about him the most."

"You don't have to live with him and his moods."

"That's true, kid; I don't."

"I just... the worst part is the not knowing. I don't know if he'll be good now or not."

"Why don't you ask Vera? And then let me know if you go somewhere else. I'll meet you there. Okay?"

"Okay."

"Shoot me Vera's address?"

"Okay. Thanks, Tommy."

Elsie pressed the button on her phone to hang up on Tommy. She scrolled to her messages, and saw the one from Vera. She couldn't help but let out a small laugh at the thought of Vera locking Nate in the car. She replied quickly.

ELSIE: Okay, can Tommy come over too?

"She's... with Tommy, I think?"

"What?" Nate slammed down the takeaway coffee Vanessa had brought them.

"Maybe? The message asks if Tommy can come over," Vera came over to sit beside Nate on the couch.

"What's she doing with him?"

"She could just want to invite him," Vanessa chimed in from a cushion on the floor. "But not actually be with him right now. Problem solve together?"

"It doesn't take a genius to see she has a crush on him. All he'd have to do—"

"Nate, honestly? I don't think you have to worry about him." Vanessa turned to him. "I had a good talk with him while you were out cold in the hospital. He's a good guy."

"You don't know what it's like to be his age and a rockstar," he shook his head.

"Really. You're saying that you would have taken advantage of a fourteen-year-old?" It was Vera who turned to him, disgusted.

"Well, *no*, but—"

"But what?"

Nate shifted uneasily. "It happened."

"What?" Vera and Vanessa almost lunged at him in shock.

"I didn't do anything..." That familiar guilt enveloped Nate. No matter what he did, he never felt like he could run from it. Well, he'd promised himself that he'd let Vera in. If she and Vanessa learned about this and wanted nothing more to do with him, so be it. "Once, I walked in on... but, I wasn't... quite *well* that night; and I didn't do anything. Do you understand?"

The two women watched him as he struggled to articulate the feelings that they could see seeping up within him. Vera remembered reading or hearing something about the drugs they were doing, the paranoia and the panic attacks that caused show cancellations as the band began to fall apart. She felt him starting to tremble next to her. Whatever he was telling them, it frightened him. She reached her arms around him to steady him.

He could tell they didn't understand, but that they wanted to. His head fell forward, and he took a deep breath in before continuing. "She was saying no. She saw me and called out to me for help. I... didn't know what to do. I *didn't* do anything. I just walked away. I should have said something, done something. And when I thought back, I should have known it was coming. I just... thought he was joking." He closed his eyes firmly, and spoke with a strange intensity — almost as if he was repeating something he'd said countless times. "I wasn't well that night. I could barely keep myself together, but... I should have done something. But I didn't stop him."

Vera looked at Vanessa, whose fists were clenched in frustration and anger. This confession had stirred up something within her, something Vera didn't know about. She wished that she'd been better friends with Vanessa in high school, closer to her. She had always seemed older and just *different*. In high school, difference is bad; as adults, difference can help you grow, help you become more rounded, help you develop: it calls you to question yourself and everything you held to be true, helps you to find balance.

Vanessa let her frustration out in a hiss, started shaking her hands out. "Yes, you *should* have," it was a statement of agreement, not one of blame.

Startled back to the present, Nate opened his eyes and looked up at her, apology and fury and shame all over his face. "So, you know that... I can't let him do the same thing."

Vanessa pulled herself back together, straightening up. "*He* won't. Tommy is a good guy, I'm sure of it," she smiled quietly to herself, then leaned forward to put a hand on his shoulder. "Nate, you're a good guy, too."

Grief clouded both Nate's mind as well as his features. He turned to Vera, who had been quietly watching him, her arms somehow around him this whole time without him noticing. There was nothing but quiet concern on her face, the same expression as when he nearly told her the first time. *I'm sure you did the best you could at the time.* This great shame at what he hadn't done, this fear that he'd be considered a monster instead of an idol; it wasn't gone — it never would be — but in this space, he was accepted.

He thought about Tommy: so attentive to him, so polite to Elsie at the ARIAs. He knew he hadn't seen anything in him that was like his bandmate, but the rumour had triggered him. "I just... I don't know if..." He took a breath, pinched the bridge of his nose between his eyes. "I'm sorry. I can't control how I'll feel about him right now."

"Why don't you take a rest. You look..." Vera paused, the pause telling more that she was lying than the lie itself, "...*tired.*"

Nate nodded, then turned to Vanessa. "I'm sorry," he said, and the weight of his tone hinted at something beyond him needing to excuse himself. Vanessa gave a terse nod, saying nothing as Vera helped him up and walked him to the bedroom. They whispered words to each other, and she closed the door behind him and turned back to Vanessa.

"I don't want to talk about it," uttered Vanessa, turning away. "When do you think Elsie will get here?"

Vera knew when to leave a subject alone. "I... I don't know, I'm not sure where she is. Oh um, I think I'm meant to let her know that Tommy can come too." She buried herself in her phone, typing away a reply to Elsie, and then struggled for a reason to stay focused on her phone and away from the situation in front of her.

They stood together in silence, both aware of their disconnect.

Finally, Vera couldn't stand it any longer. "Ness, I don't need to know what happened, but whatever it was, I'm sorry that I wasn't a better friend when it did. You've always been amazing, but especially these last few weeks... much better than Sarah ever was." Vanessa regarded her, then walked over, putting first one arm and then the other around her.

"You know, you're a pretty special person, Ronnie. I don't know if you know it, but you are."

Nate wasn't the only one who liked seeing they could make Vera blush.

Forty-Eight

⏮ ⏸ ⏭

There was a meek knock at the door. Vanessa broke away from the hug to answer it. Tommy stood in front of her, hands in his pockets, sheepishly looking behind him. He turned and, at the sight of Vanessa, spread a huge smile across his face, incongruous with the brooding look he otherwise had a habit of sporting. "Just making sure I hadn't attracted any attention on my way over."

"Come in; we're still waiting for Elsie."

"Oh, okay," he stepped dramatically over the threshold. "So uh, how's the old man?"

"Nate? He's... well I don't think you should see him right now."

"Is he okay?"

"Well, yeah; it's more what Elsie told him they were saying about you."

"What? What do you mean?"

"She didn't tell you?" Vera looked at Vanessa. "I assumed that if you were coming over, she'd told you what they said."

Tommy turned an ashen shade of his regular paleness. "What did they say?"

"Well, um," Vera grasped for words. "What did she tell you?"

"Well this guy David is saying that she was sleeping with him, but she isn't, but he's saying she did and that she's a slut," he recounted.

Vera paused, desperately hoping that he'd fill in the rest of the story, extrapolate it to include himself. Tommy just looked at her, looked to Vanessa, looked back at Vera. There wasn't anything more to the story, as far as he was concerned. She wasn't sure if she could bring herself to tell him. Vanessa came to the rescue.

"They're saying that she slept with you, too."

Tommy stared at them, horrified and fearful of what might happen if the rumours got any traction. A single, tiny burst slipped from his lips. "Fuck."

"I... I have to ask, Tommy—"

"Fuck, no! It's not true. Aw man, that would be really fucked up if it was," he ran a hand through his hair. "Fuck, I shouldn't be here. It's incriminating." Understanding rippled across his features. "Does Nate think that I...? Fuck, I wouldn't. I mean, shit. Aside from her being a *kid*, I just met her, and... man, it's... that's not me."

Vanessa nodded. "We didn't think so. But it's harder for Nate to believe."

Tommy felt the stab of disappointment in his heart. "He thinks that of me?"

"Not *you*, no. Just—" Vera trailed off. It wasn't her story to tell. "Well, it's more that you wouldn't be the first guy to take advantage of a young girl's interest."

Tommy shook his head. "I'd sooner... fucking... beat up a guy who tried to do that to her. Or anyone."

Vanessa and Vera nodded quietly in understanding. The sound of a key entering a lock creaked out from the door, and the door opened to reveal Elsie, sullen, a shadow of her usual bright self. She looked at them, from one to the other. Her lip shook.

"Your father is taking a nap," Vera said, as much for something to say as to reassure Elsie that she was safe.

"You didn't say they were talking about me, too," Tommy's voice was strained, suppressing his frustration and sense of betrayal.

Elsie wore her fear on her face, followed quickly by a flush of red. "I didn't think you needed to know."

"Kid, they're talking about me? I need to know." He looked at her through his lashes. "I'm under a lot of public scrutiny, which it seems your dad has done a good job of protecting you from, until now. I don't want schoolyard rumours to ruin either of our reputations, kid."

"What do you mean, until now?"

"Well, there are those photos of us from the ARIAs," he leant forward and cocked his head at her. "You're in the public eye officially now too, kid."

Elsie chewed her lip, nodding.

"But you can see why," he stepped over to her, putting his hands on her shoulders. "Anything that they say about me, about us, is plausible. It could get out... and wind up on some gossip website. And I'm a lot older than you, and that would look—" he yearned for the right word, but settled on the easiest, "—*bad*."

Elsie looked at him, her eyes large and dewy. "I don't care that you're older than me. They shouldn't care! Dad's older than Vera and that's okay. Right?" She lifted her hands and clasped his elbows, feeling his warmth, his sinewy arm muscles. Vera covered her face with her hands and wished she wasn't there. Vanessa couldn't look away from the train wreck in front of her, but stood at the ready to intervene.

Tommy released her shoulders, and shook her hands off. "Elsie, it's not just that I'm older than you, kid. You're *fourteen*."

"We can wait. I'll be fifteen soon!"

"Elsie... No," Tommy shook his head, turning away from her and stepping away. "You're not getting it," he was at a loss of what to say. He didn't know how to explain it; even worse, he wasn't even sure what he should explain. He looked to Vera for support. Vera just shook her head. He looked to Vanessa. Vanessa pressed her lips together, just as unsure of what to say.

Elsie looked from Tommy to Vera and Vanessa. When she realised that she'd inadvertently confessed her interest to Tommy, the rejection hit her suddenly, and made her want to bury herself. It wasn't bad enough that she was being teased about being easy, but the one person she would have liked to be interested in her had just completely shut her down.

Without turning to her, Tommy steeled himself to be as clear as possible, and hope that the heartbreak could still give way to friendship. "Elsie, I don't want to hurt you, kid. You're a smart girl, so I'm going to be completely honest with you. I hardly know you, and it was cool to hang out and talk, but," he sighed and turned to her, knowing the sting of pain that was going to come after his next line. "I see you more like a... little sister. Do you think we can still be friends, though?"

Elsie simply nodded, channelling Vera in her own attempt at controlling her feelings. She knew that if she said anything, she'd break. She just sniffed a little, and smiled weakly. Vera stepped over to her, opened her arms, and let Elsie lean into her.

"I just—" He sighed. "I want to help you, kid. And I don't want to hurt you. I mean, I don't want *either* of us to get... hurt."

Vanessa shifted on her feet. "Tommy, could I maybe talk to you outside for a minute?"

Tommy was glad for a reprieve from what had grown more uncomfortable than he could imagine. He nodded, and reached out to squeeze Elsie's shoulder. She jerked it away from him as he walked past. Vanessa gave him a sympathetic glance and guided him outside.

The door opened and closed again. Their voices were muffled outside. Elsie didn't look up at Vera. She just sniffed a bit and pressed her lips together.

"I know exactly how you feel, Elsie."

`Elsie resisted the urge to lash out at Vera, to tell her that it was impossible for her to know how she felt— she'd got the man of her dreams.` But she also knew that there were many times that Vera hadn't had her affection returned, and knew that her own father had pushed Vera away barely a few nights before. At least Tommy had been blunt with her, and hadn't been mean or cruel.

"Do you think he's being honest with me? He doesn't *like* me?"

"I think it's best to just believe him." All those rejections she'd endured came in handy for something, finally. "You'll just twist yourself up if you try to hold on to the idea that he secretly likes you." She looked down into Elsie's face. "I know you probably still will. I used to do that a lot. It was almost never worth it."

Elsie blinked, nodding her head violently.

Vera turned her towards her, holding her firmly. Elsie couldn't control her emotions anymore, and cried into Vera's shoulder.

⏮ ⏸ ⏭

"So, *Tommy*," Vanessa turned to him. "First, housekeeping. You honestly see her as a little sister?"

Tommy cocked his head, weighing up his answer. "Well, yeah. And I know opinions of people change, but..." The vagueness of his phrasing bemused Vanessa, but it was a satisfying enough answer.

"Well, let's leave it at that. I want to ask you a favour. As a," she smiled, "a big sister."

Tommy raised his eyebrows solemnly, and his hand fell on his chest. "Absolutely, man."

Vanessa opened her mouth, unsure of the best way to ask. "I've been thinking about this a lot. You're one of the good ones. Like Nate. But, there are a *lot* of guys out there that aren't."

He blinked at her. She started wandering around the house, away from the door. Tommy kept her pace. "Okay, yeah. That's true. But... what are you asking?"

She rubbed her own arm to reassure herself. "This mess at her school. You know this is bigger than Elsie, it's bigger than this one *idiot* she goes to school with. So I thought: well, Tommy's in the public view, he's in the best position to help girls like Elsie. And like... me."

"But, I don't know what you want me to do."

"You've got a loudspeaker. You're visible: you can send a message. All these years of this idea that if you're just persistent enough, you can get who you want. And heartbreak songs; revenge songs. Maybe we need, you know, 'I love you and I'm happy if you are happy,' songs. No more 'fuck you for not loving me back' songs. You know what I mean?"

Tommy nodded thoughtfully, and they continued meandering around the house's perimeter. They heard a sweet melody floating around the house, then a clash of notes, and Nate's voice. "Fu-uck!"

"Speaking of 'fuck you' songs... Sounds like he's struggling a bit," giggled Vanessa. "Poor guy."

Tommy couldn't help himself. Like a puppy, he couldn't maintain the idea that anyone would stay upset at him for long. After smiling sheepishly at Vanessa, he bounded towards the window, rapping on it with his knuckle.

Nate looked up at the sound of knocking on the glass, turning to look out the window over his shoulder. A stormy expression passed over his features fleetingly, but Tommy's charm shone through his mood. He placed the keyboard synth on the bed and stood up, heading to the window. He tried opening the window with one hand, but only managed to push it ajar enough for Tommy to grab it and yank it open. Tommy nodded towards the discarded keyboard. "You okay?"

Nate cleared his throat and put on an air of false politeness. "I'd like to apologise for the disturbance; I promise that I'm using the better of my two hands at this point."

"Seriously, man," Tommy put his hand on his chest, his rings clanking against the pendants that lay amongst his tufts of hair. "It would be my *honour* to be your musical hands, at least to help you get your ideas down." He tilted his head in compromise. "At least for a few days, until you get back to being amazing."

He held his hand out to Nate.

Hesitation licked at Nate's face.

This wasn't just about the music, for either of them. This was Tommy seeking him out, being unashamed, knowing that Vanessa and Vera had likely warned him that Nate would bite his head off; and he was unafraid — he didn't care. He was showing Nate that he trusted him, and that he could be trusted; proving that he had nothing to hide or be ashamed of. He also wasn't trying to put his work in front of Nate, trying to use his idol for his own ego or to further his career. He wanted to support and help him, to collaborate. Of course, the paranoid voice in Nate's head said, it could have all been a ruse.

Nate hadn't collaborated with anyone since embarking on his solo career; even Jason had been relatively hands-off when he'd sent through his demos. He'd been too afraid of putting his trust in another musician whose character he could so easily be wrong about, leading him to the same sort of situation he'd found himself in decade ago, complete with insurmountable anxiety, shame, and destructive coping mechanisms. He'd pulled his life back together and had been afraid of letting anyone pull it apart. Just like he'd been afraid of opening up to Vera. Just like he'd repeatedly snubbed Jason's friendship and support.

Tommy's confidence wavered. He started curling his fingers, ready to pull his hand — and his offer — away. "But, y'know, if that's not something you'd be open to, that's—"

Nate clapped his good hand into Tommy's.

The two men's faces mirrored each other as they erupted into grins.

Forty-Nine

⏮ ⏸ ⏭

"Oh man, I'm so excited," Tommy said, mostly to himself, as the wind blew in from his driver's side window, ruffling his hair almost as much as his shirt collar. "Jamming with *the* Nate Whitely!" He turned, flashing a smile at Nate, who was crumpled in the passenger seat, attempting to suppress the fear he felt at Tommy sailing through intersections between Vera's house and Nate's with the fearlessness that a man in his early twenties naturally possesses.

Elsie, sitting in the back seat, rolled her eyes. Ever since their reconciliation, Tommy had almost been more attentive to Nate than Vera ever had. They'd all agreed that Tommy would share some of Nate's caretaking, so that Vera could keep jobseeking while Tommy became Nate's literal right hand. Tommy had been following Nate around with a sort of lovesick devotion, commiserating about his hand in a way that only being a fellow musician would allow, talking about how he used to practise all Nate's songs on his school pianos. At this point, Elsie almost wouldn't have been surprised to see them holding hands and sneaking kisses later on. Of *course* Tommy would be more interested in Nate. Everyone, Elsie reminded herself, was more interested in Nate. She wasn't anyone interesting, never could be, would always be his daughter in the same way as her grandfather would always be Nate's father. Everyone in his life was relative to him, never the other way around.

"Are *you* gonna help us, kid?"

Her ears perked up, and her eyes caught Tommy's in the rear-view mirror. It wasn't the sort of invitation she wanted, but it was an invitation. "How can *I* help?" She felt like she knew the answer — it was the same thing that she had been doing for the last fourteen years of her life: staying out of Nate's way.

"You can tell us if we're any good."

The unexpectedness of Tommy's comment made Nate turn to look at him, and Elsie blush. "I don't know if I'm the best judge."

"I mean, you like *my* music, right?" Tommy grinned, though Elsie could only see the crinkling around his eyes via the mirror. "Well, it's you and the Australian public, so," he paused, pulling up in front of Nate and Elsie's house, then twisting around in his seat to face her. "So, I'd say your judgement is pretty much on the money. Come on, kid," he jumped out of the car, smiled through the back door window at her, and opened the boot to retrieve the clothes that Nate had taken to Vera's.

Nate swivelled in his seat to look back at his daughter.

"Don't worry, Dad," she rolled her eyes and unlocked the door. "I'll stay out of your way."

⏮ ⏸ ⏭

The next evening, Vera knocked on Nate's front door. She waited a while, then knocked again.

The door opened, and Elsie, still in her school uniform, grinned at the sight of her. "Is Dad expecting you?"

"He's meant to be."

"Ha, well," she stepped back, making space for Vera to step over the threshold. Closing the door behind her, she wrapped her arms around her in a hug. "He's still with his *boyfriend*," she rolled her eyes. Nate and Tommy had spent the entire day together, jamming in Nate's home studio.

"Well, it's better than him straining his hand," Vera shrugged.

"I guess," Elsie supplied a faux pout, "but it's boring." She grabbed Vera's hand and trailed in front of her, leading her to the studio. "I'm glad you're here now."

"So when are *you* going to start singing with them, Elsie?"

Elsie scoffed at the idea. She was tired of hearing it over and over, but there was something about Vera's manner that made even a tired question feel sweet. "I didn't really inherit that from Dad."

"Shame."

Elsie smiled back at her. "I know." She knocked on the door of the studio.

"I hope they weren't recording."

"Anything important and Dad would start recording at his real studio; this is just for fun, just getting down ideas at most." She twisted the doorknob and opened the door.

The two men sat side by side tinkering with the keyboard in front of them. Tommy smashed the keys and they both talked over them and each other. Nate looked up and saw Vera, and swore into his smirk. "Shit, is it time for the Changing of the Guard already? I'm afraid I'm going to have to kick you out, Tom," he stood up, half tripping over his chair in his enthusiasm to kiss Vera.

"Actually," Tommy stood up, glancing at his phone. "I was thinking of catching a movie. Tight-arse Tuesday prices! Elsie, you wanna come?"

Her ears perked up, the jealousy of how much time Tommy and Nate were spending together, gone. "Can I, Dad?"

"Sure. Nothing R-rated though." Nate's reaction surprised Vera; feeling her tense up, he gently ran his hand down her arm to reassure her.

Tommy laughed and shook his head. "Okay, kid: you happy to go now?"

"Um, sure, give me a sec!" She scuttled away, up the stairs.

Vera could delay her questions for Nate, but she had to warn Tommy. "Don't be cruel to her."

Tommy's face fell. "I'm not trying to be. Am I being cruel?" He pleaded with Vera, "Man, I'm just trying to be friends with her." He turned to Nate, eyes wide and worried.

"I know that. She should know that," Vera paused, her own memories of being strung along rising to mind. "But she might always hope. Just be careful."

"I do appreciate you being a friend to her," Nate nodded. "Between you and Vera, at least she has some people who care about her who aren't related to her." He squeezed Vera's hand. "I trust you, Tommy."

Tommy nodded, his dark eyes squinched with concern, hands thrust into his pockets.

"Ready!" Elsie had changed out of her uniform and was holding a bag, empty except for her phone, wallet, keys, and a lip balm.

Nate nodded, slapping Tommy on the shoulder. "Enjoy the movie."

Elsie bounded to the front door, opening it and letting herself out, leaving it open for Tommy.

Vera waited until the door shut, then turned to Nate. "I'm surprised you're okay with—"

"As I said, I trust him." Nate slipped his arms around her waist to pull her close to him. "So, are we still going out, or do you want to… stay in?" He kissed her, sweetly, then pulled back and looked at her the way he looked at love interests in his music clips: eyes soft, drawing her in. She let herself feel like his fan again, focused entirely on the youthful, sweet, trusting, naive yet honest feeling of 'he chose me.' In answer, she kissed him back. She pressed herself against him, twisting her fingers into his hair, her other hand pulling him back into her.

This time, she chose to focus on that sweet feeling, and didn't allow herself to be haunted by thoughts of others who had gone before her, or those who had come before him and made her fear that she wasn't enough for him. She no longer cared whether she was enough for him: he wanted her, and she was ready to go after what she wanted, too, and found herself rewarded for it. With every kiss, every touch, every little gasp, she felt his singular focus on her — and she trusted it.

His fingers found their way under the waistband of her jeans; she replied by finding a way under his t-shirt.

He looked towards the door, a coy look on his face. "Is this going to… keep going? Maybe we should go upstairs?"

Vera smiled, answering by lifting up to pull his t-shirt up and off him.

"Come on," he goaded, the fingers on his good hand twining between hers, lifting them to his mouth, peppering them with kisses; sucking on the fingertip of her middle finger. He began stepping backwards, leading her to the stairs. She watched him, looked at his shoulders, his arms, the hair sprinkled on his chest and trailing down his tummy. It was the first time she'd really had the opportunity to look at him unashamedly, feeling worthy of being able to enjoy looking at the man who she'd found herself falling for: the man who was so open and honest with his feelings, who made her feel safe to be open and honest with hers. He didn't look the way he did in the posters she once had on her walls, but he was looking back at *her*.

Nate really liked the way Vera was looking at him.

She walked past him, pulling him up the stairs, waiting for him at the top. At a step higher she was taller than him. His eyes glowed, looking up at her. She put both hands on his face, and kissed him again. He wrapped his arms around her waist, and stepped forward, pushing her backwards into the hallway. Vera absorbed his attention like a sponge absorbs water, swelling and yielding and getting heavy, pulling him back toward her. They stumbled towards his bedroom together, flicking the light on and slamming the door as they crossed the threshold.

Instinctively, Nate reached down with both hands to grab Vera's top and pull it up over her head. He yelped with pain and recoiled back, clutching his injured hand. Vera paused. "Are you okay?" He looked back at her, dropped his hand by his side, and stepped back towards her. He kissed her again, slowly, more gently. When he pulled away again, she opened her eyes, and removed her shirt for him.

"Thanks. I might need a bit more help than I like to admit." She simply pulled him close to her and kissed him, deeply.

Fifty

Elsie knew she shouldn't, but she couldn't help but be hopeful that something would happen while she sat next to Tommy in the dark of the cinema. It wasn't that she wanted him to sleep with her, or even kiss her or anything like that. She just thought it would be nice if he, *I dunno*, fell in love with her?

She just wanted someone to *choose* her; to be the favourite of someone, someone like him, who had so many else wanting him already.

She looked across at him, his pointed, sharp features lit by the light reflected off the screen. He laughed at some stupid joke in the film, and turned to share the joke with her. She caught his eye. She admired him so much: he was unashamedly so many things at once. He didn't seem to care whether people liked him or not; he just did what made sense to him.

Tommy felt himself begin to panic. There it was again: The Look. He swallowed uncomfortably, and gave all his attention to the events of the movie in front of them.

Great, Elsie thought. *Now he probably regrets taking me to the movie.* She sighed and turned back to the screen.

A movie might not have been Tommy's greatest idea, he realised now. He was thinking about how he used to go to the movies with his younger cousins, or his friends and their younger siblings; he'd forgotten that movies are also associated with *dates*. He understood now why Vera had been hinting about him being cruel. He'd just wanted to move them further away from whatever Elsie thought they could be, and move them closer to friends. Yes, he was trying to *friendzone* her. He'd tried to be honest with her, but if he wanted to keep working with Nate, he knew it was in his best interest to keep her onside. He just had to tread a very fine line.

At least he hadn't chosen a romcom or something with sex scenes. That would have been way too regrettable. But even choosing a seemingly-safe superhero movie didn't protect him from the awareness that they were together, almost alone, right next to each other. In the dark. Dilating their pupils, highlighting the contours of each other's faces: all the tricks that went into making music clips that made girls become obsessed with them. Girls like Elsie. Girls, *including* Elsie. She'd fallen for the bait like she was supposed to, but only to rack up views on social media, buy tickets to their concerts, and buy their merchandise. They weren't meant to meet in real life. He'd hoped that, considering she was the daughter of Nate Whitely, she might be so used to musicians that he wouldn't have to worry. He hated feeling that he was wrong.

He could feel the cloud of anxiety bubbling up next to him. The poor kid had been struggling with her friends at school, she'd told him the first night they'd met. She needed a friend, and he wanted to be one: he knew exactly how she felt. Still looking at the screen, he absent-mindedly reached his hand into the popcorn box that she was holding and pulled out a handful.

Elsie stared down at her lap, where Tommy's hand had just been, at the popped kernels — small and white and clumpy, salty and good for eating when you're not thinking. Not thinking. That was a good idea. Elsie passed the popcorn to him and looked up to the screen again. She'd just have to try to focus on the movie, and stop thinking about *Tommy*.

Fifty-One

⏮ ⏸ ⏭

Vera's phone chimed insistently. She reached over to see who it was, what kind of emergency warranted constant phonecalls on a Tuesday evening.

Steven.

It was like he was never going to let her go. What would he want now?

"Hello?" She sat up, rousing Nate next to her.

"Hello, beautiful," came the voice. "I wanted to check in on you. Mum said that your friend was discharged from hospital."

Said friend was lying next to her, still naked, now watching her through groggy lids. He squirmed a just-woken yawn. "Yeah, he's fine."

"Oh, that's great. That's great news. You don't need anyone to come and be a shoulder to cry on," a laugh echoed down the line. *Laughing at his own jokes— typical.*

"No, no; he's all good."

"Okay, well I wondered whether you'd like to catch up again? The last couple of times have been in less than ideal circumstances, and, um," he cleared his throat. "I'm waiting on your answer from the last time we properly spoke."

"Oh."

"I mean, I'm not *waiting*, because, you know, I've never had trouble getting girls. But they aren't like *you*."

Vera felt sick.

"But, no pressure. I mean, we can meet up just as friends. I care

247

about you, and I really missed when you weren't there for me to talk to."

"Oh, um, as friends?"

"Absolutely."

"Well, I—"

"Great, how about tomorrow? I'll take the afternoon off. Same place? You have time, right?"

"Actually—"

"Great. I'm really looking forward to seeing you. Tomorrow, same time, same place. See you then." The line went dead. Vera was left stunned. She turned to Nate, ready to tell him the story with incredulity, so they could both laugh at the idea of Steven being stood up.

Instead, his face was dark with an anger so intense that it frightened her. "You know I could hear him too."

"Well, I mean, I'm not going."

"Of course you're not."

"What does that mean? He just steamrolled me; I don't even want to go."

"You don't want to go?" Sarcasm streaked through Nate's words.

"Of course not! Why would I? And anyway, who are you to say who I can or can't spend time with?"

"Are you still… *fucking*… in *love* with him?"

"What?" Vera couldn't believe what she was hearing. "Of course not."

"Then why did you answer his call?"

"I don't know, in case something had happened."

"Something? Something? What thing? What could it be, that you would care about?"

"I don't know, something about his parents. You met his mother."

"What? When?"

"She was the neurosurgeon, Sandra."

"Wait, *what*? You got your ex's mother to treat me in hospital?"

"I ran into her and she *offered*. She's a fucking good neurosurgeon."

"So what, now you owe him something?"

"No," she sighed and rubbed her face. "It's not a big deal Nate, calm down."

"Fuck you, what the fuck is wrong with you?"

"*Me*?" She blinked at him. "Holy shit, Nate." She stood up and started collecting her clothes. She wasn't going to let herself be treated like this anymore. Not by Steven, and not by Nate. His mood switched as soon as she was out of the bed.

"Vera? Vera I'm sorry."

She turned to him, fire in her eyes. "Steven was a fucking manipulative, deceitful, abusive prick. I don't want anything to do with him. But I will *not* stay with you if you are one too!" She continued picking up her clothes. "Old habits die hard. It's hard to say no to him. I'm scared of what might happen if I do. And that goes for answering the phone as well: I do it without thinking. We lived together for *nine* years, Nate. Nine years of knowing that if I didn't answer, I'd be in trouble. Nine years of being *scared*."

Nate's mouth moved and no words came out. It was as though he was waking up from the coma all over again. She pulled on her underwear.

"I don't like being scared of you too, Nate." Hooked up her bra, scooped and swooped.

"I've been trying so hard," he said, his voice tiny. "I'm trying not to get angry. It's just so... so fast."

"I don't even care, Nate." She pulled on her pants.

"Please, please care," he begged her. "Vera, I love you."

It should have been a moment of great joy, of forgiveness, of *I love you too*. Instead, "Really?" Her top went back on, over her head, because of him. "Then act like it."

"I don't know how." The words came out instantly, unfiltered.

She turned and stared at him, incredulously. How could someone who was so in tune with their feelings, who wrote so many songs about love, not know how to act like they loved someone? And how could Steven, manipulative and selfish, seem to make her *feel* so loved?

He swallowed, afraid to say anything that might spoil the fact that he'd said something to make her stay a few more moments.

"Vera, I will love you so much, and I will do my best to..." he stopped, and thought about what he was going to say before he said it. "I *promise* I will do my best to stop and think before I go ahead and say things." Vera looked down, away from him. "I'm a shit," he added. "I always have been. Another reason why I don't deserve you, and you deserve better than me. But I promise, I will try."

She sat down on the edge of the bed, defeated. Hopeful. "Well... You're right. I shouldn't have answered the phone."

Nate looked like he wanted to say something, then thought better of it. This happened a few times, until he just sighed and said, "Thank you."

"I don't think I should answer his calls again."

Nate made a faint whining sound and finally let out, "That's really up to you, but I'd prefer if you didn't."

Vera did her best to pull herself out of everything she was feeling. The primal fear that flared at his raised voice, the panic that overwhelmed her when he so suddenly apologised again. She blinked it all away and took a deep breath in, reforming her face into a smile and an act of amusement. "I guess it's cute that you're jealous." Still dressed, she slowly climbed back into the bed, and let him put his arms around her, pulling her to him. He nuzzled her neck, and she couldn't help but let out an incredulous laugh. "*Nate Fucking Whitely*, jealous of my shit ex! Possessive of me! Who'd imagine..."

Nate pouted. "Not *Nate Fucking Whitely*, Vera. Just me."

Fifty-Two

⏮ ⏸ ⏭

Elsie sat staring out the window as Tommy drove, surprisingly carefully and smoothly, in his beaten up old car.

"Why do you have such an old car anyway?"

Tommy grinned. "This was my first car. I got it when I was sixteen. I've got a lot of memories with this car." He glanced at her. "I wouldn't swap her for the world."

Elsie nodded, frowning. "People don't make fun of you for it?"

"Sometimes," Tommy shrugged. "But I don't really care."

She looked back out the window.

"Why, don't you like it?"

"It's fine, if you like it."

"It sounds like you're okay with me *liking* it, but do *you* like it?"

Elsie turned, frowning at him. "What does it matter if I like it?"

He flashed a grin at her, but didn't say a word.

"I guess it's pretty cool. It has character." She bit her lip as she thought. "It's not flashy, but then it's kinda rough, but that's nice. It makes me feel like I don't have to be careful with it."

"It reminds me of when I was starting out," Tommy said. "You know, I never really wanted to be famous, or anything like that. I just really love music. And the guys, they told me that the best way to keep playing music was to get famous doing it."

"So you became famous," Elsie filled in.

"Nah, kid. I just kept enjoying making music, and let someone else worry about us being famous." He twisted the leather of the steering wheel under his fingers. "I kinda worry about that guy sometimes, though. Is there going to be a point where what we're doing isn't enough for him? And will that tear us apart?"

He shifted uncomfortably, feeling Elsie's eyes on him.

"Ah, I'm getting ahead of myself. I gotta focus on now, keep enjoying every moment. Right, kid?" She smiled at him, hoping there was hidden meaning in there somewhere. "Because you know, working on things with your Dad is pretty much… well it was my dream."

Elsie's face fell. Everyone was obsessed with Nate, it felt. But what about her? Was she really that unremarkable? "Yeah, it's pretty cool, for you."

Tommy struggled to understand the tone in her voice. "What about your dreams, Elsie? Do you want to get into music too?"

"No way," her voice shook. Being compared to Nate, always playing second fiddle? "I want to do my own thing."

"Oh yeah? That's awesome. What are you into?"

"Um," Elsie hesitated. It wasn't that she didn't want to tell Tommy, it was more that she wasn't really even sure. "I think robots are pretty cool. Vera's helping me with maths, because I've never been very good at it."

"Wow, kid," Tommy shook his head. "I mean, I've always been pretty good at music. It's easy to keep working at something that you're good at. Your Dad was probably the same. But you're doing something you're not good at, because it gets you closer to something you love."

Elsie blushed. "Well, I'm getting a lot better at it. Vera makes it all make sense."

"Maybe no one taught you the right way?"

"Maybe."

"It's all about keeping on going, isn't it? I mean, this life. It takes lots of unexpected turns. It's all about keeping on going."

"You should make that a song." Elsie grinned.

"You may not want to get into music, kid, but I'm sure you have an ear for poetry. So I'll trust you on that one."

A blush swept over Elsie's face, as the headlights of Tommy's car swept over the front of Nate and Elsie's home.

Elsie unlocked the door as quietly as she could. The lights were on, but it was silent inside. "They must be here," she whispered. "Dad wouldn't leave lights on if they went out. Plus Vera's car is still here."

Tommy raised his eyebrows. "Want me to scout? I'll do it in exchange for a coffee."

Elsie nodded, closed the door behind them, and tiptoed to the kitchen.

A cheeky grin spread across Tommy's face. He dramatically tiptoed through to the lounge, where he found Nate's discarded t-shirt. "Interesting," he uttered to himself, picking it up and slinging it over one shoulder. He paced to the studio, fluid as a cat. The door was ajar, and no one was inside. He turned off the light. Skipping back, he made his way to the stairs, sliding around the corner and hopping up the first few stairs, before slowing so as not to create any more sound than necessary. Only moderately familiar with the upstairs floorplan, he listened carefully as he approached different doors. Some, including Elsie's bedroom door, were ajar with the lights off. But there was one door that was closed, and the light spilled out from under it. Tiptoeing, he moved to put his ear to the door. Nothing. He knocked quietly. There was a murmur from inside, so he knocked again. "Hi, we're back," he told the door. "We're having coffee." He turned to walk away, and added as an afterthought, "I found your t-shirt, I'll leave it on the doorknob."

Elsie was standing at the foot of the staircase, holding a mug filled with milky coffee. "Find them?"

"I think so. Door closed, light on. There were definitely voices. It could have been burglars, but I didn't want to find out." He reached forward, taking the coffee from her. "My coffee? Are you having anything?"

"Yeah, I put the rest of the frothed milk in with some hot chocolate powder. It's... congealing."

"That sounds gross."

She giggled. "Yeah, maybe not the right word?"

"As long as it's *your* hot chocolate and not *my* coffee."

She walked back to the counter, rattled the spoon inside her mug, and pulled it out, covered in syrupy chocolate not yet emulsified in the milk, to lick. "Can I ask you something?"

"Sure."

"How did you get to be so cool?"

"What?" Tommy laughed in surprise. "I'm *not* cool."

"You are, though." Elsie ran her finger along the countertop. "I mean, you're super famous, you're in all these magazines, and you're just so... *cool.*"

"Elsie," Tommy walked over and draped himself against the counter, next to her. "I don't try to be. I'm just... doing my thing. I don't know." He shook his head at her, smirking. "You're cooler than you think."

"Yeah?"

"Yeah."

"Then why do people tease me so much? Why don't I have friends?" The second part of that line slipped out without her meaning it to. Elsie had also inherited speaking-before-thinking from Nate. Tommy, surprised, softened to her.

"You *do* have friends, kid. I think of you as my friend. You're fun to be around. Usually." He furrowed his brow. "Highschool sucks. Everyone gets teased, Elsie. Everyone. And if they're the ones teasing, you can bet that they're probably being teased somewhere else. No one gets that behaviour out of nowhere. I'm sure." She watched him closely, the thoughts being pulled out like a string of knotted Christmas lights. "No, I'm sure that most people are nice when they start life. But someone breaks them somehow along the way. Someone teaches them that it's how they get attention. And you know what? It becomes true for a lot of people."

"I bet you were never teased."

Tommy threw his head back in laughter. "I was a scrawny, pimply, band geek. I was not *cool.* I tried to be invisible most of the time. I just watched people a lot, stayed out of everyone's way."

"Then how come you're so... outgoing?"

"I guess, after a while, I stopped caring. Then, by the end of highschool, everyone chilled out, anyway." He put his coffee down, put both hands on her shoulders, and looked her square in the eyes. "You can't hide like me; you're bubbly, you're cute, you're the daughter of someone famous, and you're pretty freaking memorable."

Stunned, she looked away to hide her excitement over his compliment, and the intimacy of his closeness. "Elsie, just keep doing what you love. Find your tribe: find people who love the same things as you. Vera is one of them! And don't worry, in highschool you're just thrust together with people your age in your area. When you leave, you can meet people who want to learn or do the same things as you. You'll find your tribe, kid. Don't worry."

"So… I just have to wait until after highschool, and then people will be better?"

"Well," Tommy stepped away, picking up his coffee. "You can find people now. Like you found Vera. And," he paused, unsure whether he should shatter the utopia he could see he'd painted for her. "Well, there are always fuckwits. And people will be jealous of you, and want to take you down, or use you. But, just keep holding out for those who are looking for the same type of tribe as you."

"Is that why you're worried about your bandmate? You don't think he's looking for the same type of tribe as you?"

Tommy felt surprised that she'd remembered a throwaway comment that he'd made over two hours ago. "Well… yeah, actually." He pursed his lips. "He's great, he's been like the sales guy for us. You need people who are different. But I'm worried we'll end up fighting over what I want, what he wants, what the others want. But I have to keep reminding myself to not worry about tomorrow."

" You have my Dad now."

"Yeah. They say that it's lonely at the top, but sometimes you find more members of your tribe."

"Then you can be lonely together."

"Hey Elsie, great lyric."

She grinned at him.

Fifty-Three

⏮ ⏸ ⏭

Nate and Vera lay in bed together, both pretending to be asleep. They could both hear Tommy and Elsie giggling downstairs. Nate's ears were pricked to work out what was happening between what he could easily hear, and whether he needed to intervene to protect Elsie. Vera wondered whether she should join them, and tried to listen for any tell that Tommy may need a way out.

Before they both knew it, the front door opened and closed, Elsie's footsteps bounded up the stairs, and her bedroom door opened and closed, underlined by the sound of a car sputtering into life, pulling out of the driveway, and pulling away. Nate and Vera were left in the quiet dark with their own thoughts, no longer having anything to distract them.

Nate couldn't stop thinking about Steven. He knew that Steven still had sway over Vera. There was something there that he couldn't compete with, but Nate wasn't sure he could put his finger on anything specific. There was a feeling of unease that was haunting him, as though Vera was going to slip away from him no matter what he did. Steven was younger, and more handsome than he, but he also had years of knowing Vera that Nate felt was like a trump card. The only thing that Nate had on that was the same thing he had with any of his fans: the feeling that she knew him, and the idea that he knew her deeply, even though that was an illusion formed by ambiguous lyrics placed atop emotionally arranged sounds. He had that he was *Nate Fucking Whitely*. But despite her joking about it, he wasn't even sure that she actually cared about that, anymore: she seemed too smart to be tripped up by that illusion. She'd already seen the behind-the-scenes, and the truth of who he was wasn't as polished as the radio edit. And she'd come back to him.

Vera, simultaneously flattered and yet made uncomfortable by Nate's jealousy, heard him sigh, which she interpreted as him being unperturbed by the outburst of emotion that had shaken her earlier that evening. She wasn't unfamiliar with the pattern (even if Nate had executed it out of order): fight, then flatter, then fuck. It was something Steven had done so many times, bending her to his pleasure. Thinking back, she started wondering whether it was something that he deliberately used to do, just to break up his usual tactic of steamrolling and seduction. No one appreciated her like he did — but her experience had taught her that him saying that wasn't actually stretching the truth. In hindsight, she could see just how much he'd tried to protect her from finding anyone who *could* appreciate her more than him. Nate's reaction to Steven's call worried her. Was he going to do the same thing: try to possess her, as long as it made him feel good? Was he going to control her and keep her for himself, rather than allow her to build back the version of herself that she might decide is who she wanted to be? If Steven took Ronnie, would Nate try to keep Vera?

Alone in their separate thoughts about the same man, they both felt themselves retreating and hoped that, in that moment, the other would reach out in some small but meaningful way.

Nate believed that even if Vera stayed the night, she would just end up retreating back to what he thought she really wanted: not the validation of being desirable to a stranger whose personality she'd constructed from a strange voyeuristic admiration, but finally having the man who she'd shared so much with — the one she couldn't contain before — want her, and only her, and for their relationship to be the shape she'd stayed nine years with him hoping for. Nate wasn't stupid. He'd seen the photo of Vera with Steven when they were young, knew how much history the two of them had, and knew how little of any connection between himself and Vera was real or tangible. He'd been with fans before, he knew what it was like. Who he was in their head wasn't who he really was, and it was only a matter of time before this idea of him would come crashing down. He'd become used to it. But, he was getting tired of it.

Vera felt increasingly anxious next to Nate. She'd only just got out of one relationship with someone who wanted to hold the power — was she getting into another one? Was *nice* just a euphemism for *pushover*?

Did Nate view her as someone who would be easy to manipulate, who he could control and keep for himself, locked up in the tower of isolation he'd built for himself? She could feel herself trapped — the sense that she couldn't leave without upsetting him made her uncomfortable staying. And what would be the big deal if she answered her own phone? What would be next: screening her calls; snooping? It was her turn to sigh, and she turned around to face Nate. His eyes were open, looking at her in the moonlight.

"You're awake, too?"

Nate grunted, shielding his thoughts yet revealing that he was shielding something. He watched her, waiting for her to open her mouth and tell him—

"Maybe I should go home."

Bingo.

Vera could read the look on his face: betrayal. There were a lot of other emotions and thoughts, but that was what strung them all together. "Nate?"

"That's fine," came the response, another grunt that hid his anger at being right that she was going to leave him, yet again. He didn't know, of course, that he was wrong about the reason why.

Vera bit her lip, stuck in a loop of whether she wanted to leave, or that she should because it seemed like he wanted her to. She couldn't tell whether this was some sort of game he was playing, or if she was missing something. Her anger grew steadily with each circular thought that swam in her mind. She wondered whether she should tell him how she was feeling, but felt like they'd already talked about it, and that she shouldn't say anything more.

"If you want to go, go."

"Do you want me to go?"

Of course he didn't, and he felt that she should know this already. He took a shaky breath in — and out. "I don't know why we're talking about this. If you're going to *leave me*, just... *leave*."

There was a bite to his tone that broke Vera's heart. She felt disoriented. She sat up, pulling herself away from him to buy herself some space. She wondered whether he was throwing her away again: was his claim to love her earlier that night just a ploy to make her stay around a bit longer, to keep her in his control? Had they even known each other long enough to know about *love*?

She looked back over her shoulder at him. He was looking at his broken hand, fiddling with the bandages. She sighed, releasing all her confusion, and started collecting her clothes for the second time that night. She considered asking if she could see him again, but wasn't keen to have him snap at her again.

Nate watched her dress: turned away from him, facing the window. He felt both disappointed and validated that he was right about her wanting to leave for the night. He hoped that she would stop, turn around, change her mind, and show him that she *wanted* to stay with him. He sat up, swinging his legs to the side of the bed, facing away from her.

Vera sighed, her hopes that he would say anything to show that he *wanted* her to stay with him, dashed. She turned towards the door, trying to avoid having to look at him. She felt ashamed and embarrassed, confused, angry, and disappointed. She didn't want to have to say goodbye to him.

As she started towards the bedroom door, Nate stood up and, in a last-ditch effort, stepped in her way, reaching out to put his good hand on the doorknob. Instinctively, her hand went up and landed on his chest.

He didn't want her to leave, and she didn't want to leave.

They studied each other's faces in silence, both hoping the other would read their thoughts and make the connection. If their vision hadn't been so clouded by needing to be seen, they would have seen The Look in each other's eyes.

Instead, they both only looked with distrust. Vera dropped her eyes and took a step back, gave Nate a half smile, breathed in courage, and shakily told him, "Goodnight, Nate." He looked away as he opened the bedroom door, daring her to leave and hoping she'd stay.

Before he could decide how best to respond, she was already gone.

Fifty-Four

⏮ ⏸ ⏭

The next morning, Tommy was back, unquestioningly wanting to spend as much time with Nate as possible. A small part of Nate hoped that the knock on the door would be Vera, but it was hard to be disappointed when the door opened to reveal Tommy holding bags of French pastries.

"I didn't know what you liked so I got some of everything. You and Elsie and Vera can have first pick because I've tried pretty much all of them and they're just... *awesome*," his head tilted in mild embarrassment. "This place is down the road from me. I love it."

Nate smiled in appreciation for Tommy's enthusiasm. "Don't worry, you'll have second pick: Elsie's already gone to school, and, uh," he rolled his lips together and swallowed to cover any hint that something could be wrong. "Vera's not in for breakfast."

Tommy considered Nate's words, then spun around to look outside. "You know, I *totally* missed that her car isn't here. Huh." He looked back around to Nate, serving him a cocked brow and cheeky grin. "Her loss."

"You could say that." Nate turned back to the kitchen. "Coffee?"

"Yeah, sure," Tommy dropped the pastries on the kitchen bench. "Wait, so, Vera?"

"Had a lot of things to do today, I guess."

"Man, jobseeking *sucks*. How lucky are *we*?"

Despite the negotiation of Tommy spending time with Nate instead of Vera, Nate had completely forgotten about her job search. He was so used to his own self-imposed routine of self-employment and surrounded himself with others who were the same, that he'd almost forgotten that *most* people actually have to spend a third of their waking lives being a slave to someone else, just so they can get by. He'd taken for granted that what Vera had been doing every day was *not* simply wasting time in the cafe, but creating for herself a routine of jobseeking: she'd made jobseeking her job until a real job was secured. Nate actually couldn't remember what it was like to jobseek. He remembered what it was like to struggle to get gigs, and he vaguely remembered working at the local supermarket for easy money, but he'd hit fame early enough that he hadn't really ever had a career aside from music, and even then it was never commercial commissioned music.

He slipped a pod in the machine, stuck a mug under the nozzle, and pressed the button.

"Engineering, wasn't it?"

Nate looked back over his shoulder to Tommy, who was poking through the bags on the bench. "Um, yeah." Somehow, he'd managed to forget what Vera even did.

"What type? Chemical? Electrical?" Tommy extracted a chouquette, popped it in his mouth, and leant back against the table. "I don't think I ever asked her."

Nate felt himself going red. He realised that, despite his conscious decision to expose her to his vulnerabilities, he'd failed in his part of learning much about her in return. It was his old habit of keeping himself emotionally uninvested in anticipation that she would leave him. He knew that the more he learned about her, the harder he would fall; and the harder he fell, the more it would hurt when she left. If he knew more about her, there would be more to remind him of her when she was gone. Instead, he made sure that he knew she was nice, but knew nothing of her achievements, her failures, her struggles and triumphs. In short, he knew little beyond a generic and benign description that should have come from her grandmother, not from him. His fear of Steven always knowing her better than he ever could was starting to feel like it was his own self-fulfilling prophecy. "Milk?"

"No no, just black."

Nate knew he couldn't weasel out of answering. He had to think: what had Elsie told him? Elsie was intent on robotics, and he knew that Vera hadn't studied that, but had something similar to it. He didn't want to risk getting it wrong, so he just told Tommy what he knew for sure. "I think she's looking to change, actually."

"Wow, really?" Tommy raised his brows as he took the mug from Nate. "Different engineering or different path entirely?"

"I'm not sure *she's* sure." Nate wasn't exactly lying.

"Well, if she's trying to move into doing something she loves, then that's great."

"Yeah."

Tommy's enthusiasm was starting to fail. Nate had been on-edge since he'd got there, and all his attempts at light conversation had seemed to build the walls higher. "Hey, are you okay man? You still wanna do this today?"

"Oh, yeah. Yeah, definitely, today is great. It's..." Nate stopped himself before anything came out. "It's nothing."

"You sure?"

"Oh yeah. Just slept badly. You know," he raised his bandaged hand and pulled a face at it. "It kinda hurts sometimes."

"Oh, right, yeah."

"And itches."

"Itches? Is that normal?"

"I think so, it's just healing."

"You sure?"

Nate had successfully shifted focus from Vera. "Yeah, yeah."

"We should take it easy though, I mean I wouldn't want you to hurt yourself more."

"Well, I appreciate your concern."

Tommy's face crumpled into a grin. "Anytime, man. Anything you need, I'm here for you."

⏮ ⏸ ⏭

Tommy lifted his hands from the keys suddenly and clicked his fingers. "You're worried about Elsie, aren't you?"

"What?"

Tommy nodded. "That's it. That's what's been distracting you! Aw man, you should have said something."

"Er—" Nate hesitated. He *hadn't* been worried about Elsie. He hadn't thought about her. He'd been too busy thinking about himself and Vera, and how he was right to be jealous of Steven, but it wasn't Vera or Steven who were to blame, but him.

"Come on, you're transparent," Tommy crowed triumphantly, his chest puffed out. "These lyrics, man. About '*wishing I was there with you, take away what you went through*'?" He threw his hands forward in a ta-da gesture, his bracelets jangling from the movement like windchimes. "And '*things you don't want me to know, have to give you time to grow,*'? You big softie, *that's* what's been bugging you today."

"Oh, um," Nate was relieved to have an out. "Yeah, I don't really know what to do about it." He was glad that he didn't have to lie or cover anything up about this line of questioning. "You know, I want to protect her, so much. I just—" He hesitated; he'd forgotten how easy it was for him to let in someone he was musically involved with: the creative vulnerability lent itself to more vulnerability. It was one of the reasons he'd refused to collaborate with someone for so many years — what would happen if he let them in? He considered Tommy, so much younger than him, not a father, and yet seemingly so much like himself all those years ago: trusting, honest, open, pure in his love of music and so keen to collaborate selflessly — and genuinely caring about other people. Nate hoped that he was right about him.

"You don't want to make it worse by trying to make it better?"

"Exactly."

"Yeah, I understand, man." Tommy trilled his fingers on the piano. "Why don't I go talk to them?" He looked back up at Nate and shrugged. "I mean, I'm not *the dad* coming to tell off some kids. I'm…" He thought back to what Vanessa had said to him. She was right, he was in the best position of influence. These kids looked up to him in the way that he'd looked up to Nate. "I'm someone they'll listen to."

"Mmmm. If you think it will help her. I wish I could tell you what to say."

"Nah man, I got this." Tommy grinned at Nate, and wrapped his arm over his shoulders. "I'll do it this afternoon. And it means so much to me that you trust me with this. Promise I won't fuck it up."

Fifty-Five

⏮ ⏸ ⏭

Elsie dragged her feet as she walked to the cafe. She didn't understand why Nate had asked her to stretch out her suffering by meeting at the cafe instead of her just going straight home like she had yesterday. Trailing behind her were a clump of her *frenemies*, including David and his fans. Since he'd 'scored' with Elsie and revealed her as a slut, he'd gained the admiration of the other pimply brats who could never compare to the few boys for whom puberty had kicked in both earlier and more kindly.

They had made a habit of going to the cafe, with or without Elsie, so for them, this was a less remarkable day than the ones where they watched her walk seemingly the wrong way.

"Are you gonna hang out with your dorky old maths tutor?" David received a set of sniggers for his bold statement. Elsie pouted. She considered defending Vera as not dorky and more than just a maths tutor, and nicer than any of them would ever be, but she didn't have the energy to do it. "Where is she? Is she the one who taught you to be such a *slut*?"

Elsie bristled. She just had to get through this. Hopefully, they could just leave immediately, and her Dad wouldn't mind—

Oh no. She *really* hoped that Nate wouldn't be there. He'd probably try to do some crazy Protector-Dad thing, which would just make things worse. She paused; would it be worth stopping David from going in? She looked up — it was too late. She shut her eyes tight and prayed that Nate, if there, wouldn't recognise David. She heard gasps from the girls, and when she opened her eyes, everyone had stopped. What had happened? She pushed her way between them to see what — or who — they were looking at.

Piercing green eyes met hers. The sullen face erupted into a broad grin of recognition.

"Hey, kid!"

Elsie felt herself go red, her ears hot.

"Y-y-you're that Tommy guy," David stuttered.

"Yeah man, or at least I was last time I checked."

To the casual observer in the cafe, it must have looked like some strange gang confrontation. One against many: the one, smiling and confident, draped casually against the counter; the many, shaken and defensive, clumped at the entrance. Fortunately, there wasn't really anyone else in the cafe apart from the barista, who Tommy had been enjoying casually flirting with while he waited.

"So, uh," Tommy didn't generally enjoy awkward silences, and usually took it on himself to break them. "My shout for coffees?"

"What about hot chocolates?" Hazarded one of the girls, bespectacled, carrying a clarinet case, and glad that the heat was off her and on Elsie.

Tommy looked at her with the affection reserved for a fellow band outcast. "Of course, darling." She blushed despite the micro-glares she received from the girls higher up the pecking order. "But, can we please sit down or something so I can stop standing?" He backed towards a booth where he had dropped his leather jacket when he'd arrived earlier.

Elsie hesitated, unsure of what would happen.

"What's wrong, kid?"

Her eyes flicked back, indicating David. Tommy nodded knowingly, then threw the decoy line.

"Don't worry, your Dad's fine. He's just chilling with Vera, and I'm going to be the one driving you both home after dinner. I'm gonna be your big brother for the night!"

David and some of the girls giggled. Elsie closed her eyes, wishing herself away.

"I don't get what's so funny?" Tommy was good at playing dumb. It was one of the things that made him a delight for interviewers — he would happily play along with whatever their angle was, but never used all the rope they gave him.

"Well it's odd to refer to yourself as her 'big brother' when you're sleeping with her," the bespectacled girl blushed through the entire confession, garnering more glares.

"I'm *sleeping* with her?" Tommy played absolutely dumb and unflappable. "Who told you that?"

She looked down at her clarinet case and bit her lip while her glasses slid down her nose.

"I mean, *you're* not in my bedroom, so you don't know what I get up to at night." He flashed a knowing smile that flustered the girls and made the boys want to be him — or want to beat him up. "So, who is your source?" He stepped towards them, this real, flesh-and-blood-and-scent-and-sweat man who they'd only seen on television and YouTube. His tone, his energy, was getting darker and heavier, more brooding, and more like his stage persona. He looked at them one by one, staring them down like a drill sergeant.

They all maintained their strength, the fear of this stranger's wrath weak compared to their fear of the repercussions within their social sphere.

Tommy sighed. He gave it up. "I just don't want any of you to be buying into that shit. You can hear from the horse's mouth: I'm not sleeping with Elsie."

"You only know her because you wanted to meet her Dad." He'd taken his time, but David had stepped up, challenging his rival using his usual combo of undermining and embarrassing. His chest was puffed, his head was raised, the angriest of his pimples glistening and threatening to burst on Tommy at his command.

"Yes, you're right," Tommy smiled as his agreement disarmed David. "That's *exactly* how I met her. But it's not how or why I consider her my friend."

One by one, they looked at Elsie, who grew redder by the second.

She wished that she could just disappear into nothing. This was worse than Nate being here. Nate would have just made a loud mess and been a dorky overprotective crazy Dad. But Tommy was allowing for too much space between each string of words. Any moment now, the truth would come out. "Maybe we should go, Dad's probably waiting for me."

Tommy, unsatisfied, had to give up. Their fidelity to each other was too strong for him; and anyway, he never had been a great interrogator. "I guess you won't be getting those free coffees and hot chocolates."

"It was Elsie." It seemed that only one voice ever had all the information. The drive for hot chocolate was strong.

Tommy's eyes locked onto those two glass barriers. The eyes behind them, swollen by the lenses, blinked once, earnestly. There seemed to be no reason for her to lie: she could have ratted any of them out and got a free hot chocolate. Shaking his head, he reached into his pocket, pulled out his wallet, and leafed through until he found a five dollar note. He walked back to the counter and placed it down, sliding it towards the bemused barista with a quick smile. "One large hot chocolate." He turned to Elsie, his unflappable veneer scarcely concealing his feelings of disappointment, betrayal, and embarrassment. She looked smaller than usual, as though she were trying to fade into ether. She wasn't even trying to refute the charges laid against her. "We're going. *Now.*"

He snatched up his jacket and strode for the door, patting the clarinettist on the shoulder on the way past and making her flush even redder than before.

Elsie wasn't used to the idea of Tommy being angry at her. She expected him to launch into a barrage of fury and accusations in the same way that Nate did, but this simmering ire frightened her more. This would not be a flash in the pan — this threatened to reach boiling point and overwhelm her. She rushed out of the cafe before him, glad to leave behind the audience greedy for gossip that made them all feel better about themselves.

Fifty-Six

⏮ ⏸ ⏭

Nate sat in Tommy's car outside of Vera's place, trying to plan what he wanted to say to her, wondering whether she'd even want to talk to him. He'd sent her a message earlier to tell her that if she wanted to talk about what had happened last night, they would have some time because Tommy was going to meet Elsie at the cafe. He'd received a simple '?' followed shortly by:

VERA: I'm not sure thats a great idea but shes your daughter

Vera wouldn't be expecting him. He hadn't actually replied to her message at all. For all he knew, he'd knock on her door and *someone else* would be there. It worried him. Maybe it would be okay if they really did just call it quits, once and for all? He could let her get back to her life, whatever that was, and he could focus on music with Tommy, and Elsie could continue spending time with Vera without whatever was going on between her and him. It would be safer that way. She wouldn't be able to slip away from him again, she wouldn't be able to leave him, because she'd already left. He'd be alone again.

Being alone was something he'd become used to, a safe discomfort. He could cocoon and not worry about being a disappointment or being disappointed. It was just him, and Elsie, and that's it.

But, nothing bad had happened since he started to let Tommy in. Tommy was a good guy, Vanessa was right. Vanessa was a good friend to Vera, too. So there, that was fine. Everyone would have their good friend. Vera could be a good friend to Elsie — if he hadn't fucked it up.

But it was better to fuck it up now, when there was still time for everyone to recover.

His mind wandered back to the night before. He'd expected to see the admiration fade from her eyes, the disappointment filter through, turning to disgust, as his insecurities spilled out. He'd expected her to start pulling away from him. The moment she realised that he was a real person, flawed, fearful, prone to emotional outbursts, not whatever she'd imagined him to be all those years ago. He knew this was what getting to know someone was like, but he always seemed to have a longer fall from grace than most people. Who he seemed to be in his most romantic songs only hinted at a snippet of his entire emotional world.

But that wasn't what he saw. He saw betrayal in her eyes. A pain. Yes, disappointment. But, he realised, it wasn't about her idea of who he was, but about how she hoped to be treated. She wasn't pulling away as much as she was standing up for what she deserved. When she'd told him about how her ex had made her feel, she let him into her world a little more. It was stupid, he knew, but it frightened him just how much there was to know about her, just how little he actually knew about her. She liked coffee, was good at maths, was an engineer (type to be confirmed), and had an ex who was hanging around and who knew everything there was to know about her. He was also younger, handsome, and from the looks of things, rich. Not that the rich thing mattered, because if that's all Vera was interested in, Nate was sure that he'd win that particular battle easily. But worrying about that was just Nate worrying about things that didn't matter in an attempt to distract himself from worrying about the things that did.

He stopped himself. What was he *really* worried about? The panic he'd felt about Vera answering Steven's call — he was someone she knew through and through. She'd known him and stayed with him for nine years, despite — or perhaps, because of — how he'd shaped her, intimidated her into something less than she was. Even now they were apart, even though she said she hated him, she still answered his call. She said it was fear, but there was a loyalty to her that he could see. The idea that she could love him was the only explanation that Nate could find in the moment; that she loved him and would go back to him, despite it all. But, Nate wondered, maybe Vera could be just as loyal to him despite his failings; he had to make sure, however, that it wasn't out of fear of him. And while he'd found himself more in control of his emotions around her, he still knew that he had more work to do if he was going to make sure she could feel safe with him. The answer, then, was to stop feeling so worried about Steven having power over her, and instead focus on giving her the space and safety to let her unfold herself, and loving every part of her that they discovered together; just like he wanted to be accepted for all of who he was by her. That's what he wanted to offer her — if she let him.

A bang on the roof of the car woke Nate from his train of thought. He jumped and turned to see Vanessa smiling in, her curls framing her face like a golden halo. She reached down and opened the door.

"Hi! Why are you sitting out here? Did she throw you out?" The line was delivered as a joke, but Nate's face showed that there was no irony in it. "Oh, shit, what happened?" She squatted down next to him, reaching out to touch his arm.

"I don't know, Ness." He shrugged and shook his head in denial. "This is just too hard. I've never been good at this."

Vanessa cocked her head at him, but said nothing.

"You've known her for *years*, right?"

"Well, highschool, yeah. And since then, probably about the same as you. Why?"

"I just need someone who knows her better than I do to tell me what to do."

"Not sure I'm the best person, but... Okay. What's going on?"

"I guess," he thrust out his bottom lip and searched for words among the clouds through the windscreen. "I got worried that she's going to go back to her ex."

Vanessa let out a snort of laughter and staggered back. "I'm sorry, but— *The Arsehole*? No chance."

"Really." Nate shifted in the seat so he could turn to face her, and looked down his nose at her. "Why'd she meet him a few days ago? And answer his call last night? Look, I don't blame her. He's a good looking guy. And he's young, and," he stopped himself from saying any more, afraid of showing Vanessa too much of his underbelly.

Vanessa could see the fear all over him; in his face, his wide eyes, the tension in his jaw, his shoulders hunching up around his ears. She reached out to put her hand back on his arm. "Oh Nate," she squeezed his shoulder. "It's okay. This is just what she's like. She gives everyone another chance, even when they don't deserve it. A chance to explain themselves, a chance to make amends. She's—"

"Nice."

Vanessa nodded. "Nice." She stood up and leaned against the car.

"I'm sure there was nothing in it. There were probably about fifty missed calls and she panicked. She's not gonna go back to him. He's trying, though. That jerk fucking basically stalked her to the hospital. I had to distract him to get him away from her. But look," she pulled out her phone to show Nate, and scrolled through messages that she'd received from Steven. "Creep stalked me on Facebook. But, ha, he's an idiot if he thinks I'm not going to honeytrap him to get him the hell away from her."

Nate looked up to Vanessa. "Does she know about this?"

"Oh, I told her, yeah. It's pretty funny. Sometimes he says horrible things about her, as though I'm not going to show her. What a dumbarse." She laughed, scrolling through some of the tastier messages before a thought crossed her mind. "So, let me guess: you got jealous and snapped at her?"

Embarrassed that he was so easily read, Nate bit at his thumbnail and nodded.

"Yeah, okay. Well, from what she's told me about Steven, I can see why that would be a sore spot for her. You wanna make amends?"

Nate was about to reply, but caught his breath. His reasoning regressed, and his fears came back up. "I don't know. What if I can't get over this? What if I'm just hurting her more?"

"So you'd rather let her go."

"Maybe."

"Well, I can't say that I haven't made that decision before. But she didn't love me. She loves you, whether she'll say it or not. It's *so* obvious in the way she looks at you, how she talks about you."

But, he thought, *she left last night.* Maybe he had been deluding himself, maybe she was just infatuated with the idea of him after all. "Yeah yeah, she loves *Nate Fucking Whitely.*"

"No; she loves Nate, Elsie's dad, who is — and I quote — *super nice.* Nate, who Vera is worried she's not enough for. Nate, who couldn't remember her, and she was in tears over for fear that *he might never love her again.* Should I go on?"

"I've been an arsehole to her, though."

"Not more than *The Arsehole.* And I'm sorry, but that title's already taken." Vanessa's attempts at cheering him up fell flat.

"What if she doesn't want me back? What if she decided that I'm not worth it? "

"Well if she doesn't want you back, but you still try, then you won't be hurting her. But if she *does* want you back and you don't talk to her?" Vanessa shook her head. "*That's* how you hurt her."

"And what about *The Arsehole*? What if she changes her mind about him? Gives him one more chance?"

"Well! You'd better go in there and show her that you're the better option — before you lose *your* chance."

He pursed his lips, still afraid and unsure of how to proceed.

"Want me to chaperone? She's expecting me," she held out her arm to him.

He sighed, stood up out of the car, and closed the door behind him.

Fifty-Seven

⏮ ⏸ ⏭

"Why on *earth* would you say such a thing?" They were almost halfway to Vera's house when Tommy stopped mid-step to question her. It was the first time he'd said something to her since the echo of giggles heralded their departure from the cafe.

Elsie feared the look that would be on Tommy's face, the fury she knew would be in his eyes. She knew that if she ran, she'd have to explain it to Vera and Nate, whether she went to them or not. She was out of options. There was nowhere to run, there was nowhere to escape to.

"Elsie. Look at me."

She didn't want to.

"Elsie." Tommy stood in front of her, placing his hands on her shoulders and bowing his head down to catch her eyes.

Reluctantly, she turned her face up to him, and opened her eyes. There was no rage twisting his features; just fear and betrayal.

"Saying that was such a *stupid* thing to do, and you're *not* a stupid girl. So, I just want to know why," his fingers curled into her shoulders, and his confident voice shook. "Why would you tell them *that*?"

Elsie looked away from him, trying to shrug his hand off her. "I just wanted them to think I'm—"

"Think you're what? A *slut*? Sleeping with someone *seven* years older than you? Sleeping with," he half-hissed, half-whispered the rest: "a *predator*?"

"No," she wiggled out of his grasp, but not his questions. "No, you're... not! I.. I just thought... Well, I mean... if they already think I'm sleeping with *David*," she let out a shiver. "I might as well change the story and make it someone *worth* sleeping with." She looked at nothing, and least of all, him.

Tommy dragged his hands over his face and through his hair, stepping back away from her.

"When they asked me... I said yes. I'm sorry, Tommy. I didn't even think that it could look bad, until you said it. And then it was too late."

He nodded, then shook his head. "You know you just made that whole thing worse for yourself."

"I just wanted to be *cool*," she studied the grass sprouting up around her shoes. "Like you."

"I was going to *help* you."

"Tommy, I'm sorry."

"Fuck," being reminded how this could look, he suddenly looked around, searching for sniper paparazzi. "What if someone spreads something? What if someone's seen us?"

"It's just schoolyard bullshit, Tommy. No one will believe it."

"No one will believe it when it's come from *you*? Who I took to the movies? The daughter of Nate Whitely, whose home I have been going to *every day*? Don't you know what it will be like for me, having to defend those accusations from the media? What your father will have to say so it doesn't look like he put you in harm's way? What he might think of me? It doesn't matter if it's true or not: once it gets out, it will be everyone's memory of me *forever*. That's how these things work. No one will want to touch me. It won't matter what I've done until now. You fucked me over. *You*."

Elsie felt the sobs rising in her throat, choking her, making her eyes water. Before she knew it, she was convulsing with tears, standing on the side of the road.

Tommy sighed, blinking away his own tears, running his hands through his hair. "Fuck. I'll sort this out. Your *friends* know you lied to them, so at least we don't need to clear that up. But don't go saying anything stupid like that *ever* again, okay?"

She crumpled where she stood, making herself into a tiny ball of legs and tears on the curb.

"Oh Elsie," Tommy broke and sat down next to her. He picked a fat piece of grass from where it was growing between the cracks of the curb and began stripping away its fleshy green sides until there was almost nothing left. He twirled the stub between his finger and thumb, cracked his neck, and let out another sigh. "Let's not tell your Dad, okay?"

She pulled her head up from between her knees, wiped the tears off her cheeks, and attempted a smile through her quivering lips.

Fifty-Eight

Vera was perching on her couch. She wasn't sure what to do, so she'd just shut herself in so that she could *process* and asked Vanessa to come by after work to help her work through everything. When she'd read Nate's text, she'd considered replying in so many ways: telling him that maybe she didn't want to talk yet, telling him that he scared her sometimes, that she didn't want to be controlled or possessed, trapped in the way that Steven had trapped her. She had stared at her phone, hanging up each time Steven tried to call her to ask where she was, and why she'd stood him up. She didn't want to find herself in another situation where she'd lose herself to the person she was with. Maybe it had been too soon to get into another *relationship*; maybe she needed to spend more time on her own, unpacking herself and trying to remember who she was before Steven shaped her into... whatever was left of her.

She held the picture of her with Steven. He looked even more handsome than she remembered, in a dark, brooding, kind of way. Tommy could learn a thing or two from Steven for his stage persona! But then there *she* was, so fresh faced, so much spirit and personality, but with a look about her that seemed so innocent and trusting. *There* was the side of herself that had been shaped in school, some combination of self-preservation from her time at home and the person who had thrived in her refuge of school with her tribe of awkward teenaged peers. There was something about her that felt to most like she was too sure of herself to really let anyone in: the self-protection had looked like confidence, the emotional suppression leaking out only in ways that hinted that she could break, like a plaster statue painted to look like marble.

She thought back to the night when Ness had taken this photo; the first night that she and Steven were officially together as a couple. She was so excited, and he was so proud of her: his stoic conquest. They followed each other around all night. She thought it was romantic at the time, was so happy that she had someone who wanted to be with her all the time. She didn't realise at the time how it might lead to him being possessive, controlling, and trying to diminish her so that no one else would be interested in her; meanwhile, he wasn't opposed to encouraging others to be interested in him.

Vera just couldn't put herself in that situation again. While she didn't want to be someone's second choice, she also didn't want someone who tried to keep her away from everyone else.

She knew Vanessa was going to leave work early, so she wasn't surprised when there was a knock on the door. She put the picture on the coffee table absent-mindedly and went to let her in. She opened the door to a sheepish-looking Nate, with Vanessa smiling apologetically behind him.

"Vera," Nate was frightened that it was too late. She didn't look glad to see him. "I hope it's okay that I'm—"

"How did you get here? You're not supposed to drive." Concern reverberated through her words, not anger, not sarcasm.

"Tommy. He's with Elsie now."

"Oh, right… of course." Vera shrunk, making space for them to pass.

"Give him a chance, Ronnie, *please*," Vanessa whispered in her ear, reaching down to squeeze her hand. Vera returned a defeated smile.

Nate, stressed from the pressure he was placing on himself, glanced around Vera's home, trying to gauge her mental state from her surroundings. It wasn't hard to find the photo of her and—

"Urgh, *The Arsehole*." Vanessa said as Nate picked up the photo. "I remember that night. I didn't like him then, and I don't like him now."

"You should have said something."

"As if you'd listen. Look at you in this photo. As much as I hated him, you seemed happy."

"I was." Vera felt increasingly uncomfortable, Nate still looking at the photo.

"You're like a different person," he said, sitting down on the couch. It wasn't said with disappointment, or disgust, or anything negative. It was just a clean observation — he could see it, just like she could. The person he'd spent the last few weeks failing to get to know and the person in the photo seemed more like sisters than the same person.

"I guess you could say that's *Ronnie.*" Vera sat on the coffee table, across from him.

Nate nodded. "She seems nice, too." He looked across at her shyly.

Vera blushed against her will. She refused to be weak, to once again give in so easily.

"Ronnie's pretty cool. She has great taste in music, too; but, ha," Vanessa had let herself into the kitchen and was rattling around looking for mugs. "She has the *biggest* obsession with that *Nate Fucking Whitely* guy."

Vera blushed even harder. She covered her face with her hands. Nate could hear her choked breathing; he watched as she shouldered her tension. Cold regret flushed his face, tiny needles prickled around his ears, and his throat turned sticky and heavy. He cursed himself for trusting Vanessa — he knew he shouldn't have come here.

Suddenly, Vera took a deep breath in, pulled away the tears from her face, and looked at him with a hopeless little smile that crept into the corners of her mouth while apology and pleading took her eyes. "Nate - I think you should go."

Fifty-Nine

⏮ ⏸ ⏭

Elsie couldn't bring herself to follow Tommy back to Vera's home. Once again, she had nowhere in particular that she could go. "Wait."

Tommy turned around. His jaw was tight from clenching; his eyes still showing signs of frustration. He stared at her, waiting for an explanation.

"I... I don't think I can go back yet."

Tommy sighed, shifting his weight. He'd noticed Elsie's pattern of doing anything she could to avoid anything that scared her. He knew that right now, she was scared of what he might tell Nate, and how he might react. She was scared that the truth might disappoint Vera and Vanessa. She was scared that she would lose everyone. Tommy may not have been a genius, but it didn't take a genius to imagine exactly what was in Elsie's head. But, he was sick of it and didn't feel in the mood to give her a way out. She'd seriously betrayed his trust by using him to try to make her own life easier. He was understanding, but he wasn't sure she took the situation seriously. As upset as she seemed, was she only upset because she knew she was in trouble, or because she understood that she'd hurt him, risked both their reputations? She was just a teenager, he had to remind himself. She was *fourteen*.

Elsie couldn't help but think how much Tommy suddenly looked like the version of himself that he put on display when he was performing, rather than the person she'd got to know over the past week. His gaze flicked off her and to something behind her.

"Whatever. See you later," he said to her, then nodded to the short-sighted clarinettist, who had come to a halt before reaching Elsie.

Elsie watched Tommy turn and walk away, his hands stuffed into his pockets, before she turned around. "What do *you* want, Carmen?"

"To apologise."

Elsie snorted, her dismissal flicking her face like a nervous tick.

"I'm sorry I said it, Elsie." The hot chocolate churned like delicious blood money in her stomach, souring her mouth.

"You're just greedy and wanted a hot chocolate."

"I guess. I don't like lies, either. But... Why did you say you were sleeping with him if it wasn't true?"

"You're an idiot, Carmen," Elsie sat down on the side of the road, hoping that she could use an insult to avoid the question. Unfortunately for her, that tactic didn't work on Carmen, who had been teased since she was eight.

"Make me less of an idiot, then." She sat down next to Elsie, placing her clarinet case on the floor next to her. She turned to Elsie and pushed her glasses up her nose. "Why did you make that up?"

"D'you really think I slept with David?"

"I don't know. I mean, I don't know you that well, and you seem so mature, so... I guess? I have no reason not to believe it?" She blinked at Elsie. "Did you?"

"No."

"Oh."

Elsie shifted, finding a way to sink even lower into herself. "Everyone believed *that* lie, so I wanted a better lie to make the first one go away."

"I see," Carmen nodded, looking out across the street. "I guess you *did* try to say that you didn't sleep with him."

"Why didn't anyone believe me?"

"Well, I can't speak for everyone, but I think it's because they just thought you were playing it down." She turned back to Elsie. "Why would he say it if it wasn't true?"

"Because he's a loser and I didn't like him back?"

"Oh."

They sat together, staring out across the road.

"Well, look. The losers are sitting together." David was standing on the sidewalk behind them. "I knew they couldn't have gone far."

"What the hell, David," Carmen stood up at the sound of his voice. "Can't you just leave us alone?"

"No, he can't," Elsie stood up. She steeled her gaze at him. "You know what? I don't care anymore. I'm sick of it."

"Sick of what? Being such a lying *slut*?" David looked for reassurance amongst the group that had followed him. He only saw what he wanted to see, basking in his imagined superiority and support. "You were a shit lay anyway, Tommy's lucky he isn't really sleeping with you."

"Oh... just... FUCK OFF, David!" Elsie cracked. "You know who else is lucky? Me. Because I don't feel that I have to shit on other people and put them down to make myself feel like I'm someone worthwhile. And I'm even luckier because I didn't have your disgusting pimply face anywhere near mine. You wouldn't even know what I'm like because you didn't sleep with me. I didn't say much before because I felt *bad* for you, and no one wanted to believe me so I just thought if I was quiet it might go away. But you know what? I don't care anymore," she looked to their peers, standing in a group to the side. "He made it up about me because he didn't like me saying no," she turned back to him, stepped closer to him. "You didn't want to look like a loser in front of everyone, so instead you had to shit on me. You just wanted to *punish* me for not saying yes to you. You made it so uncomfortable for me that I felt I *had* to make that up about Tommy. If I was going to be a slut, I at least wanted someone *decent* to have slept with. And now he's not even my friend anymore." She looked back at Carmen. "I'll own *that* stupid move. That's my fault, I know that. I did a dumb thing. But if I'm admitting I did a dumb thing, I might as well just get it all out."

She turned back to David, leant down to him, and poked at the air in his face. "It's not fair what you did to me. You're an arsehole and I don't regret turning you down *at all*. I feel sorry for whoever you end up with because you're going to shit on them every time you don't get your own way." She looked among the group, half stunned, half stifling giggles. She sighed, shook her head, and turned back to see Carmen, who was looking at her with admiration. "I'm going home. I'm not wasting time on losers anymore."

As Elsie walked past her, Carmen scrambled to pick up her clarinet case. "Elsie, wait. Can *I* come with you?"

"Sure." The two girls walked away together in silence. They'd walked about five steps before they heard laughter erupt behind them, intercut with calls of *'Loser! Loooooooooser!'* They turned around, both afraid that they were the ones being laughed at. Instead, they saw the other kids poking and laughing at David. They looked at each other and smiled. Carmen looked back to the road ahead, while Elsie considered the clarinet case.

"So Carmen, you're into music?"

She tilted her head, her glasses slipping down slightly. She knew who Nate Whitely was — her Mum had been a massive fan of his. And if Elsie had grown up with him as her father, surely she would be someone who wouldn't tease Carmen for being a band geek. "Yeah. I know the clarinet isn't a cool instrument, but I don't care. They make us do classical at school, and I hate it but I know the foundations are important if I really want to play like Doreen Ketchens. Oh, I just *love* New Orleans Jazz." Her eyes sparkled with delight.

Elsie smiled at her. "I have no idea what that is. But I know some people who might, or will be just as happy as me to learn about it. Wanna come over and play me your favourite song?"

Sixty

⏮ ⏸ ⏭

"Vera, please..." Nate reached out to her as she stood up. "I... came to say I'm sorry."

"Sorry doesn't mean much to me anymore." Vera took the photo from him as she walked past.

"Vera... I'm not like him. I won't—"

"It's not that. I just don't feel like I know who I am anymore, and I don't want to have to hide myself because of you."

"I don't want you to."

"You *scare* me, Nate. When you get like that. And it reminds me... Not just of him, but..." She shook her head. Ness, getting a sense of the same sorts of things she'd picked up from Vera during highschool, went to her side. She took the photo, put it down, and wrapped her arms around her.

Nate stared at his hands, picking at the bandage. Quietly, with great control, he said to himself, "I don't want to hurt you."

"You do, though."

"I know." He'd been through this before. He'd pushed so many away because he couldn't control himself. The thing that made him perfect for making honest, raw music that allowed millions to resonate with him was also the thing that kept him alone. The only thing that kept Elsie intact was that she was like him, and she knew that he never, ever wanted to actually hurt her. They just blew up at each other and it would boil over with no harm done. The only problem came when he couldn't deal with his emotions and turned to some substance to numb the pain or hide what he was going through from other people. That was something he had chosen to stop after Elsie's birth, along with a whole lot of therapy. He slipped occasionally, but his general control was one thing he was proud of. But, he'd never got as far as properly managing his emotions. He'd never had reason to. Until now. "I'm sorry I'm not the person you hoped. I'm not the *Nate Fucking Whitely* you imagined."

"Nate..." Vera covered her face with her hands. "It's not about that. It's never really been about that. Who you were years ago, who I — a kid, like Elsie — imagined you to be: you think I thought that's who you'd be, really? I'm so, *so* far from who I was when I thought that about you. No, Nate. You're just someone I like. I didn't expect anything of you. I don't expect anything of you. But, I like you. I like the you that is a good Dad to Elsie, who really cares about her. I like the you who did anything he could to pay me back for a coffee. The you who loves coffee, but never drinks it because he's too busy listening to me. The you who pulled back to give me space when I freaked out. The you who gave Tommy a chance despite fearing the worst of him. The you who wants to make this work. But—"

"Vera, I know I've said this before, but I don't deserve you," he smiled at her, but his eyes were clouded with tears. "It was only a matter of time until you realised this." He turned away again. "And I don't know what you've been through, but I understand if I'm not good for you."

Vera watched Nate, sitting crumpled on the couch. It was like she could see the weight of the world on him.

He hung his head, then threw it back, leaning back against the couch. "You know, I've already been through all of this in my head, *so* many times. I knew it wouldn't last."

"So, you're going to give up?" Ness looked between them. "That's it?"

Nate sat upright, imploring Ness to understand. "I tried giving up. I tried to try again. Vera," Nate stood up and turned to her, his hand on his heart. "I'm *trying*. I promised you that I will love you, and I meant it. But I don't want to hurt you. I will... I will try, if you give me a chance. Deep breaths and all that. Therapy again," he looked at Ness. "I don't want to give up. But I will, if *she* wants."

Vera swallowed, then looked up to see both Nate and Ness watching her. "I... don't know." It felt hopeless to her. Maybe Nate was right, maybe there was no point. Maybe they were both too broken. But they were honest with each other. There was that. So perhaps that was where they could begin. "Maybe, if you explain... Why did you get so upset last night? I just don't understand why you'd think that you'd need to worry about Steven."

Time to think. Time to put words to those feelings. He laughed at how nervous he felt. "Okay. This is hard." He looked at her; she was trying, too. "I've been so scared of letting you in, but I want to open up to you. And that's part of it. I'm scared that I'll open to you completely, and I'll learn so much about you, but no matter what... I'll never know you as much as he did. As he does," he looked down at the picture frame, still in her hands. "That he'll always have a part of you that I can't get to. That as much as you call him 'The Arsehole,' as much as you hate him, that part of you will always go back to him. And I know — you've explained it already. But that's why. I'm scared that he's had such an impact on your life that I'll never be able to have you completely."

Vera regarded him as he looked down at the photo again, his eyebrows tilted up in the middle. "Nate, you've had a bigger impact on my life than he ever could. I grew up listening to *your* music."

"But that wasn't actually *me* in your life, was it?" Nate shook his head and raised his hands to wave away that line of thinking. "But that's not what I meant at all. This isn't about *me*." He stood and reached out to take her hand into his. "I mean, *I* never got to know *Ronnie*. And somehow you're now Vera. I like Vera, but somehow *he* took Ronnie away and... kept it. I can see her there," he pointed at the photo, "but I can't see her *here*. Sometimes I think I do, but then she's gone again."

Vera frowned at him, but not because of him.

Nate worried that he had offended her. "I know we all change, but ..."

"Ronnie, he changed you and we all know it." Vanessa let go of her and took the photo out of her hands.

Nate watched Vera flinch when Vanessa used her old nickname. "I'm scared that you'll want *her* back, and you'll go to him to find her."

Vera looked between them, unsure of what to say. Without wanting to, she started wondering whether that was why he'd gone with Sarah as well. If she hadn't changed, would she have been enough for him? But she'd just wanted to be what he'd wanted: she wanted to be what made him happy. So all the tiny nudges away from one behaviour and toward another shaped her into Vera. He'd been able to sculpt her, but he'd overworked her to the point where uniqueness had been lost. Was Nate right? Was there still a part of her that wanted Steven's affection, even though he disgusted her now?

She looked up to see Nate watching her quietly, his luminous eyes searching hers for understanding. He gave her a brief sympathetic smile, and his thumb brushed over her knuckles reassuringly as he waited for her response. She looked up to Vanessa and saw the same look reflected on her face.

A knock on the door interrupted them.

"That'll be Elsie and Tommy," Nate sighed.

"I'll get it, you two stay there." Before Nate had a chance to reply, Vanessa put down the picture frame and slipped out to the door, opening it, stepping outside to find Tommy without Elsie, and closing it behind her.

A dark look of near-distress had passed over Vera's features, and she was looking at where Ness had placed the photo. Seeing this, Nate hesitated. "What are you thinking?"

Aware that she hadn't said anything for a while, Vera took a deep breath and tried to smile away the forming tears. "You don't want to hear what I'm thinking."

"Whatever it is, I want to know."

"What if you don't like it?"

Nate pursed his lips. He knew what she was getting at. "Then it's my problem, not yours. Tell me. Consider this my test."

"Well, I don't know if I told you, but," Vera wasn't sure whether she wanted to tell Nate about how she felt about Steven. She didn't think it was fair, especially when he was already so sensitive to hearing about him. She looked at him again — he was nothing if not earnest. She closed her eyes; she could bring herself to tell him, but she didn't want to see his reaction. "I came home one day to Steven in bed with my best friend. I don't know how long he'd been cheating on me. And with Sarah?" She shook her head in incredulity, still unable to look at him. "Who could I trust again? *She* was my best friend in highschool, not Vanessa." She shifted, the emotion struggling to escape. "And they just didn't care how I felt about it. I'm sure he wanted to have us both, I trust that. He told me that he loved both of us, whether that was a lie or not. And Sarah was fine with it all. But that's when I realised that neither of them really cared about me. That's why I left him," she straightened up and looked straight into Nate's eyes. "That day you walked in on us in the cafe, he was telling me that he'd found *her* in bed with someone else. So if she was into open relationships, I never knew, but that's fine for her. Apparently, it wasn't fine for him, he wanted to be the centre of everyone's life." She finally squeezed Nate's hand back. "I only went to talk to him because I thought I might get closure. I never wanted him back. I knew he never really cared, and he never could."

"Okay," Nate said, biting his lip. He was trying his hardest to really focus on her, to listen to her words, to not let his mind catch on to some small wisp of an idea and let his flare into something that it wasn't. He closed his eyes and thought about what she said — and more importantly, what it meant: he was the one she was choosing here, not Steven. And he had to trust her on that, the way he'd learned to trust Tommy. Tommy was no more his predatory bandmate than Vera was his ex-wife who had left him with a tiny daughter to raise on his own. He swallowed, opened his eyes, and smiled at her, gently, slowly, as she watched him carefully. "Well, I promise I'll never do that to you. I'll always be honest with you. And all I ask is that you be honest with me, and I'll trust you."

"The worst part," she pulled her hand away from his, sat down on the couch, and wrapped both her hands around her waist as though she was nursing a fatal wound, "Is that I'd tried to be everything he wanted, and it wasn't *enough*. You're right, you and Ness. I'm *not* Ronnie anymore; as much as Ness calls me that, as much as he calls me that, as much as Sarah calls me that. As much as his Mum calls me that. Vera was a name that one of my old bosses used to call me, and it's what my parents call me. I never liked it. But every time I thought of myself as *Ronnie*, because I only heard it from *them*, I wanted to get as far away from it as possible, because it wasn't enough for him. I wasn't enough. I couldn't introduce myself to you as *Ronnie*." She shook off the tension of carrying all that inside. "Does that even make sense?"

Nate was listening, but he was looking at his hand: the cast that was stabilising his bones, that was getting in the way of his music, challenging his status as a musician. "Yeah, it does. But," he looked back at her. "Maybe you were never going to be enough for him. But there was something in who you were when you first met that made him think there might be."

"Maybe." She smiled at him. "You always did have words that could make me feel better," she marvelled at herself, feeling like she did when she was in school, finding solace in his words. "You know, when I met you and Elsie, I remembered a touch of what it felt like to be Ronnie again. But, that just made me realise how far I'd strayed from her. And even then, I was barely coping, putting on a brave face, making up an idea of who Vera might be. I don't know who I am under all of that. Nate... I don't know who I can be for you."

"I don't want you to try to be who you think I want you to be," Nate sat down next to her and placed his good hand, palm-up, on her knee. She took a deep breath in, let out the anxiety of the last day, and took his hand.

They sat together quietly for a while, vulnerable but grounded.

He glanced over at her, and saw just how small and lost she looked. It was like the night he first came to her place, looking for Elsie. He wanted to reach into her and find a way to help her out. "So, once upon a time, I was a very significant part of your life, supposedly. Unfortunately, I don't seem to recall any of it, and I don't think it'll come back to me on its own this time. Care to let me in?" Nate looked up at her, his eyes shining at her as though from the cover of a magazine like she would have picked up from a Newsagents just under twenty years ago.

Vera blushed when she saw his mock-seriousness break into a kind smile. "Okay. Let me think." She closed her eyes and thought back to highschool. She couldn't help giggling — a crack in her facade. "This feels so embarrassing. Okay, well. I remember sitting outside the art room," she started.

"You did art?"

"No, I was horrible at it. But it's where we used to sit." She smiled as she thought about her little group. "Me, Ness, Sarah, and this other girl, June. Sarah was boy-mad. Ness was always like one of those puppies who was going to grow into a big dog, gangly and her hair was a mess. I know, it's hard to see her now and imagine her as awkward; but, we all were. June was really determined, really focused on her studies. I don't know where she is now. Maybe Ness kept in contact with her? I'm not sure. Apart from Sarah and I, we all went our separate ways... though now I think that might have more to do with Steven than I realised. Anyway, I remember Sarah had brought in her little portable cd player — you know the ones that were like Walkmans, but for cds? And she and I shared the earbuds and listened to *Still* for the first time. And I remember, because my parents had been *really*..." She hesitated, afraid to let him in to something even deeper in her past that she wasn't quite ready to revisit. He squeezed her hand and wrapped his other arm around her shoulders, reassuring her that he was there with her, giving her the strength to continue. "They'd been really *bad*." She swallowed away the emotion that caught in her throat. "And it wasn't anything specific in the lyrics, and I know it didn't really relate, but something about the music just made me feel like I wasn't alone."

Nate understood now what she'd meant when she told him that he'd already made so much music that it didn't matter whether he made more or not: it wasn't that she was downplaying his grief, it was that his music had, and would continue to, affect others. He knew she didn't understand what making music meant to him, but he hadn't — until now — understood what his music had meant to her.

"I remember going looking for that cd," she continued, smiling to herself. "It was a Sunday and we were all hanging out. There was this clothes shop next to this little record store that I loved going to, and it always just seemed so cool and adult. After we found the cd, we were feeling so bold that we went into that shop and tried on so many things." She giggled, turning red.

"Did you buy anything?"

"Yeah, I got this dress that I thought was *so cool*, it had like this newspaper print on it. That whole 6os revival era," she laughed, remembering a version of herself that didn't have to try to be something for someone. "I never had a place to wear it — I remember wishing you would tour so I could wear it then. Imagine if we'd met then, Nate? Would you give me your autograph?"

She finally looked straight at him. He was watching her with a soft affection, and let out a quiet laugh at her question. She felt giddy, young, the weight of the last decade slowly lifting. Its oppressive force may have lifted, but the events didn't have to be forgotten or erased. She realised that she didn't have to choose between Ronnie or Vera: that was a false dichotomy. They were both parts of the same whole — of Veronica — and this was something that was breaking apart and coming together in the last month that she'd been spending time with Nate, whether she'd noticed it or not. As she felt herself let go of the tension she didn't know she carried, she saw a shift in Nate's expression.

Nate watched Vera as she began to glow, thinking about this moment years ago when she was Ronnie — the kind of girl that was always called the cool girl, the nice girl, whose unabashed sense of self was too much for any guy who wasn't mature enough to value it, or needy enough to desire it. "Wait, I can think of something even better," he said and fumbled for his phone. "Sorry, I'm going to be a bit clumsy with this." He turned the camera on, switched it to selfie mode, and struggled to hold it in front of them.

"Oh… I always dreamed of having a photo with *Nate Fucking Whitely*!"

He gave her one of his lopsided, cheeky smiles, and she blushed: the memory of her lost self reigniting her true self. "Anything for a fan."

She laughed as he struggled and almost dropped his phone. "Nate… let me help you." She took the phone from him. He wrapped his arm around her again, and she took the photo before he was ready. "Whoops! One more?"

Nate took his phone back after she took the second photo, and they looked at them together. Looking at Vera, he mentally compared it to how she looked in the photo of her with Steven: older, wiser, more experienced; but, captured in this photo he could finally see both Ronnie and Vera, which together made her Veronica. As for himself, he was clearly no longer the wild, pretty-boy rockstar he used to be when she idolised him. He scrolled back to the first photo Vera had taken, ready for a laugh. Despite her mouth being open and mid-laugh, she looked great and was looking at the camera. But he had been caught in the moment of wrapping his arm around Vera, and was still looking at her. The way he felt about her was written all over his face; they could both see it.

There it was: the Look.

www.ingramcontent.com/pod-product-compliance
Lightning Source LLC
Chambersburg PA
CBHW051131190726
48290CB00006B/1796